D0192294

HITLER'S NIECE

A NOVEL

Ron Hansen

Perennial

An Imprint of HarperCollinsPublishers

A hardcover edition of this book was published in 1999 by HarperCollins Publishers.

First Perennial edition published 2000.

Designed by Elina D. Nudelman

The Library of Congress has catalogued the hardcover edition as follows:

Hansen, Ron.
    Hitler's niece : a novel / Ron Hansen. — 1st ed.
      p.   cm.
   ISBN 0-06-019419-7
   1. Raubal, Geli, 1908–1931—Fiction. 2. Hitler, Adolf, 1889–1945—Fiction.
 3. Germany—History—1918–1933—Fiction.   I. Title.
PS3558.A5133H58   1999
813'.54—dc21   99-12656

ISBN 0-06-093220-1 (pbk.)

02 03 04 ❖/RRD 10 9 8 7 6

For Bo

CONTENTS

CHAPTER ONE
LINZ, 1908

She was born in Linz, Austria, on June 4, 1908, when Hitler was nineteen and floundering in Wien, a failure at many things, and famished for food and attention. Within the month she was christened as Angelika ("Ahn-GAY-leek-ah") Maria Raubal, in honor of her mother, Angela, Hitler's half-sister, but the family was soon calling the baby Geli ("Gaily"), as she was to be known all her life.

Hitler first saw his niece at a Sunday-afternoon party after the June baptism in the Alter Dom cathedral in Linz. Angela heard four hard knocks on the front screen door and found Adolf on Bürgergasse in front of the Raubal house, looking skeletal and pale in a high, starched collar and red silk bow tie and the ill-fitting, soot-black suit he'd worn at his mother's funeral in December; his wide, thin mustache so faint it seemed penciled on, his hair as chestnut brown as her own and as short as a five-day beard. With unquestioning love, Angela invited him in and hugged him, but it was like holding wood. And then she saw that hurrying up Bürgergasse from the railway station was his only friend, August Kubizek, whose father owned an upholstery shop in Linz. Angela hugged him, too, saying, "We've missed you, Gustl."

"And I, you."

She called to the kitchen, "Leo! Paula! Look who's here!" And then she noticed that her half-brother held a silk top hat in his hand and was absurdly twirling a black, ivory-handled cane, as if he were a gentleman of plenty. "Aunt Johanna's here, too," she said. "And the Monsignor."

"Oh, Lord," Hitler said.

Swerving out of the kitchen with a tankard of beer was Leo Raubal, Angela's husband, a flinty, twenty-nine-year-old junior tax inspector in Linz whose jacket and tie were now off. Everything Hitler loathed about his dead father, Leo Raubal professed to admire, and he seemed to be imitating the late Alois Hitler as he said, "Why, it's Lazy himself! The bohemian! Rembrandt's only rival! Aren't we *honored* to finally have you here!"

"Leo, be nice," Angela said.

"Who's nicer than I? I'm Saint Nicholas! I'm a one-man charity!"

Hitler's twelve-year-old sister, Paula, who suffered frequent trials with mental illness and would be nicknamed "The Straggler," hung back in the kitchen, winding string around a fist and flirting a stare at Kubizek, whom she was fond of, until Hitler held out a present to her. "I have a gift for you, Paula!"

She scuttled forward in once white stockings and took the package, irresolutely staring at a festive wrapping of tissue paper that Hitler had hand-painted.

"You can tear it," he said.

"But I don't want to."

"Oh, for God's sake, do it!" Leo Raubal said.

She tore off the paper and found underneath it a fat and difficult novel, *Don Quixote*. "You say the title how?" she asked. Hitler told her. She opened the book, and inside, where she hoped for a sentimental note from the older brother she worshiped, or even a "To My Dear Paula," she instead found Hitler's handwritten list of other books in history, biography, politics, and literature that would possibly benefit her. Her face fractured with disappointment as she said, "Thank you, Adolf," and hurried to put *Don Quixote* away.

"What a treat," Raubal told Hitler. "Girls really go for things like that."

"She's all right?"

Raubal touched his head. "She's all *wrong* up here."

Aunt Johanna Pölzl, the wealthy, hunchbacked, forty-five-year-old sister of Hitler's late mother, walked down the hallway from a bedroom. She smiled. "I was taking a nap with Leo Junior when I heard your voice, Adi."

"My favorite aunt!" he said. "My sweetest darling! Are you feeling well?"

"Oh, just tired," Aunt Johanna said. "I'm used to it." She held out her left hand and he kissed it, as did August Kubizek.

Angela got the baby from a bassinet and held the tiny girl up to Hitler's face so he could kiss her on the forehead.

Jiggling Geli's left hand with his index finger, her uncle said, "Aren't you pretty?" She gripped the finger in her fist. "Will the fräulein allow me the pleasure of introducing myself? My name is Herr Adolfus Hitler."

"Your uncle, Angelika," Angela said, and shook the baby, trying to get her to smile, but Geli only stared at his hair. "See? She loves you."

"And why not?" he asked.

Leo Raubal called, "August Kubizek! Would you like some good beer?"

Walking into the kitchen, Kubizek said, "Clearly I have some catching up to do."

"Won't take but a pitcher," Raubal said.

Hitler stayed in the front room as Angela gave Geli to Aunt Johanna and went into the kitchen behind August in order to get out the potatoes in jackets. Canting back into the pantry with a full stein of beer was a stout and white-haired monsignor in rimless glasses and a pitch-black soutane with red buttons and piping. "Wel-come, Herr Kubizek!" he too loudly said. "Are you liking the Con-servatory of Music?"

"Very much, Monsignor."

"The child's a miracle at music," the old priest told Raubal. "You play, what, violin, viola, piano. . . .   What else?"

"Also trumpet and trombone."

"Amadeus Mozart," the old priest said.

Angela got a braising pan out of the oven and put it on an iron trivet on the kitchen table. "We have potatoes in jackets here. And herring rolls in the icebox."

Raubal handed Kubizek a stein of beer and a cold skillet of sliced kielbasa in ale, then focused intently on his high forehead and his soft, feminine face. "And what does our Adolf do in Wien while you study your music?"

"Oh, he works; very hard. Even to two or three in the morning."

Raubal was astonished. "At what?"

"Watercolors of churches, parliament, the Belvedere Palace. Reading in Nordic and Teutonic mythology. Writing of all kinds. And city planning. Adolf strolls around the Ringstrasse in the after-noons, carefully observing, then redesigns sections of it at night. Amazing things, really. Architectural drawings for a new opera house. And plans for a high-level bridge over the Danube here in Linz."

Raubal smirked. "Dare I presume no one pays him for this?"

"We have made friends with poverty, so there is no urgency."

Raubal told him, "You know what Hitler's poverty is? An orphan's pension of twenty-five kronen per month plus a loan from his Aunt Johanna of another thousand."

Angela asked, "Are you going to want anything else to eat?"

She was ignored. "And what is my salary," Raubal continued, "the hardworking husband and father of two children and the guardian of his crazy sister? Ninety kronen per month. Don't talk to me about your friendship with poverty." Raubal turned to the priest. "Nine-teen years old! And a thousand kronen to play with!"

"A fortune," the monsignor said.

Kubizek fixed his stare on the beer inside his stein. "Wien is expensive," he said.

"You get germs from money," Paula said. The twelve-year-old walked as softly as a kitten to a kitchen chair and sat. "Torrents of them all over your skin."

Raubal stared at his sister-in-law for a moment, then turned to the monsignor. "And this is what I have to put up with."

"Well, it's never easy, is it," the old priest said.

Angela went back into the front room and took the baby from Aunt Johanna. Hitler watched as Geli squirmed and widened her mouth and finally cried in a worn, soft, cranky way, like a hinge that needed oiling. "She's hungry," Angela said, and eased down onto the sofa where she mindlessly unbuttoned her blue dress and offered the infant a full and aching right breast. And then she realized that her offended half-brother had fled into the dining room where he looked out a window with his hands locked firmly behind his back. She remembered him hiding in his bedroom as he dressed, or holding his mouth in malaise when she talked about childbirth, that he was squeamish about anything having to do with the body.

She called to him, "You have to give me your new address before you go. Where are you staying?"

"A few minutes from the Westbahnhof, in the Sixth District. In a flat at Stumpergasse 29."

While the baby nursed, Angela wrote down his address. "And your landlady?"

"Frau Maria Zakreys. A Polish woman. Hungarians are shouting all day next door. Upstairs are Slavs and Turks. The Habsburgs have made Wien an Oriental city."

Wearily Aunt Johanna slumped to the right in a wing chair, her forearm on her forehead. "Are you not liking this apartment, Adi?"

Angela watched Geli feeding and heard Adolf holding forth about the city. Almost every night he went to the Burgtheater or the opera—*Tristan und Isolde* just yesterday, and *Der fliegende Holländer* on Thursday—but he could afford it only because August got free tickets through the conservatory. Otherwise things were so expensive he'd had to hock his winter coat. And others were worse off than he was. Small wonder that the city was thought to be filled with *Raunzer*, grumblers. It was a hard and dangerous place to live.

Aunt Johanna tut-tutted while Angela forced Geli to try her left breast. And now Hitler was pacing around the dining room table. Did Aunt Johanna know he'd walked the streets of Wien for a full afternoon and not found one true Austrian? Really. Yesterday he'd gone into a café to read a newspaper and found many hanging on canes, but in Czech, Italian, Polish, and Croatian, not one in German! Equality of the races, pah! It was shameful. Hitler half-turned, but saw Geli was still feeding, so he faced the hanging portrait of Alois, his strict, pompous, irritable, authoritarian father, who'd died in 1903.

"Evil is rife there!" Hitler said. "One night August and I saw a hair-raising play called *Spring's Awakening* and I felt it necessary to take him to Spittelberggasse and the sink of iniquity—"

"The sink of iniquity?" Aunt Johanna asked.

"Houses of prostitution," he explained.

"Oh dear."

Angela thought of him as a misogynist; she wondered if he'd ever even held hands with a girl. She smiled and said, "You shock me, Adolf."

"I have no interest in contracting syphilis, I assure you. In fact, August and I have solemnly vowed to keep forever pure the holy flame of life. But if it is my goal to form the ideal state, I have an obligation to investigate from afar those festering and illicit monuments to the perversion of our times."

Aunt Johanna frowned. "Who can *fathom* what you're talking about?"

Angela grinned at Geli, who was forgetting to nurse, lost in a fog, her tiny and affectionate hand as delicate as a moth on the huge white urn of Angela's breast. Was it possible to feel more love than this for a child and not faint with ecstasy? Would there ever be a time when Angelika was not essential to her? She heard the three men howling in the kitchen and she wondered if whatever was said was truly funny, or was it Leo's *Schadenfreude*? Leo who clapped when waiters dropped plates, who found all falls hilarious, who often teased children to tears; Leo who first got interested in Angela Hitler because he'd heard she was fine *Hausfrau* material and a jolly woman who loved to have a good laugh. She was twenty then, and strong and pretty in a square-jawed way, and oh so eager to get out of her stepmother's house. And now she was twenty-five and, she thought, much had changed.

Aunt Johanna was talking, and then Adolf. Angela heard him say, "We face a gloomy interior courtyard. Even in the afternoon I have to light a stinking kerosene lamp in order to sketch."

Angela asked her half-brother, "Why aren't you painting at the academy of fine arts?" And she heard a shifty moment of quiet before she looked up to find that Adolf had turned from the dining room window with his hand inside his jacket. Crossing spitefully to her, he pulled out a folded sheet of paper that he sarcastically ironed out on the sofa arm next to Geli's head.

"Official judgment," it read. "Adolf Hitler, born Braunau am Inn, Upper Austria, on 20 April 1889. Religion: Catholic. Father: civil servant (deceased). Education: four forms, Realschule. Sample drawings: Inadequate; few heads."

"You weren't accepted?"

"You're quick, aren't you, Angela."

"Oh, Adolf. I'm so sorry. Was there nothing you could do?"

Aunt Johanna offered, "Learn to draw heads?"

Controlling his temper, he said, "I went to the director. Professor Siegmund l'Allemand. A Jew. He thought I had little talent for painting, but ought to consider the school of architecture."

"And?"

"I admitted I quit taking classes here at sixteen and didn't have my diploma." And then, his face flushed as if he were seething, he began ranting first about the intransigence of the officials at the grueling four-hour exam, and then about their being petty bureaucrats, all of them old-fashioned, fossilized civil servants. Without taste, without fairness, without common sense. With no loyalty to their heritage.

Aunt Johanna sighed. "You realize, of course, that if you'd studied at a technical school you'd have matriculated by now? But no, you're an *artist*, you won't listen to anybody. You're as pigheaded as your father was. You go your own way, thinking of no one else, just as if you had no family. My sister died six months ago, and this is your first visit."

Hitler fell melodramatically to his knees before her and in a high, whining, sniveling voice, his face rolling against Aunt Johanna's thigh, confessed his failings, his fecklessness, his fruitless talent; confessed, too, that it was shame and vanity and his wanting so desperately to please her that had frustrated his good intentions. And now he felt doomed to waste his life in the filth of questionable surroundings, frostbitten in winter, feeble in the heat of summer, his youth wholly lost, penniless but for the paintings he sold and too proud to ask for financial assistance, having only Sorrow and Need for companions.

Aunt Johanna softly petted his hair. "There, there now," she said.

Angela thought, *The Mommy routine.* While growing up with him, she'd all too often watched Klara give way to his miserable abjection and lamentations, and now she could abide no more. She buttoned her dress, lifted Geli to her dish-toweled left shoulder, and gently patted the baby's back as she walked to the kitchen.

The monsignor was wiping tears of laughter from his eyes and her husband was fully intoxicated and addleheaded on the floor. Angela got a platter of Russian eggs from the icebox and put a jar of gherkins next to it on the kitchen table. Leo got up, filled his mouth with an egg, and hunted in the gherkin jar with his fingers. Angela got out a fork. August Kubizek was sitting beside the kitchen sink, saying, "No sooner do we go partners on a ten-kronen lottery ticket than Adolf begins fantasizing that we've already won. A sure thing. Endless talking about how we'd rent a house across the Danube, he'd furnish it to his own taste, paint his own trompe l'oeil on the walls, make the house our own conservatory. We'd also hire a lady of exquisite culture and placid temperament to be our chatelaine. Elderly, of course; for as he put it, he wanted 'no prospects to be aroused of a kind unwelcome to us.'"

Raubal winked as he asked, "Could it be young Hitler has a religious calling, Monsignor?"

"You give me goose flesh, Herr Raubal." The old priest peered through the bottom half of his glasses at the baby girl and smiled as he petted her flossy brown hair with his hand. "She's fallen asleep," he whispered.

"I'd better go put her down."

Kubizek was saying, "And then when the lottery winner was announced, and it wasn't us, Adolf was destroyed. Annihilated. It was unjust, he shouted. Authorities had stolen the prize from us. All he could do was lie in a dark room for two days. And I realized, 'What a fantastic imagination! Others' wildest dreams are reality to him!'"

Angela walked to the hallway just as Leo Junior was toddling out of the children's bedroom, crabby with wakefulness. After she put Geli down in the crib, she hiked Leo up on her hip so the two-year-old could rest his forearms and chin on the railing and watch his sister doze for a while, her cheeks working furiously on her thumb. Then Angela changed and groomed her son, and took him to the kitchen like a gift, but found that Hitler had taken off his jacket because of the heat and had moved from Aunt Johanna to the company of men.

The monsignor was saying, "And confirmation was worse. Whitsunday, 1903, 1904?"

Without interest, Hitler said, "1904."

"Of all the boys being confirmed, he was the sulkiest, the most unpleasant, the most ill-prepared; as if religion were a giant bore for him, and confirmation repugnant. We had to drag the words out of his mouth." The monsignor filled his stein again as he asked, "You don't go to Mass or confession anymore, I'll wager."

Scoffing at the notion, Hitler said, "I have been a pagan all my life."

Raubal hit him on the head with the flat of his hand.

"Ow!" Hitler said, and worried his hair.

"Monsignor is trying to save your soul."

The old priest turned to Raubal. "At the confirmation party he ran outside to play Red Indians with nine-year-olds. And him fifteen."

"It's of a piece," Raubal said.

"Leo," Angela cautioned, "manners." She turned to Adolf. She was six years older than her half-brother and fondly remembered the sunny days when she'd put him in a stroller and parade with him, pretending he was her child. Ever since then she'd been able to forgive him anything. She touched his wrist. "Are you hungry, Adolf?"

Her half-brother unhappily examined the potatoes in jackets, the cold kielbasa, the Russian eggs, the gherkins, the herring rolls, a hunk of Gouda cheese, and, complaining that it was Jewish food, asked Angela to please make him *Mehlspeise*, a flour-based, meatless dish.

She was heading to the pantry when Raubal shouted, "Don't *cook* for him! Eat what we eat, Adolf!"

Kubizek finished his beer and stood. "You have a piano. Why don't I play us something?"

Excitedly, Hitler said, "We'll do a duet!"

The party moved to the front room where there was a magnificent Heitzmann grand piano that Hitler's mother had given him when it seemed to her that Adolf was full of fabulous talents that needed only to be stirred. Kubizek sat on the right side of the bench and deftly handled the primo parts, while Hitler hunched over the left half of the keyboard and hammered the secondo score of Antonio Diabelli's "The Pleasures of Youth." Enthusiastic applause at its conclusion encouraged them to try a minuet by Franz Joseph Haydn, but Hitler struggled enough that when they finished, his sister Paula frankly said, "We want to hear August alone now."

Hitler got up from the bench, but not without saying, "It's my piano, you know."

Raubal suggested that Kubizek honor the monsignor by playing something by Anton Bruckner, the former organist at the Alter Dom in Linz.

"Anton Bruckner," the old priest sighed. "He could turn any church into a cathedral." And then he sat heavily on the sofa with Aunt Johanna as Kubizek interpreted *Symphony No. 7*.

Angela tipped the wing chair on its hind legs and pulled it to the sofa, then sat with little Leo on her knee.

The party listened in silence to the piano for a few minutes. And then Aunt Johanna tilted toward Angela and in a hushed voice said, "Adolf asked me for his inheritance."

"What inheritance?"

"Whatever I intend to give him when I'm gone—he wants it now. Yours, too. Says he'll pay it all back when it's time."

Angela let her fidgety son get on the floor. "And what did you say?"

"That I didn't know what was worse, his greed or his effrontery."

"Are you talking about me?" Hitler asked. His hands were folded behind his back as he listened to his friend, but his head was turned to them.

"Have you no ethics?" Angela asked.

Hitler faced his Heitzmann grand piano again.

Too *beschwipst* with beer to pay attention to the music, the monsignor asked Aunt Johanna, "What nationality is Pölzl?"

"Moravian," she said. "Czech."

Angela said, "So is Hitler, we think. From Hidlar, or Hidlarček. Meaning 'small holder.' Aunt Johanna's sister and my father were both from the Waldviertel region of Austria."

"The village of Spital," Aunt Johanna said.

"Close to the Czechoslovakian border," Angela said.

The monsignor folded his hands on his stomach. "I see."

Kubizek heard their talking and halted after the first few pages of the score. Without irritation, he said, "Well, you get the idea."

"Continue, Gustl!" Hitler exclaimed.

"It's too hot to concentrate," Kubizek said.

The monsignor was still interested in genealogies. "And your grandmother went by what name, Angela?"

"On my father's side? Maria Schicklgruber."

"A good Austrian name. And your grandfather?"

And then Hitler was there, his hands folded in front of his fly, his forehead wormed with a vein of fury as he asked, "Confession, is it? In public?"

"Watch your tone," Raubal said.

Angela told the priest, "We don't know."

The monsignor thought for an instant and put it together. "Your father, Alois, was illegitimate?"

Raubal said, "We heard their grandmother was a maid in the house of a man—"

Hitler shouted, "You don't know! It's gossip! Reckless speculation!"

Raubal asked him, "Why are you always so noisy?" And he continued, "Of a man named Frankenberger and got pregnant. Whether by him or his son, we aren't sure."

"You aren't *sure* of anything," Hitler said. "It is *not* a true story!"

"It happens so often," the old priest said. "A girl without money. And the tedium, the proximity to a boy her age, the promise of wealth."

"We're going, Gustl," Hitler said, and he went to get his jacket, his silk top hat, his ivory-handled cane.

"We'll change the subject!" the monsignor called.

Angela got up. "Don't be like this, Adolf!"

"What shall I be?" he asked. "Without shame?"

Leo Junior waved his hand and said, "Bye-bye, Uncle Adolf."

Hitler firmly fixed his top hat on his head and tilted onto his cane as he asked with a false smile, "And what kind of name, Monsignor, is Frankenberger? Why have you failed to ask that? I wonder, is it Jewish?"

"Could be."

Hitler withdrew to the front door and halted to say, "I have seldom had so unpleasant an afternoon. And I won't again. I shall have nothing further to do with my family."

And then he fled the house as Leo Raubal whistled and clapped his hands.

Chapter Two
Schleissheimerstrasse 34, 1913

Worried that Adolf was dead or dying, Angela Raubal left Leo Junior with Paula and took her five-year-old daughter to München in the fall of 1913 in hopes of finding her lost half-brother, who was wanted by federal authorities in Austria for failing to register for military duty.

Angela was then, at thirty, a widow of three years' standing. Leo Raubal had died unexpectedly from a simple bronchial catarrh in 1910, and his wife had only inherited three children to take care of and a civil official's monthly pension that hardly paid the rent.

August Kubizek had attended Leo Raubal's funeral Mass in Linz and, afterward, the reception for friends and family at the house on Bürgergasse, frankly expecting to find Adolf there, and forlorn when he didn't. While sitting with Angela on the sofa, Kubizek told her that in the fall of 1908 he'd gone away for eight weeks of training with the Second Austro-Hungarian Infantry Regiment, and when he'd gotten back to the flat on Stumpergasse in November, he'd found that Hitler had abruptly moved out and had left no forwarding address. And still no letters or postcards had arrived from his friend.

"Of course there'd been differences of opinion and horrible rows," Kubizek told her, "but with Adolf that was quite normal. I've been pondering the situation for a long time now and I haven't discovered the slightest reason for his hurt feelings or his silence. He'd never so much as hinted at our parting, even in moments of anger. I feel so despised and alone."

"I, too," Angela said.

Kubizek remembered that Leo had just been buried and said, "Oh, I'm so sorry. I'm being insensitive. Your loss is far greater."

Angela grimly said, "Yes, it is."

With few job opportunities in Linz and, as far as she could see, no available men with the fortitude to marry a widow with three children, Angela finally was forced to move the family to Wien in 1913, finding work as a chambermaid in a one-star hotel. She still had not seen her half-brother for a long time, and she'd received only one letter, and that one so formal and unfamiliar it had seemed a form of sarcasm.

But Paula was becoming a weekly rebellion, and the children needed the firmness and safety of a father, even if he was one as childish and hot-tempered as their uncle. So Angela finally did what August Kubizek had failed to do earlier, going to the central registration office at police headquarters in Wien where she discovered that Adolf Hitler's last known address had been at Sechshauserstrasse 58, where he'd listed his occupation as "Writer." But that was three years ago. The only other police form he'd filled out had a blank line after "Address."

She went to Sechshauserstrasse, where an older woman in the building thought she'd seen Hitler sleeping on a park bench one night, and suggested Angela try the hostelries that served the poor.

She did that, going systematically from one to the other over the next few days before finding on Meldmannstrasse a hostel known as the Männerheim. A few of the homeless men there remembered Hitler well, for his offensive clothes were so ferocious with lice that they'd been forced to hold him down to his bed while they stripped him and scrubbed all he owned with kerosene. Others remembered him shouting venomously against the Habsburgs, singing "The Watch on the Rhine" as he shaved, chilled to the bone because he'd sold his winter coat in the fall, concentrating on watercolor postcards of famous buildings that he'd sell to tourists on the street, or hanging around an occult bookshop in the Old Quarter. And that's where she went next.

She wanted to exit as soon as she entered the shop, for it stank of old food and dirty shirts, flecks of dust hived in the fusty air, and an insane chaos of books and pamphlets were heaped on the floor or sloppily jammed in close bookcases that seemed a jolt away from tipping. Charts for astrology and alchemy were on the walls, and there were framed photographs of weird and glaring people she hoped she'd never meet. She heard a man say from a storage room, "Who is it?" She gave her name, and immediately the owner hurried forward through the draped doorway and with both his damp hands held hers as he introduced himself as Ernst Pretzsche. A hunched little man far smaller than Angela, he seemed all too fascinated that she was Hitler's half-sister, inching ever closer to her as he talked about his dear friendship with Adolf and her own beauty, while the only thing she could think was that his face was like a toad's. She asked him where Hitler was, but he seemed not ready to tell her yet. Holding his hand to his heart, he exclaimed, "To have such a genius as a relative! I won't pretend I don't envy you, Frau Raubal. Young Hitler! That self-confidence, that passion, that force of will, those mystical eyes!"

"Have you seen him lately?"

Pretzsche simply wiped out a cup with his handkerchief and filled it with cold coffee for her, then offered Angela the stool behind his cash register as he told her his own history, saying he'd grown up in Mexico where his father was an apothecary and a weekend anthropologist who'd studied the magic rites and blood cult of the Aztecs. "But you don't like the black arts," he said.

"You can tell?"

His facial expressions swam from one to another, as if holding on to just one was a feat of coordination. "You need not patronize me," he said.

"You haven't told me yet where Adolf is."

"You don't believe I know him?" he asked.

"But I *do*."

"Stay!" he said, and scuttled down an aisle. "I'll show you a book he sold back to me!" And he produced a foxed and tattered old copy of *Parsival* by Wolfram von Eschenbach, telling Angela that Eschenbach was a thirteenth-century lyric poet whose famous legend about the Holy Grail had been the inspiration for the nineteenth-century opera by Richard Wagner.

She took the book from him and saw Adolf's signature inside the front cover. And then she turned a few pages and was shocked to find Hitler's handwriting all over them, filling all the white space as he commented on the text, corrected phrasings, cited other authorities, heralded a useful footnote with an exclamation mark and dismissed another with "NO!"

"Was this a favorite book?" she asked.

"Oh yes," Pretzsche said, "but so were a hundred others. Ancient Rome, yoga, hypnotism, astrology, phrenology, the Eastern religions, Wotan. Unfortunately, he couldn't afford to buy books. So I took pity on the boy and let him borrow."

"But why was he poor?"

Pretzsche fiddled with a fountain pencil in his shirt pocket as he looked to the front door. No one else was there. "Maybe he gambled, or lost it on women. Maybe he was paying a tutor. Who knows what happens to money?"

Angela gave him back his coffee cup and got up from the stool. "You haven't seen him for a while?"

"A full year. Maybe longer."

"Have you any idea where he'd be?"

A faltering smile squirmed onto his wide mouth as he inquired with quaint innocence, "Are you still unmarried, Frau Raubal?"

She headed for the front door.

"Wait!" he called. And when she didn't, he called, "Bavaria!"

She turned. "Where?"
"Aren't there artists there?"

■ ■ ■

Riding west through Austria with five-year-old Geli in a second-class railway car, Angela lifted up a picnic basket and got out a lunch of Wienerwürstl, rye rolls, sweet mustard, and white radishes. She told her daughter that München was short for *bei den Mönchen*, "at the home of the monks." Cowled Franciscan friars had been brewing beer there in the twelfth century. And now there were hundreds and hundreds of breweries.

"Are we going to see somebody?" Geli asked.

Angela said, "You don't remember your uncle, do you?"

Geli shook her head.

Angela told her all about him. She was six years older than Adolf, she said, and had grown up up thinking of the tiny boy as her plaything, a favorite doll. She'd called him *Schatzi*, Sweetie. But he was a *Muttersöhnchen*, a mother's darling; she often vied with Frau Klara Hitler to hold or coddle him, and both found it easiest to talk when Adolf was the subject. Klara Pölzl had been serving as Angela's mother's maid when she'd gotten pregnant, and she'd been four months along when Angela's mother died and Klara married Alois Hitler, her uncle. Twenty-three years younger than Alois, the obedient girl never thought of him as less than a superior being and throughout their marriage addressed her tyrannical husband as "Uncle." If he were away and she needed to scold, Klara would point to his rack of meerschaum and calabash pipes as a sign of authority. Angela told Geli that the family had lived for three years in Passau am Inn in southern Germany, and she'd frequently heard Adolf describe his childhood there as the happiest years of his life. You could still hear a hint of a Bavarian accent when he talked. She confessed that she'd taught herself to kiss at twelve by kissing him, and when she'd been flooded with love for a high school boy who'd hardly known she existed, she'd found a kind of self-fulfillment in offering her affections to Adolf, fondling him, telling him how

handsome he was, how gifted and intelligent, how worthy of everything. Oh, how she had adored him then! Even their father, Alois,
who was hard to please and had chased his first son, Alois Junior,
away from home with his carping, was flamboyantly proud of Adolf,
helping his friends remember the high grades his son won at the
Benedictine school at Lambach, how he sang such a glorious tenor
at the choirboys institute, how he had a head for facts of all kinds as
well as a hand at art. But Adolf only recalled his father's chidings,
his criticisms, his canings. "And he recalls nothing but his mother's
saintliness," Angela said. And then she added, "Will you always
think of me as saintly?"

Geli smiled. "Uh-huh."

At the Hauptbahnhof, the main railway station in München,
Angela asked a woman selling used jewelry on a blanket where the
writers and artists stayed. "Everything is in Schwabing," she was
told.

She therefore took her little girl on a six-block tram ride into the
district and got off at the first café, where Angela began holding up
to idlers there an old photograph of an unhappy Hitler in the
Realschule at Steyr. Within the hour, in front of a Schwabing
cabaret called The Eleven Executioners, she'd found a white-
bearded sidewalk caricaturist who, once he'd ascertained that she
was not a creditor, told Angela he was not particularly a friend but
that he sometimes talked Communism with Adolf Hitler and
thought he sold his watercolor versions of postcard scenes at the
Kunsthandlung Stuffle on Maximilianstrasse. And at the gallery she
finally learned that her half-brother lived at Schleissheimerstrasse
34, above the Josef Popp Tailor Shop.

A friendly Frau Elisabeth Popp welcomed Angela and Geli to
Germany and, just to confirm that it was the same Herr Hitler, got
out a registration form he'd filled in with his fast, slashing, handwriting style on May 25, 1913. "Adolf Hitler," it read. "Architectural Painter from Wien."

"An Austrian charmer, he is," the landlady said. "Ever so gallant
and funny. But can't he be a mystery? You just never know what he's

thinking." Frau Popp thought he was out now, but she took them up to his third-floor furnished room to wait for him there. She confided to Angela on the way up that she need not fear, Herr Hitler was quiet, pleasant, helpful, and fastidious, and she'd never once seen him with kangaroos.

Angela thought that rather faint praise until she determined that "kangaroo" was slang for "prostitute."

The landlady unlocked his door with a skeleton key. "Often he stays home for days at a time, hardly eating or drinking, his head buried in those books of his. Shall I stay with you?"

"We'll be fine," Angela said, and Frau Popp walked sideways down the sheer cliff of stairs.

The flat was furnished with a feather bed, a lavender sofa, a petroleum lamp, a ladder-back chair and a dining table, and matching oleograph prints of a schnauzer and a dachshund. Angela installed Geli on the sofa where she swung her legs and dangled her unlaced shoes from her toes as her mother hunted for food for them. She found only a mostly finished tin of English biscuits and four chocolate-covered almonds in a box. She gave Geli a biscuit, then wandered to the dining table and its high stack of books on loan from the Bayerische Staatsbibliothek. She lifted off something titled *Das Kapital* and feared the worst as she flipped through the pages, but was relieved to find none of his crazy handwriting inside. She began reading the first chapter but found it hard going, then heard the flat's door open.

Angela turned and tried to find Adolf the wolfish, skinny Artist there, five feet nine in height and no more than one hundred twenty pounds, with injustice in his milk-white face and his hand still theatrically on the door handle as if he would soon slam it. His fairly clean but unshorn hair was in avalanche at his frayed green collar, his first try at a full goatee was like a child's crayoned jeer on a face in a poster, and his hand-me-down clothing was as weirdly pied as a jester's: ankle-high shoes with broken laces, a yolk-yellow waistcoat underneath a too tight and short-wristed purple suit, a green shirt, a blood-red tie.

The landlady seemed to have prepared Hitler for his family being there, for he acknowledged the little girl on the sofa with flitting glances, then scowled at the book in Angela's hand as he walked in, saying, "I have been immersing myself in a doctrine of destruction called Marxism."

"Is it politics?" Angela asked.

"Everything. Economics, politics, culture. A world plague."

Angela looked at the book beneath it, Jörg Lanz von Liebenfels's *The Book of German Psalms: The Prayerbook of Arios-Racial Mystics and Anti-Semites*. And beneath that was a book by Berthold Otto, *The Future State as a Socialist Monarchy*. She heard in her head what her late husband would say and couldn't help but ask it. "Will you make money with all this reading?"

"Dear Frau Raubal," Adolf said with an insincere smile, "Who knows for certain what will or will not be of use to him in life?"

Geli was fiddling with a shoelace, and afraid to look at her uncle. Sitting jauntily next to the little girl, he waggled her knee with his hand. "And you are Angelika all grown up?"

With great seriousness she held up her right hand, her five fingers spread. "I'm this many."

"So old! I am all my fingers and toes, two eyes, two ears, and not yet a nose. What is that?"

She giggled, but shrugged.

"Twenty-four," he answered. Crossing his legs, he held his higher knee with his hands as he inquired of Geli, as of a waitress in the Löwenbräukeller, "And you, Fräulein Raubal. What have you been reading? Anything good?"

Geli seemed full of regret as she said, "I don't know how to read yet."

Angela asked, "You are liking München, Adolf?"

"Absolutely! " he said. "And Schwabing is the capital of the arts in Europe."

Angela looked at his easel. On it was a half-finished painting of the Cuvilliés Theater. On the floor was a fine if academic rendering of the sixteenth-century St. Michael's Church, where the Wittelsbach royalty were buried.

"I haven't turned pious," Hitler said. "Churches sell."

Angela held up a penciled sketch of the Hauptbahnhof for her daughter and asked, "Have you seen this building, Angelika?"

She shook her head.

"But you did! Where did we get off the train?"

"Oh."

Angela frowned at a watercolor of the Sendlinger Tower. "Why are the people so tiny?"

"I have trouble with proportions," he said, flushing with petulance and embarrassment. "Why are you here?"

"Are you aware that Austria has a compulsory service law?"

"Angela! You surprise me. You're working for the Austrian government now?"

"Look at what I have been getting in the mail!" She got an official document from her purse and handed it to him. It indicated that Herr Hitler was to present himself for Austrian military service in Linz within a fortnight. If he failed to comply, he would be prosecuted, and if he was found guilty of having left Austria with the object of evading military service, he would be fined heavily and imprisoned.

Adolf folded the official document and handed it back to her. "I have no fear of prison."

"Oh good," Angela said, "because the police tell me you'll be arrested at the border."

"And why would I go back to Austria?"

"Us!"

"Who's that?"

"Your family!" she shouted, and watched him chew his fingernails as she urged him to find a real job in Linz or Wien, to register for his Austrian military duty, and to help in taking care of his childlike, seventeen-year-old sister.

And then it was Adolf's turn to argue, and she found she was no equal to his flame as he wildly paced all around the flat, his hands flying, his voice a screech as he harangued his half-sister about a hopeless Austro-Hungarian army composed of gypsies and mongrel people, about Wien, the home of the despicable Habsburgs and their Babylon of mixed races, and about his own Wagnerian genius as a thinker and artist that she wanted quelled with grinding labor and drudgery.

It was the tyranny of anger she'd grown used to with him. Angela begged him to see things her way, but she hated her own whining tone as much as she hated his nastiness and scorn, which reminded her so much of their father's, and so she finally did what his mother would do. "Dear Adolf," she said, "you're so worked up. Are you hungry?"

Obviously he was, but he wouldn't say so.

"Shall I get us some groceries? We can talk later, when we've eaten. We'll all feel better then."

With anxiety he again noticed his niece on the sofa. "Don't stay away long."

"Shall I take her, then?"

Hitler shrugged. "I have no company here usually. I'm a hermit. She won't be a nuisance?"

"You'll be good, won't you, Geli?"

"And quiet?" he asked.

The little girl looked at her mother in fright.

"She'll be fine," Angela said.

Hitler shoved his forelock left with his right hand. "Kindergarten isn't man's work, you know."

Angela sighed, got her hat and purse, and went out.

A sheet of paper with handwriting on it was weighted down by an inkwell on the sill beside his bed. The little girl pointed to it. "What's that?"

"A poem," he said. "About my mother. She's passed away."

"Oh," she said. And then, "Will you read it to me?"

Uncle Adolf sighed, but twisted to get it. "'Think of It!'" he read. "That's the title."

She was listening with great seriousness.

"'*When your mother has grown older, / And you, too, have grown older, / When what was formerly effortless / Now becomes a burden, /*

When her dear loyal eyes / Do not look out into life as before, / When her legs have grown tired / And fail to carry her anymore— / Then lend her your arm for support, / Accompany her with gladness and joy. / The hour will come when, weeping, you / Will join her on her last journey! / And if she asks questions, answer her. / And if she asks again, have patience. / And if she asks another time, speak to her / Not stormily, but in gentle affection! / And if she cannot understand you well, / Explain everything joyfully. / The hour will come, the bitter hour / When her mouth will ask no more!'"

She finally said, "Oh."

"A good poem?" her uncle asked.

She gravely nodded.

Hitler slid the sheet of paper under the inkwell again, and then he seemed to faint, falling backward onto his feather bed and throwing a forearm over his eyes.

"Are you sad?" Geli asked.

After a few seconds, he said, "Tired."

The sofa fabric was making her thighs itch, so Geli slid off. "I'm hot," she said.

"Darling, I have to rest a little."

She heard a ticking clock on the windowsill and walked to it. She put her ear to its face. She got up on tiptoes and looked out the window to a playground on the other side of Schleissheimerstrasse, but no children were in it. She found three paintbrushes in a full glass of water. She slightly lifted the tallest one and watched a faint strand of blue paint float from it and change into smoke, and then there was nothing but tinted water. She watched her uncle to make sure she was being good. His fists were clenching and unclenching. His hands were fair and hairless. One ankle-high shoe was still on the floor, the other was rucking the quilt. She squatted and stared underneath the bed. A high stack of magazines was there. She pulled out the top one and held it in her lap as she sat on the shellacked planks of the floor. She traced the big letters on the front cover.

"*Ostara*," her uncle said.

She looked up and found him critically watching her from the feather bed with the *Those are mine* face that she often got from her brother.

"Ostara is the ancient Germanic goddess of the spring."

With great effort she turned the pages of the magazine, finding a puzzling cartoon of a pretty blond woman whose clothes had fallen off and who seemed to be crying and hitting with her fists a hairy human being or ape who seemed to be trying to lie on top of her. "What's happening?" she asked.

"It's what Jews do to Aryan virgins. You wouldn't understand."

She turned a page. "What's it say?"

"'Are you blond?'" he read. "'Then you are a culture-creator and a culture supporter! Are you blond? If so, dangers threaten you!'" Hitler got down on the floor beside his niece and held up other magazines in the stack. "The 'Race and Welfare' issue," he said. "And here's one on 'Sexual Physics, or Love as Odylic Energy.'" Then he guided Geli's forefinger under the fancy lettering as he read the front page of another: "'The Dangers of Women's Rights and the Necessity for a Masculine Morality of Masters.'" Hitler went to another. "And here's my favorite, Angelika. 'Judging Character Through the Shape of Skulls.'"

"Why is it your favorite?"

Hitler's hands fell upon her head and felt all around underneath her hair, saying in a ferocious voice, "Because I can tell if Angelika's naughty or nice just by feeling the knobs on her noggin!"

Hitler's niece squealed with delight.

■ ■ ■

When Angela got back to the flat with groceries, she found them still on the floor, wildly laughing as their hands inched along each other's flushed faces. "I have food for us," she said.

Hitler raked a hand through his flowing hair as he sat up. "What kind?"

"Leberkäs, sauerkraut, and strudel."

"And coffee?"

"Chicory. And milk. Many things."

She started putting the food away and Hitler held Geli close as he stage-whispered, "This is what it is to have a mother!"

Chapter Three
The Corporal and the
Schatzkammer, 1919

Late in the first year of the Great War, Angela was pawning an emerald necklace for food money when she happened upon a shop window that displayed a famous press photograph taken in München in August 1914. The photo featured a huge crowd gathered at the Feldherrnhalle, the Hall of the Field Marshals, to register their wild enthusiasm for the alignment of Germany with Austria in a war against Russia and Serbia, a conflict that they thought would be over within a few weeks. And Angela was surprised to find Adolf there in the front of that rally, white-faced and frail, his hair now short, his hat lifted high in a cheer, happier than she'd ever seen him. She found out that Adolf had formally petitioned Ludwig III for permission to enlist in the Bavarian army and, in spite of his general unhealthiness, had been accepted as a volunteer. Even though it meant forfeiting his Austrian citizenship, Hitler was overjoyed, and he later wrote Angela, "I am not ashamed to say that I fell to my knees and thanked Heaven with an overflowing heart for granting me the good fortune of being allowed to live at this time."

Angela in fact got few letters from her half-brother in the four years of the war, but Hitler was in regular correspondence with his former landlords, Josef and Elisabeth Popp, and they often forwarded news of him to the Raubals in Wien. And so they heard from Elisabeth Popp that Hitler was with the Sixteenth Bavarian Reserve Infantry Regiment. She told them that his friends called him "Laced Boots," called him "Adi." And now he was a *Meldegänger*, an orderly and runner between headquarters on the front, "functioning," as he put it in one letter, "as a field telephone," the favorite target of snipers. "My highest goal," he wrote, "is to follow my superior blindly and contradict no one." In occasional postcards from the Popps, Angela heard that he was in Ypres, Belgium; in Messines; in the battle of the Somme. His favorite food, he'd told them, was zwieback toast and honey. Sergeant Max Amann had gotten him to paint the officers' dining room. A superior's report noted that he was "modest and inconspicuous," which he took as high praise. He'd found a lost white terrier he'd named Little Fox. Schopenhauer's *The World as Will and Idea* was in his backpack and he was memorizing it.

Even at Christmas, when Angela expected some private summary of his year on the front, she got only one poem:

> *I often go on bitter nights*
> *To Wotan's oak in the quiet glade*
> *And with dark powers form a union!*
> *The moon offers spells and magic*
> *And all who are defiant in daylight*
> *Are made fearful and insignificant!*
> *Shells and guns and bayonets*
> *No longer have power over me!*
> *I am Wotan and in charge*
> *Of my own destiny!*
> *Enemies waving their shining swords*
> *Are all changed into pillars of stone!*
> *So the false ones part from the real ones*

As I consult the ancient nest of words
And find formulas of blessings and prosperity
For the pure, the just, and the good!

Angela heard secondhand that a shell had wounded him, and in the field hospital he'd been awakened by a nurse, the first female he'd seen in two years. And then he was healing in Beelitz, outside Berlin, where he found "only hunger and dire misery." Children were drinking coffee because there was no milk, and cats were being called "roof rabbits." And then he was in the Ludendorff offensives on the Somme, on the Aisne, and on the Marne. Just before the Armistice she heard he'd been blinded by a gas attack near the village of Werwick. Another letter forwarded from the Popps reported that he was "fit for field service" again and was living in "the pigsty of the Türkenstrasse barracks" near his old Schwabing neighborhood. Angela heard that Frau Popp had taken a calf's head vinaigrette to him and that he'd finished it in one sitting. She said Hitler wouldn't say what he was still doing in the army, but he'd told her he was stunned to hear that the Raubals never got his letters. *Liar*, Angela thought.

Then, six years after Angela and Geli had last seen him in München, Hitler showed up, on a furlough, at their flat near the Westbahnhof in Wien. Geli was then eleven and her uncle was thirty, and handsome, she thought, in his polished boots and gray, high-necked tunic and a faintly perfumed, gull-winged mustache known as a *Kaiserbart*. She peered closely at his hero's medals as he proudly described them to his niece and his admiring thirteen-year-old nephew: the Iron Cross, first class; the Iron Cross, second class; the Military Cross, third class, with swords; the regiment's diploma for conspicuous bravery; the Medal for the Wounded; and the Service Medal, third class. And then he let Leo feel through his gray woolen trousers the gouge that a shell had torn in his left thigh. Even after four years in the war, Hitler had gone no farther in rank than *Gefreiter*, a lance corporal, owing to his Austrian background, he told Leo, and to the circumstance that his preferred and dangerous job as a runner could not be held by someone with a higher rank.

His twenty-three-year-old sister Paula hesitantly brought out
their finest porcelain tea service and simpered and curtsied to him
before going back into the kitchen to help Angela with the Austrian dessert that was called *Kaiserschmarren*. And then Leo was sent
to the bakery for rolls because their only bread was the wretched
stuff made of potato peelings and sawdust.

And so the choreography of family allowed his niece to be alone
with Hitler in the parlor, watching silently and starstruck as he sat
forward in her father's old chair and held a Dresden teacup and
saucer rather daintily in his hands, letting the tea become lukewarm
and then cold as he talked and talked about the endless war of attri-
tion that Germany would have won were it not for the pacifists and
slackers and traitors who had signed the armistice.

She imagined this was how it was to have a father or a husband.
To be affectionate, first of all, to tell him how gallant he looked, to
offer him spice cakes or strudel, to loll in a heated parlor, to hear his
voice and be the still pond on which he skimmed his opinions. She
tried to seem poised. She found herself adjusting her stockings and
her skirt, but he failed to notice. She otherwise kept her ankles
crossed and her hands folded and her head tilted in fascination.
When she lost track of what he was saying, she'd gently smile and
Uncle Adolf would be encouraged to go on with his monologue.

Often in Belgium, he told her, they were forced to hide from
heavy artillery fire for days on end. In cold trenches of crumbling
mud. With water up to their knees. And so it was a relief to charge
forward, hearing the first shrapnel hissing overhead. Watching it
explode at the edge of the forest, splintering trees as if they were
straws.

"We observe it all with curiosity," he said. "We have no idea yet
of danger. We crawl forward on our stomachs while above us are
only howls and hisses. Shattered trees surround us. Shells explode
and hurl clouds of stone, earth, and sand into the air. Even the
heaviest trees are torn out by their roots. We get to water, a stream,
and though it offers some protection, we find it choked in the
yellow-green stink of poisons. We cannot lie there forever, and if we

have to fall in battle, we choose to be killed as heroes. We attack and retreat four times. And do you know, Geli, from my whole company only one other soldier remains, and finally he also falls? And so I am alone. A shot tears off my right coat sleeve, but I remain safe and unscathed. Quickly I find a hiding place. At two o'clock in the afternoon others join me and we go forward for the fifth time, and finally we occupy the forest and the farms. We slaughter all the animals, until the fields flow red with blood. Within a few days, we withdraw."

Seeming exhausted, Hitler slumped back into her father's chair and sipped his heavily sugared tea, waiting for his niece to respond, but she didn't know what to say. She thought she'd failed to understand him, for his story seemed full of awfulness softly rendered, but his face was pink with vibrancy and his freakishly pale eyes were finely tuned on hers.

"We used to read about the battles in school," she said. "It was horrible. The girls used to cry."

Hitler held his stare for an uncomfortable minute more. She worried that he was trying to read her mind. And then slowly, like a man just getting used to his body, he curled to his left to gently put his Dresden teacup and saucer down on a shined side table, the clack as faint as when good teeth meet.

"Another time I was eating my dinner in a trench with several comrades," he said. "Suddenly I seemed to hear a voice saying to me, 'Get up and go over there.' It was so clear and so insistent that I obeyed mechanically, as if it were just another military order. At once I got to my feet and walked twenty yards along the trench, carrying with me my fork and my dinner in its tin can. I found a shell box and sat down on it to go on eating, my busy mind being once more at rest. Hardly had I done so when a flash and a deafening boom came from the part of the trench I had just left. A shell had detonated over the friends I'd just been with. All of them were killed."

"We're so glad you're still alive," she said.

Leo rushed into the flat with the rolls and flinched when he saw

Geli alone with their uncle. "Wait for me, Uncle Adolf," he said. "Don't tell her anything more." But when he took the rolls into the kitchen, Angela told him to get changed for dinner. Walking down the hallway, Leo called, "Two minutes!"

Confidentially, Hitler leaned forward and told his niece one more story. "October," he said, "1918." In Belgium, near Werwick, his infantry regiment, filled to overflowing with defeatists and pessimists and future deserters, had been attacked by British artillery with a poison called mustard gas and his regiment was forced to retreat. Hitler had lost his voice and his face had swelled like a penny balloon until he was blinded. At a hospital in Pasewalk just outside Berlin, he'd heard the news of Germany's surrender in the forest of Compiègne, and his heart had ached as it had only once before, after his mother had died in the agony of cancer. Would he ever see again? The question was no longer that. The question was: Would his beloved motherland die as his mother had?

At that point Uncle Adolf placed a surprisingly damp hand on her knee as he said, "But, Angelika, as I was lying on my cot that night—and you must picture it: frightened, confused, full of hatred, in the blackest state of despair—a miracle came to pass! Like Joan of Arc, I heard voices. Each one crying out, 'Save Germany!'"

Geli giggled, for she thought he was kidding, but his face was serious and his eyes were aflame with fury. She thought for a second that he might strike her.

But he controlled his emotions and calmly said, "To be sure, it's peculiar. Quite out of the ordinary. But you see, when I opened my eyes, I was no longer blind! And I vowed then and there that I would become a politician and offer my life in the hope of changing Germany's fate."

"A politician?" she asked. She thought they were all aristocrats. She felt his hand staying on her knee. Would he waggle it as he did when he was teasing?

"You see what these stories have in common? I am a child of providence, Fräulein Raubal." He released his hand and smiled. "You will hear much about me. Just wait until my time comes."

■ ■ ■

Adolf failed to offer Angela money for food though his soldier's pay
had accrued to a tidy sum on the front and the Raubals' poverty was as
obvious as the canning jars they used for glassware. And yet she made
him such a feast that even Adolf noticed, he who was like an infant in
his alertness only to himself. Tucking a napkin at his throat and fanning it over his medals and ribbons, he smiled at a dining table filled
with Tyrolean dumplings on sauerkraut, red beets in a horseradish
cream, and four squabs on a bed of celery stalks and onions. And he
said, "Such prodigality, Angela! Where is the fatted calf?"

"Well, it's not like we often see you, Corporal Hitler."

A fierce glare was flung at Angela, but then it softened as Hitler
chose to pinion a squab with his fork and vulgarly dump it onto his
dinner plate. And then he sawed so hard at the fowl with his knife
that the flames trembled on their candlewicks. *Would he be sucking
his fingers next?* Angela thought. The Raubals just stared, until with
a strictness and confidence worthy of his father, Hitler said without
lifting his gaze, "Everybody, begin."

Eating did not halt his talking. Only his listening seemed
affected. Inquiry about Angela's or Paula's jobs, other opinions, or
the children's hobbies and schools never occurred to him as he told
the Raubals and his sister that for a while he had served as a fence
guard in a prisoners-of-war camp, near Traunstein, on the Austrian
border. But higher-ups had become aware of his perspicacity and
loyalty to Germany, even if it was now a republic headed by Jews,
and he had been sent back to München to confirm the fidelity of
Reichswehr soldiers by spying on the fifty or more organizations of
Communists, Anarchists, Socialists, Centrists, even the Bavarian
Royal party—politics being one of the few industries that flourished
in postwar Germany. Technically an education officer, he had taken
courses in propaganda and politics at the Ludwig-Maximilians Universität, where he'd been fortunate in that all the lecturers were,
like him, nationalists, anti-Left, and anticlerical; and he could now
say with certainty that four years of war had been the equivalent of

thirty years in a university. "I have a doctorate in sorrow, a doctorate in treachery, and a doctorate in the ways of the world. I have no use for whatever subject is not included in those."

Hitler told them he was now a proud member of the "Instruction Commando," and regularly giving talks to Reichswehr soldiers on "The Conditions of Peace and Reconstruction" and "Social and Economic-Political Slogans," which were meant to ignite their German patriotism. And he had heard many compliments from his audience, who called his talks "spirited" and hailed him as "a born popular speaker."

Paula bluntly said, "You think you got all the talent in the family."

Adolf ignored The Straggler and turned to Angela. "But I have no talent in cooking," he said. "My older sister got all that."

"Wasn't I the lucky one," Angela said, and rose to collect the dinner plates. And Hitler was talking again. Angela saw that Paula was openly yawning, Geli's chin was on her fist as she dully fiddled with her fork, and Leo was staring wide-eyed at his uncle, as if thunderstruck by Hitler's ability to take such pleasure in himself while offering only boredom to others. Angela bent to kiss her son's head and thought, *You all are also a fortune that Adolf is squandering.*

■ ■ ■

Waking at noon on Saturday in Angela's room, Hitler was astonished to find no one but Geli still in the flat. Angela and Paula were at work—he was not interested enough to ask where—and Leo was at soccer practice in the Wurstelprater park. Geli watched him dither for an hour, sitting and getting up again, hunting for food in the icebox, agitatedly stalking by the front windows, holding up framed photographs of distant family that he frowned at—having forgotten their names—and noisily put down.

Geli asked, "Was there something you wanted to do, Uncle?"

"Something important," he said, and turned to her. "But I suppose I can't abandon you here."

She did not say that she was eleven years old and often alone in the flat. She instead connived to be with him by saying, "You could take me."

And so he did. Hitler did not tell his niece where they were going, he just strolled gracefully ahead of Geli up Rotenturmstrasse to Sankt Stephansplatz, dourly accepting the praise of Austrians who tipped their hats to his Iron Cross. Geli wore a favorite navy blue sailor dress, with a blue bow and grosgrain ribbon in her lilting, light brown hair, and she thought she looked pretty, but Hitler's far-off stare failed to find her. She tried to hold his hand, but he withdrew it. At times she was forced to skip to keep up. When he turned onto Spiegelgasse, she asked him, "Are we going to the Hofburg?"

"Well, not all of it, of course. Only the Schatzkammer. Have you been there?"

She shook her head.

"Shocking," Hitler said. And then he confided that he'd found a dear friend in the Thule Society, an occult group of deep thinkers in München. They'd taken the name "Thule" from a long-forgotten island in the North Atlantic between Scandinavia and Greenland that had been the origin of Nordic civilization and of a master race of blond, blue-eyed vegetarians. The friend he'd found had told him he *must* visit the Schatzkammer.

She worried about the odd interests of males. She asked, "Was it a boy friend or a girl friend?"

Hitler halted at the insinuation he heard, then understood her. The friend, he said, was Dietrich Eckart, a poet, a playwright, and the editor of the anti-Semitic, anti-Republican, anti-Bolshevik weekly *Auf gut deutsch* (In Plain German). "We are seeking together a national messiah."

And then they were at the Hofburg, the common name for the Imperial Palace of the Habsburgs and the former Austro-Hungarian Empire, which was now in foundering pieces. The Weltliche Schatzkammer was a treasury within the palace, and was filled with crowns, sceptors, jeweled ornaments, weighty robes, and the other fineries of majesty. But as Geli walked the aisles of the museum with her uncle, she got the impression that Hitler was disgusted by either the wild extravagance of royal wealth or by the hundreds of Czechs, Hungarians, Croatians, and Jews who were crowding around the displays, for he did little beside frown and fan imagined odors from his face until they got to the official crown of the Habsburg emperors. Then he hoisted Geli up higher so she could see the rubies and sapphires on it as he told her, "Everything wrong with Austria begins here. Who could remain a faithful subject of the House of Habsburg when they chose as their insignia the crown of Bohemia rather than the magnificent crown of the German emperors?"

She said, "Uncle, I don't understand why you wanted to come here."

And he put her down. "You will." Walking on, he furiously sidestepped through an official party of foreigners, hurried past a few more exhibits, and then halted in front of a glass case on which was a sign that read: HEILIGE LANZE. Lying on red velvet behind the glass was a leather case and within it was a hammered iron spearhead, blackened by age, a nail tied to it with gold, silver, and copper wires.

"What is it?" Geli asked.

Hitler would say nothing. He folded his arms and stared in a funereal way, as if right then he could tolerate only his own thinking.

The girl found a hand-printed placard that stated that many considered the *Heilige Lanze* to be the Spear of Longinus, reputedly used by the Roman centurion to thrust into the side of Jesus as he died at the Crucifixion. A nail thought to be from the Cross had been attached to it in the thirteenth century. Otto the Great had once owned the lance, but he was just one of forty-five emperors who'd taken possession of it between Charlemagne's coronation in Rome and the fall of the old German Empire one thousand years later. Each had believed in the legend that whoever held the spear held the destiny of the world in his hands.

"Are you interested in history?" Geli asked.

"In power," he said, and then he stood there in silence, shaking; and he stayed that way, lost to his niece, until the Schatzkammer closed an hour later.

CHAPTER FOUR
THE BEER HALL PUTSCH, 1923

Months passed, and then the Raubals got a letter from Lance Corporal Hitler telling them that he was enrolled on the staff of the "Press and Information Bureau" of the Seventh Army District Command, and working for a Captain Ernst Röhm. And they'd become such fast friends that each was soon calling the other by the familiar "*Du,*" which had helped Adolf to achieve some useful importance among the officer corps.

One night at the Brennessel Wine Cellar, Röhm and Dietrich Eckart, the famous translator of *Peer Gynt* and "a co-warrior against Jerusalem," had invited him to join the forty members of the German Workers' Party, saying they needed a good public speaker like him who was also a bachelor—"so we'll get the women"—who was shrewd in politics and firm in his convictions, was not an officer or an intellectual or in the upper class, and who'd proven he could face gunfire, for the Communists would try to kill him.

At first Hitler had been unimpressed by the faltering party—it was "like a high school debating society," he wrote in his memoirs, and "club life of the worst sort"—but the High Command thought it offered a good defense against the antimilitary and antinationalist sentiments of the working classes, and the Command had promised him all the financial support he would need. And so he'd become a member and was now chief of propaganda, with his own Adler typewriter and with former sergeant Max Amann as his business manager in a "funeral vault of an office" in the Sterneckerbräu beer hall on the Herrenstrasse. With Röhm's help, theirs was now a party of soldiers, he wrote Angela, and often one could see whole Reichswehr companies marching through the streets in civilian clothes, hunting down and bloodying those he called "Germany's enemies," by which he meant Bolsheviks, Weimar Republicans, and Jews.

A few weeks ago, he wrote, in the great feast hall of the Hofbräuhaus, he'd talked heatedly for two and a half hours to a hostile audience of about two thousand Communists and Socialists. But they hated the ineffectual Weimar Republic as much as he did, if for different reasons, and by the time he'd finished there was frenzied applause for whatever he said. "Walking away from that meeting," he wrote the Raubals, "my heart burst with joy, for I knew a great and fearsome wolf had been born, one who was destined to rage against that flock who were the pitiful seducers of the people."

The Raubals received another letter in July 1921, informing them that he was now a private citizen and was renting a flat above a drugstore at Thierschstrasse 41, not far from the Isar river. On his insistence, his organization was now called the Nationalsozialistische Deutsche Arbeiterpartei (NSDAP), the National Socialist German Workers' Party, but was primarily known by an acronym formed from the first and sixth syllables, Nazi, which was, he told the Raubals, Bavarian slang for "buddy," for, "We are friends of the common man." It was he who had designed their blood-red flag with the black Old World peace symbol of the hooked cross or swastika, now reversed on a white field in order to represent chaos and conflict, "for we are at war."

Within the last year, he wrote, he'd been the featured speaker at eighty mass meetings, harping on the financial collapse under their

Jewish-Marxist government in Berlin and arguing for a change to a "patriotic dictatorship." It was he alone who had been responsible for the burgeoning growth in the party's membership to three thousand people, and yet the founders feared his prominence and the influx of so many full-throated former soldiers into their meetings, and had sought to enfeeble his influence by an alliance with a socialist group in Augsburg. "Hearing of that, I faced them down by offering to quit. Without me, they knew there was no future for them, and so they went the other way." In fact, in a fulsome letter the party had noted his great successes, his cunning, his sacrifice, and his "unusual oratorical abilities" and had offered to make him its first chairman, dispensing with further parliamentary debates and the confusions of democracy. And so he was now called its führer, its imperious and omnipotent leader. Which was, of course, as it should be.

"And he asks how we are," Angela said, folding up his letter.

Leo smirked. "And says how much he misses us?"

"That isn't funny," Geli said.

Their mother said, "Adolf is so busy, he just forgets about others."

"But isn't it nice that he's doing so well," Paula said. "With no skills or education."

Leo's uncle mailed the high school boy a flyer announcing the party's gymnastic and sports division, which offered such things as boxing, hiking, and soccer games to its youthful members, and harnessed their strength "as an offensive force at the disposal of the movement." At the bottom of the flyer in Hitler's own handwriting was "Are you interested?", along with the notation that the name had just been changed to Sturmabteilung (SA), or Storm Detachment. The feisty young men in the SA, he wrote, were being given uniforms of Norwegian ski caps and brown shirts and swastika armbands to "infuse them with feelings of solidarity and discipline." Captain Ernst Röhm was their commander, and "he thinks of them as his private army, though their allegiance is solely to me."

Leo Raubal *was*, in fact, interested in the Sturmabteilung, but primarily because he wanted a father so badly and because his famous uncle finally seemed interested in him. Working after school and on weekends, Leo saved enough money to purchase a railway ticket to München for the first Reich Party Day of the NSDAP on January 27, 1923.

The Ruhr Valley, which was Germany's foremost manufacturing and mining region, had just been invaded by one hundred thousand French and Belgian troops on the pretense that Germany had failed to fulfill the outrageous obligations of the Versailles Treaty in its huge shipments of coal and timber. Angry Germans were fighting back through strikes, massive demonstrations, passive resistance, and sabotage, and as a consequence the *Rentenmark* lost such value in the world market that in a few weeks it fell from the already inflated seven thousand marks to the dollar to almost fifty thousand to the dollar. Within eight months the *Rentenmark* would be practically worthless at one hundred thirty billion to the dollar. Currency values were changing so frequently that factory workers tossed their wages to their wives as soon they were paid so the women could hurry off and buy groceries before prices went up again. The Weimar government was forced to use forty-nine office boys carrying huge wastepaper baskets filled with notes just to pay a railway bill. Children stayed indoors because they had no stockings. Coal was so precious that houses went unheated. There was epidemic unemployment, chronic hunger and illness, chaos in the streets, nihilism and purposelessness, and of all the chancellors, industrialists, generals, and quarreling politicians who spoke for the foundering Reich, only Adolf Hitler seemed as personally offended as the people, and the National Socialists achieved greater esteem the more he furiously protested Germany's avalanche of misery.

Wearing his new Norwegian ski cap and riding proudly in his uncle's car as Hitler went from town to town in Bavaria, Leo heard his uncle speak at twelve huge public rallies on January 27th, offering Germany only two choices, that of the red star of Communism or the swastika of National Socialism. Leo later told his family of the fanatical excitement of the people for Uncle Adolf and of his own awe in watching six thousand storm troopers hold themselves in rigid attention as they listened to Hitler talk on the windy Marsfeld, withstanding the ferocious cold through sheer effort of will. Röhm saw to it that Leo was given a copy of his uncle's speech, and in the flat in Wien afterward Leo would quote his uncle saying to the Sturmabteilung, "You who today fight on our side cannot win great laurels, far less can you win great material goods. Indeed, it is more likely that you will end up in jail. But sacrifice you must. He who today is your leader must be first of all an idealist, if only for the reason that he leads those whom the world is trying to destroy. But dream I will." The crowd was ecstatic. Afterward, Leo said, Hitler had taken him to the fancy Carlton Tearoom on Briennerstrasse where he talked with his intimates on a host of subjects. Leo told Geli and Angela, "Everybody listens with reverence to anything he has to say. What an extraordinary person!"

Angela herself heard no more of her half-brother until November 1923, when she read the headlines of an Austrian newspaper saying that General Erich Ludendorff and Adolf Hitler had attempted a putsch, or revolution, in Germany.

It seemed that on Thursday night, November 8th, cabinet ministers who were scheming to restore the Wittelsbach monarchy in Bavaria had been on stage at a mass meeting of three thousand people sitting at the timber tables of the Bürgerbräukeller—where a stein of beer cost one billion marks—as Commissar Gustav von Kahr had tendentiously condemned Communism, putting many in the audience to sleep. At precisely half past eight, Captain Hermann Göring had invaded the hall with twenty-five storm troopers carrying machine guns. Women screamed, tables were overturned, brass steins rang across the floor, and fleeing men were struck down. Wearing a black, long-tailed morning suit, as if it were a formal wedding, Hitler had strode toward the stage, gotten up on a chair, fired a Browning pistol into the ceiling, and shouted, "Quiet! The national revolution has broken out! The Reichswehr is with us, and the hall is surrounded!"

Hitler had then ordered into a side room Reichswehr Lieutenant General Otto von Lossow, the military commander of Bavaria who was, he thought, an ally, Colonel Hans von Seisser, head of the state police, and Gustav von Kahr, the head of government, and there he'd promised them all high-level appointments in a People's National Government that would put the former quartermaster general Erich Ludendorff in charge of a great national army that would march on Berlin just as Benito Mussolini and his Blackshirts had successfully marched on Rome thirteen months earlier. All three were older aristocrats of high rank in the Reichswehr, and they had looked at the thirty-four-year-old former lance corporal with contempt. Hitler had held up his pistol and threatened, "There are still four rounds in this. Three for you, my collaborators, if you abandon me," and he'd held it to his forehead, "and one for me if I fail."

An angry, fifty-eight-year-old General Ludendorff had then arrived in full regimentals and with all his decorations. While he thought Hitler had gone too far in a unilateral way, he did think revolutionary change was necessary in Germany, and he'd sought a private conversation with the three politicians to work out concessions.

Hitler had hurried back to the stage and heard whistles, catcalls, and jeers, but he had first assured the crowd that the cabinet ministers were now fully behind him and then, with his wily instincts for mass psychology, had found all the right things to say to convert the various factions in the hall, hinting that he might restore the Wittelsbachs by praising "His Majesty Crown Prince Rupprecht of Bavaria," and haranguing about the Weimar Republic and the despised Prussians who ruled that sinful Tower of Babel in Berlin, where "we shall establish a new Reich, a Reich of power and glory, Amen!"

It had been an oratorical masterpiece. Within a few minutes, the crowd was completely his. A historian there said it was like "hocus-pocus, or magic," it was as if he'd turned them inside out, "like a glove." "Loud approval roared forth, no further opposition was to be heard."

General Ludendorff had brought out the cabinet ministers, who'd formed a gentlemen's agreement to join a coalition government, and the tearfully ecstatic crowd began singing "Deutschland über

Alles" while a blissful Hitler went about the hall, shaking hands and accepting cheers. And to Gustav von Kahr, whom he'd just threatened to shoot, he had promised, "Excellency, I shall stand faithfully behind you like a hound!"

Hearing him, one skeptic had turned to a cowed policeman and said, "All that's missing here is the psychiatrist."

After midnight Captain Röhm and the SA had taken over General von Lossow's headquarters on the Schönfeldstrasse, "enemies of the people"—mainly Jews—had been taken prisoner, and the police had been told to wait and do nothing as the six bridges of München were blockaded with machine guns, the infantry school of one thousand officer candidates affiliated themselves with the Nazis, and a few Brownshirts scoured the telephone directory for names that sounded Jewish, then went to their addresses and assaulted them.

Waiters had been cleaning a Bürgerbräukeller that still held a few hundred drunken storm troopers when Hitler, who'd made his headquarters there, found out that Ludendorff had permitted the cabinet ministers to go free, for they'd promised their cooperation, and "an officer," Ludendorff had frostily told the corporal, "would never break an oath."

Hitler had fallen heavily into a chair, flummoxed and disheartened, feeling his revolution was now doomed, and he'd heard further bad news from Berchtesgaden, where Crown Prince Rupprecht had coldly rejected Hitler's messengered offer of the post of regent ad interim and instead had sent Commissar von Kahr the order to "Crush this movement at any cost. Use troops if necessary." By three a.m. all of Germany's wireless stations were sending out the message that von Kahr, von Seisser, and von Lossow had repudiated the Hitler putsch, and that their expressions of support, extracted at gunpoint, were invalid.

Word had gotten to the putsch headquarters in the Bürgerbräukeller at sunup that Röhm's headquarters were under seige by Reichswehr and state police troops. Claiming "the heavens will fall before the Bavarian Reichswehr turns against me," General Ludendorff had suggested a parade into the heart of the city to win the people to their side, and had then sipped red wine as preparations were made.

A band of musicians was supposed to form in the front and play marching songs, but they'd neither been paid nor been given breakfast, so they'd offered a raucous version of Hitler's favorite march, the "Badenweiler," and had then skulked off. Which left in front Ludendorff in his formal helmet and a brown overcoat, Hitler in his white trench coat and slouch hat, and beside him a confidant, Max Erwin von Scheubner-Richter, followed by Alfred Rosenberg and Hermann Göring, then the hundred men of the "Stosstrupp Adolf Hitler," a bodyguard that was a forerunner of the SS and was outfitted with carbines, hand grenades, and steel helmets as large as kettles. Easing along behind them was an automobile with machine guns on its backseat, then there had been a full regiment of the hung-over SA, holding rifles from which the firing pins had been removed, and perhaps a thousand shopkeepers, workers, officer candidates, and university students, "all higgledy-piggledy" as one witness said.

Wet snowflakes had been falling on a cold, gray noon as the putschists walked through the Marienplatz, where the Nazi flag had been flying atop city hall, and toward the gray, high-arched, Italianate Feldherrnhalle, where a hundred green-uniformed state police were forming a blockade. Scheubner-Richter had shaken Alfred Rosenberg's hand and said, "Things look ugly," then had linked arms with Hitler and taken off his pince-nez, telling his friend, "This may be our last walk together."

The parade had begun singing "O Deutschland hoch in Ehren"— "O Germany, High in Honor"—and those with carbines and bayonets had leveled them on the waiting police. Hitler had shouted, "Surrender! Surrender!" And then someone had fired a shot and a police sergeant was killed. The police had hesitated, and then, a fraction before the shouted order to do so, had fired a salvo on the parade. Scheubner-Richter had been killed with those first shots, and as he'd collapsed he'd pulled so heavily on Hitler's arm that he'd dislocated Hitler's left shoulder. Ulrich Graf, Hitler's bodyguard, had flung himself in front of Hitler and been hit eleven times before falling, but had lived. Alfred Rosenberg had crawled to the rear. Old soldier Ludendorff had thrown himself flat to the street at the first sounds of gunfire, hiding behind Scheubner-Richter's body until there was silence, and had then gotten up again and frowned as he'd marched forward, his hand in his left coat pocket, still confident that no one would shoot him. They had not.

Hermann Göring, who as a flying ace had won Germany's highest medal for valor in the war, the *Pour le Mérite*, and wore it ostentatiously over his fine, black leather jacket, had been hit in the upper thigh and groin. On his hands and knees he'd gotten to a hiding place behind the lions in front of the Residenz Palace where a friend had found him and helped him to the house of the first doctor he saw, at Residenzstrasse 25. The friend had asked if the owner would help them. "Of course, I'll give aid to any wounded man," Dr. Robert Ballin had said. "But I call your attention to the fact that this is a house of Jews." And still they'd gone inside.

Twenty men were killed, four of them police, and hundreds were injured in a skirmish that had lasted less than a minute. Of the sixteen Nazis whom Hitler would finally make heroes and martyrs, four were merchants, three were bank officials, three were engineers, and there had been a hat maker, a locksmith, a headwaiter, a butler, a retired cavalry captain, and a judicial official of the Bavarian Supreme Court whose bloodstained draft of a new Nazi constitution had been found folded in his pocket.

Quickly as that the putsch was over. A journalist would later call the day *Kahrfreitag*, Kahr Friday, a play on the German for Good Friday, *Kar-freitag*. A few revolutionaries had run off to a nearby girl's academy and had scrambled under the beds to hide from the police; others had fled to a *Konditorei* and had concealed their weapons in pastry ovens and flour sacks; some had just returned to their jobs as if they'd only been onlookers.

With Dr. Walter Schultze helping him, Hitler hurried away in agony, his hair falling over his face, white with failure and shame, and got into a yellow Opel automobile that had a red cross painted on its side. An old friend, Emil Maurice, got behind the wheel and drove them south toward the Austrian border as fast as he could. "What a fiasco," Hitler sighed, then said nothing more until Murnau, where he remembered that Ernst Hanfstaengl, the party's foreign press secretary, owned a country home not far away, in Uffing, on the lake called Staffelsee.

They went there. The quiet was stunning. The fields and lawn were white with snow. A farmer was walking his brown milk cows along the five-foot-high granite wall that surrounded the house. Emil Maurice and Dr. Schultze hunkered low in the Opel as Hitler trudged up to the front door and was greeted by Egon, a three-year-old boy whom Hitler often played with, and who knew him as Onkel Dolf. Egon yelled upstairs for his mother and Frau Helene Hanfstaengl came down. She was a pregnant, serene, and glamorous American woman of German descent with whom Hitler thought himself in love. Without saying anything of the putsch, or why his left arm was in a sling, he kissed her hand and meekly asked if she would let him stay for the night, and she put him up in an attic room. And it was there, still threatening suicide, that he was arrested by the police on Sunday night and taken to Landsberg fortress.

Ernst Hanfstaengl himself had fled to Rosenheim, on the Austrian border, where a physician's secretary helped him find his way across the frontier illegally. And he was surprised to later learn that the führer had selected Uffing rather than Austria for his hideaway. In fact, Hitler's odd reluctance to go back into his homeland again only became a greater mystery for Hanfstaengl when, in 1938, at the time of Germany's Anschluss with Austria, he heard that the Geheime Staatspolizei, the Gestapo, took it as one of their first obligations to haul off from police headquarters in Wien a box of dossiers having to do with Adolf Hitler in his twenties. And those who knew what was in them were soon found dead.

Urged by Lorenz Roder, Hitler's lawyer, to stay away from Germany for a few more months, Herr Ernst Hanfstaengl hid in the house of a National Socialist in Salzburg until the ennui was so great that he journeyed east to look up his leader's family just out of curiosity.

The Raubals owned no telephone, so they weren't listed in the Wien directory, but through a few inquiries Hanfstaengl found out that Frau Angela Raubal worked full-time in the kitchen of a Jewish girls' hostel in the Zimmermannsdamm area. Angela was highly thought of there, he was told. She'd once quelled an anti-Semitic rally in front of the hostel simply by the challenging force of her presence, and she prepared meals that were so perfectly kosher that an Orthodox rabbi brought Jewish housewives to the hostel kitchen to have her show them how it was done. A girl at the hostel thought the Raubal family was renting a flat on the fourth floor of a five-story building on Blumengasse, near the Westbahnhof.

Imagining Angela a formidable lady, the female version of the tyrant Adolf could be, Ernst Hanfstaengl took along as gifts of homage a box of Empress chocolates and a book of art reproductions that his family's firm published, *Old Masters in the Pinakothek*, and visited the Raubals' flat on a Wednesday afternoon in December. Children already old with misery forlornly watched him as he went up scuffed wooden stairs as cupped as spoons with wear, watched him, too, as he waited in a filthy hallway for one of the Raubals to answer his knock. And then he heard, "Who is it?"

"Herr Hanfstaengl, my lady. A family friend."

Paula Hitler hardly opened the front door five inches as she warily peered up at him. "Which side?"

"Adolf's."

She slammed the door and called, "Angela!"

Hanfstaengl heard Angela hurrying down the hallway, and then she opened the flat's door wide. She was far less like Hitler than he had expected, just a handsome, solid, ill-used *Hausfrau* of forty, the kind of charwoman his wife would hire on streetcorners whenever their city house wanted cleaning. "Ernst Hanfstaengl," he said. "I'm the party's foreign press secretary."

She disliked Hitler's politics, he could tell, but she tried to hide it by considering her chafed and reddened hands. "We heard about the riot. And the arrest. How is Adolf?"

"We lost some dear comrades in the fighting, so he's sick at heart, but otherwise well. You know how he thrives on adversity."

She didn't. A flicker of unease seemed to cross her face, as if she were unused to the size and heartiness of men. "Won't you come in?" she asked, but then flushed and withdrew farther from him as he filled the foyer.

"Oh, I forgot," he said, and handed her his gifts.

"Chocolates! And a book!" Angela cried, as if she'd just noticed them. "You are too kind."

"You're tall, aren't you," Paula called. She was a stout woman of almost twenty-eight. She was hiding behind the icebox in the kitchen so that only her tilted head showed. She was just a little fuller in the face than Adolf; otherwise the resemblance was obvious.

Hanfstaengl doffed his hat and smiled. "You must be Fräulein Hitler!"

"Oh, yes; must be, forced to be, had no choice." She fell back from view and called, "We don't have any money! You go away now!"

"Quiet, Paula!" Angela shouted. She turned back to Hanfstaengl and with chagrin confided, "She's strange, you know." His frown told her he didn't know; Hitler had hidden that. She realized it was the hour for *Kaffee und Kuchen.* "Shall I take your coat?" Angela asked. "We still have some coffee, I think."

But Hanfstaengl was focused on the squalor of the flat, seeing Leo's foul straw mattress in the hallway, the old three-legged green sofa that was Geli's bed, and the few frail pieces of other furniture that hadn't yet been sold. "I hope you will pardon the observation, Frau Raubal, but it looks like you have had a difficult life here lately, just as we have had in Germany."

She told him, "We all get to eat at the hostel, so we have it better than most."

"We have lost a war," he somberly said, "and the world won't let us forget it." Then his gaze shifted farther down the hallway, and Angela saw that he was smiling at Geli.

She'd been studying geometry on the floor of the bedroom that Angela shared with Paula, but she'd been so intrigued by the American accent she'd heard that she'd hastily fussed with her hair and changed into her finest gray wool skirt and the pink angora sweater that Angela thought was too formfitting for a girl of fifteen. And then she'd sashayed out to find in the foyer a homely but jolly man with a jutting jaw and underbite, fully six feet four in height, in a chalk-gray English suit and black cashmere topcoat, a gray fedora in one huge hand, his brown hair oiled slick and middle-parted and still grooved by his hat.

"And you must be Angelika," he said. "Aren't you pretty!"

"My friends call me Geli."

She felt her hand lose itself in his as he introduced himself first as

Herr Ernst Sedgwick Hanfstaengl, and then as his friends and family knew him: Putzi, a childhood nickname that meant Cutie. "Say it, please."

"Putzi."

"And so we are done with formalities," he said, and offered Geli's hand back to her.

Angela held up the gift box and said, "Look, Geli, chocolates!" And then she shouted to the kitchen, "Paula, won't you have some?"

"Hah!" Paula said.

Putzi Hanfstaengl's hand found Geli's forearm as he tilted toward Angela to offer, "You know what I would like to do, Frau Raubal? Rather than have coffee with you here, I'd far rather take your family out."

■ ■ ■

Leo Raubal was still at his high school, where he assisted the night janitor, and The Straggler preferred to stroll Stadtpark as she always did, one hand in a sack of crushed zwieback toast, hunting in vain for pigeons to feed. So only Angela and Geli went with Hanfstaengl to the swank Café Sacher for mocha *mit Obers* and their famous Sacher torte.

Riding there in a taxi he cordially lectured Angela on *The Protocols of the Elders of Zion*, a little pamphlet that Adolf insisted she read in order to understand fully who the party's archenemy was. With an intensity she associated with high school acting, Putzi informed Angela that the Jewish Nationalist Movement of the Zionists had been founded at a congress in Basel, Switzerland, in 1897. Ostensibly their intention was to lead the Jews back to a homeland in Palestine, he told her, but in their secret sessions the Zionist elders had been hatching a heinous plan for a Jewish conquest of the world. Each of their speeches had been recorded in shorthand and the collected papers had been sent by courier to Frankfurt am Main where they were to be stored in the archives of the Rising Sun Lodge of Freemasons. Czarist secret police had somehow intercepted them, however, and the pamphlet had been published in Russian just before the revolution. It was then that Alfred Rosenberg, a Baltic architect who was often called "Hitler's co-thinker," had fled to München and, fearing that a Jewish conquest was already well under way, had joined the National Socialists, for whom he had translated the text into German. The famous automaker Henry Ford had been so shocked by the protocols that he'd had them published in America under the title *The International Jew*.

"And what do they say?" Putzi rhetorically asked. "'We'—the Jews—'shall create unrest, struggle, and hate in all of Europe and thence to the other continents. We shall poison the relations between peoples by spreading hunger, destitution, and plagues. We shall stultify, seduce, and ruin the youth. We shall use bribery, treachery, and treason as long as they serve the realization of our plans. We shall paint the misdeeds of foreign governments in garish colors and create such ill-feeling toward them that the people would a thousand times rather bear a slavery that guarantees them order than enjoy the freedom offered them by others.'"

Angela frowned. "Are you saying this is occurring right now?"

"Oh, so you've seen it in Austria as well?"

"The Jews I know aren't like that," she said.

"There are Jews and there are Jews," he said. "I would only caution you to be suspicious." Putzi found his fountain pen, tore out a page from his address book, and wrote on it *The Protocols of the Elders of Zion*. He handed it to Angela and watched with satisfaction as she dutifully put it in her purse. And then he saw Geli in the front seat, hiding a yawn. "All this grown-up talk," he told her with a smile. "We *do* go on, don't we?"

"I wasn't really listening," she said. "I was just enjoying the ride. I haven't been in a taxi before."

They were in front of the Sacher, and as Putzi Hanfstaengl got out his wallet, he grinned and said, "We'll make this a night of firsts."

Coffee in the Sacher Café was a first for Angela, too. She found herself frightened by the high prices on the menu, the haughty ladies in furs, the Old World opulence of the furniture; and she was embarrassed by her faded dress with its cooking stains on the front, the shine on a green gabardine overcoat that she'd bought before the war, the hair that she'd been cutting with kitchen shears since the hard times after the armistice. She was forty, and just four years older than Putzi Hanfstaengl—whom she could not call by his nickname—and yet she felt dull and male in his company, without fascination or joy. She forgot the Jew-hating after a while and found herself liking this huge, generous, genial man; she even liked his ugliness—it gave a flavor of wry comedy to whatever he chanced to say. But he seemed to find it hard to unfasten himself from Geli's admiration, and he seemed to be talking only to the girl when he said he was from an old family of art dealers and publishers on the Continent and in America, that he'd graduated from Harvard and had belonged to the Hasty Pudding Club, that he'd worked on Fifth Avenue in New York City for twelve years, then had returned to Germany to work on a doctorate in eighteenth-century history, that he was German on his father's side and American on his mother's, that his grandfather had been a Civil War general and a pallbearer at Abraham Lincoln's funeral.

Angela thought she ought to know that name; she glanced anxiously at Geli. *Lincoln?*

Without shifting her fond gaze from Putzi, Geli said, "A president of the United States."

"I was just thinking that," Angela said.

But that was only the beginning of Angela's being left out. Geli flirted with him outrageously, giggling at the faintest humor, finding reasons to touch his hands, flattering him with awe.

"I first met your uncle at the Kindl Keller beer hall," Putzi said. "While I had some misgivings about him and his program, I was utterly conquered by his oratory. And I recalled something that Teddy Roosevelt told me long ago when I visited him at his Sagamore Hill estate. The former president told me it was wise in my business to buy only the finest art, but I ought to remember that in politics the choice is often the lesser of two evils. And so I became a member of the party."

"The lesser of two evils," Angela said. "High praise."

But Hanfstaengl was too focused on Geli to hear her. Confessing that he and his wife, Helene, had taken Hitler on as their joint project, Putzi told how they'd spruced up her famous uncle, found him a tuxedo and a good tailor, taught him the graces of the dining table, and forbade him from adding four teaspoons of sugar to one of Prinz Metternich's finest Gewürztraminer wines. "I haven't yet got him to change that postage stamp of a mustache, though. He looks like a fourth-form schoolteacher or a bank clerk who lives with his mother." Putzi told them he'd offered Hitler their parlor for his afternoon reading, invited him to parties with their wealthy friends, cheered him up by banging out Wagner preludes on the piano "with Lisztian *fioriture* and a fine romantic swing."

The headwaiter refilled his coffee cup and then he continued, "While in the first days of his remand at Landsberg, Hitler followed the Sinn Fein of Ireland in trying a hunger strike. Roder, his counsel, got in touch with my wife, and Helene forthwith sent a message to Adolf saying she hadn't prevented his suicide in Uffing just so he could starve to death in the fortress. Wasn't that exactly what his enemies wanted? Well, Hitler has such a great admiration for my wife that her advice turned the scale, and he's far fitter now."

"You have our thanks," Geli said.

Putzi tilted forward in a bow while saying, "And you have *my* admiration."

"Will you be staying in Wien long?" Angela asked.

Geli glared, as if she'd heedlessly thrown cold water on a cake.

"Oh no," he said. "Who can work here?" And he offered his observations on the gaiety and frivolity of Wien, falling into French to say, "*Elle danse, mais elle ne marche pas.*"

It was left to Angela's fifteen-year-old daughter to translate: "The city dances, but it never gets anything done." And then in the way of teenaged girls with their mothers, Geli added, "French." She smiled at Putzi. "I want to hear you speak English."

Hanfstaengl gave it some thought before saying in English, "You are quite the saucy morsel."

Geli grinned in fascinated ignorance at Angela. "Did you understand him?"

Angela shook her head.

Hanfstaengl said, "I told her she was not unattractive."

Angela stared glumly at Geli and said, "Yes, it's true, isn't it."

Only then did he turn to the older woman. "You often hear gossip in high society about Herr Hitler and glamorous women, that he fancies this one, that he's marrying another, but I assure you, Frau Raubal, there's absolutely no substance to it."

Angela grimly asked, "Why are people always assuring me that my family has no love life?"

Geli sighed loudly, then fluttered her eyes at Putzi in apology.

"Well," he said. "We're having such a lovely time I hate to have it end. Shall I try to get us seats at the opera?"

Geli nearly shrieked, she was so thrilled. "Oh, *could* you?"

Putzi stood up from the dining table and said, "The concierge of the Sacher Hotel is famous for finding tickets when none are available."

Angela watched him lumber through the dining room to the hotel lobby, then she frostily said to her daughter, "You *shock* me, Angelika!"

She smiled. "Only because I have such an electric personality."

"Carrying on with a married man."

"We were just talking, Mother!"

"You're fifteen years old! The thought of you at twenty gives me goose bumps!"

"Well, that's easy: Don't think."

Angela furiously hit the dining table hard with the flat of her hand. Cutlery jangled and Geli jumped with fear. Heads turned in wonder throughout the Café Sacher.

Tears filled Geli's brown eyes as she thickly asked, "You know how long it's been since I've had any fun at all? Why can't you just let me *be* this one night?" She sniffed, and got out a handkerchief. "It probably won't ever happen again."

She's right, Angela thought, and said nothing more. She watched a handsome couple on Kärntnerstrasse get into a horsedrawn carriage. She ate the last of her Sacher torte. And then the last of Geli's. Then Ernst Hanfstaengl was there again, huffing with breathlessness but holding up three opera tickets in triumph. "*The Merry Widow,*" he said.

Geli felt sure he was making fun of her mother, but she couldn't help herself. She laughed.

At Christmastide the Raubals got a card from Ernst and Helene Hanfstaengl featuring a fine reproduction of Raphael Sanzio's *Madonna of the Chair* and saying in a note how much Putzi had enjoyed meeting them in Wien, and that in a porkpie hat and fake muttonchop whiskers he'd sneaked back into Germany through a dangerous railway tunnel near Berchtesgaden known as the "Hanging Stone."

Within the card Putzi included a journalist's newspaper account of a living tableau that a group of artists had created at the Blute Café in Schwabing. Called "Adolf Hitler in Prison," it featured a jail cell and snowflakes falling behind a barred window as a dark-haired man hunched at a desk with his face buried in his hands. A hidden chorus softly sang "Stille Nacht, Heilige Nacht" as a female angel gracefully carried in an illuminated Christmas tree and placed it on a table. Looking up in surprise, the prisoner showed his face "and the crowd in the café gasped and sobbed, for many thought it was Hitler himself." When the lights went up, the journalist had noticed some wet-eyed men and women hastily putting away their handker-chiefs.

After she'd read the account aloud to Angela, Geli was aston-ished to see that her mother's face was streaked with tears. "Are you *weeping?*"

Wiping her cheeks with her palm, Angela said, "I just wish you children could have gotten to know your Uncle Adolf better." She got the Christmas card from Geli and displayed it on the fireplace mantle. "And I suppose I'm crying because I'm ashamed that it was strangers who first pointed out to me what an admirable man my brother is. The family always, *always* underestimated him. No won-der he was so distant."

■ ■ ■

In February 1924, Adolf Hitler, Erich Ludendorff, Ernst Röhm, and seven codefendants went on trial for *Hochverrat* (high treason) in a classroom of the old brick infantry school. Hitler was the first to be called to the dock and immediately accepted full responsibility for the putsch, regretting only that he had not been slaughtered along with his fallen comrades, and consigning "the other gentlemen," including General Ludendorff, who was pompously there in full dress uniform, to the weaker, subordinate roles of those who "have only cooperated with me." Calculating that the conservative judi-ciary preserved nationalist sympathies and despised socialism, just as he knew the police and army did, Hitler immediately upset judicial proceedings by becoming the accuser, arguing in a strong, baritone voice that he was not a traitor but a patriot, that he alone was trying to lift Germany up from its oppression and misery, that he alone was forming a bulwark against Communism in whatever form it took.

In front of a huge international press corps, Hitler proclaimed that "the man who is born to be a dictator is not compelled; he wills. He is not driven forward; he drives himself forward. There is nothing immodest about this. The man who feels called upon to govern a people has no right to say: 'If you want me or summon me, I will cooperate.' No! It is his duty to step forward."

Employing his mastery of rhetoric and effrontery, he thoroughly dominated the little, goateed presiding judge, the three thunder-struck lay judges, and a chief prosecutor so harried by the hoots and jeers of university students that he began offering platitudes to the principal defendant, congratulating him on his self-sacrifice, his military service, his private life that had always been proper in spite of many carnal temptations, and calling Hitler "a highly gifted man who, coming from a simple background, has, through serious and hard work, won for himself a respected place in public life."

Hitler held sway throughout the forty days of the trial, inventing himself as a popular hero as he shouted ridicule, interrupted testi-mony, and orated at one point for four whole hours—about which the presiding judge meekly explained, "It is impossible to keep Hitler from talking."

The *Münchener Neueste Nachrichten* noted in an editorial, "We make no bones about the fact that our human sympathies lie on the side of the defendants and not with the November criminals of 1918." The jailers were said to be uncertain as to whether to watch him or wait on him. Women were bringing flowers to him. A female follower requested permission to take a bath in his tub. One of the panel of three lay judges was heard to say after a speech, "But he's a colossal fellow, this man Hitler!"

In accordance with German law, he was given the final word, and he told the court: "It is not you, gentlemen, who pronounce judg-ment on us. That judgment is spoken by the eternal court of history. What judgment you will hand down, I know. But that Court will not ask us 'Did you commit high treason or did you not?' That court will judge us, the Quartermaster General of the old Army, his offi-cers and soldiers, men who, as Germans, wanted and desired only the good of their people and fatherland; who wanted to fight and die. You may pronounce us guilty a thousand times over, but the goddess of the eternal court of history will smile and tear to tatters the brief of the state's attorney and the sentence of this court; for she acquits us."

The Raubals followed the judicial proceedings in the *Münchener*

Zeitung and were shocked that the stuffy and querulous Erich Ludendorff, who'd condemned Adolf during the trial as a foreign agitator,
was acquitted of high treason, and Wilhelm Frick, a collaborating
police chief, and Ernst Röhm were condemned but released, while
Adolf and the other codefendants were found guilty of the charges
against them, and Hitler was sentenced to four and a half years in
the prison at Landsberg am Lech—precisely the length of time he'd
served in the war, and the number of years between his resignation
from the Reichswehr and, as it was now called, the "Beer Hall
Putsch."

Within days of the sentencing, Angela got a letter from the
presently illegal Nationalsozialistische Deutsche Arbeiterpartei,
signed *für den Führer* by Alfred Rosenberg, saying that Herr Hitler
would benefit psychologically and in the court of public opinion if
the Raubals were to reestablish family ties with him. While party
officials thought it would be fitting for Leo and Paula to stay in Austria, they wondered if Angela and Geli would be so good as to visit
Adolf soon at Landsberg am Lech. Included with the letter were two
round-trip railway tickets and what seemed to Angela a generous
amount of money "for miscellaneous expenses."

"What do you wear to a *prison?*" Geli asked.

They went in funeral dresses and black veiled hats, going to
München in a first-class railway car, and then an hour west by taxi
through the mists of the forests above the Lech River. The fields
were still white with snow and the sky was as gray and close as a kettle lid. On a hill outside the handsome medieval village of Landsberg was a fortress of high stone walls and watchtowers that
surrounded the old gray buildings of what was now a penitentiary.
There common criminals were jailed in one part and those considered political prisoners in another. Adolf Hitler was being held as a
traitor in cell 7.

Walking Angela and Geli inside, a friendly prison guard named
Franz Hemmrich took them past the dining hall where forty-five
Nazis ate their meals at five linked tables and where Hitler would sit
regally at the head in front of the hanging red flag and swastika of

the party. And when they were going upstairs to cell 7, Hemmrich confided to them about Herr Hitler's good manners and magnetism, how firmly he governed the other prisoners so there was never any fuss, how he'd given all his guards boxes of Lindt truffles to take home to their wives, how he was like Saint Paul in chains: You knew that if the jail fell down, you would still find Hitler obediently waiting in his cell. "To be frank, I hated him and his program just a few months ago," Herr Hemmrich said, "but the warden forced me to listen in as he talked to his friends, to find out what he was plotting, and he made so much sense to me that within a few days I joined the party. Others here are doing the same."

When they got to cell 7, the guard unlocked the door, hollered "Heil Hitler!" and kissed Angela's and Geli's hands in good-bye, just as it was Hitler's habit to do.

They heard Hitler talking when they walked inside, but he was behind a closed door. Angela was surprised to find that the cell was like a white-walled gentleman's club and filled with so much food it looked like a fancy delicatessen. Well-wishers from all over Germany had mailed Hitler fruit baskets, homemade strudel and tortes and cakes, Rhein and Mosel wines, Westphalian hams, brown rings of sausage and salami, Andechs and Franziskaner beer. Angela lifted off her veiled hat as she went to a four-paned window of old glass and iron bars and saw a fine but wrinkled view of frosted trees along the Lech River and a garden on the first floor. An old Remington typewriter was on a walnut secretary against one wall, and a ream of white bond paper was beside it, patiently waiting for words; the four chairs were made of cane and rattan, and a bookcase held works by Bismarck, Nietzsche, Ranke, Treitschke, and Marx. A crown formed with sprigs of green laurel leaves was tacked onto one wall, and on the floor was an old front page of the London *Times*, obliterated with Hitler's offended comments and juvenile caricatures of Jewish faces. One of the Landsberg prisoners knew English, Angela saw, for he'd translated into German a journalist's opinion that "the Hitler trial has proved that a plot against the Constitution of the Reich is not considered a serious crime in Bavaria"—about which the prisoner offered a fairly obvious and vulgar joke on the constitution of the queen. *With time on their hands*, Angela thought, *men turn into boys*. She heard her daughter say, "What a lot of loot!" and she turned.

Geli, too, was now hatless. She'd tucked a pink sugarcane in her cheek as she held a mandolin she'd found and strummed a chord with a plectrum. "We have been far too law-abiding, Mother."

"Are you thinking we ought to trade places?"

"Aren't you?"

Angela said, "We'd be in a tailor shop here. We'd be doing dishes. Adolf has always had a way of getting extra consideration."

A tall, fierce, officious man in loden-green hiking clothes looked out from the room where Hitler was talking. "You are the Raubals?"

"Yes."

Angela briefly saw Adolf holding forth before the man softly shut the door behind him. He held out his hand to her. "Herr Rudolf Hess," he said. "His personal secretary." He shook her hand hard once while formally bowing. And then he did the same to Geli.

They felt like Prussian officers just in from the front. They both gave their first names.

"The leader is conferring with Count Rudinski," Hess said, as if they'd surely know the name. "Won't you please sit?"

They did, as did he, effeminately crossing his legs at his thighs but holding himself firmly upright with an air of stiff-backed confidence, his square-jawed head tilted high. His hairline was receding, but his black hair flowed back from his forehead in waves that women got by marcelling theirs with hot irons. Angela had never seen eyebrows that were so much like heavy objects, that so darkly shaded his deep eyesockets that his irises were as obscured as brown pebbles dropped in snow. His mouth was a wide, thin line and tightly shut in order to hide the buckteeth and overbite that stole from him the look of high intellect he wanted. Ill at ease with their silence, he offered, "Would you like some food?"

"Shall we hire a truck?" Angela asked.

Geli giggled behind her hand.

Hess faintly smiled, as though he'd missed the humor, and then he lifted and seemed to weigh a Thüringer cervelat in his hand. "We get these gifts, and I know we aren't finished. The party is forbidden in Germany now, Hitler is forbidden to speak, the hierarchy is in disarray; and yet we find such public sentiment in our favor that we can only look at our prison stay as a mild interruption in our heroic march toward destiny."

"You sound like Adolf," Angela said.

"You flatter me," said Hess. And then, in the Nazi way, he began talking at length about himself, saying he'd been born in Alexandria, Egypt, five years after Hitler, the son of a wholesale importer. He had gone to business school in Switzerland, and had worked in Hamburg for his family. Then the archduke and his wife had been killed in Sarajevo and he'd become a lieutenant and shock-troop leader in the First Bavarian Regiment before joining the air corps. Losing interest in commerce after the armistice, he had enrolled at the university in München and had had the good fortune to have as his mentor Herr Professor Karl Haushofer of the Geo-Political department, the author of the theory of Lebensraum.

She hadn't heard of it.

"Simply that the future of a culturally dominant but land-starved country like Germany necessitates the annexation of states in eastern Europe."

"I see."

To make a long story short, in 1920 a German millionaire who'd fled to Brazil but still had great love for his country had offered a significant cash prize to the most worthy essay on the theme: "How must the Man be constituted who will lead Germany back to her former heights of glory?"

Angela got up and took an orange from a basket. She began peeling it.

"Eat, yes. We have so much," Hess said. And then he continued, "It was precisely that question that was preoccupying me in my political studies, and so on paper I constructed a messiah who would lead the Aryan race to its rightful place in the world. He would strike one at first as an ordinary man and have his origins among the masses so he could understand them psychologically, but he would be a genius, of course, with superb talents and intellect, and would have nothing in common with them. He would be a fantastic public speaker, all fire and personality. Currents of electricity would flow from him. Worrying about nothing, not even the fate of his friends, he would not shrink from bloodshed but would unhesitatingly march forward with hardness and an iron will, trampling whoever blocked his path in order to achieve his goal in all its purity."

"Did you win the contest?" Geli asked.

"Certainly, Fräulein Raubal. With much praise." And then Hess fell into distraction as he watched her licking the sugarcane.

She smiled. "What did you buy with the money?"

Hess shook his head free of the question and got back on track. "The point of the story is that quite soon after the competition, I happened to attend one of Herr Hitler's speeches for the first time ever, and I was absolutely stunned. He was sheer genius, pure reason incarnate, everything I'd hoped for and imagined—but *here, now.* Tears streaming down my face, I ran home to my fiancée and screamed in ecstasy, 'I have found the man!'"

Then the office door opened. Hess hurtled to his feet. Count Rudinski was chuckling as he walked out of the office in a sable coat and hat, wrapping his neck twice in a long orange scarf. Hitler was just behind him, in knee-high woolen stockings, leather lederhosen, and a collarless white shirt, his hands holding the gift of *The Collected Poems of Stefan George.* "Rudi, you must listen to this," Hitler said, then stiffly held the book far out from his face to try to read the front-matter inscription without his glasses, but couldn't. "Well, you read it," he said.

Rudolf Hess announced, "From Frau Winifred Wagner in Bayreuth: 'Dear Adi, You are the coming man in spite of everything. We all still depend on you to pull the sword out of the German oak.'"

Count Rudinski smiled. "A lovely sentiment from a great lady."

"It's a glorious inscription," said Hess.

"You think? And true, too. Count Rudinksi just now brought it to me."

Hess took the book from him and shoved it among the others. The good-bye lasted a full minute more, during which time Hitler offered no acknowledgment that his half-sister and niece were there. Only when the count was gone did he grin at Angela and give her his hand. "Good evening, Frau Raubal!" Then he gently touched Geli's light brown hair. "And to you, Fräulein. I'm happy you're here."

"We like your pantry," Geli said.

Hitler winced and held his hands to his soft belly. "Oh, it makes my stomach ache! Look at how fat I'm getting! I can't fit into my pants!"

Angela failed to argue the point; he looked paunchy. "Aren't there prison sports in here?" Angela asked. "Or gymnastic exercises?"

"Well, yes," he said, "but what would it do to ideals and discipline if I joined with the others in physical training? A general cannot afford the affront of being beaten at games by his infantrymen. Anyway, I shall again get the weight off by speaking."

"What jobs are you forced to do?"

"Oh, I'm far too busy for labor." Hitler lifted off the lid from a box of marzipan sweets and popped one in his mouth. "Are you in communication with Alois?" he asked.

She tore off an orange section and ate it. "Our brother, Alois? It's been fifteen years."

"Well, he's in Hamburg now, selling razor blades. He married a woman named . . ." He frowned at Hess.

"Hedwig Heidemann," Hess said.

"What happened to Bridget in England?" Angela asked.

"You see, that's the problem. Alois is still married to her."

To clarify things, Hess gave the word for it: "Bigamy."

"Thank you," Angela told him. "I have a tiny brain."

Hitler found another marzipan, but on second thought put it back. "The office of the lord mayor of Hamburg has called Alois in for questioning. And Alois has written a letter to his first wife requesting that she have their marriage legally dissolved." Hitler expectantly held out his hand. Rudolf Hess went to the secretary, got out a sheet of typed paper as well as Hitler's glasses, and gave both to him. "We have his wording from our Hamburg friends," Hitler said, and holding his folded glasses up in one hand, shook out the paper. "To Bridget Hitler our older brother writes: 'Don't think that I am at present a rich man, for to tell you the truth I am not. But I have got the chance to get rich by the aid of my brother's reputation. This chance will be lost forever if I am found guilty, and if I am sentenced.' And he goes on, 'You must help me or they'll put me in jail. This bigamy charge is mainly embarrassing, for should the newspapers learn about it they're going to use it against my brother.'" Hitler handed the page back to Hess. "Quite true," he said. His face was suddenly as red as a beet and his forehead was throbbing with veins. "'By the aid of my brother's reputation!' And here I am, in prison, fighting for my life! Alois is *destroying* my reputation! I *cannot* have this! I *won't*! Any member of my family—"

Rudolf Hess had begun whistling an old regimental song about the flower called Erika.

Hitler glanced at him as if he'd forgotten his part; then he glanced at Geli and remembered. "Would you come into my office, Angela? We have to talk further."

Angela put an orange slice in her mouth as she went with him, and Hess shut the door, then sat with his hands chafing his knees, his face fraught with shyness and discomfort.

Geli inched up the hem of her funeral dress to look surreptitiously at her shins and ankles. She'd shaved her legs for the first time that morning and worried that she'd done a poor job of it. She decided it would do.

Silence seemed to paint the room a bleaker color. And then Hess finally said, "We have them right where we want them."

"'Them'?"

"We hear the people in München are still in favor of a parliamentary monarchy."

Geli told him, "We were in München for only a few minutes."

"You aren't interested in politics?"

Geli shrugged.

"Are you interested in astrology?"

She was only fifteen and not quite certain if there was a difference between astrology and astronomy. She said yes, she was interested in the stars.

"I'm the mystic in the party," Hess said, and he grinned in a way she thought goofy. "Well, no one surpasses Hitler," he continued, "but I'm perhaps more adept in *The Secret Doctrine* and contact with the higher spheres."

She was trying to decide what she disliked more, his shameless deference to her uncle or his sober prissiness.

"Shall I read to you from his book?" he asked.

"You mean he's writing one?"

Hess got out a diary from an upper drawer in the secretary. "On the frontispiece is his motto," Hess said. "I quote: 'When a world comes to an end, then entire parts of the earth can be convulsed, but not the belief in a just cause.' And below that he has written: 'The trial of narrow-mindedness and personal spite is over, and today starts—*My Struggle.*' We're thinking that last bit may be the title. Or: 'Four and a Half Years of Struggle Against Lies, Stupidity, and Cowardice.'"

"Couldn't he be more specific?"

For a fleeting, agonizing moment Hess was like a dog besieged with thought. Then he said, "Oh. I see. You're joking."

Cell 7's door was unlocked again, and the guard allowed in a prisoner carrying a high-backed chair that might have been a throne. His red-flannel shirtsleeves were rolled up and his biceps bulged like coconuts. His face turned toward Geli as he hauled his heavy load and she saw that he was a black-haired, handsome man in his late twenties, with a boxer's tightly muscled build, features that seemed Corsican or Greek, and skin that even in jail was ginger brown. She'd never seen such huge, gorgeous chocolate eyes in a full-grown man. Like a fawn's. "Where does he want it?" he asked.

Hess pointed to the crown of laurel leaves. "Under there." And then he said, "Emil Maurice. His chauffeur. And this is Fräulein Raubal."

She held out her hand but stayed seated, afraid that if she stood she'd be taller than he was. Emil Maurice grinned with fractured and jagged teeth and said, "*Je m'appelle Emil. Enchanté.*"

"*Et moi,*" she replied. "*Je m'appelle Geli.*"

"She speaks French!" Emil cried.

"She'll grow out of it," Hess said. "She's young."

They all heard Hitler shouting. They couldn't hear the words.

"Won't he ever *cease?*" Emil asked.

Geli laughed, but Hess was horrified.

In a fair imitation of Hitler's gestures and voice, Emil held Hess's face in his hands and said, "Oh, my Rudi! My little Hesserl! Did I offend you?"

Hess flung away his hands, saying, "Quit it!"

Emil smiled at Geli. "We're tired of each other already, and we have years to go." Emil flopped into a chair, his knees spread wide, his hands holding the rattan seat in front of his crotch as he stared frankly at the only girl in the fortress.

She was intrigued by him, but embarrassed. She looked at the floor. She heard a squawk from the planking as Emil yanked a free chair next to his own and quietly asked, "Won't you sit next to me, Geli? We'll talk."

"Don't!" Hess shouted. Whether to Emil or to her she wasn't sure.

Her face felt hot enough to char paper. She felt afloat on a raft of pleasant wooziness. And then the office door opened and Angela walked out.

"We have to go, Geli," Angela said.

She got up. Emil winked. "Shall I say good-bye to Uncle Adolf?" she asked.

"We have to go," Angela said.

Walking outside the fortress, they saw the headlights of the waiting taxi flash on and off. They got in. And when they were on the highway to München and there was only a high horizon of black forest behind them, her mother put a hand on the upholstery beside her, like a purse she could have if she wanted it. Geli tried to find her face, but she was a block of night in nighttime. "We'll have money for furniture and new clothes," Angela said. "Others will handle our rent. Paula's last name shall be Wolf from now on. She'll have a flat of her own."

"Why?"

Angela thought for a while, then said, "It is necessary."

CHAPTER SEVEN
MÜNCHEN, 1925

She visited München for the first time without Angela in April 1925, going there on a high school outing with a girl's choir called "Seraphim." She knew that her uncle had been paroled in December, so as soon as she and a friend, Ingrid von Launitz, got settled into their room at the first-class Königshof Hotel, Geli tried to telephone him at his Thierschstrasse flat, but she found that his number was unlisted. She then boldly decided that she and Ingrid would walk to the flat, thinking that if she failed to find Hitler there she could at least leave a note.

"And if we *do* find him?" Ingrid asked.

"Well, he'll have to be friendly to us," Geli said. "He's a politician."

They found a druggist's shop at Thierschstrasse 41, but just above it was a three-story town home where they were greeted by Frau Maria Reichert, a friendly widow whose house it was. She was a hale and heavy woman in her late thirties, and the foyer with its white upright Bechstein piano gave evidence that she had formerly been well off. But she confessed to the girls that she was now a *Mädchen für alles*, a charwoman, and was renting out rooms for an income in these hard times. She told them as she walked to his flat just off the hall that her favorite renter was Geli's uncle, whom she called "that funny bohemian." She knocked twice and sweetly called, "Herr Hitler!" then withdrew.

And then there he was. Although it was four in the afternoon, he seemed to have just gotten dressed and shaved, for his starched, collarless white shirt looked like it was just out of its box, he was in purple carpet slippers and freshly pressed blue serge suit pants with leather suspenders, and Geli could smell Chlorodont toothpaste. Ingrid blushed to see the much-talked-about man; Geli stiffly held out her hand and offered him the old Bavarian greeting, *Grüss Gott*, "You greet God."

Hitler frowned at Ingrid behind her, then focused his irritation on his niece. "And so, is this Fräulein Raubal at my door?" he asked. "What a surprise, your appearing here completely unannounced."

She heard the formality in his tone and answered, "I do beg your indulgence, Herr Hitler. My friend Fräulein von Launitz and I are here with a singing group from Wien. We thought you'd be offended if we did not at least say hello."

"Of course," Hitler said, then looked back at the interior of his flat, found it satisfactory, and invited them in.

The flat was just one long room; his own watercolor sketches of architecture were tacked to the green walls, flaking pages of paint were falling away from the ceiling, and the floor was a worn green linoleum hidden here and there with ugly other-color throw rugs. His headboard obstructed half the window at the far end, and hanging above it was a photograph of his dead mother, Klara, when she'd been just a little older than Geli. The only other furniture was a plain chair and folding table and a tilting bookcase constructed with bricks and unplaned planks with rusty nails still in them. *Was he truly as poor as this?* Geli took it all in, and told her uncle, "This place was never new."

Hitler was about to object, but then realized she was kidding. She saw he did not take kindly to it. Seeming to see his room for the first time, as she did, he said, "I'm hardly ever here, Fräulein Raubal. And it can be beneficial for a workers' party to have a leader who seems a little down-at-the-heels." He held out a box of English toffee to her, but she shook her head. "I have no kitchen. Otherwise I'd heat some tea."

Hitler shyly offered Ingrid the box of toffee and, far later than other men Geli had seen, finally noticed that the girl was gorgeous. And then he fastened his stunning silver-blue eyes on Ingrid's, holding her in an unrelenting gaze in which she could do or say nothing. She seemed amazed and bewildered. She flushed and her lips faintly parted, as if she were awaiting a kiss, and only when she fluttered her eyelids with weakness and looked to the floor was she able to catch her breath. Ingrid later told Geli that she was embarrassed to have been so spellbound by him, but she'd never felt such intensity in a stare. Even days later when they were in the railway car heading back to Wien, Ingrid confessed with utter seriousness, "Looking into those eyes of his may have been the greatest moment of my life!"

But Hitler seemed to grow bored with his hold on the girl, and shifted around to his niece. "You said you're singing here?"

"With our high school group."

"And what's its name?"

"Seraphim."

Her uncle smirked. "My Angelika, with the angels! You're a soprano?"

"Yes."

"Where are you singing?"

Ingrid too urgently said, "At Wilhelmsgymnasium, Herr Hitler. With the boys there. Eight o'clock. Won't you come?"

"But I am so terribly busy tonight," Hitler whined. "Will you both be singing again?"

Geli told him they would be, at three tomorrow, at the Theatine Church.

"Well, I can't be seen in a church," he said. And then his face was nettled with insight. "Oh no, you're not singing *The Messiah?*"

"Yes."

"Handel! That Englishman!"

She reminded her uncle that George Frideric Handel had been born in Germany.

"And he was a failure here, wasn't he? While finding success in Dublin and London. Oh, they know their own." Hitler shot his sleeve to look at his wristwatch. "I shall not pretend I'm sorry to miss *The Messiah* tonight, but would it be possible to have a little more time with you this afternoon?"

"Certainly," Geli said.

"Walk with me to my office, will you?"

While he got out of his carpet slippers and put on a hard white collar, Ingrid sidled up to her friend and whispered, "Don't you think he's handsome?"

She shrugged, then signified his foolish little mustache by holding a finger beneath her nose. Ingrid giggled and agreed. Geli tilted her head to the left to read the titles in his bookcase: both volumes of *My War Memoirs* by General Erich Ludendorff; *My Life* by the composer Richard Wagner; *On War* by General Carl von Clausewitz; Houston Stewart Chamberlain's two-volume *Foundations of the Nineteenth Century*; Franz Kugler's biography of Frederick the Great; a collection of heroic myths by someone named Schwab; four volumes of Oswald Spengler's *The Decline of the West*—sober books that her uncle could claim he was reading, if asked. But on the first shelf were books that felt more authentically his: thrillers such as *The Crimson Circle* and *Sanders of the River* by an American named Edgar Wallace; twenty Wild West juveniles by the wildly popular Karl May; erotic picture collections that an Eduard Fuchs had titled *The Illustrated History of Morals* and *The History of Erotic Art;* and a flimsy, worn pamphlet called *The Protocols of the Elders of Zion.* She heard her uncle ask, "Did your father purchase his title, Fräulein von Launitz?"

She told him, "We inherited it."

Geli surreptitiously opened *The History of Erotic Art* as her uncle said, "Old wealth, then! Would you like to join the party?" She heard Ingrid giggle.

A bookmark was just above a frightening painting by Franz von Stuck of a beautiful and frankly staring dark-haired female with skin as white as pastry and a face that Geli would have guessed was Jewish. Her hands seemed to be tied behind her back. Easing up between her lewdly opened thighs and undulating around her naked torso was a gigantic sleek black python whose fierce head hung over her shoulder to nestle just above her round left breast. She seemed to be taking dull pleasure in its weight. The title was *Sensuality*. Geli was mystified. Why was this erotic? What did her uncle see that she didn't? She heard Hitler telling Ingrid about the hikes and picnics the National Socialist German Workers Party organized for the young, for whom life, he knew, was now so boring, but Geli could not shift her gaze from the vexing picture, though it was making her feel a little ill. And then Hitler called, "Er, Fräulein Raubal? Will you tie my tie?"

She closed the book. "You can't?"

"I have trouble with it."

She felt his chagrin as if it were catching. "I think I would have had to grow up with a father to know how."

"I can do it," Ingrid hurriedly said, and Geli watched closely as her uncle hesitantly offered his throat to her and oddly held his breath as she tied a four-in-hand, flushing with panic when she got one part wrong, and falling back with relief when she finished.

Sheepishly eyeing his niece, he put on a blue serge suit coat, a calf-length black cashmere overcoat, and a black slouch hat that could have had a former life in the Old West.

Geli told him, "You look like a desperado, Herr Hitler."

Without humor he thanked her for reminding him, and got a handgun from underneath his pillow and slipped it into his overcoat pocket. "I have to worry about assassination all the time," he told them.

Halfway up Thierschstrasse was the finance office of the Eher Publishing House, and the official party newspaper, the *Völkischer Beobachter* (People's Observer). Walking there, Hitler took joy in telling the girls how he took over the weekly with an interest-free loan from Herr Ernst Hanfstaengl of six hundred American dollars, a fortune in Germany then, but shrewdly paid off the loan a few months later with fantastically inflated deutsche marks, "so I got offices, furnishings, Linotype, paper, and two American rotary presses for the price of a peppermint stick."

"But I thought Putzi was a friend of yours," Geli said.

Hitler's face was full of childish wonderment over what the objection could possibly be; then he informed his niece that Herr Hanfstaengl was also a good Nazi. "Willingly, with no regret, a good Nazi gives all he has to his leader."

And then he held open the front door to the finance office, and followed the girls inside. Geli saw Max Amann hastily put out his cigarette, get up from his cluttered desk, and proudly offer a straight-armed version of the Italian Fascist salute as soon as he saw her uncle stroll in. Hitler's former sergeant major in the List Regiment, and a graduate of a business college, Amann was a short, gruff, and often irritable man in his thirties with crew-cut hair, a brown inch of mustache that frankly imitated his leader's—who'd soon order it shaved off—and a face that seemed as hard and cruel as cinderblock. But he softened with adoration whenever Hitler was near. Quickly ignoring the girls, the grinning business manager held out forms and letters for Hitler's signature and tried to illustrate with a wide green ledger some financial problem that the unofficial publisher ought to be aware of. But Hitler wouldn't even sit, for a film of dust was on his favorite chair. Everywhere files and papers were heaped and scattered around Amann. An hourglass spider hurried across his hand-cranked adding machine. Everything he touched seemed to have turned into an ashtray.

Hitler sighed as he signed his name twenty times with a Mont Blanc pen, then curtly told Amann that the office stank of tobacco and escorted the girls outside. "Well, that's done," he said, as if he'd finished a hard day.

Geli told her uncle that she felt sorry for Amann, that he looked like a hound in a kennel visited only at mealtime.

Hitler laughed. "I'll have to tell him that."

"Will he enjoy it?"

Quizzically frowning at her, Hitler said, "*I* will," as if that were enough.

They strolled farther, to the Schwabing district where on Schellingstrasse, a few blocks from the university, Hitler waved to a short, buoyant man inside the Hoffmann Photography Studio at number 50, then held open the door to the Müller Printing Press, the editorial offices of the *Völkischer Beobachter*.

Putzi Hanfstaengl and a few men in brown shirts stood and offered the Nazi salute when they saw their leader walking inside behind the girls, but it was only Rudolf Hess who also shouted out, "Heil Hitler!" Geli found it puzzling that *Heil*, "well-being" or "salvation," an old Teutonic salutation that was unfashionable in Austria, was now being associated with her uncle's name; but he seemed not at all embarrassed by it, and in fact received their Fascist salutes with haughty nonchalance.

"You may sit," he said, and took off his slouch hat and coat. Looking around he asked, "Where is Herr Rosenberg?"

Hess said, "He just went out for coffee."

Stamping his foot, Hitler played a child as he wailed, "But wasting time in cafés is my job!"

Everybody laughed too loud and too long.

Hitler turned to his niece. "Have you seen our paper?"

She hadn't.

Hess handed him an old issue with the headline "Clean Out the Jews Once and for All," and Hitler held it in front of himself as he fulsomely congratulated Hanfstaengl for thinking up the American format, the slogan beneath the masthead, *Arbeit und Brot*, "Work and Bread," and for his getting a *Simplicissimus* cartoonist named Schwarzer to design the masthead. *Simplicissimus*, Hitler explained to Ingrid, was a famous satirical magazine with a pronounced hatred of the National Socialist Party, so he thought of Schwarzer's—and Hanfstaengl's—contribution as a great victory. The huge Hanfstaengl gracefully bowed to Hitler's praise, which could not have been new, while Geli saw the forgotten Hess fuming

with hurt feelings and anguish. *And now he must do something extra,*
Geli thought.

Hess surged forward and told the girls, "We have been thinking
about calling the months by their heroic old Germanic names. We
would call May *Wonnemonat,* which means 'month of delight.' Rather
than June, why not *Brachmond,* or 'fallow moon'? October would be
Gelbhart, or 'hard yellow.' And *Nebelung,* 'mist,' for November."

"I find the idea ridiculous," Hitler said. "We are a party of the
common people, not mystics." And as Hess's face fell, Hitler turned
to an interior page to show the girls a cartoon he thought hilarious,
of a handsome Germanic knight on his steed hauling away from his
fortress a squalling, fat priest and an ugly Jew whose nose was as
large as a gourd. The knight was ruefully thinking, "Must we always
have to deal with these two?"

The girls looked at each other: *Why is that funny?* And then
Ingrid quietly hinted, "We have to go practice."

"What was that?" Hitler asked.

Geli smiled. "Sotto voce."

"But I have so much yet to show you!"

"I have the morning."

"Excellent!" her uncle said.

Putzi Hanfstaengl grinned and asked, "Are you aware that morning generally comes before noon?"

But Hitler kissed the girls' hands and insisted, "You have my word
of honor that I will be at the Königshof Hotel for you at nine a.m.
tomorrow!"

■ ■ ■

Instead Geli was met in the hotel lobby by a shy young man in a
trench coat who introduced himself as Herr Julius Schaub, Hitler's
adjutant. A former shipping clerk at the Eher Publishing House,
Schaub was a tall, sullen, old-seeming man of twenty-six with slicked-
back hair, ears like handles, and staring eyes that he kept focused on
the floor as he shook her hand and told her, "My job is to do whatever
the leader asks. And he has asked me to give you a tour of München."

"But he promised me he would do it himself."

Schaub flickered a smile and asked, "Did he swear to God when he said that?"

"He gave me his word of honor."

Schaub shrugged. "It's the same thing. It means he strongly wishes he could oblige you. He cannot; I can. Shall we go?"

Hobbling through the lobby and outside, he told her that his feet had been frozen on the Russian front in 1917 and that he'd lost his toes. "You are so young you may not know it, but the German army was undefeated on the field. Yet we lost the war. We were sabotaged by the higher-ups at home." Schaub considered her jacket. "Are you going to be cold?"

"No."

"Don't complain then." He held open the passenger door to an old green Selve automobile. "Your uncle's old car," he said. "Herr Hitler is so generous that he gave it outright to me when he got his Mercedes eight-seater from his friends, the Bechsteins." She sat inside, and he added, "I hope you aren't bothered by the smell. The front seat is stuffed with seaweed."

"In case you get hungry later?"

"Are you making fun of me?"

"I was teasing, Herr Schaub."

"You are glib, Fräulein Raubal," he said as he got in the car, and then he hunted for what *he* was. "I am—"

"You are prickly, Herr Schaub."

Concentrating hard, he frowned through the windshield and finally pronounced, "I find life a chancy and tragic affair, worthy of serious attention."

She smiled. "You can say that while sitting on seaweed?"

Schaub was so offended he hardly looked at Geli again as he headed to the famous sites in München. "We are called 'the City of Good Nature,'" he said as he drove. "'The Capital of German Art,' 'the Athens on the Isar,' 'the Moscow of our Movement.' We are nearing eight hundred thousand people, and less than four thousand Jews."

She gave him a strange glance that he ignored. Schaub took her first to the Feldherrnhalle, where, as he put it, "our Nazi martyrs were killed in 1923"; and then through the woods and meadows of Englischer Garten, which was "five kilometers long from north to south," he said, "and the first public park on the Continent." Then it was the Glaspalast, which housed industrial exhibits and had been constructed by King Maximilian II in imitation of the Crystal Palace in London. There was little to see now at the fairgrounds of Theresienwiese, he told her, but in mid-September it held Oktoberfest, the largest public festival in the world.

Schaub saw that she wasn't paying attention, so, just for something to say, he asked if her singing went well, then failed to listen to her reply. At the botanical gardens, he confessed he'd given up cigarettes to please her uncle, but he badly wanted one now, as if she'd brought on that terrible craving. She walked through the huge Cathedral of Our Lady on her own, and when she came out, Schaub had been stewing for too long. Getting up from the cold stone steps, he told her, "You have heard of religious zealots, Fräulein Raubal? Well, Adolf Hitler is my religion." And that was all of his conversation for another hour. Often he simply put on the brakes and with gravity pointed to a building as he named it—the Egyptian Museum, the Pinakothek, the Wittelsbach Residenz—then heavily stepped on the accelerator again. His tour ended northwest of the city at the huge baroque palace and five hundred acres of parkland built by the Wittelsbach royalty at Nymphenburg, where he was as silent as a bodyguard as they strolled through the villa and galleries and around a green lake where children played with sailboats. Taking out his pocket watch, Schaub frowned at the time and said, "I have orders to take you to Maximilianstrasse."

"Why?"

"We have to buy you finer clothes. My leader says you look like a waif."

Maximilianstrasse was the high-fashion district and full of the Italian shoes and haute couture dresses she'd seen only in glamour magazines. She was so giddy with the hundreds of choices that she

tried on fourteen pairs of shoes while Schaub sighed in the chair
beside her, and she later felt him simmering as she finally let a shop-
girl decide which of the five elegant gowns she was fretting over she
ought to buy as Hitler's gift. To pay for it, Schaub got money out of a
dirty envelope with NSDAP printed on its front, stingily put one bill
at a time on the glass countertop, and when he carried the box outside he took off the string and saved it in his trench coat pocket.

"Well, that was fun," Geli said.

"Was it? We are National *Socialists*, not National *Capitalists*."

"I have been poor all my life, Herr Schaub. My uncle gave *you* a
car."

Schaub failed to find a reply until she got into the green Selve
again. Then he faced her and with half-throttled misery said, "I
have no friends." And then he turned to start the car.

■ ■ ■

The girls of Seraphim joined boys from Wilhelmsgymnasium in performing *The Messiah* at the Theatine Church that afternoon and
were supposed to stroll through the Altstadt that evening, but when
Geli got back to her room, she found a message from the concierge
saying her uncle was speaking that night at the Hofbräuhaus am
Platzl and was inviting his niece to hear him. And to wear her new
clothes. She got the faltering permission of her teacher to go, and
she was talking with Ingrid and four other friends in front of the
Königshof Hotel when Hitler's sleek red supercharged Mercedes
Compressor arrived beside them as softly as fluid. Envy filled her
hushed friends' faces when they saw handsome Emil Maurice hurry
out from behind the wheel to gallantly hold open the right-rear
door for her. She got in with false majesty, and fluttered a queenly
wave to her friends as the Mercedes headed off, leaving them to
wander their high school around the Marienplatz and the shut-up
stalls of the Victuals Market.

Her uncle failed to say hello as he tilted into the far-side window
of the backseat in order to hold a page up to the fading sunlight of a
quarter to eight. Wearing a gray velour fedora and gray wool suit

with a soft-collared American white shirt and uninterestng tie, he
looked like a financier as he oriented his black-framed glasses higher
on his nose and frowned at his notes.

Sitting in the front-right seat was a White Russian with flawless
German who turned and grandly introduced himself to Geli as Herr
Alfred Rosenberg, editor-in-chief of the *Völkischer Beobachter*,
which he unnecessarily told her was the official newspaper of the
Nationalsozialistische Deutsche Arbeiterpartei. He was a finely
dressed widower of thirty-two with heavily pomaded dark hair, but
he was also sallow, serious, faintly foul-smelling, and vain for no dis-
cernible reason, and within a few minutes she could see he was
wholly deferential to Hitler, who paid him no heed at all. Rosenberg
asked her, "Have you heard your uncle speak, Fräulein Raubal?"

"My mother says he was trying it even in childhood."

"Humorous," he flatly said. And then he looked at Hitler lov-
ingly. "Oh, what an orator! Your uncle is better than opera!"

She looked at him. Hitler simply turned a page.

"My own gift is writing," Rosenberg said.

She felt an ellipsis he wanted filled. "Shall I pry?" she asked.

Her uncle chuckled, but continued scanning his notes.

"Well, only articles and pamphlets up to now," Rosenberg said.
"The Tracks of Jewry Through the Ages?"

She shook her head.

"Of late I have been laboring on a book about the biological
necessity of war. Soon the blood spirit will cry out and world revolution will sweep away all falsifications as the soul of the blond,
Nordic race is awakened under the sign of the swastika."

She hardly heard a word, so stunned was she by his halitosis. "But
who of us here is blond?" she asked.

Rosenberg faced the front again. "You probably wouldn't understand my pamphlets. They're not for females. Quite scientific."

Without irony, Hitler said, "Herr Rosenberg is the party's intellectual."

Emil Maurice slyly shifted the rearview mirror to find her in it. He
smiled, then changed lanes in traffic to pass a fruit vendor's cart

being pulled by a horse, then peered at her again. He smiled. Watching Emil watching her, she faced forward with a stiffened neck and formally folded hands and a look, she hoped, of insouciance.

The Hofbräuhaus was filling up when they got there. Hitler quickly hid his glasses as twenty urgent Sturmabteilung men in their late teens and twenties rushed to the famous car when they saw it. Each was in jackboots and jodhpurs and brown shirts, with the *Hakenkreuz*, or swastika, insignia on a red armband. Hitler fondly smiled at them, as a father would his children, waiting for them to hold back the surging crowd before he got out and gracefully strode toward the Hofbräuhaus entrance under the Nazi salute, his dog whip in his left hand. Rosenberg followed him, and then Geli and Emil, his hand gently riding her waist as he guided her forward.

She heard the crowd wondering aloud who she was. Ever stilted and serious, Rudolph Hess pompously bowed toward Geli as he conferred with Max Amann at a folding table stacked high with the first volume of Hitler's memoir *Mein Kampf* (*My Struggle*). It had just been brought out by the Eher Publishing House, which the party owned. The price for the book was twelve reichsmarks, whereas the price for the old *Völkischer Beobachter* daily she'd seen had been eight billion *Rentenmarks*. Much had changed.

She saw an unconscious man being hauled out of the Hofbräuhaus by the ankles, his face an affluence of blood. She heard havoc to her right and shouts of "Red scum!" as three storm troopers chased onto a tramway a frail man in his sixties whose misfortune it was to resemble Lenin. She looked away in horror as each took turns hitting him, and when she looked back again he was just a bleeding heap on the tracks, trying to find a tooth.

But she forgot the violence in the festivities. Teenaged girls were handing out pretzels, and singing men were sharing a tankard of beer. Everywhere there were red-and-black political banners and posters: of Nazi hands holding out tools to job seekers under the words "Work and Bread"; an illustration of a Nazi fist strangling a frightening black python underneath "Death to Lies"; a fierce eagle astride a swastika held up by the masses, and over it "Germany Awake!"; and a sketch of three scowling soldiers haloed by a swastika and the phrase "National Socialism—the Organized Will of the Nation." Above the front doors of the Hofbräuhaus was a freshly painted sign that read NO ENTRY FOR JEWS.

About four thousand people were crammed inside the hall and interior garden, the greater percentage of them forlorn middle-aged men who seemed to be former army officers, civil servants with dueling scars, schoolteachers, waiters, clerks and shopkeepers, factory workers and farmers, some in the lederhosen, jackets, and feathered hats that was the Bavarian national costume; and in the front rows were old ladies in fine dresses and hats, a few of them knitting as they waited. Emil called them "The Incorruptibles." A greater part of the crowd, though, was comprised of high school students, fraternity brothers from the university, even children—the majority of those wearing Nazi pins were under twenty-five. Collection baskets were being passed from hand to hand, as in church. Everyone seemed to have a tankard of beer and a cigarette or a pipe, and some were stooped over paper plates of bratwurst and sauerkraut. Tobacco smoke hung in the hall like filmy curtains of gray and blue.

Emil told her she would be sitting far away from the main stage because there were generally fights at these rallies, and ferocious arguments over nothing. She was installed, therefore, in an upper loft in the hall. With her there were journalists slouched in their chairs, some wives or mistresses of party members, a harried waitress with tremendous breasts filling orders for food, and, in the farthest corner, a stern priest in a black suit and Roman collar watching Emil leave.

She leaned over the railing of the balustrade to observe Emil as he fought through the crowd to join Julius Schaub as a bodyguard while Rosenberg and Hess huddled with her uncle and other party officials by the stage. Hitler was the only one not talking, a fact he seemed to find irritating. She was fascinated that so many people there seemed excited about hearing him speak, for from this distance he seemed wary, officious, and ordinary, like a concierge in a hotel that had fallen on hard times.

She heard a man say, "You must be important." And she turned to find the priest leaning on a cane held in his left hand, his black fedora in the other. He was a fit, broad-shouldered man of fifty, a few inches over six feet in height, with steel-blue eyes, a wild shock of graying brown hair, and the hard, weathered face of a frontline infantry soldier. He further explained himself by saying, "Wasn't that one of Hitler's friends?"

"His chauffeur," she told him. "Herr Hitler is my uncle." She saw the hint of a wince before the priest forced a wide smile and hunted for a calling card in his suit-coat pocket. "Would it be an impertinence if I introduced myself?"

She took the card and read, "P. Rupert Mayer, S.J., Maxburgstrasse 1, München." "You're a Jesuit, Pater Mayer?"

"And you must be a Catholic."

She held out her hand to him, and he shook it as she said, "Angelika Raubal."

Shifting his cane to his right hand, it knocked his knee, and he must have seen her shock at the sound of wood striking wood, for he told her, "In the Great War, I was a military chaplain with the Eighth Division. A grenade forced the surgeons to amputate my leg."

"Oh, I'm so sorry." She half turned out the chair next to her. "Would you like to sit, Pater Mayer?"

"Your uncle would find that highly inappropriate, Fräulein Raubal." Crinkling his eyes, he smiled in private merriment, though his mouth was little more than a wide, flat line. He told her they went back a long way, Herr Hitler and he; to 1919 when they'd both participated in a public debate in München on the false teachings of Communism. Corporal Hitler had been an "education officer" then and had followed Mayer to the platform and said, "We have had a religious attack on Communism from a priest; now I shall attack it politically." And he had electrified the crowd. Even Mayer had been carried away. But beneath the brilliance of his oratory, the Jesuit had found ideas that were so disturbing that he'd begun attending Herr Hitler's meetings whenever he could. "And now I have heard a hundred times what Adolf Hitler has to say," he told her. "I regret the offense to you, his niece, but your uncle is a dangerous man."

Geli reddened in defensiveness, but the priest simply wished her a good evening and limped off to his faraway seat. Then the hall lights went black and Rudolf Hess stiffly walked onto the spot-lighted stage below, his sunken eyes zigzagging beneath his fabulous eyebrows, and in his shrill, frightened voice he went on and on with his fawning introduction, flattering Hitler so fulsomely that people began to rhythmically stamp their feet with impatience. Hess finally turned to his leader, offered the Fascist salute, and shouted, "Heil Hitler!" And then, as his followers cheered and five hundred inflamed storm troopers jumped up as one and yelled over and over again, "Victory, salvation!," her uncle walked onto the stage.

Without looking at the crowd, Hitler put his pages of notes faceup on a plain table there, diffidently arranged and squared them, and coughed softly into his fingertips in a way that Geli thought of as prim and effeminate. He seemed at first as reluctant to speak as Hess. He held his stare on the floor and stood a little behind the table, as if he'd totter without its support. Quiet settled on the audience and he uttered in a guttural, hardly intelligible bass voice a few sentences about the crisis they were facing in this twentieth century. She could see others leaning forward just as she was, frowning as they tried to hear.

Then both the timbre and the volume of his voice began rising, and in a good High German that was often tinged with Austrian slang and pronunciations, he gave his own interpretation of their motherland's plight since November 11, 1918. "When we ask ourselves today what is happening in the world," Hitler said, "we are obliged to cast our minds back to the kaiser's abdication and his flight into Holland." And then he reminded them of how the armistice had been signed by weak-lings and criminals in Berlin, stabbing a knife in the back of the great German army when it was on the brink of victory. Communist Spartacists had incited a revolution against the Weimar Republic, but were quelled in hundreds of street battles by the Ehrhardt Brigade and other soldiers in private armies, many of them now his loyal and necessary storm troopers. But while they were shedding their blood for their friends and families, European and American enemies humiliated, in fact, sought to murder, their precious motherland with the Treaty of Versailles—"the treaty of shame," he called it—compelling Germany to take sole responsibility for the war, and calling for fantastic reparations payments, the theft of 13 percent of its territory, and the occupation of the Rhineland and Saar by Allied forces. "The hands that signed that treaty shall wither!" Hitler shouted, and his audience leapt to its feet in wild applause.

Waving them down and quieting, he reminded them that the Weimar government had foolishly tried to fulfill those war debts that were impossible to meet by simply printing more money, hence its currency had soon become worthless. An American dollar could purchase a little more than four German marks in 1914, about eight and a half in 1918, and well over two hundred *billion* five years later! Hard-won savings were lost, factories were shut down, houses were sold to foreign investors for the price, to them, of a cup of tea.

We are on the right track again, Hitler said. Errors in policy have been corrected. But we are still being preyed upon by the four horsemen of hunger, illness, unemployment, and loss of national pride. There were Europeans at Versailles who wanted the "pastoralization" of Germany. Shall we permit them to do that? Have we, in fact, become sheep? And when he got them shouting no, his face turned fiendish as he threatened, "I'll haul all those bargain-hunting, pact-making sissies right off the political stage." Which was followed by tumultuous applause.

And so on. The history was familiar to Geli and everyone else in the Hofbräuhaus, but her uncle's recitation of it was stunning in its conviction, its poisonous wit, its passion. Shunning rationality, he sought the peoples' faith with his own certainty. Hard questions were given easy answers. Objections were overcome with insistence. Opinions difficult to accept were continually repeated. Every complex issue was simplified. Every suspicion of paranoia was offered due consideration and respect. The ill-educated in the audience got the impression that they finally understood politics.

Geli looked at her watch and realized an hour had passed since her uncle had begun speaking, and there was no sign he would soon quit, but the people seemed rooted in their seats, fully absorbed in what he was saying. She felt almost as if they'd furiously turn on her if she stirred, for he was healing them in his peculiar way, acquitting them of hostilities in the war, justifying their fury and spite, holding up as praiseworthy their most petty and shameful emotions, for hatred, fanaticism, and mercilessness were not only good but obligatory if the Aryan nation was to find its rightful place in the world. Exalting warfare and struggle as "the father of all things," insisting that death in battle was a soldier's highest duty, stressing his own ruthlessness and brutality, frankly admitting the intolerance of his ideology, Hitler was far less a politician than a ferocious prophet of wrath.

Geli later learned that each of Hitler's ten or twelve large foolscap pages of notes contained fewer than twenty words, which served as cues for what would be ten or fifteen minutes of his rant. Each of his speeches was no less than two hours long and frequently closer to three, obeying the rules of a Wagnerian symphony in its fiery construction. Watching her uncle from afar, she saw how he kept the crowd, like his friends, off balance, first quarreling with the right wing for their feudal economic system, their meanness and class prejudices, their fears in the face of adversity, and then attacking the left wing for their facile thinking, their lax moral values, their abandonment of the great Germanic traditions. Without saying so, he gave the crowd the choice of agreeing with him or of being annihilated by his contempt, and they found themselves in his sway.

She saw that her uncle could do what cannot be faked: He honestly, deeply, majestically felt the hurt, the shame, and the outrage of being in Germany in the first quarter of the twentieth century. Hitler's gift was to make his hearers feel he was speaking to each one personally, heart to heart, and that he was proudly one of them, a Völkischer—ill-educated, ill-favored, from humble beginnings, a failure in all his undertakings, just another wounded, unknown soldier,

and he had suffered precisely as they had. And yet he foresaw a glorious future for them if they would put their complete faith in him as
their führer. "One is either a hammer or an anvil," he shouted. "The
only choice is between Hitler and death, victory or destruction,
glory or ignominy. We shall be rich or we shall be poor. We shall be
conquering heroes or sacrificial lambs. We shall be hot or cold, but
those who are lukewarm shall be damned."

Even beyond the inflammatory wording, Geli saw that Hitler cap-
tivated his audience with a skilled actor's talent for histrionics: his
fists at his heart when he talked of his patriotism; his face ravaged,
his shoulders shrugging beneath their heavy burden as he talked
about Germany's afflictions; his hand reaching upward, his face
transfixed, as he talked about seizing the future. Often, though, he
stood like a soldier at ease, his hands folded protectively in front of
his crotch, his head high, his face reddening, his voice an orchestra
of primal emotions as he shouted out his enmity for the Weimar par-
liamentarians, the Communists, the industrialist war profiteers, the
intellectuals, and the Jews, promising that all the enemies of the
people would one day be "*beseitigt,*" eliminated. And in case there
was any question about who the foremost enemy was, Hitler finished
his second hour with one long harangue against those he called "the
Hebrew defilers" and the "ferment of decomposition."

Everything wrong in Germany, he said, was wrong because of the
secret Zionist conspiracy to conquer the world. The Jews were para-
sites; they were vermin. They had stood by idly as Aryan soldiers
died at the front, they had forced the armistice, fostered Communism, put their signatures on the "treaty of disgrace," and gotten fat
on Germany's misery in their black markets. And now they were
manipulating financial affairs, miseducating the young, radically
changing the sciences, filling the humanities and arts with their
ugliness and degeneracy, polluting Aryan blood with intermarriage.
With a rage verging on hysteria, his face running with sweat, his
shirt soaked through, his voice growing hoarse, Hitler shrieked, "I
will pull out the evil of Jewry by its roots and exterminate it!"

Was this why he had invited her here? Was he aware that Geli had girlfriends who were Jewish, that Angela worked in a Jewish hostel and Paula in a Jewish firm? Was he trying to change that, to make them regret it? She felt he was screaming at her personally, like an unhinged, upbraiding father in the midst of four thousand witnesses. She was chagrined. And she was shocked by other feelings as well, for if what he said was hateful and terrifying, it was also electrifying. Each sentence was being cheered now. Half of those in the hall were on their feet. Even grown men joined the high school boys in getting up on the tables to hoist their steins to him and yell their enthusiasm. Geli saw a girl faint with ecstasy. Elderly ladies were weeping with love of him. Cold weather was not as real as the thrill she felt around her.

Quickening his tempo, Hitler heatedly pounded out the final paragraphs of his speech in a rhapsody of words, offering the people food, order, full employment, European supremacy, and a complete end to the confusions and upheavals of democracy. ("I feel the heat of the audience," he later told Geli, "and when the right time has come, I hurl a flaming javelin that sets the crowd on fire.") And so he heightened his outrage, forging ahead with rhythmic, pounding sentences, his face as red as blood, his fists clenched, his neck straining, until, in a final orgasm of words, he grandly offered them himself as the messiah of the Germanic people. "I shall be your leader," he screamed. "And ours shall be the kingdom, and the power, and the glory! Amen!"

With that the four thousand affirmed him in such a giant voice that the hall's rafters shook. Quickly Hitler saluted his Sturmabteilung, signaling his Brownshirts to link arms and roar out the national anthem, "Deutschland über Alles." While the exultation was still at its highest pitch, Hitler weakly escaped from the stage, but the hurrahs and singing and banging of tankards continued. And though Geli felt that the priest in his faraway seat was watching her with disappointment and scorn, she joined the others in wildly applauding her uncle. She couldn't help it. She was enthralled.

■ ■ ■

Emil Maurice got hold of her hand and hurried Geli down hidden stairs to the outside, where the Mercedes was thrumming, its running lights off, and Julius Schaub was behind the wheel. Waiting in front of it was a taxi. While Emil gave Schaub instructions, Geli opened the passenger door to congratulate Hitler, but was stunned to find he'd fallen asleep, his mouth hanging open as if he'd been slain. His gray suit coat was off and his white shirt was so wet with sweat that she could see through it. And the odor was hideous, like a hellish whiff of skunk and offal. Geli held a hand over her nose and mouth as she shut the door.

Emil smiled. "We'll go in the taxi."

She heard the thousands still singing as she got in the backseat with Emil and he leaned forward to give the taxi driver an address in the fashionable district of Bogenhausen. When Emil sat back, his right knee widened against hers and did not withdraw. "Were you amazed by the talk?" he asked.

She was. "Mesmerized."

"Exactly. Max Amann was his first sergeant, and he says Hitler was quite an oddity in the trenches. 'The White Crow,' they called him. Constantly serious. Didn't drink or smoke. Wasn't interested in women. Took duty at Christmas so he wouldn't have to join in the festivities. Even then, though, he could talk politics for hours. 'Spinning,' Amann called it. You look at his writing and it's not very good. Dull; hard to read. Ugly grammar and misspelled words . . ."

Exiting traffic from the Hofbräuhaus was tying up the street. Emil hunched forward to give the taxi driver instructions before familiarly sitting back against her thigh and finding his train of thought. "But when Hitler speaks, it's hypnotic," he said. "You have no will of your own. Only his. You forget to think. You give up your liberty. You submit. And you find the faith you lost. Hear him once and you become a friend of the party. Hear him twice and you become a fanatic." Emil grinned like a boy as he said, "Won't Germany be glorious when Hitler's in charge?"

She only felt his thigh firmly against hers. She agreed by nodding. Emil watched as the taxi got onto Maximilianstrasse and headed east toward the Isar.

"We're going to the house of Herr Heinrich Hoffmann," Emil said. "We're having a birthday party for Hitler now because he'll be in Hamburg on April twentieth."

"I ought to know this, but how old will he be?"

"Thirty-six. And you?"

Geli thought about trying twenty, but admitted, "I'll be seventeen in June."

Emil took that in like a factor that he hadn't considered, then focused on Geli so intently she lost the rhythm of her breathing. "I often go out with girls that age." And then he turned away, saying, "Your uncle, too. Old ladies and girls."

She was aching with questions about Emil's girlfriends, about Hitler's, but figured they were all too invasive, and she knew men were often chary with their thoughts. She silently watched the city streets until the taxi turned left onto Ismaningerstrasse. She then asked, "*Whose* house is it?"

"Heinrich Hoffmann. Hitler's official photographer. And his wife, of course. Also there's a little boy named Heinrich, and a sassy daughter, Henrietta. She's thirteen."

Wryly she asked, "And you often go out with girls that age?"

"Even *I* have limits."

She smiled. "At least it's a beginning."

Within a few minutes they were on a leafy street lined with cars, and halting in front of a magnificent house that seemed to have forty windows filled with light.

Enormous numbers of cakes, candies, and birthday presents were on an intricately carved table in the grand entrance hall. Many inside the side parlors wore dinner jackets and the finest dresses and jewels. All the Brownshirts were absent. Waiters in old Bavarian livery were offering trays of canapés and champagne. Emil felt out of his element, so he took Geli to Herr Hanfstaengl, who was finally *in* his. Putzi got her a tulip glass of champagne and then she was over-whelmed with names and titles as he gaily introduced her as "Hitler's niece" to his beautiful blond wife, Helene; and to a socialite named Gertrud von Seydlitz; the former wife of Olaf Gul-bransson, a cartoonist; Frau Hoffmann, the harried and heavily jew-eled hostess, who had a little boy on her hip; and Minister of Justice Franz Gürtner, a stern man with a gray mustache and a pince-nez. She met a factory owner's widow, Frau Wachenfeld-Winter, from whom her uncle was going to rent an Alpine house near Berchtes-gaden, and her wealthy neighbors there: Edwin Bechstein, of the Berlin piano company, and his wife, Helene, who, though she was little more than ten years older than Adolf, gladly called herself "Hitler's mommy."

Putzi then took Geli to a red parlor where she met Paul Nikolaus Cossmann, editor of the *Münchener Neueste Nachrichten*, who was talking to William Bayard Hale, an American classmate of Wood-row Wilson at Princeton and a retired European correspondent for the Hearst newspapers. Emil Gansser of the firm Siemens & Halske in Berlin gave Geli his card; Joseph Fuess and his wife invited Geli to their jewelry shop in the Corneliusstrasse; and Jakob Werlin, the München representative of the Daimler Works in Stuttgart-Untertürckheim, who told Geli that her uncle's custom-made Mer-cedes must have cost twenty thousand marks. And then there were Frau von Kaulbach, the stout widow of the acclaimed Bavarian painter; a sitting and quietly inebriated Prince Henckel-Donners-marck; a flirtatious railway official at the east station named Lauböck; Quirin Diestl and his wife, who owned a stationery shop near the Regina Hotel; Frau Elsa Bruckmann, who was the former Princess Cantacuzène of Rumania and the wife of the foremost pub-lisher in München; and Erich Ludendorff's far younger second wife, Frau Doktor Mathilde Spiess Ludendorff, who magisterially pro-claimed her hatred for Jewry and Christianity, and was going on and on about a new German religion that she and her husband were founding, and that had its origins in the old pagan Nordic gods.

Walking away from them, Putzi slyly told Geli, "The Frau Doktor's specialty is mental diseases."

Geli smiled. "It probably helps to have had so many herself."

"Hah!" he said. "Precisely what I was thinking."

Another voice said, "And now I shall quiz you on all the names."

She turned and found a jovial, blond man of forty in a tuxedo, a few inches shorter than she was, his face flushed with alcohol, his wide shoulders slanting left off a twisted spine. "You are Herr Hoffmann," she said.

"You knew!"

"The host always has an air about him."

Ebulliently he said, "So sorry. I shall have all the windows opened at once."

Hanfstaengl begged Geli's forgiveness for leaving, kissed her right hand, and was gone.

She told Hoffmann, "My girlfriend and I saw you yesterday on Schellingstrasse, inside your photography shop."

"Was that *you* with Herr Hitler!"

A pretty and fairly tipsy girl of thirteen slinked up in a quite adult fitted evening gown and linked her arm inside her father's as she kissed him on the cheek. She wore pink lipstick on her pouting mouth; her chestnut-brown hair was in a chignon. She looked like the high school girls of Paris, flat-chested but soigné and athletic, willfully alluring, with the fretful expression of the frequently disappointed. Hoffmann introduced the girl as "My daughter, Henrietta," but she put out her hand and said, "I'm Henny."

"Geli Raubal," she said as she shook the offered hand, and when she saw the girl's puzzlement, Geli added, "Hitler's niece."

"Interesting," Henny said, as if that indeed was. She took in Geli from shoes to hair and tilted into her father as she said, "You have beautiful breasts."

Geli just blushed and said, "Thank you."

Hoffmann hastened to say, "My dear frank child did not mean to embarrass you, Fräulein Raubal. She was raised among models and actresses."

"Don't you think?" Henny asked him.

"It's true, of course," Hoffmann said. And then he steered their conversation toward Geli's views of München.

"I haven't seen much, just what I could on a short tour today."

"Who took you?" Hoffman asked.

"Herr Julius Schaub."

Henny said, "Not much of a talker, is he."

"Herr Schaub's idea of good communication is to stare at feet other than his own."

Henny and her father laughed so loudly that others at the party quizzically turned. "Aren't you delightful," he said. "We must get to know each other." With that he got another glass of champagne for himself and guided Geli into his library as Henny tagged along behind them. And then he did all the talking, first showing Geli his book of photos, *A Year of Revolution in Bavaria*, then the King Gustav of Sweden gold medal he'd won at the Malmö exhibit, the Great Silver Medal of Bulgaria, and other awards he'd been given for progress in the art of photography. While doing so he told her that his father had been court photographer to King Ludwig III, and so he'd naturally fallen into the job and become a war photographer on the western front. Afterward, with the troubles in the Weimar Republic, he'd sold his photography studio for what he'd thought was a fantastic price, "but the nation's purchasing power so declined that when the first half of the debt was paid, all I could buy with it was a reflex camera. And by the time I got the second half, it was not sufficient for even six eggs." Two friends and he had formed a company to make a silent film comedy about a hairdresser whose homemade potion put great manes on bald heads until the hairdresser's assistant—unfortunately played by no Charlie Chaplin—caused much to go awry. "Germany did not find it funny." While living a hand-to-mouth existence, he had joined the Nazi Party, with membership card number 427, and soon thereafter was sent a telegram from an American agency offering one hundred dollars for a photo of Adolf Hitler, a fortune then. And he'd found out that there were hundreds of others seeking photos of the famous man, of which there were none at the time.

Henny was slumped on a sofa, her forearms folded, her shoeless feet up on a coffee table. Wearily, she said, "To make a long story short—"

Hoffmann sighed. "Children have no patience. In hasty conclusion, I obtained the leader's trust and got a photograph of Adolf Hitler on my big thirteen-by-eighteen Nettel camera. And would you believe I sold the negative internationally for twenty thousand dollars?"

"You can buy all the eggs you want now," Geli said, and the girl on the sofa giggled.

"And that is why I am celebrating your uncle's birthday. I owe all I have to him. Everything. I have been his only photographer since 1923. All others who try have their plates smashed by the SA. And it is my monopoly—to say nothing of Herr Hitler's kindness—that has furnished my family with this house, our servants, my Daimler and Opel, my Berlin pied-à-terre at the Kaiserhof Hotel."

Emil stood in the doorway of the library and said, "He's here."

Henny shot up and scurried out with her father. Emil waited for Geli to join him. All the partygoers were happily crushed around the grand entrance hall and cheering as Hitler trudged up the stairway, rings of tiredness under his eyes, in a formal black tailcoat, starched shirt, bow tie, and patent leather shoes.

Emil pointed out to Geli a glowing film actress from Berlin who was flaunting her body in the sheerest of gowns. Willingly a gift. "We've put together a surprise for him," Emil whispered.

When Hitler entered the hall, the partygoers wildly yelled, "Happy birthday," and he smiled, oh so briefly showing his square brown teeth, but then the film actress rushed forward and kissed him full on the mouth as people hooted and whistled and called out jokes. Hitler only stiffened at the laughter and frightened the actress with his glare, and when she shyly retreated from him, his face was white with rage. A cold stillness fell over the house as he sternly evaluated his well-wishers, then turned around and stormed out.

Without him, the party ended.

CHAPTER EIGHT
HAUS WACHENFELD, 1927

Adolf Hitler first became acquainted with the Obersalzberg region of Germany when he vacationed at the Pension Moritz in August 1922, registering as Herr Wolf. Doktor Sigmund Freud and the Austrian playwright Doktor Arthur Schnitzler were also staying there, but he knew them to be Jews and failed to introduce himself. Even in summer the Alpine air was as pure as fresh snow and he would pace the balcony late at night inhaling it until his chest ached. Salt that was mined in nearby Berchtesgaden was generally thought to be so health-giving that he gave himself long, hot footbaths in it just before bed at night and again in the morning when he hungrily scanned the papers for news of himself. Hiking up the northern slope of the Hoher Goll for a solitary noon picnic, he could see green farmlands and white stone villages far below, the sandstone tints of Salzburg twenty kilometers to the north, the jagged slate-gray peaks of the massive Untersberg and Watzmann mountains, the Wittelsbach palace where Crown Prince Rupprecht lived in Berchtesgaden, and, farther west and south, the azure waters of the great Königssee.

The village of Obersalzberg held a post office and fire department, horse stables, a ski lift, a Dresden pensioners' club, a naval officers' club, the Seitz Children's Sanatorium, six inns, twenty private homes, and eleven luxurious villas, including two owned by Hitler's wealthy patrons, Edwin and Helene Bechstein. Often dining with them when they were skiing in the winter or hiking in the summer, he talked about renting a home for himself there, and it was they who had found him the so-called Kampfhäusl, a one-room plank-sided cabin where he'd finished the first volume of *Mein Kampf* after his release from Landsberg fortress in 1924. The Bechsteins had recommended Sonnen-Köpfl to him when they'd heard that Frau Maria Cornelius was willing to sell, but Hitler hated sunshine on his face and the villa had been built to invite it. And they themselves were not yet willing to part with Weissenlehen, their home just across the road.

At last Hitler heard that Margarethe Wachenfeld-Winter, the industrialist's widow, would be renting out Haus Wachenfeld for one hundred reichsmarks a month. High up Kelstein Mountain, at an elevation of nine hundred meters, the chalet had been built in 1916 and had three upstairs bedrooms, one upstairs bathroom, a dining room, kitchen, bedroom, and sunroom on the first floor, and travel poster panoramas from every window. It was only a four-minute hike through woods to the Hotel zum Türken, so friends and aides in the party could stay there, and only a few minutes farther along the winding road that fronted the house was the Gasthaus Steiner, where they served Wiener schnitzel and Hungarian goulash just the way he liked them. Although Frau Winter would not sell it to him until 1931, Hitler fully intended to own the chalet from the instant he first saw it. Within hours of signing the lease, Hitler was moving in.

Doktor Karl Lüger, the former mayor of Wien and the publisher of *Das Deutsche Volksblatt*—a prewar newspaper that fascinated Hitler with its erotic pictures and tales of the international Jewish conspiracy—had lived all his life in a household run by his two older sisters, and Hitler sought to imitate Lüger's sham of respectability by having Angela and Geli handle the chores of Haus

Wachenfeld for him. Offering his half-sister full-time pay for far less work, and in a fashionable Alpine resort, Hitler also offered to furnish the funds for Leo to finish his studies at the Universität von Wien, and to rent a flat for his niece in München, less than two hundred kilometers to the north, so she could enroll in the university there.

Angela agreed to the offers and arrived in Obersalzberg in March 1927. Geli arrived in June, after her nineteenth birthday, and after she'd completed her gymnasium studies and received her *Abitur*.

Angela rushed out to greet her when Julius Schaub drove Geli up from the Salzburg railway station. They hugged and linked arms to walk the grounds, and Geli fell in love with Haus Wachenfeld, just as her uncle had. The first-floor exterior was white stucco, with red-shuttered windows. A balcony railed with white flower boxes was on all four sides of the chalet's wood-sided second floor, and heavy stones and lath had been laid on the wide, overhanging roof to hold fast the wooden shingles in high winds. East of the chalet there was a fenced-in vegetable garden that tilted on the hill just above the road of crushed pebbles that gave access to the underground garage. West of the chalet was a wide, slate terrace with striped canvas lawn chairs; to the north was another terrace with white-enameled café tables and chairs and with a huge red-and-black Nazi banner hanging from a mast. Clouds would often float like a soft mist while they sat there, but on that first day the weather was so fine that Geli could squint her eyes from the sun and just make out the tall white Cross on the highest peak of the faraway Untersberg.

Angela walked her daughter through Haus Wachenfeld's interior, showing her the front porch enclosed in tall, uncurtained windows to form a sunroom that was called the Winter Garden and was furnished with a heating stove, a gramophone, a grandfather clock, green ferns, succulents, palms, a crooked and hang-necked rubber tree, and soft, floral-patterned armchairs facing a round oak table. A fine hemp rug of geometric design was on the floor. All were gifts from Helene Bechstein.

The dining room was wainscotted in oak and fussily decorated

with green-leafed drapes, four watercolor cityscapes by Hitler, hanging plates of ornate design, old-fashioned and rustic chairs, and pil-
lowed corner benches that formed half the seating for a square oak
dining table with inlaid green marble. And there was more to dislike
everywhere else. Slurring the window panoramas were the dimity
curtains of the peasantry; a fake cactus and a far too literal painting
of a huge-buttocked female nude were in Hitler's upstairs room; on a
kitchen wall where a crucifix usually was in Bavaria there was a tin
tray with a picture on it of three jolly fat men hoisting steins of
foaming beer; in the bathroom was a lantern that when lit depicted
a little boy urinating; and here and there about the house were
hand-stitched pillows, dish towels, and doilies, all with swastikas or
the initials "A.H." or fancily embroidered expressions of undying
loyalty. "Aren't *they* ugly," Geli said.

Angela looked below to the terrace in a precautionary way and
found Hitler strolling head down with his Alsatian, Prinz, and Julius
Schaub, Hitler holding a dog whip of hippopotamus hide behind his
back as he talked and talked. "Ugly as sin," she told Geli. "Adolf
knows they're not beautiful things, but they're gifts from party members, so he finds it hard to let go of them, out of loyalty." She sighed
as she went back downstairs. "Our father was the same," she said.
"He shoots for love, but the arrow falls, and he only hits sentimen-
tality."

■ ■ ■

Geli was given the chores of a handmaid. Each morning she got up
with her mother at eight and helped Angela in the kitchen with
vanilla pancakes, plum cakes with cinnamon, or Austrian puff pas-
tries. She let Prinz out of her uncle's room and watched him sniff
and sign the forest trees as she walked to the Hotel zum Türken to
buy newspapers from Austria and Germany. She got the mail from
the post office box on the walk back and put what she'd collected on
a red-painted chair just outside Hitler's door. On Sundays and holy
days of obligation, she and Angela would join other workers for a
ride down to Berchtesgaden and the ten a.m. Mass at the twelfth-

century Stiftskirche, or Abbey Church, next to the Wittelsbach castle. On weekdays she and Angela would simply wait for Adolf to wake up. Around eleven Geli would generally see his forearm and hand as he got the mail and papers from the red chair, and then she would go make a fresh pot of coffee, peel and section an orange, and carry his breakfast to him on a fine silver coffee service that had been a gift from Princess Cantacuzène. When she got up to his room, Hitler would have shaved with two blades, patted his face with a liniment of aloe, and fully dressed in lederhosen, a white shirt and tie, knee-high stockings, and hiking boots, though if company were expected he generally wore his black dress shoes and a light gray woolen suit. She'd watch as he soaked his hair with Dr. Dralle's Birkenwasser, then tilted forward and combed his wet, dark hair flat to his forehead, fastidiously parted it, stood upright, and jerked his head so that his forelock fell to the left. Only then would he acknowledge her, often kissing her hand and saying how pretty she looked, at other times sulking as if she'd offended him, once shrieking in terrifying wrath because he'd found a spiderweb wobbling frailly inside the upper sash of his window.

Rudolf Hess was now Hitler's private secretary and was paid three hundred reichsmarks per month. Each day Hess would stroll up from the Pension Moritz at noon, find Hitler's reading glasses, fondly steam them with his breath, dry them with his handkerchief, then solemnly and patiently stand beside his leader on the terrace, saying not a word until Hitler had finished perusing the newspapers. Geli would carry out a tray of *Apfelstrudel* and apple peel tea, then the men would talk politics and economics while Geli folded her uncle's pajamas, tightened the blankets on his bed, collected laundry, vacuumed the floor, and wiped the furniture with linseed oil, or the window glass, mirrors, and bathroom fixtures with watered ammonia.

After that she was free for the afternoon. While listening to operas on the gramophone, she sang with the sopranos and sewed her own clothing or filled in crossword puzzles or read the continuations of serialized romances in five or six magazines. Often there were picnics with sandwiches, fruit, and mineral water; or a frowning Schaub would be forced to take her down to the Königsee for a cold swim; or she'd walk in the shade with her uncle and Prinz, and Hitler would show her how he'd used fried chicken gizzards to teach the *Wolfshund* to climb a ladder, walk on a railing, jump over a two-meter fence, heel, sit, roll over, crawl, beg with praying paws, and play dead. Each afternoon he strolled with Prinz to the same corner of his lot, picked up the same stick, and threw it in the same direction until the Alsatian had fetched it six times and they could head back to the house.

Evening chores began at eight as she and Angela cooked a late dinner. She set the dining room table with Rosenthal porcelain and Irish linen napkins, then put wildflowers in a Steuben vase that had been a gift from Frau von Seidlitz. She and Angela ate in the kitchen when guests were there, with him when the three were alone. With dinner they'd have a Liebfraumilch or a Moselblümchen wine, or, if they were dining on *Zungenwurst*, a strong Salvator beer. When they'd tidied the kitchen, they would loll in the Winter Garden with coffee and dessert and quietly listen to Wagner, or to Hitler's flood of opinions on Charlemagne, the childishness of Mozart, the physics of flight, Karl May's Westerns, future pharmaceuticals, horses—which he hated, and never rode—lipstick, which he insisted was made from wax and sewage, why red cabbage was far superior to green, why champagne caused headaches, why the children of geniuses have far less talent, of his plan to fully employ Germany in the construction of a network of *Autobahnen*, of his hopes of having a factory produce for ordinary people an inexpensive automobile that he would call the Volkswagen.

But Hitler generally avoided harangues about Jews and political strife when he was at Haus Wachenfeld, and only once that first summer was he visited by a party official other than Rudolf Hess. That official was Franz Xaver Schwarz, a former accountant in the finance section of the München city hall who had lost his job after the putsch and was now party treasurer. Clenched in his hands was a valise that stayed with Hitler when Schwarz went away that evening. Geli presumed it held the money that financed Hitler's lazy life of interrupted unemployment.

Schwarz was in his fifties and far older than other Nazis she'd met, a graying, dour man with a high forehead, owlish black glasses, and a little gray mustache. Like Hess, he was wholly and wistfully subordinate to Hitler; like Prinz, he willingly subjected himself to Hitler's gallery show for Geli, in his head multiplying two five-digit numbers, adding the populations of Germany, Austria, and England, and subtracting from them Belgium and France. Hess dutifully checked the sums on paper, found them correct, and Hitler slapped his thighs with joy, saying Schwarz was just what the party needed, the sheer intellect of an adding machine and the spirit of a *Knicker*, or skinflint.

Schwarz flushed at the scorn behind the praise and sought to change the subject by asking, "Are you going to join the party, Fräulein Raubal?"

She was trying to think of a tactful reply when Hitler fretfully waved a hand and said, "My niece is not interested in politics."

She'd never felt so fortunate, so reprieved. When their talk finally turned to foreign affairs, Geli promptly got up from the terrace table and gleefully hurried back to the house.

■ ■ ■

She began calling him Uncle Alf, and at his fondest he called her Princess. She would look up from reading and find him just glancing away, or she'd turn when she was walking and find him intently watching the sway of her dress. At times she felt unclothed by him. At other times she felt protected, cherished, and adored. She was his quiet den, his twilight stroll, his hobby. She knew Hitler was carrying her in his humming mind like a tune that would not be lost. Like a beautiful sentence from an ancient book that he'd turned into his motto.

■ ■ ■

In fair weather, Angela would shift their late-morning breakfasts outside to the terrace, and, when Hitler did not shoo them, big black jackdaws would fly down from their high mountain aeries and wait for gifts of pastry. Within a few days, to fight boredom, Geli was making a game of it, first testing how close the jackdaws would come, then flicking out a winding trail of pine kernels to see how far the jackdaws would strut through Haus Wachenfeld for more food.

She found out that the one who stayed inside longest had a hurt wing hanging so low that its right feather tips dragged on the floor. She couldn't heal him, but she named him Schatzi, Little Treasure, and trained him to hop and spin for crumbs as she whistled Strauss so it looked like the jackdaw was waltzing.

It was just the kind of slightly cruel trick to make Hitler laugh until his sides ached, and he wanted his niece to show it off to Helene Bechstein when she visited them for afternoon tea on August 12th, his dead mother's birthday; but an hour beforehand her housekeeper telephoned Angela to say Frau Bechstein preferred that they visit her.

And so in his finest navy blue suit a frustrated Hitler hiked and skidded three hundred meters down the hillside with Angela and Geli until they got to the fabulous Villa Bechstein, which would later be taken over and turned into a guest house for Joseph Goebbels, other high party leaders, and Benito Mussolini. "They also own Weissenlehen," Hitler said with enthusiasm, and hunched to point through the forest to a fine house across the road.

Angela rolled her eyes at Geli. *Such a child.*

Ilse Meirer, the housekeeper, was a friend of Angela's now. She greeted all of them at the front door, and then she and Angela stayed behind to have caraway seed tea in the huge white kitchen while, as if this were a fairy tale and their future precarious, Hitler firmly took Geli's hand to guide her upstairs to Frau Bechstein's huge, all-white sitting room.

She was a handsome, square-bodied, matronly woman in her late forties and was lying on a fainting couch *en grande toilette*, wearing only a yellow silk nightgown beneath a yellow silk robe and perhaps four hundred carats in diamonds. She offered a falsely thrilled hello to Adolf and held out both hands to him, which he kissed on the knuckles. And then with stiff formality, he introduced his niece.

"Oh, I'm so glad to finally meet you," Frau Bechstein said, but she did not hide the rivalry in her tone.

And so, in rivalry, Geli curtsied.

"Aren't you a sweet girl," Frau Bechstein said.

"At times."

Frau Bechstein hugged Hitler around the thighs and brought him forcibly against her face. "And this is my sweet boy." She let go and glided her hand along the fainting couch. "Won't you sit, Adolf?"

Obediently, he did so, his hands primly on his knees and his knees tightly together. Geli sat, too, in an Empire chair, but felt the urge to ask a history question just to see the sweet boy raise his hand. Worried and sheepish, Hitler explained to his niece, "We have known each other for seven years now."

"Oh, how he thrilled us in those first days," Frau Bechstein said. She angled her head against his chest and inhaled his smell. "Our shy young messiah," she told Geli. "We put him up in a deluxe hotel, and my husband wore tails for dinner, all the servants were in livery, and Adolf was there in his shabby blue suit, talking away half the evening about the faucet handles in his bathroom that could regulate the heat of the water. And then—it was so funny, really—when Adolf spoke to us about National Socialism, he stood up and shouted intemperately for an hour, his face contorting, his hands flying this way and that, as if our salon were a giant beer hall. And when he finished, he sat down again, thoroughly spent."

With just a hint of his threatening tone, Hitler said, "You are embarrassing me in front of my niece, Frau Bechstein."

She prettily slapped his forearm. "Oh, Wolf. Don't call me that. Call me Mommy."

Worming his eyes toward Geli, he said, "Don't humiliate me."

"We tried to adopt him as our child," she told Geli, "but were afraid there'd be a stink. Instead we showered him with money, jew-els, objets d'art. And for a while I had such hopes that Adolf would fall in love with our daughter Lotte."

"I shall not marry. You know that."

She smiled. "Whenever I see him, I melt in his presence." A hand crawled through his forelock as she admired his sullen face. "You know I would do anything for you, don't you, Wolf?"

"Yes."

"Yes, Mommy," she prompted.

She saw his head hanging in silence and seemed to remember that Geli was there. "And do you play piano, Fräulein?"

She shook her head. "I sing."

She looked at Hitler. "Would it be impertinent of me to offer her a Bechstein pianoforte?"

Waggling pianist's fingers in front of her waist, Geli said, "I'm afraid I lack a Bechstein talent."

"She hates me," Helene Bechstein said.

"Who could do that?" Hitler asked.

"Will you lie with me like we do?"

"My niece is here."

Geli stood. "I'll just be going downstairs. My mother's there."

"And so, you see?" Helene Bechstein said. She then fell back on the fainting couch and Hitler scooted forward and cuddled until his head was on the flattened pillow of her bosom. And she was gently petting his hair and humming a Brahms lullaby as Geli fled, quietly shutting the door behind her.

She hurried down to the first floor of the villa, then to the kitchen where the women were, and said, "I feel sick."

Angela looked up and understood. "Aren't they a pair?"

Geli shrugged in a gruesome shiver. "Mommy! Wolf!"

Ilse Meirer got up. "Shall I get you some cake?"

"I'm too busy trying not to imagine what they're doing up there."

"Or not doing," Angela said.

"Yes, that's worse, isn't it?" Ilse asked. And the older women chuckled as Ilse got Geli some tea.

■ ■ ■

Wearing a sleeveless and belted white linen dress in the late August heat, Geli was on the northern terrace and trying to humor her uncle by finally reading Karl May's *Winnetou* when she shaded her eyes from a shock of sunshine, and saw a green Daimler flow down the pebbled drive to the underground garage. Heinrich Hoffmann got out in white tennis shirt, white flannel trousers, and white shoes, and shouted up to the terrace, "We're here!"

"Welcome!"

"Wake up your uncle!" he said, and hauled from the floor of the car a high stack of dark photographic plates, a carpenter's hammer, and a handled leather portfolio as Henrietta got out in a pleated white tennis skirt, a frilly white blouse, and a fine white cashmere sweater tied at her neck. Hurrying up the garden path with two bottles of Kupferberg Sekt, she called, "It's me!"

"Just as I thought!" Geli called back. She then turned and saw her uncle on the upstairs balcony in his brown woolen suit and purple tie, a foam of Chlorodont toothpaste on his mouth and a hint of blood on his toothbrush. She couldn't tell if he'd been staring at his houseguests or at her. He ambled back inside.

Geli went through the Winter Garden and dining room and into the kitchen where Angela was helping the girl jam the champagne bottles into the icebox. Henny had styled her chestnut-brown hair in a fashionable bob just below her ears, and she was a full inch taller and far more developed since she and Geli had first met. Even Hitler noticed, for he walked in and watched Henny fitting Angela's ham sandwiches next to a package of flank steaks and said, "Why, you're fully grown, Fräulein Hoffmann!"

She fetchingly turned in such a way that the fabric of her blouse was strained. "You missed me, Herr Hitler?"

"Oh, my Sunshine. Each day is night without you."

She grinned and held out her right hand for his kiss. She childishly scolded, "You have stayed away from München too long."

"But why not?" he asked. "Look at all I have here!"

Widening his hands to solicit praise for his property, he seemed to include his niece, and Henny's pretty face fell into a pout. Whether from jealousy or wild speculation, Geli wasn't sure.

Wanting some sentence to tidy up the awkwardness, Geli tried, "I have been here only two months."

Henny flatly stated, "We met your mother up here in May."

Angela said, "So they know absolutely everything about you."

And then Heinrich Hoffmann sidled in with his hammer, plates, and portfolio. "Where shall we?" he asked.

"The dining room," Hitler said. "Would you girls like to see?"

Angela brought in a tin waste can as the photographer filled the table with public relations shots of Hitler in his famous trench coat, on a field of snow, hectoring an audience; dining at the Café Heck; shaking the hands of children; striding down Thierschstrasse with Prinz; holding opera glasses as he chatted with an older woman in a fox stole; worrying over an item in the *Münchener Zeitung*.

Hitler bent low over the photographs, leaning on his hands. Without looking up, he said, "You have a picture of me in spectacles here."

"Where?"

Hitler jabbed at it. "There! Didn't I tell you?"

Hoffmann flipped through his plates, found the offending negative, and smashed it with his carpenter's hammer over the waste can.

"And here. My face is puffy," Hitler said, and ticked a photograph off the dining room table.

Hoffmann got the negative and destroyed it, the glass clanging against the tin as it fell.

Hitler then held up to all of them a stark close-up of himself in a dark brown shirt and a black tie, furrows between his shark-cold eyes, his mouth held in the opposite of a smile, his facial expression that of a hate-filled man whose fierce vengeance is even now being silkily enjoyed. "This is good," he said.

Winking with irony, Hoffmann told Geli, "We're never too old to learn."

And then Hitler put together four different shots of himself as he posed in the brown hat and uniform of the Sturmabteilung.

Geli thought he looked foolish, like a child playing dress up.

"They go or they stay?" Hoffmann asked. Hitler's glare swung toward him like a farmer's scythe in wheat, and the photographer hunted for the negatives.

"Let me do it," Henny said. Her father handed her the hammer and she took joy in crashing the hammer into Hitler's face in the darkened glass, the shards raining loudly from her hand as she told them, "I'm having fun."

Angela called from the kitchen, "Ouch, such a racket!" while Geli winced at the noise and held her ears. But her uncle watched with fascination and zeal as the girl shattered the plates, urging her on by handing Henny even good negatives and seemingly growing ever more excited by the wreckage until at last the photographer angrily took the hammer from his daughter. "We seem to be hungry," he said.

■ ■ ■

Angela stayed behind at Haus Wachenfeld to have tea with friends as Hoffmann conveyed the four of them in his Daimler seven kilometers west of Berchtesgaden to the village of Ramsau and the green lake called Hintersee. Henny and Geli shook out red tartan blankets beneath linden trees and they all had a picnic of champagne and caviar, then lemonade and ham sandwiches as they watched fly fishermen in green hip waders hook trout and saibling, wrap them in seaweed, and stuff them inside their creels.

With his slouch hat cocked on his head and his purple tie flipped over his right shoulder for fear of staining it, Hitler ate salted radishes as he lazed in the shade, his brown trousers twisted high enough that Geli could glimpse the stocking garters pinking the hairless white skin of his calves. Tilting up on his elbows to watch Henny toy with a child's kitten, he told his niece the folklore that Emperor Frederick, the Antichrist of the Middle Ages, was thought to be sleeping beneath the holy mountain of Untersberg, patiently awaiting a flight of ravens that would herald the hour of victory over all of Germany's enemies and the final, long-sought unification of the Aryan nations. And there was some truth to it, of that he was sure. The first time he'd visited Obersalzberg he'd felt a magnetic force urging him to stay, and he knew that he, like Nietzsche's Zarathustra, was meant to live in these mountains for ten years, to become hard here, hard and cold as ice, rejoicing in his loneliness, forging a spirit of steel. "I will have reached my peak," he said, "when I can observe my former self with loathing and pity, and spit on the fate my stars had determined I should have."

Such pomposity, Geli thought, but she said, "You have it all worked out, then."

"I do," he agreed, and held himself up on his right elbow as he faced her, locking his hands together with the plum satisfaction of a fortunate banker. "Are you aware of the origins of the name Adolf?" he asked.

"Adolfus, I thought."

"Athalwolfa," he corrected. "*Athal* means 'noble,' *Wolfa*, 'wolf.' And now a noble wolf has been born who shall shred into bloody pieces the herd of seducers and deceivers of the people." And then he grinned with his fanged, ugly, and generally hidden smile, and she was alarmed to find that with such strange talk her famous uncle was trying to woo her.

She was confused by his flirtation and she flicked her dress farther toward her knees as she felt him float his stare from her sun-bleached hair to her suntanned neck and full breasts and waist and then to the fine blond hairs on her forearm. "Oh, listen, Uncle Alf," she said. "Singing." And she got up from the blanket to pretend she needed to find out who it was.

Wholly unaware of their führer, ten meters away on the other side of the linden trees were five roaring and sunburnt Brownshirts hoisting steins and hollering *Trinklieder* at a picnic table with two tipsy prostitutes who seemed already to have been much used. Geli was stunned as a brassy, singing woman whose hair was the color of *Weissbier* allowed the hankering man beside her to furtively hunt under her skirt as she linked the fingers of both her hands with those of the man she was facing.

"Are we invisible here?" Geli asked, but no one answered.

When the song was just about finished, a drunken practical joker farther down the table quickly hoisted up the sweater of a heavier, bleached-blond woman whose breasts seemed as huge as world globes. She hurriedly hid herself again, but Heinrich Hoffmann ostentatiously gaped and then grinned at Hitler over his filled glass of champagne. "Where are we?" he asked. "In Berlin?"

Hitler flushed as with a disclosed secret, and looked far out to a racing scull on the Hintersee. He tore up blades of grass and chewed them. Henny was still staring at the five men and the prostitutes, as if this were an important moment whose details she'd want to recall.

Ill at ease, her face hot with embarrassment, Geli kicked off her shoes and walked through a door she'd made in her mind, strolling a hundred meters from their afternoon picnic in shaded grass that was plush and cool under her feet. Sunshine whitened the denim blue of the sky and flashed off the green water as if it were a jeweler's case holding tumbled rows of gold bracelets. She joined the lukewarm slosh of the lake, lifting up the hem of her dress to wade farther out and holding still enough that she could watch with childish amusement as sudden minnows schooled by her ankles and softly tickled her skin with nibbles.

"Aren't you gorgeous!" Heinrich Hoffmann said.

She turned and saw the short, blond, wide-shouldered photographer waist high in the gray reeds of the bank, winding forward the film in his Stirnschen camera. "You took my picture?"

"Of course. Don't move." Hoffmann hunkered forward a little and took another. Winding the film, he said, "I'm getting my shoes wet." Squinting through the viewfinder, he urged Geli, "Look into the water as you were doing, but then you hear a noise and you *just* turn your face with surprise." Hoffmann performed it in a feminine way. "Like so."

"Like this?"

"Exactly. Twinkling eyes. Try to flip your hair."

She did so, and he took the picture.

"Excellent," he said. "Are you comfortable?"

"Well, I'm not a model."

He took another. "But you are! You're an enchantress! With that height, that figure, those Slavic features, that perfect white smile." Hoffmann hunched forward and she heard the shutter shear closed like a scissors. "And yet I wonder," he said, mulling it over. "Could you show the camera some more, please?"

"More?"

Hoffmann held the Stirnschen in his right hand as his left instructed her by fiddling his fingers near his thigh. "Hike up your dress just a little higher, my darling."

"Are you sure about this, Herr Hoffmann?"

"Quite sure." She complied, but he said, "Higher still. You have panties on?"

She crossed her eyes at him.

"Then please raise the dress just to your panties, Geli. High as a bathing suit would be, so we can see the beauty in that sturdy young thigh, that womanly rump."

"'Womanly' meaning fat?" She inched the hem of her dress up until she could feel it touching the joint of her thighbone.

"Alluring," he said. "Enticing to hands. Will you bend over for me a little?"

She did. "I feel like I should be beating loincloths on rocks."

Hoffmann adjusted his shutter speed and stalked his pictures, walking sideways, crouching, getting up on his toes, even surging ankle high through the Hintersee in his white tennis flannels.

"Are you taking these photos for yourself?" she asked.

"For whom do you think?"

"Uncle Alf."

She heard his silence, and the shutter again. And he said, "Worse than that. It's for Röhm's storm troopers. We'll put one in every locker."

She laughed at him then, and he got it on film.

■ ■ ■

That evening, when Hitler and the houseguests were waiting for dinner outside, Geli's jackdaw flew down to the terrace and Hitler shouted for his niece to halt food preparations and show Henny and Heinrich one of the jackdaw's tricks.

She hurried out to the terrace in a white apron and said, "We have flank steaks cooking." She then got an inch-square piece of red fabric and affixed it to a chink in the wall. She cawed a few times and the jackdaw flew to the fabric and tugged it from the chink.

"Remarkable," Hoffmann said.

"Shh," Hitler hissed. "There's more."

She cawed again and the jackdaw flew over to the café table where Geli was sitting, hopped within a few inches of her face, and let the fabric fall from its beak. "And now our good-bye, Schatzi," she said. The jackdaw held up his beak to be kissed, then took half a biscuit from her hand and flew off the terrace.

"Marvelous!" Hitler exclaimed. "Geli, that was fantastic!" And he wildly and thoroughly applauded her as she bowed first to him, then to the hoots and congratulations of Henny and her father, and then again to her uncle, whose hands were striking together long after the others had quit, his overjoyed eyes filling with tears as he raved, "She's a miracle, isn't she? She's so beautiful, so gifted! Even birds have to obey her!"

"I have flank steaks in the oven," she said, and went inside.

Within a few minutes Heinrich Hoffmann was in the kitchen, filling his wineglass beside her. They both could still hear her uncle praising her. "You're quite a hit with Herr Hitler," Hoffmann said.

She got butter from the icebox.

"You gave that jackdaw a name?" he asked.

"Schatzi."

He swallowed some Riesling, then winked as he walked outside, saying, "You ought to have named him Adolf."

■ ■ ■

The first night she'd stayed in Haus Wachenfeld, Hitler had given his niece a framed photograph of himself—his favorite gift to friends—and the first volume of *Mein Kampf*. She had happily put the photograph on her night table and had taken the book with her to bed, but had fallen asleep within a few minutes. She'd tried it again the next afternoon but found the prose so atrocious, the thought so vitriolic and contradictory, the tone so whining—when it wasn't pompous—that she couldn't get farther than the first chapter about his childhood in Linz. Each night for two weeks after that her uncle asked her how she liked his memoir, presumably trying to humiliate her into finally finishing it. She told him she was still reading, but so far it seemed quite good.

They celebrated Geli's last night in Haus Wachenfeld on September 27th, but Angela got so sleepy from Riesling that she went to bed at nine. Hitler just watched Geli reading a serialized romance as he finished his coffee, then he went upstairs, and when he walked back into the Winter Garden he had his glasses on and the first volume of *Mein Kampf* in his hand. Dragging a chair until it was facing his niece, he sat in it heavily and began questioning her. "Where was I born, Geli?"

"Braunau am Inn," she said. "1889."

"Why did I not attend a Gymnasium?"

"They didn't teach drawing there."

"And how old was I when my father died?"

"Thirteen, I think."

"What do I say in this of my mother's death?"

She couldn't recall. "Hardly anything," she said.

"My one regret," her uncle said. "But I was dictating the book to Hess, and it seemed too private and important under those circumstances."

"Naturally."

"'Chapter Two,'" he read. "'Years of Learning and Suffering in Wien.' A quotation, Fräulein Raubal: 'X was my faithful attendant, the only one that almost never left me, dividing with me share and share alike. Every book I bought roused his interest; one trip to the opera would give me his company for days; it was a never-ending battle with my unsympathetic friend.' To whom am I referring?"

She shook her head.

"Well, it's not a whom but a what. Hunger. Making hunger seem a human being was for me a fascinating literary conceit. I find it odd that you wouldn't remember that passage." Hitler hunted further through his pages and inquired, "Who produces nine tenths of all the literary filth, artistic trash, and theatrical nonsense in the world?"

She hesitated.

He held up his book and pointed to a block of print. "I say it on page sixty-eight."

"America?" she guessed.

"The Jews," he said. "And the finest things in art, science, or technology are produced by . . . ?"

She thought of galling him by saying, "The Jews," but he was in a tricky mood. "I have no idea," she said.

"Oh? Why is that, I wonder?" And then he told her, "The Aryan." Considering other pages, he halted and focused on one paragraph, asking, "The highest purpose of a man's existence is not the maintenance of a state or government, but . . . what?"

"I only have the answer from religion class."

"We're talking about *my* ideas. *My Struggle.* A book that will one day be the Bible of the German people. The highest purpose of a man's existence is *the preservation of his own kind.* Chapter Three." Hitler offered one of his false smiles. "But we both know you didn't read that far."

She icily stared at him. "Shall I tell you precisely how far I got?"

With the suddenness of a gunshot he was white with rage, and he shouted, "You *dare* to talk to me in that tone? You *dare*?"

At once she was near tears, while he was giant and ancient and uncontrolled, a hurricane of wrath. She felt her stomach growing wobbly with an onset of terror and uncertainty as she folded her arms and humbled her head. She felt he'd turned her bones into wax. She told him, "I'm sorry, Uncle Adolf. You were embarrassing me."

"And you have offended *me*! You have had the temerity to challenge *me*? Adolf Hitler!"

She knew that so much was now so out of proportion that anything was possible. She'd be sent back to Austria. She'd be locked away. She'd be denied. In a faint, thin voice she offered, "I can only say I'm sorry."

"Walk over here to me," he said.

She obediently got up from the floral-patterned chair and nearly tipped with wooziness as she went to him. Would he strike her? Would he make her kneel? She felt he could slay her with a look. She saw his trousered knees lock together and heard him tell her to bend over them. She shocked herself by giggling with scorn as she asked, "You're going to *spank* me?"

Then his left hand flashed up and he hauled her down so hurtfully by the hair that she did what he wanted, squinting her watering eyes tightly shut and locking her knees as she tilted forward, letting his left hand firmly grip her left wrist as his right flipped her pleated skirt up to her waist and struck her hard enough on the left buttock that she jolted forward. She was wearing pink satin panties and his hand seemed to scald through them with his second blow. And his third was like fire. But then he seemed to hesitate, and his fourth strike was far softer. She felt Hitler altering further as he hesitated again, and for a moment she was afraid he'd caress her. She felt sure his hand was floating over her panties, fondling a curve in the air, and then he gently tugged her pleated skirt until she was covered, and she knew the shift of power was complete.

She stood and faced him, but he shied away from her stare. "Have I learned my lesson?" she asked.

Hitler was not an unintelligent man. "Yes," he said. "I'm afraid you have." And then it was his turn to be embarrassed. Calling for Prinz, he escaped her watching by roughhousing with the hound, and he pretended not to notice when his niece walked haughtily upstairs.

In October she moved into a white, furnished room in the Pension Klein at Königinstrasse 43, in the Schwabing area of München. The house faced the west side of the Englischer Garten so she had a third-floor view of green lawns and horse paths from her desk, and it was just a short walk from the Ludwig-Maximilians Universität, where Angelika Raubal was registered for premedical courses in biology, chemistry, zoology, and English.

Geli began each morning with a buffet breakfast of hard rolls, fruit, and hot chocolate in the pension's dining room, then got her textbooks and, with a friend named Elfi Samthaber, walked up Veterinärinstrasse to the first-floor lecture hall of the university for an eight o'clock biology class. She went upstairs for a far smaller class in English, and afterward was free for an hour, generally going to the Café Europa on Schellingstrasse, near Heinrich Hoffmann's photography studio and the editorial offices of the *Völkischer Beobachter*. She did not try to find her uncle there, for it was not yet noon.

She was an affectionate, fun-loving woman with a gift for female friendship and an affability with men, so she would not have been without company for long anyway, but the fact that many of the university students were fanatically pro-Hitler meant she was often the focus of attention. She'd be offered Italian coffee, and handsome young men with fresh dueling scars would huddle around and tire her with questions about her Uncle Adolf—whom the *Münchener Neueste Nachrichten* was calling "the uncrowned king of Bavaria"—while her female classmates looked on with jealousy and Gauloise cigarettes held near their faces.

She freed herself from observation only by heading to the first-floor laboratory of the science wing for chemistry. She finished her English homework just before zoology class, and after that strolled to the south end of the Englischer Garten where her famous uncle would be in the fashionable Café Heck on Galerienstrasse, holding forth to a group of six or seven passive, reverential men at his *Stammtisch*, his reserved and increasingly popular table in the farthermost corner on the right.

She would see him agitatedly glancing around the café even as he talked, hunting for some sign of his niece, and as soon as he saw her, Hitler's face would shine with glee and he would promptly stand up, as would the others. "And here is my Princess at last," he'd say, and kiss her on both hands. All talk of politics would cease—"We do not mix business and family," Hitler had objected once—and he would order a late lunch for them both while courteously inquiring about her classes. She'd practice English with Herr Hanfstaengl, she'd say nothing to Herr Rosenberg, who fiddled with his fork or wristwatch whenever she was around, she'd ask Herr Hess about Ilse, whom he'd just married; she'd hear from Herr Hoffmann about Henny's high school functions, and she'd perhaps be introduced to a visiting *Gauleiter* (a party regional governor) from Essen or Mecklenburg. She'd try to be charming and Hitler's men would try to seem enchanted and after she'd eaten she'd find a reason to exit so they could all get back to their worries and scheming.

She'd study from four until eight if her uncle was free for the evening, or until ten if he was giving a speech, and then she'd put on a fine dress and talk with the other boarders in the parlor until Emil Maurice was impatiently there at the front door, Hitler's Mercedes idling behind him on Königinstrasse and Hitler either in it, drumming his fingers, or still in his shabby bachelor's flat on Thierschstrasse getting changed for their night on the town. After the cinema or opera, they'd dine at the Café Weichard, next to the Volkstheater, or the Osteria Bavaria, the garden restaurant in the Bayerischer Hof Hotel, or the Nürnberger Bratwurstglöckl am Dom, and then, well past midnight, Emil would return Geli to the pension and take his employer to the Café Neumaier near the Victuals Market where he'd talk with worshipful old friends until three or four in the morning.

Weekends she was Hitler's from noon until night. Often Henny Hoffmann would join them and they'd lunch at the Carlton Tearoom on Briennerstrasse, and Hitler would flatter them with fulsome praise for their beauty, and charm them with funny imitations of his pompous subordinates. Then they'd stroll through the galleries and the jewelry, shoe, and millinery shops off the Odeonsplatz, or the high-fashion stores on Prinzregentenstrasse. Geli was new to luxuries and having money, and with a flirtatious tyranny forced her uncle to wait like a forbearing husband as she tried on twenty hats then settled on a beret, or dotted her wrists with French perfumes and held them to his fussy and defenseless nose.

With his niece Adolf Hitler was often affectionate, softhearted, and helpless. Emil Maurice would lean against a fender of the Mercedes-Benz with a cigarette and watch his otherwise fearsome boss bashfully follow the tittering girls as they went from one shop to the next, and in the late afternoon he'd be fascinated to find the führer tilting toward him under a high stack of parcels, chagrined but grinning— fatherly, flushed, and perfectly content.

Emil himself was enthralled by Geli, but at first he tried to give the impression that being with her was his duty when Hitler was away. But one Saturday morning in late October Emil simply showed up at the Pension Klein and told Geli her uncle was on party business in Berlin. And then he hesitantly asked if she'd like to visit the famous Auer Dult flea market at Mariahilfplatz, across the Isar river.

She wanted to further furnish her white room, so she went, and they found a *Halali* hat for Emil, and for Geli a fairly good Köhler sewing machine, a faintly worn Axminster rug, and a fine, gold-plated Tellus clock that wasn't working, but that Emil, a former watchmaker, said he would fix, and did.

Emil drove her to the Haidhausen district and a pub called Löwen-Schänke where they shared a late lunch of hard rolls and salami and tall steins of Spatenbräu. He took off his white *Halali* hat and told Geli he'd been born in Westmoor in 1897, so he was eleven years older than she was, and a former *Unterfeldwebel*, or sergeant, on the western front, where he had been put in charge of a reconnaissance patrol because his family were originally French Hugenots and his father had forced his children to learn the language. Without a high school *Abitur* or even a lesser *Matura*, Emil had had few work prospects after the armistice; he was just one of the injured millions and had found and lost a dozen jobs—as a horse dealer, a butcher's apprentice, a watchmaker, a nightclub bouncer. Anything. And whenever he was out of work, he was a street fighter for the Ehrhardt Naval Brigade, paid to heckle Communist speakers and disrupt rallies during Spartakus week. "What we wanted, we didn't know," he said. "But what we knew, we didn't want." And then that changed in 1920 when he'd first heard Adolf Hitler speak. Immediately he'd joined the party as number 19, and had been given the job of *Ordnertruppe*, whose duty it was to protect her uncle at mass meetings. "I was the first SA man," he said. "The very first storm trooper. And I still would gladly die for him. A former soldier like I was, with no education, no money, no family, really, and he knew what I was feeling, the furies inside me, the fears and longings, the things that were ugly, and he made them seem right. Even glorious. It's never intellectual or head-to-head when Hitler talks. Always heart-to-heart. And so I could *feel* how much he hated the same things I did: the Weimar Republic, Bolshevism, the Reichstag, unemployment, inflation, crime and disorder—"

"The Jews?" Geli asked.

Emil reddened with irritation. "Are you thinking I'm Jewish?"

She was stunned. "I just thought that was part of his program."

"Are you an Anti-Semite?"

She shrugged. "No."

Emil smiled as her uncle did, with falseness and condescension. "In time," he said.

"Are you Aryan?" she asked.

"Naturally. But I hear party members talking. 'Look at Emil Maurice,' they say. 'Look at that Alfred Rosenberg.' And others, too. 'They're trying to hide that they're Jews by hating them.'" Emil drank from his stein with his hot stare held on her. "Even about the leader they say that."

She was fearless in the face of contention, but was fundamentally a conciliator. She slid off to friendlier terrain. "I remember when I first saw you at Landsberg am Lech," she said. "Your skin was so dark. I thought you looked Corsican, or Greek."

Emil grinned. "Yes? Is that good?"

"Excellent," she said.

He hunched forward on the pub's table, his chin on his hands, conquered by flattery. "Was it love at first sight?"

"Well, I was sixteen."

"And easy to please? Tell me, Fräulein Raubal: What did you admire most about me?"

"Your eyes," she said. "They seemed so big and gentle and chocolate brown."

"Your eyes, too," he said. "They're like a poem."

She laughed. "They rhyme? They're a couplet?"

Emil flopped back in his chair and held up his hands in surrender. "I have no education; I told you."

She reached over to him. "No, no. I'm sorry. I was embarrassed. You're so sweet to put it that way." She hesitated a little, then smiled demurely. "What else? You have to say more."

"Why?"

"Because I'm the girl."

Emil studied her from her head to her waist, frankly but tenderly.

Without amusement. She'd never felt so caressed. Geli found herself thinking how her uncle's stare could be a persecution, a mystery, a contest he always won.

"We'll start with your hair. Wild and free, like a lion's mane."

She involuntarily put her hand to it. "And you like that?"

"Certainly."

"Just checking."

Emil squinted. "And your eyes. You're right. They *do* rhyme."

"They used to roll around like marbles, but then I got my diploma."

"I have bad teeth. No money for dentists. But yours are beautiful."

"Thank you."

"White. Even. Everything fits together so nice. And that smile! Radiant! We could turn out all the lights and still read."

"Well, maybe not you."

"It's true. Reading I don't like much."

"You're lucky you're a man," she said. "You can just sit there and look pretty."

"I haven't finished worshiping you."

"Sorry."

Emil touched his own mouth as he looked at hers. "I'm thinking of those lips, so soft and pink and feminine—"

She smiled. "But this is too much, Herr Maurice!" She felt her flushed cheeks with her palms. "My face is getting so hot!"

"Eyes follow you when you walk by. Men *and* women. Have you seen that? The admiration?"

She shook her head.

"Shall I quit?"

"Yes. Enough. I'm dizzy."

Emil's stare fell to her chest, and he smiled. "But there's so much more to describe!"

She blushed and crossed her forearms over her sweater. "And now we really can stop with the compliments, Herr Maurice."

Emil was quiet for a minute. "Would he mind it if we saw each other?"

She tried not to seem as thrilled and breathless as she was. "Uncle Adolf? Why?"

"Haven't you seen how he looks at you?"

"But he's my uncle. And nineteen years older." *Ask*, she thought.

"Would you like to go out with me tonight?"

She hesitated, then sighed, "Oh, I suppose so."

■ ■ ■

Emil took her to the cinema and a government-financed *Kulturfilm* called *Ways to Health and Beauty*, a feature-length documentary urging the "regeneration of the human race" through calisthenics, dancing, "hygienic gymnastics," and wrestling—a subject that might not have filled the theater had it not been for the fact that for much of the film the oiled actors and actresses were stark naked. Emil smirked at Geli's shock, and she hit his shoulder. "You knew, didn't you," she said, but Emil just smiled and watched, pressing his forearm and knee against hers.

Walking to the Hofbräuhaus afterward, Emil said, "Don't tell Uncle Adolf."

"Don't worry."

"Has he talked to you about the flame of life and the sin of iniquity yet?"

"No."

Emil smiled. "He will."

At the Hofbräuhaus a waitress in a Tyrolean dirndl put gray porcelain steins of foaming Hofbräu in front of them, and Emil told Geli what it had been like chasing around Berlin in the old days. "We were all poor, but Hitler found party financing in Switzerland; just a few hundred francs, but a fortune with the exchange rate then, and we took it with us. We were in a cabaret and I was scouting for girls to join us at our table—that was my job as his driver—when a fellow introduced himself as a judge and told me he knew of a far more interesting nightspot. We took the underground with him and found ourselves in his home: fine furniture, family photographs of officers on the walls, and his wife serving us a champagne she'd made with spirits and lemonade. And then the judge brings out his two daughters, maybe fifteen and sixteen years old, and Hitler about faints because they're naked. No clothes on at all, and they're squirming around in front of us in some kind of Egyptian dance, and the judge is waiting for us to make him an offer. Well, Hitler jumps up and starts shouting that this was what he was going to change, this was how Germany was being destroyed by the Communists and the Weimar Republic and so on, a twenty-minute version of his speech. And pretty soon the whole family is weeping and wanting to join the party, and when we go out the judge insists we take his gift of Havana cigars. But this was Berlin in 1922 and the cigars turned out to be cabbage leaves soaked in nicotine."

"And *why* are you telling me this?"

Emil blushed. "I'm not betraying him, if that's what you're thinking." The horns of a band began blaring so loudly in the festival hall that Emil was forced to hunker forward to be heard. "We used to go watch bare-breasted girls in boxing matches. Hitler was thrilled. And that's when I put it together. He likes to look, but won't touch. Women and sex, they frighten him, I think, and so he's standoffish, he seems a prude, a perpetual bachelor. At that judge's house, with those naked girls, at first I was thinking how high-minded and moral he was, but then I saw that he was just squeamish."

"And if he hadn't been there, what would *you* have done?"

Emil smiled. "Oh, well; who knows?"

She fixed a cool stare on him. "That's why I asked."

"Watch? Yes. Offer money for more? Unlikely."

"Do you always do what he says?"

"Sure. Naturally."

"Why?"

Emil seemed honestly puzzled, then he grinned at her for a minute as if waiting for some telltale hint that she was joking. "Are you trying to tell me you *don't* do what he says?"

She felt a guilty twinge saying it, as though it were a lie, but she insisted, "No. I do as I please."

Emil considered her as if she were rebellion and will-of-its-own and whatever else it was he'd subtracted from his life. And finally he said, "Well, maybe that's what he wants, then."

■ ■ ■

They were in the parlor of the Pension Klein. The house lightly snored in the silence, and the flakes from the first snowfall of winter softly ticked against the windows. Chewing gum was the latest fad from America, and Emil gave her a stick of Wrigley's Spearmint. Quoting the billboard ads, she said, "Pleasant and refreshing."

Emil thought hard and remembered the other line, "The aroma lingers."

She patted his knee to praise him.

Emil inched closer on the sofa and asked, "May I kiss you?"

And Geli said, "Yes, please."

■ ■ ■

At first they didn't tell Hitler they were seeing each other, but for a selfish, cold, and insensitive man he was fairly intuitive, and within a few days he seemed to have noticed a new significance in their glances, the way she would stay in the car just a little longer than necessary, as if Emil were her air, how she seemed to find her harbor not far from him when they were in a room. And so he started talking about the Nazi hierarchy and all the bachelors in it. "We need wives," he told Emil, "families." And as Emil drove and Hitler wore his leather flying cap in the front seat, he'd embarrass his niece by mentioning unmarried women whom Emil ought to consider. Fräulein Christa Schröder? A beauty. Or who was that contralto at the Cuvilliés Theater? Fräulein Marika Kleist? And what about that girl at the Carlton Tea Room? Fräulein Meiser, wasn't it? Leni Meissner? Which?

"Leni Meiser, I think," Emil said.

"And?"

Emil found them all wanting.

Hitler sighed in frustration. He turned to his niece, in the backseat. "Any ideas, Geli?" he asked.

"Well, it's hard with him so ugly."

"We'll just keep looking," Hitler said. "Surely there's somebody you'd like, Herr Maurice. Somebody to have little Aryans with? We'll go to city hall for the wedding. We'll get Franz Gürtner to officiate. And we'll all get to be such good friends. We'll have spaghetti together at your house every night."

Emil smiled. "She can't cook, my leader. Women I like can't cook."

"But my Angelika, for instance! She cooks, she cleans, she sews her own clothes! And beautiful, too! Why not find a wife just like her?"

Emil found Geli in the rearview mirror. Geli gazed out the window.

Hitler folded up his itinerary and held his hands in his lap as he said, "I myself have overcome any need for women. But I find nothing more sacred than the flame of life awakened by holy love. We must remember, though, that the flame only burns when lit by a man and a woman who have kept themselves pure in body and soul. And when their love is magnified by the presence of children, the sins of iniquity that have destroyed our nation fairly scream out in their doom."

"And the sins of iniquity would be?" Geli asked.

"Oh, that you would never learn," Hitler said.

■ ■ ■

With nothing being mentioned, Emil and Geli began holding hands around Hitler's friends, and one night took the risk of hugging as they strolled to his *Stammtisch* in the Café Heck after the cinema. Rudolf and Ilse Hess were there with Putzi and Helene Hanfstaengl and Heinrich Hoffmann and a photographer's model named Kristina. She was wearing a swastika pin. The gentlemen were all in white ties and tails, and the ladies in sheath dresses and opera tiaras. And the party turned and beamed at Emil and Geli as if they were children shocked awake by hearty toasts from the dining room.

Winter was finally there in earnest. Geli's cheeks were as wind-chilled as if she'd been skiing, and she'd gone without gloves so she could feel Emil's hands in hers. Hitler formally stood up, kissed her knuckles, and was startled. "But your fingers are cold as silverware, Geli!"

"I feel warm," she said.

"I'll bet you do," said Ilse Hess, and she watched with fascination as Emil went to the *Herrens*.

"What film did you see, Fräulein Raubal?" Putzi Hanfstaengl asked.

"*Metropolis*."

Rudolf Hess tilted toward the führer to inform him. "About the alliance between labor and capital," he said.

"And what Jew directed that?" Hitler asked.

Heinrich Hoffmann said, "Not a Jew. Fritz Lang. A first-rate director."

"You liked it?" Hitler asked his niece.

"Oh yes. It was stunning."

"Whose metropolis was it?"

She shrugged. "It's imaginary, I think."

With certainty, Heinrich Hoffmann said, "It's Philadelphia."

White-jacketed waiters brought over two highly ornamented dining chairs, and Hitler ordered Emil's to be situated near his own, and his niece's inserted farther away, between Ilse Hess and Helene Hanfstaengl so "the women can talk about hairdressers and clothes and romantic novels."

"Oh do sit," Putzi's American wife said as she held out the chair to Geli. And then she added in English, "And fill us in on your love life."

Geli knew just enough English to shyly grin.

Hearing a foreign language, Hitler frowned, but then he turned in his chair to his private secretary and told Rudi what a marvel his niece was because she could follow the fiction serials in twelve magazines and newspapers simultaneously. "And she always knows how the stories fit together. She even notices when an installment is missing."

Geli turned and found Ilse Hess interestedly staring. "What's your sign?" Ilse asked.

"My *sign?*"

"Astrologically."

"I'm Catholic. We don't believe in astrology."

Ilse smiled indulgently. "What's your birthday?"

"June fourth."

She sat back. "You're a Gemini then. I'll have to do your chart."

Waiters put china and glassware in front of Geli and filled a flute with champagne. She heard Hitler holding forth to his followers about the joy of having such glamorous female company as he dined. "Women have always been such a comfort to me," he said. "I have always found that feminine beauty lifts me from my doldrums and helps me put aside the cares that the world so often hands me. Whether she is intelligent or original is quite unnecessary. I have enough ideas for both of us."

Helene Hanfstaengl sighed at his gracelessness, and softly asked Geli in German, "Are you in love?"

Geli thought for a few seconds, furiously nodded, and then she and the women laughed.

Kristina, the photographer's model, asked, "Are you talking about the man you walked in with?"

"Hitler's chauffeur," Helene Hanfstaengl said.

Kristina fascinatedly looked over her shoulder as Emil walked from the *Herrens* to his chair near Hitler. "He's very handsome. Is he French?"

"Corsican," Geli said. She saw that Herr Hoffmann was now telling a joke, but Hitler was divided in his listening, flicking his worried attention between Emil and her, trying to be a jocular man among men yet wanting even more to hold his niece's voice next to his ear, like a seashell with an ocean's roar. She heard Helene ask in English, "Are you kissing yet?"

Geli answered in first-semester English, "Yes. But many time kissing not. Uncle watches." She pinched her thumb and first finger a few millimeters apart. "Little only."

Hearing them, Putzi Hanfstaengl widened his knees and hunched into their group, his white tie falling loose. In English he whispered, "Who's kissing whom?"

"Emil and Geli."

Clownishly dropping his jaw, Putzi tilted his ugly head to his wife. "And how will our smitten corporal take that?"

"Why should he care? Women don't matter to him. He's a neuter."

Ilse asked Geli in German, "What are they saying?"

"I have no idea," she said, but she did.

Waiters put down hot plates of food in front of Kristina and Ilse and Helene. Heinrich Hoffmann was full of satisfaction as he sat back to be served and continued his story, telling it now only to Emil Maurice and Rudolf Hess, whose hand failed to hide his buckteeth as he smiled. Geli's uncle was glaring at her across the dinner table as if she'd betrayed him, his white face seeming about to fracture with hurt. Hoffmann finished his joke by shouting, "Hold the lion!" and the men howled with hilarity, and Hitler joined in, too, repeating Hoffmann's final words and folding over with laughter, laughing so hard that he took out his handkerchief and wiped the wetness from his eyes.

■ ■ ■

She was scheduled to take the afternoon train to Berchtesgaden and share Christmas with Angela at Haus Wachenfeld, and so at noon on December 21st Hitler visited her white room at the Pension Klein, staying in his coffee-brown leather trench coat and slouch hat as he scanned her science textbooks and turned the handwheel on the Köhler sewing machine on her desk. A chart of the periodic table of the elements caught his attention, and he seemed at once to hate it. Swatting his right trousers leg with his dog whip, he asked, "Are you enjoying your studies, Geli?"

She said she was, but heard the heartlessness in it, as did he.

"We call it the Talmud high school," he said, "there are so many Jews there."

She shrugged. "They're smart."

"Are your studies difficult?" he asked.

"I have so much reading to do. And memorization."

Hitler flinched a smile. "And you don't have much time for either."

Emil, he meant; the friend he envied, the rival he revered. She put a pfennig in the heater and watched the coils warm into radiance as she buttoned up a pink cardigan and hugged the chill in her torso.

"Are you thinking of Emil now?"

"Always," she said.

She felt a soft nudge against her forearm and saw that her uncle had taken off his hat and was jutting out a present that was the size of a fountain pen in a box.

"I have something for you," he said.

She took it from him and smiled. "Well, it's too small to be a photo of you."

Saying nothing, her uncle sucked his right little finger as he often did when he was nervous.

She tore off the silver foil wrapping and opened a jeweler's box to find a fourteen-karat-gold chain and swastika pendant. "Oh," she said. "Thank you."

"And now you can take off that other thing."

She was still wearing the crucifix, on a fine steel chain, that she'd gotten at her confirmation. She took it off to please him, and he fastened his gift around her throat. She felt his hands hover just above her shoulders, his face tilt close enough to inhale the fragrance of her freshly washed hair.

"Love has made you even more lovely, Geli."

She touched the swastika and said, "Won't the girls at school be envious." She felt him withdraw from her and sink down on the white-enameled bed, his leather trench coat talking with each move. She turned and he was lying back as he so often did, as if in a faint, one forearm flung over his forehead, one hand hanging to the floor.

"I hate the Christmas holidays," he said. "Have you any idea why?"

"No."

"Of course you don't. You weren't even born."

"Oh," she said. "Your mother."

"Today is December twenty-first. She died precisely twenty years ago today."

She sat forward on her desk chair. "Uncle Adolf, I'm so sorry."

"Cancer of the breast," he said. And he told her that Klara had been just forty-seven. She'd gone through a mastectomy, but they'd still found cancer in the tissue. A Jewish doctor had told them their only chance of a cure was to continually saturate the wound with iodoform, which burned into her skin like acid. Even now he could smell its foul, hospital odor. Klara had clenched her teeth on a towel so she wouldn't scream. When it entered her bloodstream, she couldn't swallow. When he'd offered her water, it had tasted like poison. They'd installed her in the kitchen, Aunt Johanna and he; there was no heat in the rest of the house. They'd torn down a closet and hauled in a sofa so he would be in perpetual attendance, and would hear her moan in her sleep. "I was in hell."

"But wasn't it good for her, having you there?" Geli asked. "Wasn't she happy for the company?"

Rolling to his side, he crushed a pillow under his head and squeezed his forearm between his knees. "I was eighteen, and she changed me. She was so brave, Geli. So tender and considerate. Unflinching. Without complaint. We put up a Christmas tree and filled it with candles, and she fell asleep in their flickering glow. I was sketching her face just after midnight when she died. Angela found us at sunrise."

Geli got up and gently knelt by him, a handmaiden to his grief. "And you still feel the loss?"

He childishly turned his face into the pillow, childishly nodded his head.

"Are you crying?" She heard nothing but a false kind of wailing, a boo-hoo-hoo. "Don't, Uncle Adolf." She put a hand into his hair and trained it back. She kissed his shoulder. "You'll make me cry, too. You don't want that."

Wildly thrashing, like a fish in a net, Hitler tore away from her and hiked up his dark trench coat to hide his face. "Don't look at me like this!" he shouted.

With fright she got up from her knees and faced the window. A female equestrian in fur coat and jodhpurs trotted a gelding through the fields of the Englischer Garten, the horse sinking to its fetlocks in the snow. "Are you all right, Uncle Adolf?"

She heard his shoes find the floor, heard him sigh in a halting way, his face perhaps in his hands. "She was everything to me. And now *you* are. I have such fears—"

"You needn't—"

The floor shook as he fell to his knees behind her, hugged her thighs, buried his face against her buttocks. "If only I had someone to take care of me!" he wailed, his words like hot, moist handwriting on her skirt.

She felt his hair with a hand. "I'll take care of you."

"Will you?"

Clarification seemed necessary. She told him, "You're my uncle."

"I have no friends, no family—"

"You have me. You have Angela and Paula."

She felt him shaking his head. "They don't love me! I need love!"

"*I* love you."

She felt him withdraw from her, still on his knees, his hands riding his thighs. And then he stood as an old man does, finding his balance, hurting and huffing, then collecting himself. "I have to find my hat," he said.

She gave it to him without turning.

"I do hope you're happy, putting me through all that."

She turned. His scowl was as red as a scream. "I didn't—"

"You have made me look ridiculous," he said.

"I'm confused, Uncle Adolf. I—"

And then he smiled. His hand oh so gently groomed her hair and fondled her cheek and chin. "Aren't you pretty," he said, and put on

his hat. "I have rules for you, Princess. Each reasonable and generous. One, I still expect your obedience, your loyalty, and your company. Two, I will be in charge of when you go out with Emil and
when you do not. Each of you separately must ask my permission.
This is what fathers do for their daughters. Three, you shall keep the
relationship secret from the public. You shall not be photographed
together. You shall not be seen with him at the university or in the
cafés. Four, you shall continue your studies until I say otherwise. You
may give them up, but not to get married, and if so, you'll need my
permission. And five, you are nineteen years old. You cannot marry
for two years. When you're twenty-one, we'll see."

And then he walked out, and she sat on her bed. Weak and
exhausted.

CHAPTER TEN
Hitler's Friends, 1928

Of his friends in the National Socialist hierarchy, she was fondest of Herr Doktor Paul Joseph Goebbels, but only because he seemed fondest of her. They met in March 1928, when the thirty-year-old Goebbels, *Gauleiter* of Berlin and editor-in-chief of the weekly newspaper *Der Angriff* (The Attack), journeyed to München on party business and later wrote in his diary: "Yesterday I met Hitler, and he immediately invited me to dinner. A lovely lady was there."

Geli had heard that he was a former floor man on the Cologne stock exchange and a facile writer of fairly high intelligence, at first politically far left of the Nazis but now a frenzied campaigner and zealot for Hitler, who had affectionately said of him, "Our Doktor is all flame." So she'd fashioned in her mind a man far different from the one she saw at their first meeting in the Osteria Bavaria, for he seemed a scrawny juvenile of thirteen, just over five feet tall, weighing no more than one hundred pounds, his head too big for his body and his brown hair creamed against a skull that was cadaverously there just beneath his face. Limping to their table in his overlarge

white trench coat, he tilted steeply to the left due to a childhood illness, osteomyelitis, which had caused his left leg to halt growing
and stay four inches shorter than his right. And yet he seemed to
think himself handsome and jaunty, and his eyes feasted on Geli
with a lickerish stare as her uncle introduced them.

"Aren't you lovely," he said.

She said, "Enchanted, Herr Goebbels," and offered her hand.

"Herr *Doktor* Goebbels," he corrected, and though he was smiling, she felt rebuked. But he was so amiable otherwise, and his huge
and luminous black eyes betrayed such tragedies in his youth, such
scorchings to his psyche, such an aching to charm and fascinate that
Geli forgave him his haughtiness. And she did find him fascinating,
for he was cultured, quick, an intellectual, and funny, if malicious;
his voice was a beautiful baritone, as rich and sonorous as a full-
throated church organ; his fine hands were faultless, those of a skillful pianist who'd never risked injury in work or game of any sort;
and he modestly admitted that his play *The Wanderer* had just a few
months earlier been performed at the Wallner Theater in Berlin.

She'd never met a playwright before, and said so, and then she
was fearful she'd sounded too impressed and unpoised.

"And he's a novelist, too," Hitler said. "Won't Eher be publishing
it this year?"

Doktor Goebbels bowed to him. "With your help."

"And its title?" Geli asked.

"*Michael: The Fate of a German*. It's just a little thing in the form
of a diary, about a young intellectual eager to grasp life with every
fiber of his being. Who finds his calling among workers in the
mines."

"I'm in it," Hitler said, as if that were only fitting and reasonable.

Doktor Goebbels graciously bowed again. "You are Germany's
fate, its man of destiny. The novel would be hollow without you."

The fawning continued throughout their three-course meal. She
thought her uncle was in one of his fouler moods as he flitted from
subject to subject, his insights floating somewhere between the
banal and the just plain weird, but Geli saw that Doktor Goebbels

hung on his every word, hardly eating, as full of adoration as one of Hitler's hounds. And when Hitler excused himself to go to the *Herrens*, Doktor Goebbels confided, "When he speaks, it's so simple, but so profound, so mystical, full of infinite truth. It is almost like hearing the Gospels. Like hearing the final word on whatever topic he's chosen. I feel shudders of awe." He smiled. "All night I have been fighting the urge to genuflect to him."

"Self-control is a good thing," she said.

Doktor Goebbels lifted a goblet of Chianti and softly gazed just over its rim at Geli in a way he might have thought seductive. "You are a very lucky girl," he said.

"And why is that?"

"With his elementary strength, you can walk safely in the abyss of life. With him, you have at your side the conquering instrument of fate and deity."

"Oh; I knew that. I just wanted to hear you say it."

"Amusing," he said, and winced a smile, then swallowed Chianti and resettled the goblet on the table. And then there was silence between them. She watched a red tear of wine ever so gradually trickle down the stem and cross the base of the goblet until it stained the white tablecloth. She found him focused on her face. "Would you like to visit me in Berlin?" he asked.

"I have a boyfriend," she said.

With disdain, he said, "Oh yes, Hitler's chauffeur." And then he added, "I say that without disdain, you understand. Emil Maurice is an Old Combatant. He took part in the putsch."

"We're in love."

"And there he is, sitting outside in the car," he said, and scowled at the shame of it. "Waiting for us to finish. Wondering what that devil Herr Doktor Goebbels is up to."

"And what *are* you up to?" she asked.

"I invite you in all innocence. With no tricks up my sleeve. An American expression. Won't you come up with your uncle next weekend? We'll attend to party business, and then I'll show you the city. Berlin is magnificent."

Hitler strode back into the dining room and seated himself.

Geli leaned toward him and lightly touched his jacket sleeve. "Uncle Alf, Herr Doktor Goebbels has invited me to join you in Berlin next weekend. May I please?"

Hitler's right hand held hers to his forearm as he smiled at his *Gauleiter* and said, "Our Doktor always finds ways to make me happy."

■ ■ ■

Although the party furnished Hitler with a suite on the third floor of the first-class Hotel Kaiserhof in Berlin, just across from the Reich chancellery, Geli and Angela—whose presence he'd insisted on—were installed in the filthy and fourth-class Gasthof Ascanischer in order to give journalists a fitting example of party frugality. And to further make his niece's misery complete, Hitler had decided that Julius Schaub rather than Emil Maurice should escort them on their railway journey north.

Seeking to avoid Schaub's company, mother and daughter took their own cold-weather walking tour of Berlin on Saturday, starting out by mistake on Nollendorfplatz and hurrying past dance halls and underworld bars and a fire-red building called Erotic Circus. Even in the morning there were prostitutes standing together in threes, chattering about their children, and dressed just like housewives on their way to the grocery. Angela said, "I ache so for them. In the misery we're in, how can they marry?"

"I couldn't ever do that," Geli said.

Angela softly patted her wrist, saying, "Oh what a comfort you are to your mother."

They finally reached the Emperor Wilhelm Memorial Church, then visited, for Geli, the Zoologischer Garten, strolled through the Tiergarten to the Brandenburger Tor and the Reichstag, and took a taxi to Wittenbergplatz, where Angela's brother, Alois Jr., had just opened a restaurant.

She hadn't called ahead to warn him, so he was shocked when he carried forward menus and found her in the vestibule with a niece

he'd never seen. Alois was the illegitimate son of Franziska Matzels-
berger, Alois Senior's kitchen maid, whom their father had married
just two months before Angela was born. Although he was only one
year older than Angela, Alois seemed closer to sixty and, with his
walrus mustache, thin, graying hair, and skeptical squint behind
rimless glasses, he looked far more like the photographs Geli had
seen of her grandfather than he did his half-brother, Adolf. The
worrisome qualities that Adolf had somehow made work for him,
Alois hadn't; he seemed merely vulgar, selfish, pompous, and con-
niving, like a stuffy waiter who steals from the till, or a civil servant
who alters the rules for a fee. Sharing fireside coffee and sandwiches
with them, he seemed avid for news of Adolf, for he was sure their
fortunes were connected and he felt it was his turn, as he said, "at
the trough." "And who knows? We could even become friends, once
he gets over the bigamy business and his fears that I'll damage his
good reputation."

Angela quickly grew tired of Alois and his all-too-obvious disinterest in Paula or the Raubals, and she told him they were going to
the Deutsches Historisches Museum. Alois allowed them to pay the
bill, saying he'd treat them to a fine dinner next time, and they went
outside to Wittenbergplatz.

"Well, that's an obligation fulfilled," Geli said.

Angela was nearing forty-four and was thirty pounds heavier than
the woman in Linz who had given birth to Geli, and so she asked,
"Would you mind if I went back to the Gasthof now? I have to get
off my feet."

And when they got to their room, there was a message from Emil
Maurice saying, "I really miss you," and another from Doktor
Goebbels saying there was a sudden change of plans, that the führer,
whom they'd not yet seen, would be having dinner with Edwin and
Helene Bechstein, the film actress Dorothea Wieck, and Herr Rein-
hold Muchow, Doktor Goebbels's chief of organization for the
Berlin Gau, and Herr Muchow's wife. Would it be an impertinence
to offer himself as their sole company for the night?

Angela thought she'd had about as much fun as she could stand, so she gave Geli permission to go out with him, provided Julius Schaub went along.

"Oh, Mother!"

Angela held up her hand, brooking no further argument. "Adolf wishes it," she said. "And in Wien once, I was a girl."

Wearing a double-breasted suit to widen his body, Doktor Goebbels was sitting in the front seat of an unfamiliar car when a characteristically gloomy Julius Schaub honked the horn for Geli in front of the Gasthof Ascanischer. The Doktor, as he called himself, gaily got into the rear with her and stayed allergically far away on the ride to the fashionable Charlottenburg district, filling the time with vanity about his doctorate in Romanticist drama from Heidelberg University, as if she'd arranged the night just to talk about the playwright Wilhelm von Schütz. They headed first to a filled restaurant where the Tyrolean chef, himself a Nazi, insisted they have his Colchester oysters and *Adlon*, a honey-glazed breast of duck. And then the Doktor had Schaub ferry them to a nightclub where they drank the Berlin specialty of *Weisse mit Schuss*, or wheat beer with a shot of raspberry juice, and watched an American *Negerin* sing "Madiana" and "La Petite Tonkinoise" while all but naked.

Doktor Goebbels confessed, "Any female excites me to the marrow. It's horrible. Like a hungry wolf, I prowl around them in pursuit of satisfaction. I can be at an elegant dinner, completely engaged in conversation, but in my fantasies I find myself assessing the attributes of the female guests or imagining how my host's wife or daughter would be, nude and in bed."

"And here I am, wearing you out again."

He smiled. "At the same time, I am timid, like a child. Afraid of rejection. I do not understand myself."

"Why don't you get married?" she asked.

"And become bourgeois? And hang myself within eight days?" Doktor Goebbels waved to a cigarette girl, bought a pack of Aristokrats, lit two in his mouth with the flame of a backhanded match, and attached one of the cigarettes to Geli's mouth in a vaguely sexual gesture that seemed so glamorous the fine hairs stood up on her forearms.

Inhaling his cigarette deeply, he expelled wisps of smoke as he asked, "Haven't you found me to be completely amiable and charming, Fräulein Raubal?"

"Were you trying to make a good impression?"

"Certainly. You *are* Hitler's niece."

She fetchingly asked, "And what have you been resisting?"

"It's far too shocking for words."

On the nightclub stage a female troupe in headdresses and gauze see-through tunics was now performing an Egyptian dance to the music of Erik Satie.

"Would you like to go back to my flat?" he asked, and his tone was so silky and enticing that she flushed with nervousness. "I'll only fantasize, I promise you."

"Will Herr Schaub be joining us?" she asked.

"Must he?"

"I feel so sorry for him, just waiting for us in the car."

Doktor Goebbels sighed.

■ ■ ■

Julius Schaub took off his jacket as soon as they got to the flat, and he found a bottle of Schultheiss beer in the icebox as the Doktor popped open Taittinger champagne. Schaub squatted by a high stack of thick RCA Victor records, hunting for "*Yats*," or jazz, and, finding none, tuned an American Crosley radio to a station that was playing Bix Beiderbecke and the New Orleans Rhythm Kings. And then he dourly sat on the floor by the speaker as if he were alone in the world.

Doktor Goebbels was like Hitler in thinking the highest order of entertainment was his talking about himself. And so Geli learned that he was from the Rhineland; that his childhood nickname had been Ulex, short for Ulixes, the shrewd hero of the Trojan wars; that his family was petit bourgeois—his father was a factory accountant—and had fervently hoped he'd become a priest, and that he was estranged from them now because of his hostility to the Catholic Church. Like Hitler and others in the party, he'd volunteered for military service in the Great War, but unlike them he'd been rejected because of his "infirmity" and was so frustrated and ashamed that he'd tried to kill himself with a hunger strike but had been rescued by his mother. And then his dream had become that of being a journalist for the *Berliner Tageblatt*, and he'd sent the editor-in-chief, a Jew, twenty or more articles. And each of them had been rejected. "I'll have the last laugh, though. I'll be humiliated no more." While he had once been a radical socialist, he told her, hearing Hitler talk had forced him to further examine his political thinking, and now the conversion was complete.

Watching him talk she'd had to shake from her head the anti-Nazi doggerel she'd heard: "Oh God, make me blind / that I may Goebbels Aryan find." She asked, as a distraction, "Were you recruited by my uncle?"

"In a way. Are you aware of the writings of Johann Wolfgang von Goethe?"

She said she was even though she wasn't.

The Doktor quoted, "'Half did she drag him / Half he gave himself to her.'"

She wondered at the oddness of the feminine pronoun, but simply said, "Ah-hah."

Julius Schaub was hugging his knees like a boy, his eyes tightly shut, listening hard to Mamie Smith singing "Crazy Blues," though he could not have understood a word.

"And what do you do for the party?" Geli asked.

Doktor Goebbels gave it long thought and said, "I orchestrate opinion. I offer the masses the savior they have been yearning for, and I offer Hitler confirmation of his call to greatness." Tugging himself up from the sofa, he lurched across the flat in his hard-swaying gait, his left leg seemingly no more than a cane as he hitched along. "Shall I read to you from my diary?" he asked.

She gave no reply and he seemed not to expect one, for he took a notebook from the bookcase and found the pages he was looking for. "In 1926 I visited our dear and revered Herr Hitler at the Pension Moritz. Delightful! Three whole weeks in his company. Here, for example, from July twenty-fourth. '*The Chief speaks about racial questions. It is almost impossible to render it. You had to be present. He is a genius. I stand before him deeply shaken. That is how he is: like a child—dear, good, full of compassion. Like a cat—sly, clever, and smart. Like a lion—roaring, powerful, and overpowering. A real fellow, a man. He speaks about the structure of the state and of political revolution. Thoughts that I have harbored secretly but have never pronounced. I feel overcome by something like true happiness! This life is worth living! His parting words to me were, "My head will not fall before my holy mission is fulfilled." That is how he is! Yes, that is how he is! I lie sleepless for a long time.*'"

Doktor Goebbels looked up, inviting sounds of approval, but Geli was occupying herself by filling her sherbet glass with champagne.

"And this," he said. "'*In darkest distress a star has appeared! I feel bound to him to my last breath. My last doubts have vanished. Germany will live! Heil Hitler!*'" Excited by his own prose, he flipped through other pages and halted. "'*There may come a day when all around us breaks apart. We shall not break. The hour may come when the mob around you will slaver and scream, "Crucify him!" Then we shall stand firm. Men of iron, we shall exclaim and sing: "Hosanna!" Then you will see around you the phalanx of the last guard, who will not know despair, not even in death, for that guard of iron men will not want to live if Germany dies.*'"

Was this her uncle he was talking about? Geli was mystified. "Aren't you idolizing him just a little, Herr Doktor Goebbels?"

Shoving his diary back in the bookcase, he said, "I have no desire for friends, Fräulein Raubal." And then he faced her, his left hand on his hip. "I desire instead a leader. With him I am linked unconditionally. Without him I cannot live. When I needed to be needed, he needed me. When I wanted to be known, he knew me. And if that isn't love, it feels like it. And so he may humiliate me, or ignore me, or scold me, but I shall always love him and only be challenged to further and greater efforts to please him."

Julius Schaub finally made his presence felt with vigorous applause.

■ ■ ■

She did not meet Hermann Göring until May 1928, but she'd heard a great deal about him, for, next to her uncle, he was the most famous Nazi in Germany. She was told by Putzi Hanfstaengl— whose job as foreign press officer obligated him to know—that Göring's father, the first governor of West Africa and a former consul general in Haiti, had been sixty-four years old when Hermann was born in 1893, and had named his son after a friend who was a wealthy Austrian Jew and who flagrantly took Hermann's mother as his mistress. The child had been raised by aunts, and his first memory of his mother was when she forced herself on him when he was three and he had screamed in fear at her kiss.

"Even then," Putzi told her, "our Göring claims that he wanted only to be a soldier." At first assigned to an infantry regiment after his graduation from the Royal Prussian Cadet Corps, Lieutenant Hermann Göring later joined the air corps and gained fame in the war as a fanatically brave fighter ace, flying Fokker biplanes against the British Sopwith Camels. After his twentieth victory in the air, Lieutenant Göring had been awarded Germany's highest military decoration, the *Pour la Mérite*, or Blue Max, and had become a national hero. Commander of the Richthofen Flying Circus at the time of the armistice, he had bargained away his future pension in exchange for the higher rank of *Hauptmann*, or captain, but had soon found that his status as an officer was hateful to some when he'd been attacked by Communists in Berlin who bloodied his face and tore off his medals and insignia.

With few job opportunities in Germany, he'd gone to Denmark and collected fees for aerobatic stunts, then become a commercial pilot for Svenska Lufttraffik airlines. Crash-landing in a field, he'd staggered to a castle where he'd met and fallen in love with the motherly Carin von Kantzow, whose father was a member of the Swedish nobility, whose mother came from a family of Irish brewery owners, and whose officer husband had stoically put up with their affair in order to have control of his young son.

At the Osteria Bavaria, Geli heard from Rudolf Hess that Captain Göring had rejected an offer to join the Reichswehr so he would not have to defend "the Jew republic," and that for a short time he and Hess had attended a few university classes together in München before Göring lost interest in academics. Cynical, defeated, and embittered, Göring on his own had chanced upon a political rally in October 1922 and heard a former frontline soldier with an Austrian accent talk feverishly about his hatred of the Jews and of his call for revolutionary action in Germany, and he'd felt compelled to meet this Adolf Hitler.

Hess told her that her uncle had been overjoyed at their meeting, for he'd thought Captain Göring was just what the party needed: a famous holder of the *Pour la Mérite*, and a fattish but still fairly handsome Nordic he-man with ash-blond hair and hawkish blue eyes; a regal, nonchurchgoing Protestant only a little more cultured and educated than himself, and a cosmopolitan from high society and wealth—though he and Carin's lavish ways were funded by loans and the sale of her jewelry. Within a month Hitler had made Captain Göring supreme leader of the Sturmabteilung, which was then just two thousand of the unemployed who eagerly fought Communists in the streets; and within the year Hitler was offering Göring his *Vollmacht*, or authority, to head the party in his absence.

With Hitler harrying them about observing the proprieties, Göring had finally married Carin in 1923 and they'd taken possession of a villa furnished by her lovelorn former husband. And then there had come the putsch, when Captain Göring had become conspicuous not only for his bravery but for his bloodthirstiness and brutality, for he'd told his storm troopers to gain respect through terror and had ordered them to kill at least one man in every neighborhood of the city to frighten and cow the people. "Wounded savagely in the groin," Hess said, hinting at the full extent of his injury, "Göring was taken to Austria after the Feldherrnhalle massacre. And then we lost track of him."

Emil skimmed a stone on Kleinhesseloher Lake, in the Englischer Garten, and told Geli that that wasn't so, but that some in the party were jealous when forty thousand photographs of a helmeted Göring sold out after the putsch. And when party officials heard he'd taken his agonies poorly, chewing on his hospital pillow and perpetually groaning, that he'd become addicted to Eukodal, a synthetic morphine injected intravenously, and that he was, furthermore, penniless, they'd wanted nothing further to do with him.

Around midnight, when Emil had drunk a few too many Doppelspaten, and he knew party officials were with her uncle at the Café Heck, Emil scared and excited Geli by sneaking her into the Nazi offices on Schellingstrasse and showing her the file on Göring. "Look at who he is," Emil said. "The fraud."

In the file was a poorly typed German translation of a 1925 confidential psychiatric report by Doktor Hjalmar Eneström of the Långbro Asylum for the Criminally Insane in Sweden. Eneström claimed his patient H.G. had inflated self-esteem and was fundamentally lacking in moral courage; that he was sentimental and talkative, suicidal and domineering, colossally vain and full of self-loathing; belligerent, weepy, troublesome, and strongly affected by any palliative, even table salt; that he thought he was the target of a Jewish conspiracy; that he faked or exaggerated his withdrawal symptoms from morphine; that he hallucinated about Saint Paul, whom he called "the most dangerous Jew who ever existed" and about Abraham, who he dreamed had offered him a promissory note and three camels if he would halt his war against the Semitic people; that he would be finished politically if news of his insanity ever got out in Germany.

Emil smiled. "And that, of course, is perfectly true."

Geli was disturbed. She hadn't seen the schemer in Emil. "Are you threatening to use it?" she asked.

"Am I going to *blackmail* him?" Emil shrugged. "Maybe not. But I have to protect myself if the vultures come. And so I have a photograph of the letter, just in case."

She later thought of vultures when she heard Doktor Goebbels delight in telling how a hangdog Göring had returned to Germany in 1927 to sell parachutes in Berlin for the Swedish company Tornblad, and had suffered the ignominy of finding that his name had been erased from the party's membership rolls and of having to apply again, "like some lowly farmer from Worms." But Doktor Goebbels had watched "His Corpulence" use whining, flattery, threats, and fawning obsequiousness to gradually insinuate himself far enough into the party and Hitler's good graces that he had been permitted to have his famous name inserted far down on the list of those men the National Socialists were putting up for the Reichstag elections of May 20, 1928.

"Will they vote for him?" Doktor Goebbels asked. "I do hope not. It's crowded at the top."

■ ■ ■

Adolf Hitler gave fifty-six speeches throughout Germany in the three weeks prior to the 1928 elections and was so convinced the party and its candidates would do well that he invited his niece up to Berlin for a night of celebration after the Sunday voting. Emil picked her up at the railway station and they kissed and fondled in the front seat of Hitler's car for a frustrating few minutes before Emil had to drive them to Berchtesgadenerstrasse 16 where Herr and Frau Göring were renting a tiny apartment on the third floor.

Wild-eyed and ebullient, his belly as huge as a beer barrel beneath a shocking white suit, a white slouch hat aslant on his head, Göring waved his arms from the sidewalk to halt them, and squeezed part way through the front passenger window to firmly shake Emil's and Geli's hands, his face rouged, his wide mouth faintly lipsticked, a full bottle of Chanel seeming to waft off him in eddies. "Deputy Göring," he called himself, for he'd just learned, he told them, that the party had gotten enough votes for him and for Doktor Goebbels and ten less famous Nazis to join four hundred eighty men from other parties in the Reichstag.

"Only twelve?" Emil said, for that meant the party had lost two seats. But Göring was in no mood to have his victory diminished, and he turned to escort his frail wife down the front steps and into the car.

Carin was taller than he and flat-chested, with frizzy auburn hair and a face that was as wan as his was red. She would die of a heart condition in October 1931. Emil had told Geli that Carin was "soulful and mystical," but as she seemed to faint into the Mercedes she seemed to Geli only vexed and vicious, talking in fluent German about the hundreds of revolting Jews who'd ruined their sunset in the Tiergarten, and of the Communists who'd paraded in the streets all that week "with their crooked noses and their red flags with the Star of David on them."

"You mean the Soviet star," Göring said.

"Same thing," said his wife. And then they would brawl and buckle with Hitler's men, who were "hoisting their own glorious red banners with the proud swastikas—but without the crooked noses, of course—force meeting force until the Communists fled, leaving behind their injured comrades. Oh, how I look forward to peace!"

"There, there," her husband said.

"And how I shall hate and resent seeing all those who have snubbed and avoided us in our hard times as they slink forward and assure you that they always believed in you, dear Hermann, and why didn't you let them know you were having difficulties?"

"Well, that's changed now, hasn't it?" Göring said. "We'll have our sweet and lasting revenge."

Carin tilted forward. "Young lady? I didn't hear your name."

"Geli."

"A pretty name," she said, as though it wasn't. Carin sat back. "We've found a fantastic villa in the Schöneberg district that we can afford now. I have a white harmonium and other fine furniture that we hocked, and I have already put in an order to have it returned. Another woman can appreciate what that means."

"More housework?"

Emil shot her a look.

Carin turned to her husband. "Who *is* she, Hermann?"

"Hitler's niece."

"Ah," she said, and held her tongue until they got to the grand ballroom of the Hotel Kaiserhof.

Doktor Goebbels held aloft a glass of champagne as soon as he saw them walk in. "And here's to Deputy Göring and *his* five hundred marks per month, free railway tickets, and immunity before the law!"

"Only the beginning!" Göring hollered back, and he grinned as though they were good friends.

A hundred far more solemn party members were there in their finest clothes, the majority of the wives glumly sitting against the wall as a string quartet played all too plaintively at the far end of the ballroom and their husbands conferred in funereal tones about a party that, even with a late infusion of money from northern industrialists, had lost one hundred thousand votes since the last election.

"Looks like fun," Geli said.

Emil just surveyed the room, hunting for Hitler.

Wishing she were back in the car kissing Emil, she hopefully asked, "Are you bored yet?"

"We'll get away soon," Emil promised.

The Hohenzollern Princes August-Wilhelm and Prince Eitel-Friedrich were announced at the grand ballroom's entrance and waved to the partygoers, then gave way to their host. Wearing a white tie and tails and a peculiarly buoyant expression, Hitler strode in behind them and soaked up the roars and applause from all sides before falling into his habit of torrential talk. The partygoers circled around him. Congratulating the newly elected deputies, Hitler predicted that journalists would call them the Reichstag's twelve black sheep, but in fact they would be wolves, continually hunting for and sorting out Germany's enemies. Without a financial or political crisis in the country, the party would not find more adherents, he admitted, but in the Weimar Republic such crises were inevitable. They would just need to have patience. And though he felt the gloom they had felt when he'd first heard how the voting had gone, he'd noticed that their losses were not to the centrist parties but were to those on the far left and right. So the people were welcoming extreme solutions. The party would simply have to concentrate on teaching the public that National Socialism was the only extreme that would not ultimately fail, and would persevere and finally triumph over all opposition. And then, with his voice hinting at the strain of overuse, Hitler ceased talking, and to shouts of joy and thunderous applause he waded into the crush of party members to shake hands and hear their praises.

Emil escorted Geli toward a flourishing bar at the far end of the ballroom, but he was called by a joyless, healthless, chinless man in his late twenties who was wearing pince-nez and sitting with his older fiancée at a big round table, and Emil, for some ungodly reason, felt obliged to go to them.

And that was how Geli met Heinrich Himmler. She would later learn from Göring that Himmler had been born to a Catholic family in Landshut, near München, in 1900, the son of a much-esteemed teacher in a Gymnasium that served high society and the Bavarian royal court. An orderly-room clerk and officer cadet in the final year of the war, Himmler had never found his way to the front and would often say he regretted that, though Emil thought it likely he was just trying to fit in with the other former soldiers around him, for he fainted at the sight of blood. In 1922 he had graduated from the Technische Universität in München with a bachelor of science degree in agriculture, and with a prized dueling scar on his cheek. A job selling fertilizer for a firm in Schleissheim had enabled him to buy his own chicken farm and join a Blood and Soil group called the Artamanen, farming men. And that in turn had led him to join the occult society that was called the Thule Gesellschaft, and through it become friends with Dietrich Eckart and Captain Ernst Röhm, whose adjutant he had been in the putsch.

Emil had first met Himmler in 1925 when he'd been named the party's deputy *Gauleiter* and *Obmann*, or propaganda director, for Upper Bavaria and Swabia. Quietly hardworking and shrewd, highly organized and suspicious, Himmler had found Hitler's favor over other party officials through his loyalty, his freedom from scandal, and his methodical accumulation of facts about the friends and enemies of the führer. In 1927 Himmler had become deputy *Reichsführer* of the few hundred men in the Schutzstaffeln, the SS, which functioned as the party police; and now he'd invited Emil Maurice to his table in order to recruit him as an officer, and Geli was of no interest to him.

His glazed hazel eyes were vacant, his handshake moist, his face as bland as a thumb as he officiously introduced himself as Deputy Reichsführer-SS Heinrich Himmler. His dark brown hair was all but shaved from the sides of his head, but was scruffed on top, like a squirrel's tail. Geli was a few inches shorter than he but her shoulders were wider; he seemed without muscle, as soft as eiderdown, ineffectual and passive, but beneath the coldness and dullness of his face she felt she detected a fearsome seething and contempt that he was holding under fierce control. "You are from Wien, Fräulein Raubal," he said.

"I am."

"Have you visited the Treasury?"

"With my uncle, yes."

"And how did you feel about the Holy Lance?"

She shrugged. "It was nice. I was just eleven then."

His face twitched and he turned from her to Emil. She felt she'd flunked his test. "Shall we sit?" he said, and they did. And then he told Emil about the Aryan criteria he was establishing for those who wanted to join the Schutzstaffeln, strictly judging each applicant on the basis of his family origins—including proof of Aryan forebears for a minimum of three generations—and hereditary biology, health, physique, and physiognomy. The deputy *Reichsführer* himself would subject each applicant's photograph to his famous magnifying glass to ensure conformity to his rigid standards. The SS insignia would be a skull and bones, signifying its sworn loyalty and obedience to the führer, even if that meant death. "We'll be an elite," Heinrich Himmler said. "We'll be like Jesuits without Jesus."

"Aren't you flattered, Emil!" Geli falsely gushed. "The high honor of even being considered!"

"Are you being humorous?" Himmler asked.

"Apparently not." She leaned forward to find Emil's eyes. "What *day* did we get here?"

Emil smiled. "Soon."

Geli turned to Himmler's fiancée. She was Margarete Boden, a shy, desultory, prematurely gray woman seven years older than he was. She talked dully for a while about her faith in herbalism and homeopathy, but then fascinated Geli by saying that her fiancé had foresworn any physical contact with her until their marriage. "Oh, but it's so hard on him. 'Don't you know how I long to hold you and kiss your feet?' Heinrich says. But he also says that a wife's perpetual innocence and purity give a real man the strength never to falter in even the worst strife he encounters."

"And have you been engaged for a long time?"

"Six months now."

"Whose idea was the marriage?" Geli asked.

"Herr Hitler's. He insisted."

Rudolf and Ilse Hess strolled over and joined them. Ilse asked Geli, "Are you aware that you and your uncle have the same tarot archetype?"

"Which is?"

"The hierophant."

"Really!" Himmler said.

"Oh, *now* you're impressed." She looked to Ilse. "I have no idea what that means."

Doktor Goebbels ambled over to the table and told Heinrich Himmler, "We have further good news. Prince Viktor and Princess Marie-Elisabeth zu Wied have made inquiries about 'the Hitler movement.'"

Ilse told Geli, "The hierophant was an official interpreter of rites of worship and sacrifice in ancient Greece, and in the tarot represents the principles of learning and teaching. You're influenced by Isis, the goddess of intuition. You walk the mystical path with practical feet. I haven't finished your birth chart yet."

"And mine?" Doktor Goebbels asked as he settled next to Geli.

"I have only Herr Hitler's," she said.

Effervescent with victory, Hermann and Carin Göring found their table, but frowned at its barrenness. "We need champagne here," Captain Göring said, and he shouted to a faraway man with a tray, "Waiter! Three bottles of Mumm's! And nine glasses!" He held out a chair for his wife, then reversed another and straddled it, hunkering forward with his fleshy, pink cheeks in his palms as he watched Ilse unfold a page of handwritten notes.

She said, "The leader was born on the cusp between Aries and Taurus, just like Mussolini and Stalin, and has his sun in Taurus and Libra, so there's a fondness for the arts combined with infinite ambition. Which is why he can be tyrannical at times."

"Oh, what a *child* I become in his presence!" Captain Göring exclaimed. "I can't explain it. I'll be full of certainty and valor, but he'll turn on me and I wither."

"It's his eyes," Doktor Goebbels said. "They'll scar you for life."

Captain Göring hurriedly added, "I meant it only in a positive way, Doktor Goebbels."

"Me too," said Doktor Goebbels.

"Continue please, Ilse," said Rudolf Hess. "We're very interested."

"Quite willing to sacrifice his own happiness to a higher ideal," she said, "he is apt to put off his own matrimonial bliss for the good of Germany. And yet this may cause him fits of jealousy and self-recrimination."

Heinrich Himmler objected, "I haven't seen that."

"She used the word 'may,'" said Rudolf Hess. "A conditional tense. Merely a possibility."

"Careful, Frau Hess," Doktor Goebbels said. "There's plenty of room for you in Himmler's filing cabinets."

"I have no importance," she said, and went on, "Herr Hitler has Pluto in his eighth house, which is what accounts for his stamina and tenaciousness, as well as his wonderful influence over people. And the moon in his third house gives him marvelous powers of verbal expression."

"We found that particularly interesting," said Rudolf Hess.

"Also, 'sun trine Jupiter,'" his wife read.

"Oh good," said Himmler's fiancée.

"Sun trine Jupiter?" Geli asked.

Himmler's fiancée said, "Wealth and success."

Carin Göring said, "I'd heard that meant religiosity."

"All those things, as well as a high level of intelligence," said Himmler. "And Mars?"

"Mars square Saturn," said Ilse Hess.

"Cruelty. Egotism," said Carin Göring. She elbowed her husband. Who shrugged.

"Also, Mars trine Jupiter," said Ilse Hess. "Rudi, how would you put it?"

"We have found such a combination in preachers whose joy it is to offer freedom and truth to those who will hear them."

"Earlier I so wanted you to do my chart, Ilse," Carin Göring said. "But how can I bear it now? I'll be so *banal*."

With a sidelong glance, her husband said, "Well, that goes without saying, doesn't it?"

"We all suffer in comparison with the leader," Doktor Goebbels said.

"And here he is," Emil said.

Like schoolboys the men hurtled up from their chairs as their master walked over, his forelock fallen, his white tie cocked. Ilse Hess surreptitiously folded up her notes. Widening his arms and smiling, Hitler said, "What a joy for your leader to find all his friends sharing the same table! Would you do me the honor of having you as my guests in the dining room?"

And as they collected their things and Emil took her hand and they all strolled across the grand ballroom, Geli looked at Rudolf and Ilse Hess, Doktor Joseph Goebbels, Hermann and Carin Göring, and Heinrich Himmler and his fiancée, and she thought that if she was in fact one of them, Hitler's friends, she would be mortified.

Chapter Eleven
Picnic, 1928

She quit medical studies after her first year at the Ludwig-Maximilian Universität. She'd earned fairly good grades in English and fairly poor grades in the sciences, and after her hectic, high-living nights she too often found herself bored and cold and overtired in the heatless lecture halls and ludicrously ill-equipped labs, while being forced to continually report how she was doing academically to a scoffing, proprietary uncle who hated academics. And so she told him on her twentieth birthday, in June, that she would like to try other things in the fall.

They were in the foyer of the Osteria Bavaria, and his face became as somber as her chemistry professor's. "Well, if that's what you want," he said, and he faintly bowed to the owner, who was frantically helping four waiters set up Hitler's table on the patio.

"I think it is, Uncle Alf."

With a forced smile of affection he said, "Women ought to be mothers. *That* is their talent." And then he stalked ahead of her to his luncheon table.

She felt annoyed enough then to change her mind, but she was fearful of his scolding. She instead told him as she sat next to him, "I haven't given up on the idea of medicine. This may be temporary."

"We'll hope for the best," he said. His hand fleetingly touched her knee as he unfolded a napkin in his lap, and he immediately rose and jarred his chair farther away. "My apologies," he told her.

"Accepted."

And then Max Amann, Alfred Rosenberg, Franz Xaver Schwarz, and Rudolf Hess joined them. Each handed Geli a birthday card containing fifty reichsmarks, as if they'd voted on an affordable sum, and then Hitler gave her a flat package in white butcher paper that he'd watercolored and addressed to "My Darling Angelika." In a silver photography frame inside were four Heinrich Hoffmann snapshots of her uncle in 1926 as he practiced using his hands histrionically in accordance with the instructions of a famous clairvoyant named Erik Jan Hanussen.

"Are you pleased?" Hitler seriously asked.

She was at a loss for words.

And then the five men all fell into laughter and the owner of the Osteria Bavaria walked forward with Hitler's real birthday gift of a fancy golden birdcage and two bright yellow St. Andreasburg canaries. With joy her uncle told her, "I have decided. You'll be taking singing lessons."

She was delighted. She recalled the finch's proper name from zoology class: *Serinus canaria*. She stuck a finger inside the cage and the canaries shied from it. "With such good teachers, Uncle Alf!"

"Why not? And then in the fall perhaps with Herr Adolf Vogl, a friend in the party."

"Another Adolf?" she asked.

"There's only one, really," he said. "And now are you pleased?"

She teased, "Will I still get to keep the photographs?"

"Naturally."

She kissed his cheek and said, "I love you, Uncle Alf."

He flinched at hearing the word "love" and his hooded stare fled to four parts of the room.

"We all love him," said Rudolf Hess.

Hunting for some distraction, Hitler took the knife from beside his plate and polished it with his napkin. "And after you finish your final exams tomorrow—"

"With flying colors," said Alfred Rosenberg.

"—you should hurry and get your things together. We're going to Obersalzberg."

■ ■ ■

Heinrich Hoffmann's wife had died in the European influenza epidemic of 1928, and he was so worried about his fifteen-year-old daughter being alone and available to boys while high school was out that Hitler graciously invited Henny to stay with Geli in Haus Wachenfeld that summer.

They'd both later remember that July and August as their most glorious time in Obersalzberg. The nights were cool, the fields were green, the skies were azure blue, and the air was filled with the scent of pine and snow and wildflowers. Geli and Henny would finish their housecleaning chores by noon and have the afternoons to stroll through Berchtesgaden with chocolate ice cream in waffle cones, hike up past the treeline on Kehlstein Mountain in their hobnailed boots and feed chunks of snow to Prinz, furiously race at filling in the Sunday crossword puzzles after the Raubals came back from Mass, find hilarity in reading Karl May's Westerns aloud on the terrace with false male voices, lie flat on the floor of the Winter Garden, their chins on their fists, tuning in a faint London signal on the radio to listen hard and seriously to American music: "Ain't She Sweet," "Thou Swell," "I Wanna Be Loved by You," "You Took Advantage of Me."

Angela shifted her things to Geli's room so the friends could share Angela's full-sized bed on the first floor and watch the canaries fly around the room, and chatter and fret and giggle until one or two in the morning. With childish excitement, Henny once told the plot of a chilling film Geli had missed, a film in which a fiendish scientist took control of a prostitute and inseminated her with sperm he'd extracted from a just-hanged criminal. She became pregnant, and the girl who was born grew up to be a sleepwalking temptress named Alraune who ruined all the foolish men who fell in love with her. "You were supposed to fear Alraune," Henny said. "But it was surprising: I found myself wanting to be like her."

"A femme fatale?"

"Yes. To have that power."

Geli smiled. "You aren't a vampire or anything, are you?"

"I promise you'll be the first to know." With one hand behind her head, Henny tilted the lone tallow candle that was flaring in the darkness, and the flame deformed as white candlewax spilled onto the windowsill. "Are you still a virgin?"

Geli confessed she wasn't.

"Who?"

"Oh," she sighed, "I forget."

"In Wien?"

"Change the subject."

"Are you and Emil . . . ?"

"We aren't married, Fräulein Hoffmann."

Henny jolted up onto her elbows to fascinatedly peer at Geli. She scoffed, "Emil is suddenly moral now? Emil Maurice?"

With false and defensive prudishness, Geli offered, "With me, yes."

"Then he's afraid of your Uncle Adolf," Henny said, and fell forward onto her pillow. She spidered a few fine brown hairs from her face and seemed prepared to sleep as she said, "Who isn't."

"Your father?"

"Heinrich? Hah!"

"My mother."

"Angela? Oh, please. She'll do whatever he says. Anytime he says it. Won't she?"

Nothing was said.

Henny grinned. "What a good game: Who's not frightened of Adolf Hitler? Try to think. Herr Doktor Goebbels?"

"Definitely frightened."

"Herr Himmler? Of course, yes."

"Rudi shamelessly confesses it."

"Who else?" Henny asked. "Herr Rosenberg?"

"That toady."

"And Herr Göring's a child around your uncle."

"And wears his childishness like a medal."

"Are you?" Henny asked.

"Still a virgin? I answered that."

Henny nudged her shoulder.

Geli thought, and finally said, "No. I'm not afraid of him."

Quiet took even the sounds of their breathing into its stomach. There was only the faint hiss of the candle. And then Henny conceded, "I think that's probably true."

"What do I win?"

She was silent for a while, then said, "My amazement."

■ ■ ■

On July 28th, they celebrated Angela Raubal's forty-fifth birthday by letting her sleep in while Geli and Henny fabricated a breakfast of flambéed crêpe suzettes, orange sections and grapes, and a full pot of Italian espresso. Leo Raubal took a four a.m. train from Wien to get there in time, and was with them when they sneaked into Angela's room with the food tray and woke her by singing the first verses of a song from Mozart's *Die Zauberflöte*, Angela's favorite opera.

She was first astonished by the flooding sunshine and hunted for the alarm clock that her daughter had stolen in the night. "What time is it?"

"Half ten," Geli said. "We let you sleep."

With shock Angela then noticed her tall, nearly twenty-two-year-old son, and she started fussing with graying hair, that was as forked and twisted as seaweed. She gruffly said, "Aren't you cruel children to surprise me like this."

Leo grinned. "We thought about inviting in the others, too. They didn't know the song."

Angela heard Heinrich Hoffmann shouting a joke in the dining room, that Göring was the first man to *ascend* to a higher realm by means of a parachute. Many men heartily laughed. She held a sheet up over the front of her nightgown. "Who's here?"

"Emil came," Geli said. "And Putzi Hanfstaengl, all the way from France."

"Also my father, as you hear," said Henny. "And what's-his-name, the man who lost his toes on the front."

"Julius Schaub," Geli said.

"To be with their leader," Angela said. "Otherwise he might forget them. Are they hungry?"

Geli told her mother they'd been fed, and that the Bechstein's chauffeur would be taking Angela and her friend Ilse Meirer to Salzburg for the day, so she ought to make herself beautiful.

"And what will you do with all those men?"

"We're going to the Chiemsee for a picnic."

Aching as she got out of bed, Angela avoided foul language with the slang, "Oh green nine." And as she hobbled to the bathroom she said, "You ask too much of your old mother on her birthday."

Geli changed into a fitted navy blue sundress with a white geometric pattern, white ankle-high socks, and brown oxfords. She brushed her hair for the third time that morning and went downstairs to the dining room.

Putzi Hanfstaengl was now a Herr Doktor, having finally gotten his D. Phil. degree in history with a dissertation on the Austrian Netherlands and Bavaria in the eighteenth century; but he was talking with Hoffmann about his family firm's photography of the art masterpieces of the Louvre, a permission just recently given them by the director, Henri Verne, a nephew of the famous novelist.

"So you'll be rich!" Hoffmann said.

"If the books sell, possibly."

"We'll have to celebrate with champagne."

Julius Schaub frowned. "Always the drinking."

Joking with Hoffmann, Putzi referred to Schaub as "Il Penseroso," but it fell flat because no one else there knew Italian.

"Who'll want beer?" Geli asked, and four hands flew up.

Emil stood. "I'll help."

She shyly smiled and felt Emil watching the feminine tilt of her hips as she went to the kitchen ahead of him. Henny was filling their picnic hamper with Apollinaris mineral water and vacuum flasks of coffee and tea, so Emil hauled a full crate of Spaten out to the trunk of Hitler's Mercedes.

Then Hitler finally came downstairs and into the dining room, for she heard the other men collectively stand from their chairs and heard Putzi say, "I have the foreign press clippings here."

And then her uncle gracefully walked into the kitchen in his gray flannel summer suit and yellow tie, a red-and-black swastika pin on the suit jacket's lapel. His forelock fell as he examined the food wrapped in waxed paper: Swiss cheese and salami and hot, roasted chicken.

"Won't you make me a peanut butter sandwich?" he whined to his niece. "And put in some Bahlsen biscuits? And chocolate, and an apple tart? Make me lunch like always, Princess; nothing fancy or new."

She sighed and did as he said.

Emil and Leo wandered in and Hitler told Geli's brother what a good *Hausfrau* she was becoming. "She cooks, she cleans, she sews!"

"Rare talents," Geli said.

Leo Raubal hunted for a handmade cigarette in his front shirt pocket, held it to a flame underneath the tea kettle on the stovetop, and was inhaling it before he noticed the shocked silence and his uncle's scorn.

"We don't smoke inside the house," Emil said.

"I'm allowed," Leo confidently said. "I have rank in the Austrian SA." And then he felt his family staring at him in silence. "A firing squad offense?" Leo asked.

"We don't joke about it," his uncle told him.

Leo jarred the screen door open and flicked his cigarette outside.

And then they got into the cars. Emil and Hitler were up in the front of the red Mercedes convertible, and Henny and Geli joined

Putzi Hanfstaengl in the back where the Herr Doktor could hang his long legs over the folded-down middle seat. Hitler found linen caps in the glove compartment and handed them to his niece and the girl he called Sunshine so their hair wouldn't fly wildly in the wind, and he and Emil strapped on their cold weather leather aviators' caps. "Prinz!" Hitler called. "Ride!" And the Alsatian galloped down from the house and jumped inside the car, scrabbling his paws on the jump seat before finding a space on the floor next to Geli.

Heinrich Hoffmann, Julius Schaub, and Leo Raubal climbed into Hoffmann's old Daimler where smoking was not just permitted but was assured. And Angela waved good-bye to them from the upstairs balcony in her purple flapper's dress and cloche hat.

The Chiemsee was a fairly substantial lake with three islands, fifty kilometers northwest of Haus Wachenfeld, but Hitler maintained that the water there was three degrees centigrade warmer than the far closer Königssee, and his enthusiasm for fast automobiles was still so fresh that he considered most highway travel to be a good form of recreation; so they journeyed an hour north. Currying favor, Putzi hulked forward on the fold-down seat to pass on an invitation to visit Adolf Müller, the printer of the *Völkischer Beobachter*, whose luxurious summer home was in St. Quirin on the Tegernsee, just fifty kilometers south of München; but Hitler told him he couldn't possibly go there, for the many journalists out to destroy him only thought of the Tegernsee as a playground of the very rich.

Putzi Hanfstaengl admitted that this was true. "I have heard it called the 'Lago di Bonzo.'"

"Which is?"

"Mafia Italian for 'Lake of the Big Shots.'"

When Hitler laughed hugely, hitting his thigh with the flat of his hand, Putzi felt he could sit back. The Alsatian was standing high on his hind legs, his forelegs on the fold-down seat, and avidly sniffing the air for florid tales of wildflowers, Benzine, macadam road, finches, fences, wet meadows, and milk cows. Geli and Henny were singing American tunes they'd memorized. Putzi smilingly listened through two songs and then challenged their English pronunciation. "Some-vun to votch o-fer me?" he asked. "Yas! Vee haff no bahn-nahn-az?"

"Close enough," Henny said.

They sang "Ain't We Got Fun?" and "Ain't She Sweet?" and then they couldn't fully recall other lyrics, so Putzi filled the ride by teaching them strange American slang. A "sap" was a fool. Schaub was a "rube," Himmler a "Milquetoast," Goebbels a "wolf." Göring considered himself a "he-man." Money was "scratch" or "jack." Coffee was "joe." Whiskey was called "panther sweat." "Ish kabibble" was what you answered when you couldn't care less. In America they would both be considered "live wires," "peaches," "Janes," "skirts," "thrills," "panics," "tootsies," and "hot little numbers." Emil was Geli's "sheik"—from the Rudolph Valentino movie—and she was Emil's "Sheba."

"And what would Uncle Adolf be?" Geli asked.

"Your 'sugar daddy,'" he snidely said. But when she asked him what sugar daddy meant, the Herr Doktor told her, "It's too hard to define."

And then they were at the Chiemsee where Geli thought the far-off mountains seemed to settle into the lake like white-haired women in green bathing dresses. They parked the Mercedes and the old Daimler under oak trees and Schaub flung out woolen rugs and linen tablecloths from the trunks as Emil carried the crate of Spaten to the shoreline and sloshed out among floundering reeds to submerge the beer underwater for chilling. Leo Raubal filled coffee cups from a vacuum flask as Hoffmann handed out *Der Völkische Kurier*, the *Münchener Neueste Nachrichten*, the *Münchener Zeitung*, and the *Wiener Sonn-und-Montag* from the stack he'd collected at a Schwabing kiosk that morning, and the six men stood in the shade with tilted heads, silently absorbed in their reading, their filled coffee cups steaming at their shoes or on handkerchiefs on the fenders, their serious newspapers held as wide as the maps of continents.

The craze of nudism, or *Freikörperkultur*, excited all of Germany in the twenties, and in public parks and on lakes there were generally areas where, as a fitness author put it, "for the benefit of the race, those with high aspirations can steel and train their bodies in the sacredness of their natural condition." One such beach was on the Chiemsee. Hiding behind a scrim of sloe and scrub bushes, Geli and Henny took off all their clothes and scurried into the lake, screaming as they hit the shallows and fell forward into water that was still so cold it seemed to have teeth. They swam out to a floating dock and hung on to it to find their breath, feeling an aching chill in their feet, and then went farther out toward Men's Island and the unfinished Sun Palace of Ludwig II, sidestroking back only when Henny's face was pale with heat loss and her lips were the color of a four-day-old bruise.

And then they lay flat on their backs and naked on the fine, white sand, holding their faces into the flare of the sun, feeling water beads contract on their skin as air flowed over their bodies like cool silk. They heard the men on the other side of the sloe bushes fifty meters away, vying at skimming flat stones on the lake. Geli's brother seemed to have won with five skips, but then Geli's uncle, who hated sport, threw a stone that struck the water six times and, with him the victor, the game was determined over.

Henny said, "I was nine years old when I first met him. 1922. I was practicing the piano and hating it and I heard the front doorbell so I went to see who it was. Herr Hitler was on the front step in his slouch hat and shabby white trench coat, a frightening dog whip folded in his hand. I told him my father was taking his afternoon nap upstairs, and he kindly said he'd wait for him. And then he was so charming. We got to talking about the piano, and he stopped my grumbling by sitting down on the bench and playing a Strauss polka. You know how delightful he can be with children."

Geli shook her head. "I don't; not really. We hardly knew him then."

"Well, he is. In fact, I was so flattered by his attention that I polkaed around the room for him, but in a harsher voice he told me to quit and just listen. Then he told me old Teutonic stories about Rhine maidens and an evil dwarf named Alberich, tinkling the piano keys when he talked about fairies and pounding hard on the low notes to indicate trouble and menace. My father woke up before he'd finished his tale and I fell into a sulk. But Herr Hitler promised me he'd stop by on other afternoons when I practiced, and he did, reading his stack of newspapers for an hour or so, then playing a few songs as my reward. That's when he first called me Sunshine." With both hands she smoothed her bobbed hair back from her face and crushed water out of it. She asked, "Have you been to the Bayreuth Festival with him yet?"

"No."

She told Geli he'd taken her there when she was twelve. She'd stayed in the home of Siegfried and Winifred Wagner, and seen *Parsifal* and *Der Ring des Nibelungen*.

"Are you trying to make me jealous?"

She smiled. "Well, you get to do everything with him now."

"I'm his niece."

"Hah," Henny said.

"And 'Hah' means what?"

"Nothing; never mind."

A fallen branch was thrown into the Chiemsee, and Geli watched Prinz in full tilt after it, crazily vaulting into the water and crashing through reeds—*Phragmites*, she thought—before floundering out with the stick in his mouth and shaking furiously. Whoever the thrower was strolled behind them and the Alsatian trotted farther away.

She found she'd hidden her sex with a hand and a forearm. She relaxed. Henny was trying to sleep. Her pinking breasts were the size of sherbet dishes, her fifteen-year-old legs were as hard and lean as a boy's, a hand was idly brushing sand from her dark pubic hair. Closing her eyes Geli saw redness. She felt a faint trickle of sweat find its way down her side.

Anything was still possible. She fantasized about a future with Emil and four children and a forest cottage in the Wienerwald, south of Wien. Shaded in summer. Safe. In Austria. Or a fine, furnished flat off Grillparzerstrasse in Wien, or between the Stadtpark and the Konzerthaus, with medical offices inside the Ring. With dinners at the Korso or the Three Hussars. She'd be a pediatrician. A veterinarian. Well-off, but not rich. Or she'd offer physical therapy in a fashionable health resort like Semmering. She'd find Aunt Paula a job there. And her mother could cook. In Austria. Maybe her husband would not be Emil but a handsome doctor. Civilized, educated, and kind. With no interest in politics. With friends she admired. She'd have four children and gay dinner parties and season tickets to the opera and a weekend house in the Wienerwald. She'd have friends who were civilized, educated, and kind. She'd sing. She'd be safe. She'd . . .

She felt Prinz urgently sniffing her face and realized she'd been dozing. The Alsatian was worried about her, but Hitler called, "Prinz! Heel!" and the hound hurried back to him. Henny frankly displayed herself, as she'd seen her father's models do, but Hitler averted his head. Geli hunkered forward to hide what she could. She shaded her eyes but couldn't find her uncle's face because of the fierce sun behind him. Ambling toward them on the white sand, he was still in his gray flannel suit and yellow tie, but his shoes and socks were off and his trousers were rolled up to his hairless white calves.

With a menacing tone, he said, "Without a stitch on, two pretty girls lie naked in the sun. And whom do they talk about? Me." And then he grinned. "I should die immediately. Anything else I achieve from now on will only be a disappointment."

Geli smiled. "You heard us?"

"And watched you," he said. Tucked under his arm was a sketchbook that he nervously handed to his niece. Geli paged past some older architectural drawings of a future motorway that he'd fantasized being built between München and Salzburg, some sketches of a fantastic university complex on the Chiemsee, as well as an Art Deco restaurant that he'd slashed with an X. And then there she was in fresh pencil, her feet without the difficult detail of toes and her hands without fingers, her face canted to the side and her wild, tawny hair in cascade so that he didn't have to fail at her features. But her torso was fairly accurate, with the bowls of her breasts flat-

tened slightly over her rib cage, shadows and roundness deftly
smudged in with his thumb, her haunches wider than she'd like, and
her vulva shockingly correct but then—with embarrassment?—
crosshatched to imply pubic hair. She glanced up at her uncle and
recognized his fretfulness and diffidence, his fetching vulnerability,
his childish need to be rewarded. *And now you're at my mercy*, she
thought. She flattered him by exclaiming, "But it's excellent, Uncle
Alf!"

He beamed. "Do you think?"

"Oh, indeed."

Hitler faced the Chiemsee as she tilted the sketchbook toward
her friend.

"Sexy," Henny said.

Geli glared *Are you crazy?*

"Well drawn," Henny said.

Hitler's face was flushed, and his back was as shut to them as a
wall. "Don't humor me," he said. "It's like pity. I have far too much
talent for that."

Geli lightly stroked his shaking trouser leg. "We *do* think it's
good."

"My thanks," he archly said. "And now why don't you girls put
clothing on and fix lunch?"

■ ■ ■

Geli's brother found her rinsing dishes. "I haven't had a chance to
talk to you," he said, and so they strolled far from the group to an
impermanent dune of sand where they could feel erosion underneath
their stomachs as they lay there and watched a hot wind harry the
hurrying green waves. "Are we far enough away?" Leo asked.

"Why?"

Leo found two handmade cigarettes of Turkish tobacco in his
wrinkled shirt pocket, offered one to his sister, and lit hers with a
friction match. With fraudulent elegance she poised the cigarette in
her right hand just as her older brother did. She smiled at him as she
considered his friendly but not handsome face. His hairline had

receded in just a few years, with a hand's-width stripe of dark hair combed straight back and two fresh areas of forehead beside it, shaped like the heels of shoes. And his mustache she found unfortunate, only a little wider than Hitler's; but when she questioned him about it he said it was the fashion for teachers in *Realschule*.

"And that's what you want to be?"

"I have already been offered a position in Linz after graduation next year."

"Good for you."

"Thanks. Are you still studying medicine?"

"I haven't totally given it up."

"You aren't, then?"

"I have other concerns."

He smiled with cunning and told her his own "other concern" was a Frenchwoman named Anne whom he hoped to make his fiancée even though Uncle Adolf considered it a misalliance. "Are you seeing someone?" Leo asked.

"Yes."

"Who?"

"You guess."

"He's here?"

"Aren't you observant."

Geli's brother frowned and rested his chin on one fist, squinting as he inhaled smoke and flicked away ash. "Emil Maurice?" he finally asked.

"Awfully difficult for you."

"Well, it's not very obvious."

"Haven't you talked?"

"You weren't mentioned."

She hit her brother on the shoulder.

"Really," he said.

"Don't say it just because it's true."

"Are you in love?" Leo asked.

"I'm not sure now."

"Don't fume."

"You'd think he'd have a hundred things to ask an older brother."

"*Adolf* talked about you. 'Such a darling girl. So delightful.'"

Geli sighed. "Always the adulation."

"Uncle was my second guess."

"You don't find that odd?"

"Well, he's only your *half*-uncle. It's just that Schicklgruber blood-line, that one-quarter contribution."

"And he's nineteen years older."

"Age," Leo said. "What's *that?*"

White sunlight splintered through a palace of clouds. The far off Women's Island and its fishing boats were painted with their shadow. Geli said, "I have the distinct impression that you don't like Emil."

Geli's brother ground out the stub of his cigarette in the sand dune. "*Like* him? Actually I do," Leo said. "And I have the feeling you *like* him, too."

■ ■ ■

Evening came. Putzi Hanfstaengl fell asleep in a Bombay hammock he'd strung between trees while Henny and her father and Emil, Schaub, and Geli's brother stood in a wide star pattern in a forest clearing, kicking a scuffed white soccer ball to each other, the men with their shirts and socks and shoes off, drinking Spaten they held by the necks, smoking Herr Hoffmann's Palo cigars, scolding faulty shots and imperfect form. Hitler shouted his own corrections as he sleepily reclined on a striped folding lawn chair, a china cup of Apollinaris mineral water cradled against his chest. A wild kick rolled to him and he skidded the soccer ball slowly back with a feint of his foot. Schaub congratulated him.

Geli wedged a rug and the picnic hamper into the trunk of the Mercedes, found a still cool Spaten for herself, and strolled over to her uncle, sitting beside him on soft ferns.

"Company," he said and smiled.

"Are you happy?"

"Quite." In the European way, his familiarity with her nakedness was balanced by a formality that would have seemed stiff in a first-class hotel. Hitler frowned. "Your skin is burnt."

"All the girls get as brown as they can now. It's the fashion."

"*Really?* I had no idea."

She nodded as she drank beer. She asked, "You didn't want to swim?"

"Oh no. I might be photographed. There are few things as discouraging as the sight of a politician in a bathing suit."

"But Uncle Adolf, you'd be dashing."

"I find your innocence quite endearing."

Emil flipped the soccer ball high and Leo smacked it with his forehead flush into Schaub's face. Wide-eyed, Schaub considered a crushed cigar that seemed to have exploded, as in a cartoon, and the others fell over with laughter.

Watching them, Hitler said, "Even in groups one can be so alone. Whether because of force of mind or character or other unusual traits, one becomes aloof, different, an outsider. It's the principal hazard of leadership."

"Are you lonely?"

Hitler forcibly took in breath and sighed it out. "Often," he said. "In childhood. On the front. With my followers now. I have given up *so much* for the party, for Germany. And I wonder if it's worth it. Self-sufficiency is a fiction whose father is false pride. We in fact need someone of our own; someone with whom we can be wholly ourselves, foolish and intimate and off guard. I have such a longing for that."

"You have me," Geli said.

With wet eyes, Hitler focused on his niece, his normally stern mouth twitching as he said, "Yes. With you I can fully relax. You're so natural and free spirited. And tactile. Affectionate."

She didn't know what else to say but "Thank you."

Hesitantly touching her hair, he told her, "And I hope you have come to see me as the father you never had."

Geli's flesh tingled as she felt his fingertips graze her skull and then grip a sun-blond hank of hair inside his fist. She told him he'd been quite generous.

"My father was fourteen years younger than his first wife," Hitler said. "And twenty-four years older than his second. She was Fanni, his first wife's maid. Did you know that Alois Junior was illegitimate?"

She nodded.

"And Angela was born two months after the wedding?"

"Yes."

"And then when your mother's mother became ill with consumption, my father shifted his courtesies to his young niece, Klara, who was taking care of the children. When his wife died, he married my mother. At six in the morning, so he could get to work punctually at seven. She was twenty-five years old, and he was forty-eight. She would continue to call him 'Uncle' until he died, at sixty-six." He freed her hair. He smiled. "Had you heard all that?"

"A few times, but it's confusing."

"And that's exactly why I mentioned it." Hitler put his china cup on the grass to his right and linked his hands at his waist. "We are given the impression that good German families have their origins in a man and a woman of about the same age who first meet each other as strangers and gradually fall in love and get married. We see, though, that there are many surprising and successful exceptions to the pattern. Endless variations, really. Children born out of wedlock. A wife twenty-three years younger. A husband who is also her uncle. We are living in times that cry out for ingenuity in how our finest men and women achieve intimacy with each other."

She was farther ahead of him than he thought. A child of nine would have been. She said nothing.

Emil walked over, sheeted in sweat, and fell to his knees next to Geli. His hard muscles bunched as he dried himself with his shirt. "Are we out of beer?" he asked.

"Herr Doktor Hanfstaengl was standing on the case to hang up his hammock."

Emil turned. "Oh, I see it."

"I was just falling asleep," Hitler said mildly. He tilted his head onto his left shoulder and squinched his eyes shut as he nuzzled his chin into his gray flannel lapel.

Emil kissed Geli's cheek and left to find himself a Spaten. And Heinrich Hoffmann hushed Geli from making a sound as he hunched nearby with his Stirnschen camera in order to take a photograph. "This will be fantastic," he whispered, for Hitler seemed so fond of her, so content and youthful yet fatherly, and his niece seemed so feminine and adoring and wryly amused.

CHAPTER TWELVE
NEXT DOOR, 1929

Within a few days Hitler forced his niece to go with him to München to find a flat for her, insisting that the university students would be getting back for their fall classes soon and that the finest situations would be lost. Rudolf Hess found five rentals for them to consider in Schwabing and Haidhausen, the first of them just below the shabby apartment of Franz Xaver Schwarz, the party treasurer. Geli thought it was nineteenth century and ugly, and Hitler agreed, but that was just the start of his dissatisfactions that day. A flat near the Hauptbahnhof Hitler rejected as far too noisy. Another, he was convinced, would be cold in winter; in the fourth he hated thinking about trudging up so many flights of stairs; and the fifth on Rudi's list, he decided, was foul with the odors of its former occupant.

The Café Heck was fairly near, he said as he checked his watch, and he was hot, and weary of real estate, and so they walked to his *Stammtisch* for an afternoon luncheon. Waiters were just filling their water glasses when Hitler, whose silver eyes were persistently flitting toward the entrance, joyously smiled and half-stood from his dining chair, lifting his right hand in an effeminate wave. "Look who happened by," he told his niece. "Princess Cantacuzène."

Was he *trying* to seem deceptive? "Aren't you surprised," Geli flatly said, and turned to find Frau Elsa Bruckmann. She was the wife of the foremost publisher in München, a former princess in Rumania, and, with Helene Bechstein, one of Hitler's first socialite benefactors. Chic and worldly and confident, a grande dame in her sixties, she wore a fashionable Zeppelin dress and held a white bichon frise to her significant chest as she offered the café her Egyptian profile and then, in a fraudulent piece of acting, finally seemed to notice the führer. She at once asked the maître d' to escort her to his table, and she and Hitler both loquaciously overdid the coincidence of their meeting.

She was invited to join them and took some time in silently assessing Geli's poise and courtesies and clothing as Hitler chatted convivially about his far too short vacation in Obersalzberg—he was working, he said, on a secret book about Aryan blood and the Jews—and then told her about his fractious day trying to find a flat for his niece.

"But, my dear Adi," Elsa Bruckmann falsely protested. "How you hurt my feelings. You should have called me first."

"Are you aware of something?"

"She can stay with Hugo and me!"

"Really, I couldn't," Geli said, and she felt Hitler touch her forearm in a hushing gesture.

"Wouldn't it be an imposition?" he asked.

"We have a *huge* home," Elsa Bruckmann said. "Rooms for chess. Rooms to cry in. Rooms for polishing silver. I have to send the butler as a scout just to find my husband in it."

Hitler formally informed his niece, "Herr and Frau Bruckmann inhabit Thierschstrasse, right next door to me."

"Are you seeking my approval?" she asked.

"She wants to be on her own," Hitler said.

"A furnished room, a private bath. She can dine with us or with the servants." She joked for the fräulein, "I'll warn Hugo to keep his hands in his pockets and his hungry eyes on the floor."

Still Adolf demurred, but Elsa insisted, and Geli watched in silence and fascination until the play was over. They ate lightly due to the August heat, and then they took the Bruckmann's car to the Thierschstrasse town home. And while Hitler went next door to find fresh shirts in his shabby flat, Geli was introduced to her fourth-floor quarters and to Italian furnishings that would have suited a regal hotel. Elsa told her they used to offer their first-floor rooms as a *völkisch* salon after the war, inviting philosophers from a group known as the Cosmic Circle to educate their friends on the secret meaning of the swastika and the need for a pagan revival. "We once had a Dionysian evening," she said, "in which an ancient Corybantine dance was performed by gorgeous young men who wore nothing but copper bracelets."

Geli smiled and lamented, "And there I was in Wien, doing homework."

"We first met Adolf on one of our salon nights, and he became *our* homework. Hugo taught him how to kiss a lady's hand, and I instructed him on how to eat an artichoke or a lobster. To give him a more masculine air, we bought him his first dog whip. I suppose we'll have *you* as our project now."

Geli icily said, "Oh, you're so kind to offer, but I don't think that's necessary."

Elsa judged her for a second and said, "We'll see."

"Are you sure you want me here?"

"Quite sure."

"I have canaries," she informed Elsa.

"We have cats," the former princess said.

Their stares warred. Elsa won. Geli shifted her gaze to an Etruscan helmet on a scrolled white desk. She felt the wealth of pink silk on a quattrocento chair. "What are you getting out of this?" she asked.

"Access to him," Elsa frankly said.

"And Uncle Adolf? He gets what?"

Elsa smiled. "Control."

■ ■ ■

She often saw Emil Maurice from her fourth-floor window as he waited for Hitler in front of his flat, shining chrome with his handkerchief or just standing in Thierschstrasse with folded arms and a cigarette, avoiding even a wayward and sudden glance at the Bruckmann's cream-colored town house. Ever cagey, and in vague ways frightened, Emil seemed to Geli all forethought and geometry, figuring the angles, the odds, the tricky, male arithmetic of what would be gained versus what would be forfeited. If he drove Geli somewhere without her uncle, she would sit in the front seat and his hand would gingerly find her inner thigh, squeeze her breast, huddle her nearer for kisses when street traffic stalled, and Emil would say flattering, loving, thrilling things that gave beauty to their future. With Hitler in the car, he was cold and silent, his face forward, his manner correct, his hand even tilting the rearview mirror so he wouldn't find Geli in it.

In Emil's mind she was always subordinate to her uncle. Schaub drove them all to a picnic once and Emil sat in the back of the Mercedes with her, strumming the same three chords on his mandolin as he sang verse after verse of an Irish ballad in a falsetto voice that wanted to be a tenor. With irritation Hitler finally turned in his front seat and asked, "Does it ever end?" And Emil finished the song at once.

And they were all in a farmer's field near Dachau, sharing a goatskin of cider with six other young people around a fire, watching a scarecrow fall in on its own ash, the night above it wrinkling with heat, and fireflies of red sparks spiraling up. Emil kissed her hard on the mouth, for the first time in days. And then she heard a honking noise and saw her uncle tilting into his car and holding his hand angrily down on the horn. Emil immediately ran.

She was losing interest in Emil, and once told him so. She was alone in the back of Hitler's car waiting for Henny in front of the Hoffmann Photography Studio. Emil's face fell forward onto his forearms atop the steering wheel, and he professed how much he loved her, that this was killing him, he *ached* to have her with him, but she had no idea how difficult and dire and overpowering her uncle could be, how he could dominate any man he met and defeat the firmest intentions with the merest flinch of dismay.

Geli sighed. She said she'd perhaps only felt a *Schwärmerei*, an infatuation, for Emil after all. And then she told him, "Here's Henny. Smile."

■ ■ ■

She also heard of Hitler's tyranny from Adolf Vogl when she began taking singing lessons from him in September. Geli stood in his front parlor, idly scrutinizing framed opera programs and captioned photos of Vogl in chromatic makeup and costume, a fierce, full-bellied man with a wild effluence of gray hair, performing into his fifties in Fauré's *Requiem*, Schumann's *Dichterliebe*, Beethoven's *Fidelio*, Schubert's *Die schöne Müllerin*, and Mendelssohn's *Elijah*. And then Vogl swaggered in from his dining room, food still in his mouth, and found that Geli was alone. With relief he said, "Oh good. Your uncle's not with you." She thought that strange enough that she frowned, and he hurried to say, "Don't misunderstand, Fräulein Raubal. I consider myself Hitler's friend, his foremost disciple, and yet after only a few minutes with him, I feel exhausted and wholly depleted."

"I have heard that said."

"You aren't . . . disquieted?"

"We relate differently."

Vogl considered Geli for a few seconds. "You wish to be a Wagnerian soprano, he says."

"My *uncle* wishes it."

"And you?"

She shrugged. "I just like to sing."

"And I like making one hundred reichsmarks per month. We have much in common. Have you a song to try out with me?"

She handed him sheet music. "Giacomo Puccini," she said. "'O mio babbino caro.'"

"'O my dear daddy.' A good choice. Sweet and short."

They went into his practice room where he sat at his grand piano, and she sang poorly, mispronouncing the Italian and failing for air at the highest notes. When she finished, he was forbiddingly silent, and she smiled in embarrassment. "Well, that was faultless, wasn't it."

"We have something we can work on," he said, and got up from the piano bench to give her instructions about the anatomy of singing, his hand pressing just under her ribs so she could feel her diaphragm and then journeying familiarly between her breasts to her throat, squeezing her larynx, and softly circling her sinuses and the bridge of her nose. She smelled cabbage on his fingertips. "And now just an 'ahh' for me."

"Ahh," she sang.

"You're still in your head voice," he sang in his head voice. "We want to hear your *chest* voice," he sang in a fuller voice.

Weakly, she attempted it.

"Head high. Heels together. And now hum for me, Fräulein Raubal."

She obeyed.

"Much better. Can you feel the flow and arc of the sound, firing out from the bridge of your nose but controlled by the diaphragm? You have to make sure your voice is constantly supported. Work on the muscles. Did you know that there was a great Italian soprano named Tetrazzini who had a diaphragm so strong she could move a piano with it?"

"I have men to haul things for me."

"Aren't you funny," he said. "Oh, that famous Austrian charm."

Vogl's far younger wife brought him a tall glass of *Weissbier*, adoringly kissed his ear, and went out, and Vogl heavily sat on the bench with the beer as he investigated Geli's range, hitting the C above middle C on the piano, having her match it, and going on to the higher notes.

Geli handled that well enough, but faltered going lower than B flat, and when he insisted she find the F below middle C, she said, "If I go that far down I feel I'll vomit."

"We'll have to work on your lower register then. A good singer has a range of two octaves, sixteen notes. You have fourteen."

She flushed. "So I'm no good?"

"You can be taught, perhaps. I have a pupil who began with thirteen notes, and now she has sixteen. She *practiced*. Will you practice?"

She feared she nodded too fervently, like a child.

"Have you heard of the diva Bertha Morena?"

"Of course."

"Another one of my success stories," Vogl said. "She learned from me, she practiced and practiced, and now she's a star." He collected sheet music and closed the piano fall board as he said in afterthought, "She was Bertha Meyer then. She's Jewish." And then his face paled. "Don't tell Hitler."

"Don't worry," she said. "I'm practiced."

■ ■ ■

She'd practiced in the fall of 1927 by failing to mention to Hitler a tall, handsome, blond medical student named Christof Fritsch, wide-shouldered but skeletal, his mind full of scientific facts and philosophy, his preferred clothing a black turtleneck sweater, his favorite foods inky coffee and hard rolls, his face always as serious as a final examination. Christof had fallen in love with Geli in chemistry class and often found his way into her company when she was alone, whether she was feeding the swans in front of the Nymphenburg Palace or holding a textbook up to shield herself from the sun in the meadows of the Theresienwiese. She'd failed to convince Christof that she was not interested in politics—she was, after all, Hitler's niece—so he'd afflicted her with weighty reflections on the new parliamentary system, the Weimar Republic, and the *Volk*. On the feast of Saint Nicholas he'd surprised her with a fancy gold angel ornament he'd picked up at the famous Christ Child's Market in Nürnberg. She'd seen him on ice skates during Winter Carnival and Christof had informed her with the coldest intensity that for her sake he'd been studying the history of opera. And on May Day, 1928, Christof had sneaked into the Pension Klein far before sunrise in order to put an oak branch outside Geli's door in a folkloric sign

of his constancy. Christof was still around, writing her highly intellectual letters full of worship, passion, and his own peculiar *Weltan-
schauung*, and if she did nothing to encourage him, she did not
mention him to Emil either, and she worried about what that
meant.

She also failed to mention to Hitler a January 1929 party in
Berlin for Hauptmann Hermann Göring and Herr Alfred Rosenberg, who, to their mutual horror, shared the same birthday.

Within months of his election as a *Mitglied des Reichstags*, Göring
found out that Lufthansa Airline wanted government subsidies for
civil aviation, so for a consulting fee of fifty thousand reichsmarks per
year he agreed to pursue Lufthansa's goals, and though he would finally
give only two addresses to the Reichstag, they were fittingly on topics
Lufthansa chose. Soon he was a consultant as well for BMW, Heinkel,
and the Messerschmitt aircraft company; Fritz Thyssen of the United
Steel Works furnished the decor and zinfandel-red carpets for his
luxury apartment on Badenschestrasse in the Schöneberg district of
Berlin; and the coal magnate Wilhelm Tengelmann was giving him
money for "geological investigations." So he was happier than he'd
been since the putsch, and far more prosperous than he'd ever been in
his fairly affluent life, and he was getting so fat that there was a joke
about him that "he sat down on his stomach and wore corsets on his
thighs."

But now Göring was in his wide white suit, his eyes so scarily
bloodshot there seemed to be no blue in them, and he was confessing that he worked nineteen hours per day, his wife Carin's health
was failing, and Herr Hitler still found him chancy, suspect. As he
sweatily told Geli, "I try so hard with your uncle. I have facts and
convictions. Opinions in desperate need of expression. But every
time I stand before the leader, my heart drops into the seat of my
pants."

Doktor Goebbels overheard and in his cordial, milky manner
confided, "Even if we're powerful in our own domains, all those who
work closely with the leader are to a degree slavish and timid in his
company. This is as it should be. We should not have contempt for

our weaknesses, Herr Göring, but only think of it as a tribute to Herr Hitler's mystical strength."

"I have used up my contempt on others," Göring spitefully told Goebbels. "I have nothing left for myself."

Doktor Goebbels smiled. "A gross imbalance I shall challenge myself to correct." And he limped off.

With Goebbels gone, Göring called him "Clubfoot," and grinned hugely, like a boy of eight, as if that were high wit. Geli just stared. She wondered if he was floating on the fall and swoon of Eukodal. Sipping from his glass of Château Latour, Göring saw that Hitler was in the dining room, fully engaged with some urgency with Alfred Rosenberg, and his face changed. "I have something to show you," he told Geli. And he took her into his walnut-wainscotted study, which he'd stocked with the Langenscheidtsche Bibliothek and first editions of other books he'd never get around to reading. His favorite acquisition, though, was a gleaming round mahogany table whose four legs were sculpted to represent four gigantic and erect penises, with nipples attached to the cannonball testicles on the floor.

"Aren't you *odd*," Geli said. And then she felt Göring shift behind her, felt his huge, soft belly pillow into her back as his hands squashed her breasts. She smelled three different perfumes on him.

"My pretty child," he whispered. "You have heard the gossip that I am impotent, no? How would you like to cure me?"

"I wouldn't know where to begin," she angrily said.

"Here," he told her, and his right hand took hold of hers and guided it to the bulge in his pants. "And now, what do you feel?" he asked.

"Disgust," she said. She freed her wrist and wriggled, and he let her go.

Seemingly worn out, he sat heavily on an ottoman and melodramatically dropped his guilt-ridden face into the open book of his hands. "And you don't find me at all attractive?" he muttered.

"You're a glutton for punishment, aren't you."

"I'm such a *fool!*" he said. "A *Hanswurst!* A clown!"

"Am I expected to disagree?"

"Could it be that I'm losing my mind? I fear it's so." Weeping uncontrollably, he was a planet of grief, and though Geli felt she ought to go, she stayed, sitting far from him, on the edge of a sofa.

With the forearm of his white suit, Göring finally smeared away his tears, staining the fabric with mascara. "You could ruin me, you know."

She was silent.

The fat man falsely smiled. Only Hitler, she thought, could so abruptly alter his personality.

"Oh, the luxury of power you now enjoy! Aren't you excited? You could waltz into the dining room right now, give Herr Rosenberg the old heave-ho, and tell your uncle what just occurred here. And I? My face would be bloodied into pulp by the SA, just as a beginning, and I would be finished, homeless, out of a job, without a pfennig for Carin's medicines. To *think* you could do all that! Were *I* in your position, I would. Without hesitation."

"Aren't you clever to put it that way. Seeing how little I want to imitate you."

With difficulty he stood up. "Angelika Maria Raubal! Such a nice girl! With such vicious men around her! But you have grown attached to the good life, haven't you, darling. And you're afraid you'll do something to end it? Would Hitler believe you? Would he question why you were here alone with me?" He took out a handkerchief and blotted his face. "An enchantress, they call you. Affectionate; fun-loving; sexy. Aren't females always in some way at fault? I was in Wien a few years ago. There were girls your age selling themselves for the price of a packet of cigarettes. They seemed . . . unhappy." Göring slicked back his glossy hair and tidied his wide suit jacket as he strode heavily to his study door. And there he turned to sneer, "You won't tell," and went out.

She agreed. She would be in some way at fault. She got up and followed him out.

■ ■ ■

On the first night of Winter Carnival, 1929, she and Henny Hoffmann accompanied Adolf Hitler to a comic operetta at the Münchener Kammerspiele on Maximilianstrasse where his favorite seats in the sixth row of the stalls were reserved. Hitler was at his handsomest in his Rousselet hat, coffee-brown leather trench coat, and tuxedo, and Geli flaunted Elsa Bruckmann's snow-white mink coat and the gift from her uncle of a slinky, silver-sequined gown that, when they checked their coats, daringly revealed the flawless flesh of her back. She felt men staring, and liked it. She was not sure if Hitler did.

The girls were forced to idle in the Kammerspiele lobby for many minutes as Hitler shook hands with party members and celebrities, then, while escorting the giggling girls to the stalls, Hitler halted and told them he'd forgotten something, but he wasn't sure what it was. He fussed and fumed about it, ostentatiously feeling all his pockets for what was missing until he seemed to find enlightenment. "Ah-hah! I have it! It's just as Nietzsche says: 'Are you going out with women? Do not forget your whip!'"

Geli sighed heavily while Henny grimaced, but Hitler found himself hilarious, and soon others in the stalls were laughing because the famous man was. Congratulating them all for their good humor, he stiffly bowed from the waist and kissed the hand of a beautiful blond film understudy with Universum Film A. G. who was there with an aunt and seemed titillated when Hitler confided that he was friendly with Herr Alfred Hugenberg, the film and press lord. And from that point on, whenever Hitler thought the operetta was particularly funny, he'd swivel in his seat to find out if the film actress was joining him in the merriment. She was.

At the interval, Hitler fetched Fachingen mineral water for Henny and his niece, then left them to themselves by the box office so he could have some fervent conversation with the film actress, whose name they never got. She had, they heard, a tinkling laugh. She softly touched the silk lapel of Hitler's tuxedo as she appeared to compliment him on it, and then she winningly sipped from a flute of champagne as he seemed to launch into the subject of formal clothing.

"She's wearing sheer hose," Geli said.

"She isn't!" said Henny, for hose were still fairly rare, and frivolous, and desired. "She is."

"And lipstick. He hates that."

"Don't glare," Henny said.

Geli spun away from them. "Distract me, then."

"Are you still taking singing lessons?"

"Indeed," Geli said.

"Are you sure you really want to be an opera singer?"

"Why not?"

"To have to stand alone up there onstage in front of thousands, and sing every note perfectly by heart, and pretend you're dying or lovelorn, and fall in a heap; and then, after the curtain rings down, to have to hop up and hold those roses and cherish all that applause."

"And what were you thinking was the unpleasant part?"

"I'd hate it," Henny said.

"Oh no, it's wonderful. To be a Valkyrie on the flaming rocks, or Isolde, dying of love for Tristan. To be Salome and ask for John the Baptist's head because you want to give him a final kiss."

Wide-eyed, Henny said, "She just did. She kissed him."

Geli fought off the need to turn. "On the mouth?"

"The cheek. She's gone back inside."

And then a fresh and excited Hitler was with them, his hands finding the skin of their backs as he guided them to the stalls. "I have had a sudden change of plans," he had the effrontery to say. "Will you take a taxi home?"

Geli flushed with hurt feelings, but said nothing.

And when they were in their seats, Hitler leaned toward his niece. "One thing you ought to know about the male of the species is that for him there are two types of women: those he admires, such as those who are celebrated for fabulous wealth, social status, or fame; and those to whom he is strongly *attracted*, women who are less prominent and may even be beneath him socially, but with whom he feels he can be fully himself."

"And where do I fit in?" she asked.

At once he was flustered and shifted away. "You belong in a special category," he said.

Afterward, he did not even wait with them in the cold and slush of the filled taxi queue, but folded five reichsmarks into his niece's palm and ducked into the front seat of his Mercedes. She saw him lean forward in order to show Julius Schaub an address he'd scrawled, and then he was majestically driven away.

"Are you in need of a ride then?" a man asked.

Geli turned and found it was Christof Fritsch in his charcoal beret and gray wool coat. She smiled.

Christof took them to the Max Emanuel Brauerei on Adalbertstrasse, where Geli bought four rounds of Löwenbräu beer with Hitler's marks and Christof slammed into her as they danced a schottische and he finally fell on the floor in his drunkenness.

"Thunder weather," he said, Alsatian slang for unhappiness and surprise. Still flat on his back, Christof twisted his fists into his eyes as if trying to erase them. And then he considered his feebleness as Geli and Henny hauled him up onto his hobnailed boots and helped him to their booth.

"We really have to be going, Christof," Geli said.

"Another beer," he insisted.

"Why don't you stay? Drink coffee. Eat cake. We'll get a taxi."

In English he said, "Okay," slang she'd taught him from an American song, and then waved good-bye while saying in German, "Much love."

The taxi driver first went to Henny Hoffmann's home in Bogenhausen, far east of the Englischer Garten, then steered west toward Schwabing where he let Geli off at Isartorplatz. And she was just walking to the Bruckmann's town house in her snow-white mink and sheath dress and cold, high-heeled shoes when she saw Hitler and the film actress heading into his flat above the *Drogerie* at number 41.

She hid in a moon-shaded doorway until they were fully inside and then hurried forward to the farther, unshoveled sidewalk so she could huddle in the wind and watch his front window as Hitler first switched on a lamp and took off his hat and trench coat before helping the film actress with her fur. At first he wanted to lay the fur on his bed, but hesitated and folded it over a chair back. Apparently offering her something to drink, he got a nod and a funny reply, for he laughed hard as he twisted out the cork in a half-finished bottle of Winkelhausen Deutscher cognac and poured an inch into each of two juice glasses. She took one juice glass from him and Hitler turned around the chair with the fur and hunched forward on it. The fur irritated him, though, so he laid it on the folding table and took his seat again.

And now where will she sit? Geli thought.

The film actress found there was no other furniture but the folding table and the bed. She softly settled onto the swaybacked mattress as if that were only natural and sourly took in Klara Hitler's photograph above the headboard as she sipped her cognac. Geli jealously noticed that she had good legs, which she crossed at the knees, and she wore her blond hair in waves just like Lilian Harvey, an English actress famous in Germany. Hitler was formally upright in his chair, holding forth in his way, and the film actress was probably trying to understand why an internationally famous man lived so frugally. Still talking, Hitler got up, sidestepped to the front window, and jerked the floral drapes closed.

Shall I go in? Geli thought. Her feet were stones and her face felt as hard as stiff leather. And so she did, scuttling across the street to the Bruckmann town house, but then changing her mind and going up the stairs beside the druggist's shop where she found the foyer door unlocked. Geli took off her heels to softly walk to Hitler's flat. She couldn't peek through the keyhole, but crouched at a newly painted door and heard her uncle's baritone as he talked about his first disappointment with the party in 1920 and his fateful decision to join after all. And then he talked about his first successes as an orator, the firmness of his will in the face of opposition, how he'd conquered his enemies with the force of his personality and his revolutionary ideas. On and on he went, trying to woo her as he wooed the crowds, chronicling the National Socialist movement while the plainly bored film actress said little more than "Oh?" or "I see." Then Hitler halted his lecture to say, "Won't you take off your clothes?"

And a further shock was that the film actress apparently obeyed, lilting an unobjecting sentence of some sort and shifting from foot to foot as she tossed off her high-heeled shoes.

Continuing his self-flattery, Hitler only paused here and there to say, "Aren't you lovely" and "Yes, those, too" and "Slowly please." The film actress said once, "Unhook me"; otherwise she said nothing, or spoke so quietly she couldn't be heard.

"Walk to me now," Hitler said.

There were voices outside, and Geli saw Frau Maria Reichert, the landlady, holding a wool coat shut at her throat at the glass foyer door as she helped her frail old *Mutti* up the stairs and inside. Fat snowflakes were fluttering down like torn paper. The old mother must have asked the time because Frau Reichert said, "Midnight," and then Geli clicked past the women in her heels, offering them a *Grüss Gott*.

She hung up the mink in the vestibule and found Hugo Bruckmann sitting in the first-floor parlor in his pajamas, striking a match and holding it to the bowl of a calabash pipe. She was thankful his mood was unfit for conversation, and that the Princess Cantacuzène was sleeping poutily under an eye mask, the door ajar and a vigil candle burning just as she'd insisted on since childhood—a hex against the *Wichtelmänner*, who steal children from their beds and put changelings in their places.

She'd forgotten to cover the canaries so they were fretfully awake, sidling and turning on their perches and chewing the golden cage. She called them each by name, Honzi and Hansi, then gave them night and sang Brahm's "Lullaby" to them as she got out of her clothes. She again heard her uncle saying, "Walk to me now," and she watched the faint jiggle of her full breasts in the mirror as she did so. Wide as a gate in the hips. The chunkiness of her thighs. She was surprised by her jealousy, her loneliness, her feelings of inadequacy.

She was still far from sleep under her feather-filled comforter when she heard the foyer door slam next door, and she hurried to her fourth-floor window to see the film actress stalking through fresh snow in her heels. Geli wanted to see her face, and when she walked under a streetlight she did.

And Geli smiled, for the face was fraught and ashen and filled with confusion, as if Hitler had found the will to confess whom he truly loved.

With singing lessons at Vogl's her sole obligation, Geli was generally available to Hitler, and more than ever he sought her out. They
took cold-weather strolls with Prinz around Kleinhesselohersee in
the Englischer Garten, huddled with Bahlsen biscuits and steaming
tea from a vacuum bottle in the Apollo Temple at Nymphenburger
Park, watched old men in ski caps and many sweaters sweep snow
from the frozen canals and slide red and yellow and green curling
stones across steel-blue lanes of ice. The fields and sidewalks were
white with snow, shrubs and trees were just strokes of black, and the
skies were the gray of cigarette smoke with no more than a faint
hint of white where the hidden sun was; but she loved it that the
children carried skates to school, painted their faces, wore masks,
and that the *Volk* in general were as motley and costumed and fes-
tively gay as the huntsmen in paintings by Pieter Brueghel.

The Sturmabteilung and the Hitler Youth hosted many parties and
masquerades during January's Carnival and Lent's week of *Starkbierzeit,*
or strong beer time, and the organizations took care to invite Hitler's

famous niece, but Geli was generally forbidden to attend the affairs for Hitler's fear that she'd fall into what he called "a misalliance," and she supposed Hitler felt that his political fortunes were still too precarious to risk having his voluptuous, twenty-year-old niece by his side at formal party functions. She joined him only for opera nights at the Kammerspiele or the Cuvilliés Theater, or for full days at the cinema where he could sit in stillness and joy and fascination as he watched three feature films in succession.

Workdays for him could be little more than a noontime conference with Amann and Rosenberg in the Schwabing office, followed by Italian food at the Osteria Bavaria; an interview with a journalist at the Hotel Vier Jahreszeiten and dessert with Putzi and Hess in the Carlton Tearoom; a change into his tuxedo to hear Wagner's *Lohengrin* at the Prinzregenten Theater, then a four-course dinner with the faithful at the Café Heck, with him holding forth on any subject he fancied until closing time at two.

Weeks of leisure would inevitably be interrupted by public speaking and the pursuit of money, however, and there could be long strings of days when Geli wouldn't see him at all: He was talking to a party cell in Münster; he was rallying trade unionists in Düsseldorf; he was staying in the castle of a coal tycoon named Emil Kirdorf; he was in Mühlheim conferring with Fritz Thyssen of the United Steel Works; or he was in Essen, touring the Krupp factories with Gustav Krupp von Bohlen und Halbach. And then he'd be in München again, saying nothing of his week to Geli, offering her a stroll through the *Residenz* of the Wittelsbach rulers or an afternoon at the Glyptothek on Königsplatz where he stood for a full twenty minutes before the Aeginetan sculptures, or hunched forward, his hands locked behind his back, his spectacles far down his nose as from all sides he examined the Hellenistic figure of a sleeping satyr that was known as *The Barberini Faun*.

■ ■ ■

In March she and Henny were taken downhill skiing by him—just in time, he promised, for the finest snowfall of winter on the majestic Zugspitze, the highest mountain in Germany. Emil drove them all to Garmisch, ninety-five kilometers southwest of München, but he would not ski. And Hitler feared the party would be hurt if he himself were seen falling on the runs, so he let the girls go alone up the slopes on the condition that they stuff their telltale hair under stocking caps and fasten face scarves under their ski goggles. They then looked so much like boys that Hilter laughed until he ached, and Henny later took a Leica shot of Geli at the summit, with her hands obstinately on her hips and a scold like a lumberjack's. "And now do Gary Cooper," Henny said.

Wildly flapping her arms, she joked, "*Wings.*"

Emil and Hitler hiked through the forest in snowshoes until four p.m., when they raced each other back to the ski lodge, choosing different routes—the führer, Emil was sure, taking the wrong one. At twilight Emil was still alone, slouched in his heaviest coat on a rattan chair near the lift, finding the girls in binoculars as they slalomed down. And the three of them were still there at nightfall in flying sleet when they finally saw a furious Hitler on the blue hill, his snowshoes tossed in his wrath, tilting alternately from side to side as he sank as high as his knees in drifts, his clothing white from his many humiliating falls. Even when he was a hundred meters away, they heard him yell in forewarning, "It is not *funny!*"

Though he'd promised the girls a night in a Garmisch spa, and had filled an hour on the road lauding the health benefits of saunas, Hitler suddenly found the high prices there and in Partenkirchen outrageous, and so he sat in the front seat fuming as they headed due east to Haus Wachenfeld, getting there just before nine.

Geli had alerted her mother to their coming with a telephone call, and Angela was ready with one of Hitler's favorite Austrian dinners of Wiener Schnitzel and poppyseed cake, which he praised her for. And then Hitler shoved his plate forward and sought to embarrass both Emil and his niece by talking about a poll on feminity in a women's magazine.

"Women are agreed," he said, "that a girl should never go on a first date with a boy without female friends along. Or hold his hand until the fourth or fifth date. Are you aware of that, Sunshine?"

"I have it in needlepoint," Henny said.

"Women agree that kissing, just kissing, nothing further, ought to be a sign that the couple will soon become engaged." He smiled. "Are you counting your marriages, Emil?"

Emil stared into his coffee.

"Women in Germany think that a girl who smokes cigarettes is a whore. Their opinion, not mine. And that a good wife will be pregnant within the first year of marriage."

"I find this fascinating," Geli said.

"And that's why I brought it up," Hitler said. "Who is the happiest of men?" he asked. "Again, I am reporting the consensus of the poll."

Angela thought aloud that it might be a haughty Austrian with Wiener Schnitzel in his stomach.

"Close," Hitler said. "Women consider a fat husband with four children the happiest of men."

"And the happiest of women?" Henny asked.

"Who can tell?" Emil said.

"Your meaning?" Geli asked him.

"I was just looking for something to say."

"And there was an interesting question," Hitler said. "A mother interferes when a father is beating their child. Women consider her . . . what? Angela?"

Without hesitation she said, "A bad wife."

"Oh, very enlightened," Geli said.

"Ah, but Angela is correct," Hitler said. "And seventy-five percent of the women in Germany agree."

With a scolding glare, Angela told her daughter, "You still have much to learn." And then she got up from her chair to gather their dishware.

Ostensibly to reward Emil for his hours of driving, Hitler took him to the Gasthof Hintereck for snifters of Asbach Uralt cognac. The girls washed and dried the dishes as Angela took the weight off her feet at the kitchen table and sipped from a jigger of schnapps. "Are you still seeing Emil?" she asked.

Henny elbowed Geli; Geli silently elbowed her back. Henny turned to Frau Raubal. "You can't tell, can you. Emil's as amorous as a mole."

"Were I just looking," Angela said, "I'd say it was *Adolf* who was in love with you."

The sixteen-year-old vigorously nodded. "The hurt feelings. The jealousy. The mooncalf look when she's near."

Angela smiled. "Women in Germany agree."

"My father's models are wild about him."

Geli sloshed water on her friend as she forcefully handed her a dish.

Angela got up from the table. "Don't be too choosy," she said. "There are more evergreens than cedars." And she headed for her room.

"She meant what by that?" Henny asked.

"Uncle Adolf's as rare as a cedar. It's true."

■ ■ ■

With financial assistance from Fritz Thyssen, Hitler found the cash to purchase as the new headquarters of the National Socialist German Workers Party the fenced and gardened, three-story Barlow Palace on fashionable Briennerstrasse. He would name it the "Brown House" in honor of his SA and would hire Professor Paul Ludwig Troost, one of Germany's grand old architects, to handle the interior and exterior renovations, so his afternoons were often given over to visits to Troost's atelier, where he would venerate the architect's skill and feel jubilant whenever consulted on fabrics, furniture, hardware, and masonry.

Geli sang through all the soprano parts in Wagner, she walked Prinz when her uncle couldn't, she shopped with Elsa Bruckmann, she practiced English with Helene Hanfstaengl, she took up photography under the guidance of Heinrich Hoffmann, she celebrated the final day of *Starkbierzeit* with Christof Fritsch because Emil Maurice had taken her uncle north to a quarry. But then on a Wednesday in May her uncle found her upstairs in the Bruckmann's town house reading Thomas Mann's *Reflections of an Unpolitical Man*, and he insisted she put away the book in order to join him and Fräulein Hoffmann on a cultural tour of the Pinakothek.

He avoided the halls of Italian and Spanish art as "far too religious" and concentrated on a highly opinionated survey of the paintings of Flanders and Germany. He forced them to stare at Lucas Cranach the Elder's *Lucretia* for five minutes, then hurried them to Albrecht Dürer's *Lucretia*. Executed just six years apart, each picture featured an unfortunate female nude with a Roman face and waist-length auburn hair who for some fabled reason was stabbing herself with a dagger. Which, he asked, was superior?

"Cranach's," Henny guessed.

Hitler frowned. "Why?"

Geli said, "She's prettier. She's complex."

"And Dürer's?"

"Well, it's so austere."

Hitler focused again on Dürer's version, found confirmation of his judgment, and told them, "You're both quite wrong. Albrecht Dürer's is far better. The coldness is intentional. Look at the equilibrium in the limbs. The rigor in the face. She's architecture. This," he said, "is the most virtuous nude in the history of art."

"Which is a *good* thing," Geli informed her friend.

Abruptly Hitler strode forward and they followed him to the French wing where he hunted out François Boucher's rococo and sentimental *Nude on a Sofa,* which featured a sweet, pink-rumped girl, front forward and seemingly falling off a fainting couch. Geli secretly thought she'd been having sex and was watching her lover leave, but her uncle saw the allusions differently. "She's your age," he told them. "Unspoiled, feminine, and naïve. A debutante of pedigree. Wistful. Unsuspecting. Do you see how disorderly the sheets and curtains are? She's been in emotional torment. Even now, with that far-off gaze, that finger delicately touching her chin, she's possibly dreaming of one day falling in love. This is the finest art: sensual yet chaste."

In a hushed voice Henny asked her friend, "Why are her knees so wide apart?," and Geli fought off a giggle.

"You two," Hitler said, but he smiled.

Then he took them to see the Pinakothek's great collection of Peter Paul Rubens, standing still for a long time in front of the hurl and tangle of anatomies in *The Fall of the Rebel Angels*, and again in front of the great wheel of two frothing horses, two seething men, two Cupids, and two fleshy and pliant Venetian nudes in *Rape of the Daughters of Leucippus*.

Off to the side, Geli watched her uncle's hand float just above the canvas, following the flow of beige highlight and bister shadow on the flanks of the virgins. "I have so much to learn," he said, and he turned. "Will you let me draw you?"

■ ■ ■

Wearing, as he'd requested, a red ski sweater, a plaid wool skirt, and green knee-high stockings, she went to his Thierschstrasse flat the next afternoon at four. A failure of nerve that he sought her that way, she thought, for she knew he wanted a Lucretia, or a nude on a sofa, and she wasn't confident she'd reject him.

Widow Reichert was making tea for him, and he went to get it after he formally greeted Geli in his pin-striped, three-piece suit. The furniture, she saw, had been moved so that his folding table and chair were centered in the flat, the headboard and bed were against the curtained front window, and a stool stood in the rear in a rhomboid of sunlight just to the right of the photograph of Hitler's crazily staring mother. She heard *Der Rosenkavalier* being introduced in English by an announcer from the BBC and she saw that her uncle had acquired an American Crosley radio. She wondered if he'd gotten it from Doktor Goebbels.

Wanting attention on the folding table was an old *Skizzenbuch*, sketchbook, with occasional architectural drawings in pencil and maybe twenty skillful, patient, and surprisingly poetic watercolors of the meadows, mountains, and lake lands of Bavaria. In one, orange skies hinted at a fabulous sunset that couldn't be seen because of the forbidding fortress wall of a forest in winter. Another seemed to be of the Chiemsee, with a gray wash for the sky and Delft-blue waters, and only far away on the scumbled sand of the beach were there a few hasty strokes of his brush to suggest children playing on the shore. She carefully turned to another page and found a pleasant, sunlit village, but again viewed from a great distance and from behind a black fence and skeletal trees that seemed almost to be the bars of a jail. There were fences in many pictures, screens of trees, yawning chasms that functioned like moats, a general sense of exile and awayness, and she felt sorry for him—for his melancholy, his loneliness, his isolation, his consciousness of separation from the community and the happiness of others.

And then Hitler walked in with his tea, silently took away his old sketchbook, got a fresh one from his bookcase, and sat at the folding table. Geli was given no instructions, so she positioned herself on the stool.

"Like this?"

"That's fine."

At first he sketched too small, stroking in millimeters like an amateur, as he did when he doodled on paper place mats whenever others were talking. She saw him try her face four times before he sat back. "Look at my hands," he said as he lifted them. "They're shaking."

She rotated away from him, her hands on her thighs, her heels on a rung of the stool. "Why not just try roughing in the whole form first. Loosely. Don't be so careful."

"Oh, I see; you are instructed in art?"

"We took drawing in high school."

"Soon you'll be sketching *me*," he said in an unfriendly way. "Were you any good?"

"Tight," she said. "Tentative. That's how I know."

She was facing a framed 1896 poster for *Simplicissimus*, the illustrated satirical weekly, with an issue price of ten pfennigs. The price was now sixty. A frolicking lady in fancy Victorian dress was haphazardly holding an artist's palette and completing the final *s* in *Simplicissimus* with the paintbrush tail of a naked, pitch-black devil who was fiercely hauling her elsewhere by the waist even while he was reading.

She asked, "Are you friends with *Simplicissimus* now?"

"I just liked the poster," he said. "Hold still." She heard him finish a sketch, jostle the folding table either left or right, and with a flourish draw a few bold lines. "It's going better," he said.

"I'm glad."

"Shall we be silent? I find the talk distracting."

"The choice is yours," she said.

Thirty minutes later Hitler asked, "Are you comfortable?"

"Stiff."

"We'll stop."

She got off the stool. "Will you let me see them?"

Quickly, Hitler shut the sketchbook. "Maybe eventually. I'm embarrassed now."

"Don't be."

"They're not as beautiful as you are. I haven't the hand yet. Won't you come tomorrow?"

She did. And a week later, too. She liked it. She was flattered by his attention, pleased to so easily have the access to him that others schemed for; and she felt that for the first time he was selfless and sincere and concentrating solely on her, and that she was being seen by him just as she was.

In their fourth session Hitler seemed to find sentences on the floor as he said, "We'll be doing different poses today."

"Which?"

He still wore a full three-piece suit, as if he would be called to a finance meeting in a wink, and his hands were sorting charcoals and pencils needlessly here and there on the folding table, but he seemed far more confident of his talent and his notions of art, and there was that hint of mastery that he found after his first introverted minutes with a crowd. "Without clothing," he said. The tone was imperative. "You can take everything off in the bathroom there."

She hesitated, and Hitler sat at his sketchbook as at a fine meal, his fast finally ended. The Crosley radio was playing the American jazz he hated, and she knew it was for her. Without looking up, he asked impatiently, "Have you understood me?"

She told him, "Yes," and the yes seemed to preclude any other options. With a thrilling fear she went into his bathroom and took off her clothes, wanting to be neither fast nor slow about it. She fleetingly thought about first hiding herself in a yellow bath towel there, but that would imply indecency, she'd seem a present to be unwrapped. And so she checked herself in the mirror and with a flutter in her stomach walked out, forcing her hands to shield nothing as she faced him frontally.

There was no lift of his eyebrows, no blush, no intimation that this was salacious. "We'll be doing life studies," her uncle said from his chair. She saw that he held *The History of Erotic Art* open on his knees like an instruction manual. "We'll start with you on the stool."

She got on it. She felt a faint crack in the cold, lacquered wood.

"Still facing me. Yes. And with your hands flat on the seat."

She glanced down. "There's no room."

"Widen your legs."

She joked, "Are your eyes good at this distance?"

"They are."

She sighed and did as she was told, watching his flash of interest as he glanced between her shaved thighs for just an instant before her hands and wrists hid her sex. She was surprised that she took pleasure in that.

"Aren't you beautiful," he said.

"I'm not really. I have flaws."

"Where?"

"Well, it's not like you can see them with just your eyes, Uncle Alf. You need a microscope."

"Your flaws shall stay a mystery then."

As he frenetically sketched in silence, she listened to the jazz that he called "hellish noise" and to the slash and silty shadings of his charcoals on paper. Then he flipped to a favorite page in his history of women in such positions, and ordered her into a change. After he finished sketching her fourth pose, Hitler got up and folded and flattened a freshly washed bedsheet on the cold, green linoleum, and

Geli lay on it in whichever pose he wanted, gifting her uncle with the globes of her breasts, the intricate petals of her vagina, the secret between her buttocks, giving up any shame or worry as she got used to his greed and seriousness and wonder. She felt breathless. She felt sexy. She felt self-conscious and vain and insolent, free and reckless and criminal; and when he'd finished his drawing she felt so confused she wanted to be kissed.

With yearning she stood naked in front of him as he smiled with satisfaction and shut his sketchbook. "I did good work today," he told her.

"Will you let me look?"

Hitler shook his head. "I found out that models never do. It's a tradition."

"Who *will* see them?"

"They're only for me."

A shrinking in him made her cautious. "You won't tell Emil about them?"

"Certainly not."

"You won't show them to your friends?"

"Shall I give you my word of honor?"

"I think that would give me solace, yes."

Hitler held up his right palm and swore, "You have my word of honor that no one shall see these drawings but me."

"Thank you," she said. She held his cheeks as she kissed his forehead, and she felt him stir as if he wanted to touch her. She withdrew to the bathroom for her clothes feeling victorious.

CHAPTER FOURTEEN
PRINZREGENTENPLATZ 16,
1929

In June Hitler attended a meeting in Berlin with Alfred Hugenberg, the Prussian head of the conservative Nationalist Party and the owner of many newspapers and movie theaters as well as Ufa, the major film studio in Germany. With upper-class arrogance Alfred Hugenberg told others that he'd found the fulminating Austrian ill-bred, ill-educated, and fortunate to have gotten as far as he had in politics, and he wrongly thought Hitler could be controlled and his oratory directed to right-wing programs if Hugenberg confidentially offered him financial assistance just as Fritz Thyssen had done.

With such gifts Hitler became a far wealthier man and was far less reluctant to have it publicized. Heinrich Hoffmann shot twenty-two rolls of film as Hitler took the Raubal family and a full statesman's entourage to the horse races at the Hamburg Derby, on a cruise to the island of Helgoland in the North Sea, and on a visit to a film location in Denmark where it was he who signed autographs, not the stars.

Acquisitions became more frequent: a London trench coat and a

Savile Row suit; an erotic painting by Adolf Ziegler, the so-called "master of pubic hair" that Hitler privately titled "Nude in Distress"; and a purebred Alsatian pup that Hitler named Muck and boarded at Haus Wachenfeld so Prinz would have company. He also shifted funds intended for the National Socialist headquarters in the Barlow Palace—wasn't *he*, after all, the Nazi party? wasn't the party *Hitler?*—and urged Professor Paul Ludwig Troost, who'd outfitted ocean liners, to design for his own use weighty mahogany furniture that was constructed at the Vereinigte Werkstätte in München. And then all that was left for Hitler to do was shop for and, in September, purchase a grand luxe, nine-room apartment in Bogenhausen at Prinzregentenplatz 16 just a few blocks east of the Isar River and the Angel of Peace monument and only a little more than a kilometer from the future headquarters in Schwabing.

At dinner in Obersalzberg that night he told Angela he could not afford to pay off the mortgages on Haus Wachenfeld and Prinzregentplatz *and* furnish his niece's rent as well, so he regretted to announce that if Geli wished to stay in Germany she would have to move in with him. They ought not fear scandal or impropriety, however; Frau Maria Reichert, his landlady on Thierschstrasse, would be joining the household as his *Mädche' für alles* and would be sharing quarters there with her old mother, Frau Dachs. And since he would be entertaining a great deal now, he'd also engaged the staff services of Georg and Anni Winter, a husband and wife, as *Haushofmeister* and *Koch*.

On November 5th, after her uncle was fully moved in, Emil met Geli's train from Berchtesgaden, but was so unhappy about his girlfriend sharing a flat with her uncle that he wouldn't even kiss her. Emil failed to mention her high-fashion Rodier jersey and new tweed skirt, he failed to offer to carry the canaries in their golden cage, and as he drove her from the Hauptbahnhof to Prinzregentenplatz 16, Emil told Geli stories of the wild old days when she was still a child in Austria and timid Adolf would give him twenty marks for any girl Emil found for him.

Geli changed the subject by pointing out that in Bogenhausen she'd be within strolling distance of Henny Hoffmann's house, that four-star restaurants lined the wide avenue, and that she'd be within the floodlit glow of the stunning Prinzregenten Theater, which, she told him pedantically, specialized in Wagnerian operas and was modeled on the Wagner festival theater in Bayreuth.

"Big deal," Emil said. And he parked the car.

The five-story Prinzregentenplatz building was sand-colored granite with white-and-teal-blue trim. Two bays of oriel windows bracketed wide balconies on the second, third, and fourth floors. A gray stone frieze of Wotan was just above the entryway; green and gray tiles lined the outside wall of the formal staircase to the upper floors where the gaslights had just been changed to electric.

Emil rang the door chimes next to two tall oak doors on the second floor and asked, "Are you impressed?"

"The Raubal flat in Wien was a lot like this."

Emil smiled. "With the rats and cockroaches?"

"*Many* pets," Geli said.

And then the *Haushofmeister* was there, welcoming Fräulein Raubal and his old friend Emil, and inviting them inside. Georg Winter was a fine-boned blond in his late twenties, a former orderly for General Franz Xaver Ritter von Epp, who was now a Reichstag deputy for the NSDAP. Winter was an officious, ironic, often wryly amused party member wearing a starched white shirt, a headwaiter's black suit and bow tie, and a red-and-black swastika pin. Quietly taking Geli's overcoat and the canaries in their cage, Winter went away, with Emil behind him, and she was left staring at the herringboned oak flooring in the foyer and hallways and the freshly painted white wainscotting on the walls.

Taking off a full, white apron, Anni Winter swatted flour dust from the front of a short black dress as she walked to Geli from a far-off room that must have been the kitchen. She curtsied to Hitler's niece but introduced herself familiarly as Anni, and within their first few minutes together she let Geli know that she'd been a lady-in-waiting to Countess Törring and was an internationally famous cook, and that she felt this job was beneath her but for the chance to be so near Herr Hitler. "And how old is the fräulein?" she asked.

"Twenty-one."

"I have twenty-four years," Anni Winter said. She seemed to think she'd established the governance of an older sister.

"We ought to get along well then," Geli said.

Anni just stared. "Those who have not grown up with servants can be annoying to work for. There's so much they have to be taught."

"I'm sure you'll be the most patient of teachers."

Anni smirked. She showed her a bay parlor of four oriel windows where a tasseled floor lamp was next to a wide round mahogany table on a vine-and-pomegranate William Morris carpet. Six soft-cushioned chairs surrounded the table. Their color, Anni said, was "claret." She called a grander sitting room "the library," though there were only nine short shelves of Hitler's familiar books, including six copies of Mein Kampf, The International Jew by Henry Ford, and the collected Westerns of Karl May. A high-priced portrait of Otto von Bismarck by München's own Franz von Lenbach had been hung just above the secretary. A Wilton carpet in a tulip-and-lily pattern was on the floor, and two floral sofas were on either side of a soft leather armchair that faced an arched casement door leading to the balcony. The white Bechstein piano she'd seen in the foyer at 41 Thierschstrasse was huddled like Geli's Aunt Paula against a far wall.

"Some of these things are Frau Reichert's?" she asked.

Anni Winter frostily said, "My husband and I have not been privy to the details of the arrangement." And then she added, "Anyway, everywhere in Germany great fortunes have been lost."

The other four-windowed bay parlor was called "the breakfast room," though Frau Reichert and her mother often played cards or worked at puzzles there in the afternoon, Anni said, and, "Herr Winter may be found here with the shades drawn if he is suffering from one of his sick headaches."

"Oh, that malingerer," Geli said.

"Are you being funny?" Anni asked.

"I was trying to be."

Anni grimaced a smile. The Prinzregentenstrasse wing held a laundry room, a bathroom as plain as a plumbing shop, and the Reichert/Dachs quarters where the deaf old mother lost track of time. Anni then took her to the quieter Grillparzerstrasse wing and the formal dining room with its gleaming mahogany table and seating for eight on chairs covered with a jay-in-the-garden fabric. In the hallway Geli heard Emil's hearty laughter in the kitchen, but Anni walked beyond it and a full bathroom of white marble that she said Geli would be sharing with her uncle, and "he insists it stay immaculate."

"Which means?"

"Herr Hitler scents his bathwater with essence of pine. You may also, if you wish. His towels are brown; yours are white. His personal soap is Mouson-Ente; you are to use another brand. Hide your lotions and toothbrush and whatnot. Do not hang in here hose or what you hand-wash. Do not touch his things. Dry the faucets and sink and floor after use. Do not fill the air with perfumes, for he sneezes. I forget the rest, but he'll tell you."

"It goes without saying," Geli said.

Her bedroom was just across the hall from the bathroom. Soft green trellis wallpaper was on the walls, and the room held the furniture of a four-poster bed, a wardrobe, a dresser, and a desk that was white but for its hand-painted wisteria trimming.

"It's beautiful," Geli said.

Anni nodded. "Yes, it is."

She touched a canary-yellow floor lamp and matching desk lamp, a new, blue gramophone, and a framed and fairly good watercolor of a Belgian landscape that her uncle had painted in the Great War.

"Aren't you fortunate," Anni said.

"Oh yes," Geli said. "Uncle's awfully nice to me."

Anni went out to the hallway and into Hitler's office. Watercolors from the Thierschstrasse flat were on the walls as well as the framed *Simplicissimus* poster and a large Heinrich Hoffmann photograph of a haughty Hitler with his head tilted high like Il Duce, finishing a spellbinding speech in his Sturmabteilung uniform. Otherwise it might have been the office of a city government functionary: just a cabinet, an old reading chair, a black rotary telephone and lamp on the left side of the desk, fountain pens and ink blotter in the middle, a dictionary and an oval, silver-framed portrait of his mother on the right. She opened the drawers and found the desk empty. "And here the tour ends," Anni said.

"His bedroom's next door?" Geli asked.

"Naturally. One has to sleep." She did not show Geli the room. She said, "I have kaiser rolls in the oven," and went out to the kitchen.

Emil and Georg were sitting there, drinking Franziskaners, and Geli saw that the interior windows overlooked a pleasant green garden of shrubs and ivied trees. "And so," Emil asked, "do you love it here?"

"I do."

"Will you be happy, happy, happy?"

"Are you drunk?"

Georg Winter winked.

Emil fell forward onto the kitchen table and used it to heave himself up. "I have to go get your luggage," he said. "And then I get my leader."

Winter told Geli, "We're having a dinner in your honor tonight."

■ ■ ■

She learned that she and Hitler were hosting Rudolf and Ilse Hess, Heinrich Hoffmann and his daughter, and Baldur von Schirach, the founder of the National Socialist German Students' Alliance, who was the first to arrive for dinner. Geli was wearing a new Louis-boulanger white chiffon gown printed with orange flowers and green leaves; Schirach was wearing a black tuxedo and was holding a flute of the Taittinger champagne he'd brought. Cologne eddied from him as if he were its source.

Schirach was a tall, soft-bodied man with ice-blue eyes whose fine Nordic face seemed meant to be photographed. Twenty-two years old, he was the son of a Weimar theater director who'd died the year of his birth, so he'd been raised solely by his American mother, whose ancestors included two signers of the Declaration of Independence. He told Geli he was now studying German philology, folklore, and art history in München while assisting Herr Doktor Ernst Hanfstaengl—Baldur had been forbidden the use of the nickname Putzi—as the party's foreign press secretary. First looking around the room in caution, he confessed in English, "We actually don't get along very well." And he hesitated. "Ernst says you speak our mother tongue?"

In English she said, "Speak it I can some. A little. I need . . . praxis."

"Practice," Schirach corrected, then giggled in a high voice as he laid his free hand gently on her forearm and said in German, "Sorry to torture you, darling. The faces you make hunting for words!"

She found Schirach friendly and suave and stunningly good looking, but wide-hipped, pudgy, effeminate, and insolent in that Nazi way she associated with Göring. He told her that he'd first met her uncle in 1925, just after Hitler's release from Landsberg am Lech, and that he was party member number 17,251. It was he, Schirach said, who called for the storming of the universities by Nazi youth, and the party was now getting 38 percent of the votes there. "We'll have all of them in a few more years. With the stock-market crash in America, the Continent's economies will also be failing soon. And history tells us that our party thrives when financial conditions are at their poorest. Good heavens, are the people going to go to the Communists? They're so *dreary*."

She heard the chimes and watched Winter let in and loudly announce, "Herr and Frau Hess, and Herr Hoffmann and his daughter, Henrietta." And just then Hitler emerged in his tuxedo from the Grillparzerstrasse wing and forced his guests to tour his new apartment.

She went with them until she noticed Henny hanging back from the group. She ducked into the dining room and Henny joined her there. In a hushed voice she asked, "Don't you think he's amazing?"

Geli smiled. "My uncle?"

"Herr Baldur von Schirach! Don't you think he's so handsome you can hardly breathe?"

"It's the cologne," Geli said.

"Who's he intended for?"

"You, I think."

She brightened. "Are you sure?"

Geli found Hitler affectionately watching her from the hallway, a faintly worried smile rocking underneath his little mustache, his shining stare full of sentiment and imagination. She'd become his resting place, his lost civilization. "Yes," she said, "I'm sure."

■ ■ ■

Uncharacteristically silent throughout dinner, Hitler slouched in his head-of-the-table chair and took joy in his company, fondly gazing at Geli as she talked to Rudolf and Ilse, and lightly touching her hand when he wanted the butter or salt. With formality he finally said, "Tell me, Heinrich. How did you find the lamb?"

Hoffmann joked, "I just moved the potatoes and there it was. Ha, *ha*!" And then Hoffmann fell into an off-color story that was eventually so carefully sanitized for Hitler's sake that all that was left of it was innuendo.

Then Baldur von Schirach took up the spirit of fun by telling a story Ernst Hanfstaengl had told him about an old *Washington Post* article in which a journalist had written that President Woodrow Wilson had taken his fiancée, Mrs. Edith Galt, to the theater, and was so intent on "entertaining" her that he'd scarcely watched the play. Well, the journalist was horrifed the next morning to find there'd been a typesetting mistake in the paper so that it seemed he'd written that the president spent most of his time "entering" Mrs. Galt.

Only Schirach himself laughed when he finished. Confused faces were focused on him. Coldly glaring, Hitler turned to his niece. "Won't you help us forget this violation of etiquette with a song?"

"I'm really so sorry," Schirach said.

To rescue him, Geli stood and announced, as Schirach mouthed a thank-you, that she'd sing Mozart's "Welche Wonne, welche Lust."

What bliss, what delight. And she sang it so prettily and with such humor that there were chortles and titters until the conclusion, when the four men jumped up and wildly applauded. Tears of joy filled her uncle's eyes as he leaned forward to say into her ear as she sat down, "*This* is why you are here!"

■ ■ ■

There would be many more dinner parties, Hitler told his niece at breakfast, and many nights at the opera, so he wanted Geli to fill her closet with fine clothes.

"Oh, all right," she sighed, and at noon she took the green trolley to Odeonsplatz and bought a hair waver, two pairs of silk stockings, patent leather heels by Ferragamo, a yellow satin housecoat with pajama trousers, a Vionnet tweed coat cuffed and bordered in nutria, a Lanvin evening gown in black faille and strass, and a Lanvin silver coat with a white fox collar. She ordered them sent to the flat. And as she was walking to the trolley she saw Heinrich Hoffman wave to her from his new Mercedes-Benz and roll down his side window. Would she like a lift?

When she got in, he said, "I just heard a good one. What is an Aryan's Nordic ideal?"

"Tell me."

"To be thin like Göring, tall like Goebbels, and blond like Hitler. Ha, *ha*! Don't you think that's good?"

"Aren't you afraid of them hearing?"

"I'm a *jester*!" he said. And then he started to worry. "Don't tell, all right?"

"I won't."

Heading north on Ludwigstrasse, he said, "I have to have a nap. Too much champagne." He thanked her for the night before and said he'd never seen the leader look happier. She was the cause of that. All his friends were grateful.

"Well, he's been so generous to me. If I can give him pleasure, maybe it's more of a fair exchange."

"Ho, ho," Hoffmann said. "You sound like Eva."

"Eva?"

Hoffmann hit his forehead with his fist, as if he found himself a fool, and he smiled goofily as he said, "I have a big mouth."

"Who's Eva?" she asked.

Traffic was halted as horses hauled a freight wagon into Galeriestrasse. Hoffmann sighed and told Geli he'd hired a featherbrain named Eva Braun as a clerk and photographer's model for his Schellingstrasse studio. She was seventeen like Henrietta, and blonde, with a chocolate-box type of prettiness, and she was just out of a convent high school where she'd not done well. One late afternoon in the October just past she was up on a ladder, filing papers in a high cupboard, when Hoffmann walked into the studio with Hitler, and Hoffmann noticed that the leader was fancying Eva's athletic calves. Eva later confessed that she'd had no idea who the man in the felt hat and London overcoat was, for he had introduced himself as Herr Wolf.

"You can see how frivolous she is," Hoffmann said. "She won't even look at my photos. To her he was just an old gentleman with a funny little mustache. *Old*, at forty. And she thought he was staring because the hem of her skirt was uneven."

"Men worry a lot about tailoring," Geli said.

Hoffmann forced his car into a lane between a green trolley and a milk truck, and headed toward the Englischer Garten. Eva, he said, had been sent out for Weisswurst and Thüringer and Augustiner beer. They all ate and drank together, and just before she'd gone home to her father and mother, Hoffmann had told Eva that she'd been chatting with Adolf Hitler—whose politics her father, a schoolteacher, hated. She did not get along with her *Vati*, so she was thrilled. Within a few days Hitler visited Eva in the studio, with a flower assortment, a box of Most pralines, a signed photograph of himself, and an invitation to join him at an opera matinee.

"Which opera?"

"She didn't say."

"She's not a connoisseur?"

"Ha! Oh, Geli, you have no idea what a funny idea that is." The photographer guffawed a further frantic set of *ha*s, and headed east on Prinzregentenstrasse.

"She's superficial," Geli said.

"Well, for example, I hinted at Hitler's fondness for full-figured girls and found her stuffing handkerchiefs in her brassiere. I then told her I felt a sneeze coming on. Ha, *ha*!"

Geli hoped not to seem to be prying. "They're seeing each other often?"

"Occasionally, not often. In the afternoons." A yen of his own was in his face. *Widower's eyes*, she thought. "Evenings," Hoffmann said, "are for you."

"Is he trying to keep it secret?"

"Well, how to say it? The leader puts his things in many different boxes. We'll never see half of them." Hoffmann turned to her. "Are you offended?"

Geli shrugged and gazed out the passenger window. "Why should I be?" They rode in silence for a while, and she added, "It's not like he's my husband."

■ ■ ■

She stayed in the flat for no more than five minutes. She heard Maria Reichert vacuuming in the parlor and watched the canaries sidestep and spin on the perches, then she got up and took a trolley back to Schwabing.

She had no idea what she intended. She walked into the photography studio on Schellingstrasse and was surprised to find Eva Braun right in front of her, sorting packets of film negatives at a counter. She was a petite Nordic blond, five inches shorter than Geli. With a gymnast's body. With a heart-shaped face and a candy mouth and the Delft-blue eyes of his mother. She seemed not to recognize who Geli was. And Geli realized she'd gotten what she wanted.

"Nazi headquarters?" Geli asked.

Eva stood on her tiptoes to point across the street. "There."

■ ■ ■

She'd nightmared herself into wakefulness and was reading *Der Steppenwolf* in her yellow pajamas when she felt a mood in the room and was surprised to see her uncle just inside the door, his homburg in his hand, his gray wool suit coat still tightly buttoned.

"You're home," she said. "Where were you?"

"Talking," he said. "Talking, talking." He shied his stare from hers as he said, "It's half three."

"I'll be quiet."

His hand lifted his forelock and petted it flat. "It's not that. I'll have trouble sleeping. I finished a whole pot of green tea."

She could tell he was trying to say something else, but she was mystified as to what it could be.

Then he asked, "Would you please go wake Frau Reichert for me?"

"At this hour?"

"She'll know what to do."

She got up from her bed and tied on her housecoat. "I'll do it."

"Are those new?" he asked.

"The pajamas? I got them today."

"Thanks to me," he needlessly said. "They're beautiful."

"Thank you for everything."

Hitler hesitated, introverted and ill at ease in the terra nova of his niece. And then, as sharp as the snap of a maître d's fingers, he said, "Very good," and withdrew to his bedroom, saying as an afterthought, "Take off the housecoat."

She did that and followed him, self-consciously feeling the sway of her breasts under the yellow pajama top. She heard him say, "Stay out there for a minute," and she stood in the hallway, her hands finding no place to settle, her feet getting cold on the herringboned oak. She stepped onto the carpet runner. She heard hangers ringing in his closet; she heard drawers slide and shut with a *tock*.

"Enter, Princess," he finally said.

Her uncle's swank bedroom was fashioned after his favorite suite in the first-class Hotel Kaiserhof in Berlin, with furniture of mahogany, fixtures of gold, red suede walls, and a plush golden quilt on a high and wide feather bed. Hanging below one brass wall sconce to the bed's right was a fuzzy photograph of his mother, and twinning it on the left was a haunting painting by Franz von Stuck called *Die Sünde* (Sin). Hitler was hunched as if ill in a fire-red wingback chair, just under Adolf Ziegler's frank nude, his hands folded at his crotch, facing the bed in a white, collared nightshirt.

"What do I do?" Geli asked.

Whining it, he said, "Won't you fill my water glass for me?"

She saw a full pitcher and water glass on one nightstand and went to it.

"Say what you're doing," he said.

Would Eva do this? Would his actresses? She said, "Here's your water, Uncle Alf."

"Yes," he said, "in case I get thirsty."

She was about to turn until he said, "Don't turn."

"And now what?"

"Window," he said, as if she were slow.

"Shall I open a window for you?"

"Yes," he said, from his own storybook. "The air gets so stale."

She quelled a host of misgivings as she felt him watching the cinema of her motherly movements. She raised the sash of a far window just an inch, then another inch, and another.

"Quit."

She found half his face in a mirror—so sincere and guileless and fascinated, like a high school boy's first reverent glimpse of the swellings beneath a girl's blouse—and she felt only affection for him. She shifted to the next step by saying, "Oh, you're so tired, aren't you, Uncle Alf."

"Yes," he said in a child's voice. "I'm sleepy."

She waited.

Quietly, he said, "And you turn down the covers."

Was this what Klara did for him? She tried, "Shall I turn down the covers for you, Adi?"

"Yes, please," he said in the child's voice. "I'm so sleepy."

She walked to the head of the bed, took hold of the golden quilt, blanket, and sheet, and folded a triangle back from his fat white pillow.

Whining again, he said, "Don't do it so quickly."

"Again?"

"Again."

Geli stood tall, stooped over, held the bedding in her hands, and folded a bigger triangle back.

"Stay that way," he said.

Would a wife do this? Would a girlfriend? Would nurses, maids, secretaries do this for men they were fond of? And yes, she decided, they would, they did, hundreds and hundreds of times. She felt the travel of his interest as she held there, as she posed with her rump high, the yellow satin pajama trousers filmy against her buttocks, her elbows planted on the mattress to ease the strain of her spine.

"Aren't you lovely," he said. "Aren't you lovely." And then Hitler sighed and said, "You can go now."

She kept her eyes on the floor as she walked out, and at the door she said, "Sleep well."

"I shall, I think. Thank you." Calm and unembarrassed; as if she'd handed him a pill.

■ ■ ■

She was digging a soft-boiled egg from its shell with a teaspoon the next morning when he strolled into the breakfast room at eleven, fully rested and buoyant. Maria Reichert shuffled in with a tray of hot cocoa, hard rolls, and sticks of chocolate on a plate, and they talked like old friends about the cold weather, higher grocery prices, the difficulties a cousin of hers was having at his factory job.

"Well, we all have to pay our keep, don't we," he said.

"We do," Frau Reichert said. "If it's free it's not worth having." And she left.

"Was that meant for me?" Geli asked.

Hitler seemed honestly startled. "We were just making conversation."

She felt guilty. She could not face him. She held her coffee cup with both hands. "Will you have me do that again?"

She ought to have known he'd be ready, and would trivialize it. "Our little game?" he asked. "Our child's play?"

"That."

Hitler softly stroked her hair and said, "We shall do only what gives you pleasure, Princess."

"Others have done it?"

"Yes." He got a hard roll from a straw basket and sawed it without anger with his knife. "Don't feel in any way compelled—"

"I just wanted to know," Geli said.

■ ■ ■

What Makes Him Unhappy:

Emil, lately. My talking on the telephone. Warm rooms. Radiator heat. Empty apartment. Questions. Contradictions. Any foreign language. Horseback riding. Office work. Modern art and music. Yawns. Other men and me. Any touching. Any mention of cancer. Wetness on floor or sink. "Spicy" foods.

What Makes Him Happy:

My asking permission. Any dessert. Me here when he comes home or calls. "I find you very handsome." Head and neck massages (Wagner playing). With him at meals, even if I don't eat. Watching me shave my legs. Unending compliments. Orange marmalade on zwieback. "Noticeable" females, far younger or far older. These poses: "Bathing," "The Nap," "Venus Awakening." My hair longer than it is now. My smile.

■ ■ ■

In December she read a news article about the novelist Thomas Mann, who lived along the Isar just a short stroll from them. The Swedish Academy had awarded him the Nobel Prize for literature and afterward he'd been honored as München's favorite son with a banquet at city hall. She mentioned it to her uncle at breakfast, and without hesitation Hitler told her, "*My Struggle* is now outselling both *Buddenbrooks* and *The Magic Mountain*."

"Still, he's a great writer."

Suddenly reddening, and seeming to dare her to try another word, he said, "And he's an enemy of the party!"

She was quiet.

■ ■ ■

Just before Christmas Geli's gramophone was loudly playing Mozart's *Die Zauberflöte* and she was singing along with the aria "Der Hölle Rachen" as she watched snow strike her windows. And then she heard Christof Fritsch shout her name from the foyer. She turned off the gramophone and tilted out into the hallway. She couldn't see him, so he must have been in a parlor. She called out, "Who let you in?"

"I found the door open. Are the servants gone?"

She calculated: The Winters were off for the day, Maria was at the Viktualien Markt, and old Dachs was deaf. "Wait!" she said, and went into her room for a sweater as she called out, "I am forbidden male visitors here; I told you." Then she heard the jingle of his galoshes on the floor. She hurriedly fussed in her room, hiding underthings, and then he was large in the doorway, his beret in his hand, his blond hair in havoc, his black mackintosh flaked with snow.

"I have written you three letters and torn them all up," he said. "I need to say it face-to-face."

"Say what?"

Worn out, Christof slid down the wall and sat heavily in a university way, his ankle-high gutta-percha galoshes angled far out and bleeding water onto the fine woolen rug. When he unfastened his mackintosh she smelled India rubber, tobacco smoke, and the fading fragrance of the outdoors. She settled onto the sofa and hunched forward, her forearms crossed on her knees. Waiting.

"I haven't seen you much," he said.

"We haven't been in the same places."

"Are you confined here?"

"I go out. With my uncle."

"And not with Emil?"

"Were your letters about this?"

Christof sighed. "Earlier, before I started at the university, I thought politics was all clamor and vulgarity. The fanaticism of parties seemed so alien to the purity and simplicity of the intellectual life. This is what I was writing you last night. With the hard times in Germany, though, and the popularity of Communism, I have forced myself to look again at the strongest alternative, National Socialism. And what did I find? Energy and vitality and attractiveness to the young, Germany's future. And so two nights ago I went to hear your uncle speak. Were you there?"

She shook her head no. "I generally don't go."

"Why?"

She shrugged. "It's boring."

"Oh, but it's not! It's thrilling!"

"Are you carrying cigarettes?" she asked.

Christof got a packet and shook a cigarette out. She took it, hunted for a match, and lit it. She lifted a window as high as she could, letting fresh air and flurries of snow sail in, then sat again on the sofa, folding her legs. "Tell," she said.

"There were five thousand students there, and many respected professors on the stage, and Hitler was not a zealot, as I'd heard. The Jews were hardly mentioned. Rather, he talked in measured tones about social justice and harmony and an idealistic new world, one that sought freedom and work and bread for the masses while rejecting materialism and selfishness and class distinctions. Unlike other politicians, he appealed directly to the young, offering us a chance to join in his crusade for the good and glory of Germany if we would only follow him without hesitation. By the end, we were all elated. We felt that if he could excite us so much with just a speech, then maybe our fatherland could be saved if he was our leader. A friend of mine, a Jew, was there, and he surprised me by saying that if it weren't for the party's anti-Semitism he'd be joining them himself."

"And so you joined the party," she said flatly. "And you needed to tell me that, face-to-face."

"Aren't you pleased?"

She heard the door chimes. She cursed.

"Who is it?" Christof asked.

"I have no idea." She stood up and leaned out the open window to see Prinzregentenplatz. Hitler's Mercedes was there, gray smoke swirling from its exhaust pipe, and her uncle was huddled in the front seat, poring over a newspaper. "Oh no." She heard the foyer door open.

"Hallo!" Emil called.

As she went to the hallway, she touched a hand to Christof's mouth to silence him. "Emil!" she said. He was wearing jackboots, a gray soldier's coat, and a storm trooper's stocking cap that was pulled so low it folded out his ears. His hands were red with cold and he blew into them as he asked, "Would you like to join your uncle at the Osteria?"

"Oh, I think not, thank you," she said.

His face seemed indifferent to her answer. Then he frowned. "Are you smoking, Geli?"

She saw that she was holding the cigarette between the middle fingers of her right hand just as Doktor Goebbels did.

"Who's there with you?" Emil asked.

And then Christof was hulking in the doorway. "An old friend," he innocently said.

Emil sneered and calmly called Geli "*Meine Dirne*," a term that could be as inoffensive as "my lass" but could also mean "whore."

"We were just talking," she said.

"Well, that's how it always starts, doesn't it," Emil said. Walking forward, he seemed to find vicious joy in Christof's frail lifting of his hands, as if helplessness would pacify him.

Geli firmly said, "Don't, Emil."

"I joined the party," Christof weakly said. "We're comrades."

Emil smashed him hard in the nose and blood flew against the soft-green trellis wallpaper. Christof groaned and held his face with his hands as he knelt on the floor. Geli screamed and crouched over Christof as Emil said, "Oh, you think it's over so soon?" and he kneed him in the mouth. Christof cried out and folded over, blood and saliva drooling from him as he found a lost tooth on his tongue.

Tears streaming down her face, Geli held on to Emil's hands and yelled for him to quit.

Emil seemed to hear nothing. "So you think you can have my girl-friend, and in my leader's house?" With a strength greater than his middleweight size, Emil grabbed hold of Christof's mackintosh and lifted him to his feet before hurtling him into the doorjamb, shivering the room, then hauling him out. And then Emil manhandled him down the hallway to the foyer, yelling his hatred for intellectuals and sissies, his hands flashing out into Christof's face whenever he saw a free shot, his postwar years with the Ehrhardt Naval Brigade remembered as he threw Christof into the walls and the shaking doors of the library.

Christof fell and Emil kicked at him; then Emil wildly swung his leg again and his foot hit the wall. Even with his jackboots on, Emil hurt his toes, and he tried to walk off the pain as Christof lay in the foyer oozing blood.

And then Hitler was there with a pistol in his hand, shouting, "We *cannot* have this!"

Emil was startled, his eyes on the handgun. "Are you talking to *me?*"

"Who else? You have made my niece *cry!*"

"She was—" he started, but Hitler swatted Emil's head with his free hand, as if he were just a boy, and Emil fell miserably into a sit as Hitler railed at him for subjecting his home and his niece to such violence.

Geli screamed, "I hate you, Emil! I hate you!" And then she got a wet hand towel to hold to Christof's face.

While Emil pitied himself, Hitler went on and on, not letting up, lifting up Emil's chin with his handgun so he could shout that Emil's actions were shameful, unforgivable, an outrage against decency.

Woozily Christof got to all fours, then his feet, saying into the reddening towel, "I have to get to a doctor."

Hitler forced Emil to help Christof up, then he glanced at his niece and said, "My deepest regrets, Princess. This won't happen again."

At first she'd thought he'd be angry with her, then she saw how this suited him. Emil would be fired from his job, she knew, and Christof was no fool. She was Hitler's alone now.

Christof staggered out, hanging on to Emil's shoulder, his galoshes squeaking on the flooring.

Geli asked, "Was the pistol in your car?"

Hilter looked at the Walther in his hand. "I heard you screaming."

"Christof just came to say he'd joined the party."

With forlorn eyes her uncle glimmered a smile and said, "We needn't talk about it," as if he had much to forgive. And then he was gone and there was nothing for Geli to do but sponge the blood from the floor and the walls.

An American businessman named Owen Young chaired an international commission that sought to give Germany economic relief by amending many punitive conditions of the Treaty of Versailles. Agreeing with Gustav Stresemann, Germany's foreign minister, the commission established a ceiling of 121 billion reichsmarks in war reparations, to be paid off in fifty-nine yearly installments that would finally end in 1989. Taxes on industrial obligations, and other duties, were abolished. Arbitration was to take the place of sanctions. And the Allies would give up their occupation of the Rhineland four and a half years ahead of schedule.

All the changes only outraged the enemies of the Weimar Republic, who thought the original treaty was grossly unjust and ought to be wholly rejected rather than modified. Communists and other parties on the left joined the Stahlheim (the army veterans' party), Alfred Hugenberg's Nationalists, the Pan-German Association, the Resistance to Oppression Movement, and the National Socialist

Democratic Workers Party in urging that the agreement be voted
down in a December 1929 plebiscite.

And with no one to match him for stirring oratory, Adolf Hitler
became the featured speaker at some enormous rallies—seven thousand heard him at the Zirkus Krone—where the majority of his
audience otherwise felt no affinity for his politics. Hitler took
advantage of the opportunity to widen his popularity by saying
nothing about the Jews, having the inflammatory swastika taken off
rally posters, and concentrating on the noxious elements of the Versailles Treaty. He shouted that Germany was not guilty for causing
the war, it was only guilty of having lost it by tolerating the treachery of politicians; that while Germany was being disarmed and
shackled, the countries around it, preaching peace, were construct-
ing great armies and navies; that Germany was in no want of food
and raw goods and fuel, except for that which was being stolen from
it. "Shall we consent to pay out eighty marks per second for the next
sixty years? Shall we be slaves for three generations? Shall we continue to say yes to our oppressors? I say no!"

The Reichstag finally adopted the Young Plan anyway, but for
Hitler it was a victory, for party membership increased by forty thousand, Alfred Hugenberg's chain of newspapers had portrayed Hitler
as an ultrapatriot, and he was more than ever *salonfähig*, or worthy of
acceptance in upper-class society. Prince August Wilhelm of Prussia,
the kaiser's son, publicly joined the party in 1930 and induced
Prince Philip von Hessen, a grandson of Queen Victoria, to join the
Nazis as well.

Hitler knew that, with the worldwide depression, American cred-
itors were calling in their loans on the Continent, farms were being
foreclosed, factories were shutting down, three million in Germany
were already unemployed, and onerous taxes were being attached to
income, property, inheritances, and every commodity but beer. All
the party needed, he decided, was a major new offensive in public
relations founded on a martyr for the National Socialist cause. And
Horst Wessel, he thought, would do.

Horst Wessel was the twenty-two-year-old son of an Evangelical pastor who had rejected his father's advice and had joined the Sturmabteilung in order to fight the Communists in the streets. *Der Angriff* had published Wessel's sentimental poem "Raise High the Flag," which he'd written to commemorate those friends of his who'd been "shot dead by the Red Front and Reaction," and the party had liked it so much that Wessel set it to a tune from an old Austrian cabaret song, but "hotted up," as he put it, to fit marching time.

Wessel had fallen in love with a prostitute named Erna and had moved in with her, but they fought loudly and often, and their landlady hired Communists who were friends of Erna to harry them out of the flat. Since Wessel was famous for his viciousness in the streets, one of the Red Front militants took advantage of their meeting to shoot him in the mouth, shouting, "You know what that's for!" Three weeks later, Horst Wessel died.

With his genius for propaganda, Doktor Goebbels reported the shooting in *Der Angriff* and the *Völkischer Beobachter* so that it seemed a political assassination, and he organized a spectacular funeral at the Sportpalast in late February 1930, where he sonorously recited, "Horst is one who, leaving home and mother, lived with gentle concern among those who scorned and spit on him. Out there, in a tenement attic, in a proletarian section of Berlin, he proceeded to build his youthful, modest, caring life among depraved subhumans. There can be no doubt, he was a Socialist Christ! One who appealed to others through his generous deeds. His spirit has risen in order to live in all of us now. He is marching within our ranks. Even now he raises his weary hand and beckons us into the shimmering distance, shouting, 'Forward over the graves! At the end of the road lies Germany!'"

Then six great choirs joined in on what was now called the "Horst Wessel Lied," singing, "The banners flutter, the drums roll, the fifes rejoice, and from millions of throats resounds the hymn of the German revolution, 'Raise high the flag!'"

Doktor Goebbels had wanted Hitler there to deliver the oration and to make the occasion more politically important, but Hitler was afraid that Communists would murder him and didn't want to say so; instead he claimed he was ill, or busy, and, with the shilly-

shallying he was not yet famous for, he went into hiding for a fortnight with Geli.

She was his escape, his torpor, his surrender to the vacillation and
passivity that were increasingly part of his nature. With a Rolleiflex
he'd given her, she took snapshots of him in his Tyrolean costume
sitting on a snowbank in Obersalzberg, of him throwing sticks in the
woods to his Alsatians Prinz and Muck, of him on a wood-runnered
sled in a sweatered suit, his trouser cuffs tucked inside woolen stockings. And in each one he was smiling.

After their hikes they listened to the radio programs from
München in the Winter Garden while Angela heated saltwater for
his footbath. When she walked out to them from the kitchen, she'd
often see Geli kneeling on the floor, taking off his stockings and
folding his woolen trouser cuffs to his white, hairless calves. Angela
put down the steaming basin and her half-brother whimpered with
counterfeit pain as he immersed his feet, saying, "Oh, why do the
women in my family torment me so?"

"Because you crave it," Geli said and got up.

Hitler luxuriated, oozing contentment and shutting his eyes. "It's
true, it's true. I like it so much. I'm so happy. So, so happy."

In March, at twilight, Hitler stood at parade rest in the cold
winds of the north terrace, filling his chest with ion-rich air and
staring out at the majestic Alps and a fleet of clouds trundling in.
Geli went out to him in a cardigan, her flying skirt as tight as paint
against her legs. She put her arm around his waist, and he held out a
gloved finger to the villages below, giving each its name, as if he
were Adam. "Bischofswiesen is farthest west. Then Berchtesgaden.
Maria Gern. Obersalzberg. Marktschellenberg. And far behind it
Salzburg. East is Oberau. Hallein. Klaushöhe. Buchenhöhe."

"I love it here," she said, and she shamefully realized she was urging him to say he loved *her* here.

Instead he tried out a line of just imagined poetry. "And high
above the world," he quoted, "on the cold fastness of the Kehlstein,
I feed the needy flames of my hate."

Hurt and discouraged, Geli said, "I have to go in now."

There were midnights in Obersalzberg when she would hear his shoes in the hallway and see him hesitantly tip his head just inside her bedroom door to see if she was still awake. She'd invite him in, and often he would simply plant a swift kiss on her forehead and wish her a *Schlaf gut,* "Sleep well," but there were also other times when he'd sit against her blanketed calves and in a fatherly and official way consult with her about what she'd done that day, what she wished to do in the morning, whether she had all she needed. Then he'd softly pat her knee and get up, perfectly comfortable with just that.

She heard him arguing for an hour on the telephone in the Winter Garden one night, and then he walked into her room with a glass of Riesling. And he stood over her as he said, "There are those in the party who dislike my involvement with you. Who wish you'd just go back to Austria."

"And?"

Holding a hand over his eyes, he confessed, "I feel such love for you, Princess! I feel I could marry you!"

"Why is that so painful to say?"

Hitler turned to the frosted window and found his own face in a high, night-shaded pane. "I have to stay single," he grimly said, "so I can give myself fully to Germany. Without diminution. And yet I feel I have to watch over you, and exert a fatherly influence on your circle of friends until such time as you find the right man."

"Wherever I go, there's you there."

He smiled. "I shall choose to take that as a compliment."

She wasn't sure if it was or wasn't. She got up against the pillows and hugged her knees.

"What others see as compulsion on my part is simply prudence," he said. "I have such fears that you'll fall into the hands of someone unsuitable."

"Emil, for instance."

"An Old Combatant, but a misalliance," he said, and finished his wine. "Are you growing impatient?"

She nodded.

"Oh, how I wish," he said, and his hand found her hair, flowed down her face, and fell flat and heavily onto her right breast. She inhaled as if she'd jumped into shockingly cold water, and his hand lifted off. "Sleep well," he said, and walked out.

■ ■ ■

She was going alone to Wien in April in order to renew her visa, so her mother and her uncle took her to the railway station in Berchtesgaden. Geli would handle the government paperwork that afternoon, stay the night with old high school friends, and get back the next day, but Hitler seemed to fantasize that she was going to the Congo, and he was uncertain if he was angry or worried or full of grief in his affliction. Hitler had forfeited his own Austrian citizenship and was not yet a German national, so he was stateless and could not join her, and yet that was all he wanted then, and as Geli got ready to board her first-class railway car, he seemed to want to hug her good-bye just as Angela did. But he held back and instead stropped his hand hard and loud with his riding whip, shaking out the sting as he stalked away.

Angela asked, "Won't you consider becoming Adolf's fiancée?"

She flushed red and lied, "I haven't thought about it."

"Well, he has, you can tell. He's lovesick. Men just don't know it as soon as we do."

■ ■ ■

Often Geli felt she was in love with him, too. Adolf Vogl's wife had had a baby boy, and Geli was the first to visit them in the hospital. She took along a *Schwatzei*, or gossip egg, and touched it to the newborn's mouth so he'd learn to talk early. "My uncle says unless a girl has a child, she'll get hysterical or ill. Are you finally sane now, Frau Vogl?"

She smiled. "I haven't screamed for hours."

"May I hold him?"

"Of course."

Geli gently cuddled the newborn and held her cheek to his head as she swayed from side to side. She said, "Oh, I want a baby, too!"

Adolf Vogl's wife asked, "Whose?"

Geli just blushed. "Oh, you know who."

She smiled. "Would it be Herr Hitler perhaps?"

"He'd say I have already said way too much."

Which was true. Of the many roles Hitler played with his niece—father, confidant, educator, financier, swain—she disliked most his role of warden. Walking down the hallway one afternoon, she discovered that her uncle was back from his meetings in Essen and was in the kitchen interrogating the Winters about what she'd done while he was away. She slammed open the kitchen door and found him sitting at the pantry table, still in his chocolate-brown leather trench coat. Without hesitation, Hitler continued, "And Thursday afternoon?"

"Singing lessons," Anni Winter said.

"She left when?"

Anni tried to recall. Georg said, "Wasn't it one o'clock?"

"I'm here," Geli said. "Why not ask me?"

Smiling at her fleetingly, but with irony and mistrust, Hitler again turned to Georg and asked, "She got back from Herr Vogl's when?"

And she was at Hitler's *Stammtisch* at the Café Heck in June. Thirteen months earlier Alfred Rosenberg had finished a book that in self-flattery he'd insisted on calling his magnum opus, and he had given *Der Mythos des 20 Jahrhunderts* to his leader to read lest he find anything objectionable in it. She knew her uncle had not troubled himself to, in fact, read the book, but kept it for a full year before giving it back with the hastily penned comment "Very good" on the title page. Still, Rosenberg was elated, and as Rudolf Hess talked to Hitler about some pressing matter in the north, Rosenberg sought to give Geli a few reasons why her uncle was so impressed.

With a halitosis that forced Geli to shield her nose with her hand, Rosenberg leaned close to say that *The Myth of the 20th Century* was the fulfillment of the race theories that had first been formulated by Houston Stewart Chamberlain and Paul de Lagarde. "I have outdone them, however, for I have proven that the highest cultural achievements of the West all had their origins in ancient Germanic tribes.

And that Christianity, corrupted by Jesuits, Freemasons, and international Jewry, has destroyed Germanic culture by urging the dilution of our blood with feeble strains."

"And you call for what?"

"We need war," he said. "A cleansing."

Without thinking, Geli said, "Oh good. Begin with the teeth."

Affronted, he sat back and in full volume said, "Others have reported that you are an impudent girl. I now have confirmation."

She was stunned that Rosenberg would dare talk to his leader's niece in that way, but when she turned in outrage to her uncle, she saw that he and Hess were watching them in a tolerant silence that seemed to endorse Rosenberg's insult. Had he been put up to it?

Hitler smiled. "Men have little use for cleverness in women. We want them to be nice, little, cuddly things. Soft and sweet and perhaps a tad stupid."

Her face was hot. Her mouth was weak. She felt a flutter in her stomach. "Am I here to be corrected?"

"Only as it seems necessary."

She was near tears, so she just stared at her plate. She heard Hitler tell Hess and Rosenberg, "I find nothing more enjoyable than educating a young thing. A girl of eighteen or twenty is as pliable as wax." Geli was going to say she was nearly twenty-two, and then she remembered that Eva Braun was younger.

Rosenberg asked Hitler, "Would you mind if I quoted you to Herr Hess?"

"On this subject?"

"You were saying it just yesterday."

"I say so many things."

"If I have it right it was, 'A man must be able to put his mark on every girl. Women wouldn't have it any other way.' I find that so psychologically—"

Geli began to get up from the table.

"Where are you going?" her uncle asked.

"I feel ill."

"Sit!"

And then there was silence until a waiter finished serving them bowls of minestrone. Rudolf Hess tried to soften the tension by asking, "Who was it who said, 'For men love is a thing apart; for women it is their whole existence'?"

"I did," Hitler said. "But not in those words." And then he saw tears running down his niece's cheeks and he changed the subject.

At four in the morning she heard her door open and softly shut, and she got out of bed to find a small package wrapped in gold foil. With it was a card on which he'd sketched an ugly green dragon whose face was his own. "I am a monster," he'd written. "Will you forgive me?" His gift was a glamorous set of half-carat diamond earrings. And he was so abject all the next day, and so fatiguing in his gloom, that the Winters insisted and she finally forgave him.

■ ■ ■

There was going to be another election in September, and Hitler thought the party's chances were so good that he gave up his opera nights and the cinema and his July and August in Obersalzberg in order to campaign. Geli again took Henny with her to Haus Wachenfeld for the summer, and Heinrich Hoffmann mailed them weekly photographs of Hitler in Bremen, Darmstadt, Leipzig, or Potsdam, genially tousling the hair of blond boys, patting the sunburnt cheeks of girls in their village costumes, shaking the hands of factory workers, sitting on a tractor hitch to eat a farmer's wurst and sauerkraut, congratulating a grocer for the cleanliness of his store, scowling at a map in his chartered airplane, offering a formal bow to the older ladies whose votes he could always count on, stonily addressing a hall crammed full of his hard and lean Sturmabteilung for whom he was ever more an object of reverence. "Six speeches in a row and not a peep about the Jews," Hoffmann wrote. "We offend no one these days."

With her father's Leica, Henny took photos of Geli sitting on the northern terrace with her flowered white skirt lifted to mid-thigh so the jackdaw Schatzi could perch on her knee; of her imitating the flamboyant pose of Lilian Harvey outside the Mirabell movie palace in Salzburg; of her lying in a meadow and laughing hard with her brother, Leo, Prinz Josef cigarettes in their hands; of Geli sleeping nude on the *Freikörperkultur* beach with a flock of butterflies softly fanning their wings on her suntanned skin.

Because he feared that Communists would try to foil him by kidnapping or injuring his niece, Hitler had given handgun lessons to Geli and Henny and had consigned his Walther 6.35 and four boxes of ammunition to them so they would get to be good shots. And so they'd shoot at pine cones in the high woods near the Pension Moritz or wander farther down the Kehlstein to the horse stables of Doktor Seitz where they'd fire at tin cans on the fenceposts. They liked the maleness of it. They felt like Chicago gangsters, or like Jack Hoxie or William S. Hart in an American Western.

Walking back to Haus Wachenfeld one afternoon, Henny told her friend that she had a confession to make, that Hitler had joined the Hoffmanns for dinner a few months before. Afterward he'd played some Wagner on the piano, and the leitmotiv of Verdi's *La forza del destino*, and then he and Henny's father had gone out. She had been alone in the house when she'd heard the front door open and found Hitler hunting for the whip he'd forgotten. "Don't you find it strange that he carries that thing?"

Geli shrugged. "I have no idea what strange is anymore."

"Well, he planted himself on the red carpet of the foyer, his whip in one hand and his felt hat in the other, and with great seriousness he asked, 'Will you kiss me?'"

Geli forced herself to grin. "And you did?"

"Of course not. I told him, 'No, please, really not, Herr Hitler! Kissing you is impossible for me!' And then he left in a huff."

"Without trying to persuade you?"

She shook her head and asked, "Has he persuaded you?"

"A little."

"To have sex?"

"We just touch now and then. And nothing ever in public. We must keep up appearances. We share occasional kisses. Linking of arms. Sentimental looks. A hand to my bosom three times now. Quickly on, and then off, like a jittery boy."

"Aren't you frustrated?"

"Well, the ethics of the situation seem to be under a cloud." A jackdaw she didn't know stumbled up into the air and flew a few meters to the green lawn of the Hotel zum Türken. Calm women in white summer dresses were having cocktails under a shade tree and staring at the gun in her hand. She said, for no particular reason, "My uncle's a watcher, I think."

"Are you still modeling for him?"

Was there a betrayal that would surprise her now? Geli asked, "How did you hear?"

"We *saw*. My father and I. You can't tell it's you, really."

"Who else saw the sketches?"

"Well, many of his friends, I think. Herr Hitler was quite proud of them."

In fury she said, "He swore they were just for him! He gave me his word of honor! Am I supposed to face those people now?"

Trying to cheer her up, Henny joked, "They just know you a little better."

Howling with shame, she folded her arms over her head and cursed him.

"There, now," Henny said in a motherly way, and smiled as she flung an arm around Geli and hugged her. "It's just *art*, Angelika."

Checking a tear, Geli sniffed and said, "Oh. Easy for you to say. You're a hussy."

■ ■ ■

Doktor Goebbels organized six thousand meetings and torchlight parades throughout Germany for the 1930 campaign. Millions of books about the party were sold or given away. And in the last six weeks before the September election, Adolf Hitler gave over twenty major speeches, often in freshly raised circus tents holding as many as ten thousand. No country on the Continent had ever before undergone such furious miseducation, and the fruit of the propaganda was in the polls, where thirty-five million voted—up four million from the 1928 election—and the National Socialists won one hundred seven seats in the Reichstag, a gain of ninety-five. What the masses still called "the Hitler Movement" was now the second-largest party in the Reich.

With success came anxiousness. Hitler was wracked by stomachaches he feared were cancer, his insomnia worsened, he worried about his foot odor and flatulence; his hands, he felt, were too moist. And so a few days after the election he decided that he needed a vacation, and that he, Geli, and Angela were going to travel to Berlin for what Hitler called "a family outing with Alois," Angela's older brother.

Julius Schaub was at a jazz festival in Stuttgart, so Hitler determined they could just as easily take the railway north. Wanting a first-class car without crowds, Hitler got them to the Hauptbahnhof just before four a.m., but as it was Sunday, bicyclists, the hikers who were called *Wandervögel*, the Jewish sports clubs Maccabee and Shield, the Friedrich Jahn Gymnastics Forum, and the League of German Girls were in full scream at the railway station, waiting for trains to Garmisch, Passau, Nürnberg, and Bad Tölz.

Hitler tilted his trilby hat and hid his face from the chaotic crowds with an old *Berliner Illustrierte* as Angela got them all hot tea and Geli wandered through the railway station seeking lozenges for her sore throat.

She found instead, near a closed bookseller's stall, thirty reverent hikers in Tyrolean costume wearing badges of membership in Saint Michael's Sodality of Our Lady as they watched a consecration at a folding table turned into an altar. She hadn't been to church since she'd moved into her uncle's flat, so she stayed there, trying in vain to pray, but she was soon aware that her uncle was watching, and she walked back to the railway platform for Berlin.

Angela was wearing her cloche hat and raincoat and swastika pin, finishing her tea, and her uncle was pretending to scan track-meet news in the *Berliner Illustrierte*. She heard him snidely ask, "Still believe in the mumbo jumbo?"

There seemed to Geli no satisfactory reply.

"Oh, you and your smart talk," Angela said.

"I never found that going to church got the bills paid."

"Alois is the same way," Angela said. "Heathens, the both of you."

Hitler folded the newspaper and said, "We cannot have a strong nation if there are religions vying with us for control of the people. We need all of a man, not just a piece of him. We'll first get rid of the Jews. And then we'll rule out Catholicism. And then all the other religions. In a few generations no one in Germany will know that a Jew called Jesus ever existed." The railway cars for Berlin were shuttling into the station and he craned his neck to see where the first-class cars would be.

"*I'm* a Catholic," Geli said. "Mother is. Leo is."

"And I used to be," he said. "I have put away childish things."

■ ■ ■

A taxi took them to Alois Hitler Jr.'s third-floor apartment on Luckenwalderstrasse, and his second wife, Maimee, invited them into a purple-hued home so filled with inherited pictures and furniture that she had to sidestep them in order to put coffee on.

Angela and Geli uneasily shared the sofa and Adolf squeezed just beside his niece, his hand so squashed he at first settled it familiarly on her thigh before choosing his own. They were all facing the finest object in the living room, a new, flattering, life-size oil painting of Adolf Hitler in his Sturmabteilung uniform and his "man of destiny" stare.

"Am I *really* so dashing?" he asked.

Geli did not smile. "What they always miss in pictures is your modesty."

"And here you all are!" Alois Hitler said, zestfully walking in and widening his arms. At forty-eight he'd changed his mustache to one just like his half-brother's, but in his rimless glasses and his hard-collared manner there was still an air of the railway waiter and he seemed far too anxious to please as he waved forward from the hallway and introduced his firstborn son, William Patrick Hitler, who was on holiday from his job in London and whom he'd last seen in Liverpool in 1913.

Willie, as he was called, was nearly twenty and worked, Alois told them, as a draftsman in an engineering firm on Wigmore Street. He was a slim, fairly handsome young man in a gray tweed suit, with woe-filled eyes and a full head of brown hair brushed straight back from a high forehead. "My German not good," Willie said.

Adolf genially said, "Oh, but you are fortunate, English boy," and waggled Geli's knee with his palm. "My Geli here speaks your language like the queen."

With relief Willie sighed and said in German, "What an illustration!"

Alois corrected his "*Erläuterung*" to "*Erleichterung.*"

"Oh yes," Willie said. "What a relief!"

And Geli said in English, "Like telegrams we will talk."

"Herr Doktor Hanfstaengl and I have just written an article on the elections for the London *Sunday Express,*" Hitler told him. "And I have an interview with the London *Times* later this week. I see journalists all the time. Are you understanding my German, Willie?"

Hitler's nephew nodded and said he did.

With surprising fury, Hitler shouted, "Numskull! Woodhead! Did you think I would not hear about the American newspapers? Only Adolf Hitler talks about Adolf Hitler! I shall not have you or your mother, Bridget, or you, Alois—*no one*—think they can climb on my back and get a free ride to fame!"

Willie told his father in English, "All the Hearst fellow wanted was a picture of me. And a few questions. I didn't know that much."

All too familiar with Hitler's rages, Geli sighed and got up from the sofa. "Shall we help Maimee with the coffee, Mother?"

Angela got up, too. "I was just going there," she said.

Maimee was standing behind the kitchen door with a frightened face and folded arms, stunned by the tantrum she'd heard. "We thought he'd be grateful," she told Angela. "And the money was so good."

"Which newspaper?" Angela asked.

"The New York *American.*"

They heard Alois telling Adolf, "But I say how good and generous you were as a boy!"

"And what about my childhood 'fantasy life'? Am I in fact 'far removed from reality'? Even your lies are idiotic! Sweeping streets for food in Wien? Working in München as a house painter? A wall-paper hanger?"

"They put words in my mouth," Alois said.

Geli found dinner napkins and rolled them inside porcelain rings. She said, "Who'd have guessed a family outing could be so much fun?"

"He's under a lot of strain," Angela said.

"Why do you always apologize for him?" her daughter asked.

"Well, he's a genius," Angela said. "They're all high-strung."

"Hah," Geli said. She held open the kitchen door and peered out.

Wallowing in self-pity, Hitler clamped his forehead with his left hand as he whined, "Oh, how carefully I have always kept my personal affairs out of the press! And now people are trying to find out who I am! In my book I did not say a word about my ancestry or my family or my childhood friends, not a word, and now investigations are being made and spies are sent out to dig up our past! Even a breath of scandal will destroy all I have worked so hard for!"

Maimee got out coffee cups and saucers and Geli carried them to the dining room in a "Don't mind me" way as her uncle, who seemed precariously near tears, shouted that he was henceforth disclaiming Alois and Willie as his relations. If his sister could assume the name Paula Wolf and hide from the press in Wien, then Alois could say he was *adopted* by his father, that he and Adolf were unrelated. And Willie could go back to England and tell the Hearst people that he'd found out he'd made a horrible mistake, his uncle was another Hitler, and the famous Adolf Hitler was not family at all.

Angela walked out. "Hot coffee!"

Seemingly forgetting his anger, Hitler grinned. "And cake, I hope?"

"She made one fresh this morning, just for you."

With childish pleasure, Hitler hopped up from the sofa and flattered Maimee as Alois and Willie shared a look of surprise. Geli whispered to Willie in English, "Hot and cold. Off and on. Black and white."

■ ■ ■

Adolf ate three pieces of cake in silence as Alois and Angela talked about old times, and then as Alois played with their nine-year-old, Adolf felt restless and proposed that the family all take a stroll through the Tiergarten.

Geli said her throat still hurt and Willie opted to stay with her in the flat, listening to the BBC on Alois's radio: "Am I Blue," "You Do Something to Me," "Can't We Be Friends?" Willie finally took off his jacket and shoes around five and fell heavily onto the sofa next to Geli. She sucked on a lozenge. She could feel him hunting for words, and then in English he said, "I hope you won't think me too forward, but you're really smashing, you know. You're really the nicest of all the family."

"Thank you."

"I have a girlfriend of my own, in case you were wondering."

She said in English, "That is good for you, yes?"

"Oh indeed. Quite satisfying." With shock at himself, he added, "Not *physically*. We're not—"

She smiled. "I understand."

"Embraceable You" was playing, and they listened to it for a while before Willie said, "Uncle Adolf can be rather unpredictable, can't he? Emotionally, I mean."

"You get used to," she said.

"What's he like?"

She laughed when she thought about it. "A crocodile. Waiting and waiting. And then, in a blitz, the scurry forward. *Und die Zähne.*"

Willie translated, "And the teeth."

She shifted to German to say that for hours at a time their uncle would do nothing but chew on his fingernails and stare out a window and whistle. And then there'd be shocking activity until he took his rest again. She said he was stunningly consistent. Others stewed and worried and hemmed and hawed, but their uncle had decided things once and for all, and he would think on Thursday of next week just what he'd thought four years before, and he'd die without changing his mind. She allowed that Hitler was quite winning at a first encounter, but that was because he found all people fascinating the first time he met them. Joining his company, they'd be offered courtesies and pleasantness while being questioned about their fields of expertise, and she'd see his internal machinery collecting what he needed from them while figuring out their affections and secret longings and ways of thinking and feeling. And then he would talk to them, a flood of words, using all he'd learned, dominating their minds, and they'd be amazed by his force of will and intellect, his well of sympathy. If he wanted to charm you, you were charmed. If he wanted to persuade you, you were persuaded.

"And if he wanted to love you?"

Saying nothing, Geli jerked forward and got out another lozenge.

Willie asked in English, "Are you the only one Uncle Adolf's affectionate with?"

"So this you notice?"

"Oh my word, yes. Will you marry, do you think?"

She flushed. "We are just uncle and niece! Was this anyone saying?"

"My father."

To avoid Hitler's glare in the formidable portrait, she got up from the sofa and sat on the floor underneath the painting, hugging her knees. She shifted again to German to tell her cousin, "I owe Uncle Adolf a lot for acting as my father and for taking care of the family. I can never repay him. We'd have no home or money without him. We're all grateful. And I'm sure he's fond of me in his way. But I don't like it that he's so jealous and possessive. Often I feel enslaved by him. Are you aware of that feeling?"

Willie said in English, "I can't say so, no."

She said in German, "There are times when he can't bear to have me show interest in anything or anyone other than himself. Any moment I have to be ready to go where he wants, or halt whatever I'm doing to obey his latest whim. Even my weekly singing lessons get cancelled because he so hates to be alone. We sit in the movies all day sometimes, and then he wants to go back again in the evening. I get so bored. Or it's the opera. Night after night. I'm twenty-two. I want to have fun. With people my age. And all I ever seem to do is have dinner with older men."

"And they can be so tedious," her cousin said.

She was surprised to find herself in tears, and to find in Willie's face a flabbergasted terror that she'd go on gushing. And still she continued, "It's because wherever he goes he needs company. An adoring audience. Words fly up all around him, like a fortress of sentences. Who can get inside it? And does he listen to others?"

Willie admitted that Uncle Adolf seemed to find listening a distraction.

"Yes! And so I am a mystery to him. We all are. Undiscovered. Uncomplicated. He only wants me to be a good housewife, a pet. Even my singing annoys him. It's a wonder I give him any pleasure at all."

Willie said in English, "Well, I'm sure he'd be pleased to see he's made you so upset."

She laughed. "I'm sorry. I'm just frustrated. I have a fever, maybe. We have good times, too. And Uncle's very generous." She wiped tears from her cheeks with her palms. She breathed in. "Won't you try to forget the horrible things I said when you go back to England?"

Willie gallantly said, "I shall remember only you."

"Even when I hate Uncle Adolf, he wins. I fret over him; I'm obsessed by him; I can't get him out of my mind."

CHAPTER SIXTEEN
DAS BRAUNE HAUS, 1931

On January 1, 1931, at Briennerstrasse 45, just east of the white stone prairie of the Königsplatz, Adolf Hitler officially dedicated the Brown House as the headquarters of the National Socialist German Workers Party. When the formalities of the grand opening were finished late that afternoon, Hitler, in jackboots and jodhpurs and Sturmabteilung uniform, took Geli on a private architectural tour, first walking her around the four sides of the four-story building and tilting her head in his soft and feminine hands so she could see how the walls had been sandblasted and painted, the window balconies added, and the huge scarlet-and-black flag of the Nazis hung over its front entrance.

"You did a good job," she said.

"Would you like to know the technical details? How many hours of labor went into it, for example? How many wooden scaffolds were used, how many tons of cement?"

She smiled wanly. "Not really."

"I have all the facts memorized."

"Seeing is enough."

With a furrowed brow, Hitler viewed the Brown House from afar and said, "In the Weimar Republic, it is a foreign embassy. We'll soon be changing that." And he took her hand as he walked her through the giant bronze door past four hard-faced and black-uniformed Schutzstaffeln sentries who offered the Nazi version of the Fascist salute while shouting, "Heil Hitler!"

The floors were highly polished marble, handsome inlaid oak paneled the walls, and swastikas had been imprinted into the stucco ceiling or etched into the fine window glass. The forty regional *Gaue* were represented in the hall by their blood-red revolutionary standards, all tilted in reverence toward two bronze memorials containing the names of those sixteen Nazis killed in front of the Feldherrnhalle in the 1923 putsch.

She was taken downstairs to the chrome-bright records office where fireproof steel cabinets held the personnel files of five hundred thousand party members. "We'll stop taking applications when we have one million," Hitler said. "Either we can do it with a million or we can't do it at all."

Then he took her back up to the first-floor "Hall of Senators," where the highest-ranking dignitaries in the party would be invited for conferences, seating themselves in sixty chairs of red morocco leather arranged in a horseshoe of two rows facing, of course, the führer. Heroic busts of Otto von Bismarck, the first chancellor of the German Empire, and Dietrich Eckart, who had died soon after the putsch and to whom Hitler had dedicated *Mein Kampf*, were on pedestals beside four plaques illustrating phases of the party's ten-year evolution: its formation, the announcement of its program, its vanquishment at the Feldherrnhall, and its renewal after Adolf Hitler's release from Landsberg am Lech. Even as he showed the hall of senators to Geli, Hitler hinted that he thought it too parliamentary, too much like the Reichstag he hated, and she got the feeling it would never be used.

Wide doors opened into an elegant first-floor restaurant of soft blond light above walls of herringboned oak, gold damask chairs, and dining tables of tan marble. Waiters were still there after the afternoon luncheon, putting out Dresden china and silverware, arranging hothouse flowers in crystal vases, vacuuming the plush red carpet. Each choice of fabric, color, and ornamentation had been personally made by Hitler.

Offices for Hess, Himmler, Goebbels, Göring, Schwarz, and other party officials were on the second and third floors. Each desk was perfectly clean except for a black telephone, a writing pad and a fountain pen, and a framed photograph of Adolf Hitler. Each hallway held a huge oil portrait of the führer, and on one wall was a green map of Germany with its cities and villages pinned with black swastikas.

Hitler's office was grander and far too large, perhaps fifty strides from door to door, with a suede wall covering of reddish-brown, ceiling-high windows facing the Königsplatz, a sumptuous red carpet that felt as soft as a mattress beneath Geli's shoes, a great fireplace and a golden sofa and chairs at one end, and at the other two secretary chairs in front of a huge, ornately carved ambassadorial desk that was free of even a pencil. A full-length portrait in oils of auto tycoon Henry Ford, a secret patron, hung on a wall, a fine stone bust of Benito Mussolini was on a pedestal, and not far from it was one of Heinrich Hoffmann's haunting, ghostly photographs of Hitler, his face artificially handsome and framed in blackness, his hypnotic stare like a fiery assault.

Geli strolled by a fair illustration in oil paints of the Sixteenth Bavarian Reserve Infantry Regiment on its first attack in Flanders in 1914, and then walked to one of Hitler's many eighteenth-century paintings of Frederick the Great. She realized for the first time that the king of Prussia's left hand was effeminately posed on his hip, just as her uncle's often was.

"Old Fritz," Hitler said, and she turned. He was sitting in his high-backed chair of pudding-soft leather, his hands folded in front of him as if she were his theater, his entertainment. "Old Fritz kidnapped a pretty Italian ballerina named Barbara Campanini so she could perform nightly for him as his private dancer. But she became more than that. She was his Leyden jar, his source of energy. 'La Barbarina,' she was called. Odic force radiated from her and electrified the Prussian king, whose many obligations and long hours may have sapped his potency."

"Why don't you have a picture of *her* here?"

Hitler did not smile. "I have you."

She looked at him without blinking. "Oh yes. I forgot."

"Haven't you found by observation, Geli, that health and vigor and zest for life fairly surge from an older man when he is with an enchanting young girl? You can only agree. Wives are not the same thing at all. Wives ought to be, first of all, mothers. An older man needs a mistress."

And Eva's yours, she thought. She spun a world globe on its axis as she felt him frowning.

Abruptly standing up, he knocked the heels of his jackboots together, and raised his right hand high in the Fascist salute. "I can hold my arm up like this for hours! With only my stupendous iron will for support! At the party congress in Nürnberg, Göring tried to keep his own up for as long but failed utterly. He fell limp with exhaustion. Others would not even try."

She just stared at him.

"I have letters!" he said, and he searched his desk drawers until he found a file swollen fat with cards and envelopes. He put on his spectacles and read one. "This is from a fanatical woman named Hildegard, who also sent me a cake. 'My *dear, sugar-sweet Adolf*,' she begins. '*I stare at your pictures constantly, spreading them out in front of me and giving them a kiss. Yes, yes, my dear, sweet, good Adolf, love is as true as gold, and I can't do a thing about it.*' Et cetera."

"And you have no idea who she is?"

"This is from a Melita. '*My heart's own!*' she begins. '*I'm having a front-door key and a key to my bedroom made for you. In the next letter, you'll get the first one; and in the letter after that, you'll get the other. We must be very careful because the scum will try to kill you. But come here as early as you can, whenever you want.*'"

"Were the keys sent?"

"Who knows? Hess takes care of my mail. I have another one from a high school girl." Hitler hunted for it, read a few lines to himself, and smiled. "She calls me 'Poppet.' She talks about meeting. *'If the worse comes to the worst, our parents (because they're yours now as well) have given me permission for you to come to the house at any time so we can spend the night together.'*"

Insolently smiling, she said, "Take her up on it, Uncle Alf. I can feel the Odic force from way over here."

He took off his spectacles, folded the letter, inserted it in the file, and shoved the file inside his desk. "*Hundreds* of women find me desirable," he said.

"I think that's well-documented now."

Hitler just stared at her until she glanced away. He said, "Baldur von Schirach is hosting a Carnival party here for the National Socialist German Students' Alliance. Would you like to go?"

She toned down her excitement before saying, "Could I?"

"I'll do far better than just give you permission. I'll be joining you."

■ ■ ■

Schirach rejoiced, of course, and extorted party funds for a giant swastika ice sculpture, an effuse Swedish smorgasbord of chilled meats and fish, and a chanteuse and a six-piece band from the Resi nightclub in Berlin. Hearing the führer would be there, hundreds more students came than Schirach had planned for, a few from as far away as Heidelberg and Innsbruck, and a fascinated crowd seethed around Hitler as he shook hands and signed his autograph and Schirach spoke stirringly about him as Germany's greatest son.

"My church is no longer the altar of Christianity," Schirach shouted, "but the steps of the field marshal's hall where the blood of the Old Combatants was poured out for our sake. Their spirit lives on in Adolf Hitler, our leader and hero, in whom rests the roots of our world. Upright, firm, and modest, he remains a man like you and me, and so we love him all the more, for we know he is a genius whose soul touches the stars!"

If Hitler's niece beside him was looked at, it was with either jealousy or wonder. *Who's the girl?* they seemed to be saying. She'd lived in Germany since 1927 and still she was nothing more than an adjunct, a trifle, a plaything, a subject of gossip, an odor of scandal, a niece. She was wearing a Lanvin evening gown in black faille and strass and she felt wealthy, old, and humorless as she sat with Hitler and Schirach in their tuxedos, all three of them glumly watching the many young partygoers fusing and dancing. Then Rudolf Hess was at the entrance, his face as dour as Scotland, and her uncle rose up, saying, "I have a meeting. Ten minutes, no more."

She asked, "With whom may I talk?"

Quickly glancing at the jarred Schirach, Hitler pretended to be surprised by the question. "Anybody, of course!"

She said nothing. She did not watch him go out. She saw Henny on the dance floor shaking her head to a boy who'd asked her to join him as the band played a nonsense hit from 1928, "My Parrot Won't Eat No Hard-Boiled Eggs."

Henny seemed to see Geli with the handsome founder of the alliance and walked over, flushing a little as she tried not to face Schirach, who stood from his chair and gaily said, "Please join us, Fräulein Hoffmann."

"Will it be all right?" she asked Geli.

"Certainly."

Schirach shoved in her chair as she sat.

"Are you here alone?" Geli asked.

Wide-eyed at someone behind Geli, she shook her head.

Geli turned. Henny's hunchbacked father was merrily strolling over in his tuxedo, his arm linked with Eva Braun's. She was wearing a shirred, ankle-length taffeta gown and a black wool overcoat with a fitch collar and cuffs. She'd hidden her blond hair underneath a fitch turban by Agnès. Weeks ago the full ensemble had been featured in a store window on Maximilianstrasse. Were they gifts from Hitler?

Schirach stood. "I haven't had the pleasure, Fräulein."

She forced a smile onto her kittenish face as she shook his hand. "Eva Braun."

Hoffmann held her waist as he joked, "I have been telling everybody she's my niece." And in a silence as loud as a slamming door, he furthered his insult by saying, "What the leader does, I do."

"She's his shop girl," Geli frostily said.

"Clerk," Eva said. "And model."

"Oh, I see," said Schirach.

"Are you *drunk*, Daddy?"

"Well, others thought it was funny."

Eva and Geli exchanged glares. Eva said, "I just saw your uncle. I'm so sorry that he seemed so sad."

"Was it sadness over seeing you?"

Eva wasn't a wit. She said, "I think not."

"Was it over all the monkeys they killed for that turban and coat?"

Eva looked at the fitch fur of her cuff.

"Are *you* drunk?" Henny scolded.

In a fair imitation of Eva, Geli slacked her jaw and said, "I think not."

"Changing the subject for a moment," Hoffmann said, straddling a chair, "I was just talking to one of the students here and he told me he was having a hard time cramming for his examinations in law. Well, so I helped him out by going over the various pleas a lawyer could make for acquittal." Hoffmann found a hammered silver flask inside his tuxedo jacket and held it out. "Schnaaps, anyone?"

There were no other takers. Hoffmann tilted the flask and finished it, then hid it inside his jacket again.

"The fellow was fine for a while," he continued, "but he was forgetting the insanity defense. I said, 'Oh, come now. There's one you hear about every day. Criminals who are acquitted of violent acts not because they are minors or because they acted in self-defense, but because of . . . what?' Well, the fellow seemed lost for a while and then his face brightened with insight and he said, 'Because they are *Nazis*?'"

Heinrich Hoffmann guffawed at his joke and glanced around to guarantee that his daughter and Geli and Eva joined him in the hilarity. Baldur von Schirach squirmed uneasily in his seat, and

Hoffmann squinted at him with annoyance. "We must puncture the swellings, Herr von Schirach."

"I just didn't think it was funny, or fair."

"The leader did."

"Really?"

"Oh yes. Hitler has a fantastic sense of humor, doesn't he, Geli?"

She granted that he did seem to enjoy laughing at others' misfortunes.

Eva volunteered, "We go to Charlie Chaplin films all the time."

"And not the zoo?" Geli asked. "To see the primates?"

Eva was going to say something foolish, but Hoffmann saved her by getting up from his chair. "We ought to be going," he said.

Schirach smiled. "We want to see you Charleston, Heinrich!"

"Oh no, the black bottom's my dance," Hoffmann said. "There's a joke there somewhere. I'll have to go think of it." And he took Eva by the hand as he strolled across the floor to the hosted bar.

Geli called, "Good-bye, Monkey Girl!"

Eva glowered over her shoulder.

"Aren't you gracious," Henny said.

"She's my rival."

"She isn't."

She turned to Schirach and intensely asked, "Will you go out with me?"

He blanched. "But I was under the impression that you and Herr Hitler—"

She turned to Henny. "See? And so she goes with him to Charlie Chaplin films while I stay home alone. Who isn't afraid of offending my uncle? Who can risk his jealousy? Uncle Alf has put me in quarantine."

Seeing that she was near tears, Schirach gallantly stood. "Won't you dance with me, Geli?"

She glanced at Henny, who furtively nodded, and she listened to the Resi singer as she began "Falling in Love Again." She got up. "Yes. I would like that. Thank you."

Schirach escorted her onto the floor, and softly held her waist as he took her right hand. As they waltzed to the song with fifty others, she felt his strength and largeness, the fascinating difference in his torso and footsteps. She felt small and safe, feminine and cared for. She'd missed this. Cologne water was in his jacket and she even found herself liking that. She smiled up at him. "I haven't waltzed since high school."

"Am I too clumsy?" he asked.

"Not at all. You're very graceful."

"Well, my parents were in the theater."

"Mine were in the kitchen."

Schirach laughed. "Aren't you funny!"

She found herself self-consciously counting steps as Schirach hummed along with the singer. She felt his soft belly forcing their turns. She asked, "Have you seen *The Blue Angel?*"

"Twice," he said. "Wasn't Marlene Dietrich marvelous?"

"My favorite was Emil Jannings."

"Oh, but his Professor Unrath was so stuffy and middle class and sad. All I could think of him was 'He is the Germany we are rebelling against.'"

"At least he was in love. She was so callous and insolent and sadistic."

"Well, there are those who find that—"

"Mesmerizing?" she asked.

Schirach laughed. "Are we on the subject of your uncle again?"

She shook her head, then tilted it farther toward his chest as she sang Marlene Dietrich's famous song, "'Men cluster to me like moths around a flame. And if their wings burn, I know I'm not to blame. Falling in love again. Never wanted to. What am I to do? I can't help it.'"

And finally the song ended, and the singer was generously applauded, and Geli felt a funneling stare from off the floor, and she knew who it was but failed to turn. She forced him to embarrass himself by walking out to her like a fuming emissary, a lane widening as the many dancers fell back, his shoes as loud as wood in the hush. And then she did turn, and his face was as white as a faint, canceling any hint of his wrath for the sake of all his children there. "We are going now," Hitler said.

Schirach was still young enough to be surprised. "My leader," he implored, "it's just ten o'clock. I have access to a car. Won't you let me get her back to your flat in an hour or so?"

Clenching his jaw, Hitler held the large twenty-two-year-old in his scalding eyes until Schirach's fortitude, his friendliness, the flush in his feminine cheeks were all gone. "She is with *me*," Hitler said, and she followed him as he went to where Rudolf Hess was holding the coats.

■ ■ ■

They were driven to Prinzregentenplatz in a silence as great as that of a closed museum, his anger trying to disfigure everything he glared at, he in the front seat, she in the back. She ran up the stairs ahead of him and when she got inside the flat heard Maria Reichert call from her quarters, "Fräulein Raubal?"

"Yes."

"I have four messages for Herr Hitler."

Hitler was just then walking inside. He frowned at his niece, then went to Frau Reichert, and Geli hung up her overcoat, got a beer in the kitchen, and went to her room, firmly locking the door. She put Verdi's *Requiem* on the gramophone and took her canaries out of their cage, lying flat on the bed as she watched Honzi and Hansi fly wildly from wall to wall and then find the fingers she held out just above her face. She kissed their beaks. She cheeked their feathers. She finished the beer.

She heard Hitler in his office next door, railing over the telephone at Himmler, then Göring, then Doktor Goebbels. "Won't any of you ever think for yourselves?" he shouted, and slammed down the receiver just for her. She heard him stewing in the hallway outside her door, and then she heard him in the library at the white Bechstein, childishly pounding out the overture to Wagner's *Rienzi* until she finally lifted the needle from "The Chorus of the Hebrew Slaves" in Verdi's opera *Nabucco* and there was peace.

She got into her pink flannel nightgown, glanced down the hallway, and hurried into the bathroom. She urinated, washed her hands, cold-creamed her face, worked up a froth with her toothbrush and her uncle's Clorodont powder, then opened the mirrored vanity cabinet above the sink and carefully put her things on the second shelf, his on the first. She found an old towel in the straw hamper and polished the chrome faucet and handles, wiped spots of water from the mirror and the porcelain. She stowed the towel away again and flicked the lock on the bathroom door.

Hitler was there, frail and woeful and still in his tuxedo. "This is not enough," he said, and fell to his knees. His face flattened against the flannel just below her heart, thudding now like his shoes on the staircase, and he said, "Oh, Geli, this is not enough. This is not enough."

"What isn't?"

"This!"

"The way we are?"

"We *aren't*."

She felt his petulant breathing like moisture, and she found herself softly petting his chestnut-brown hair, though her palms, she knew, would glisten with oil. "What would be enough, Uncle Alf?"

Like a little boy begging for a pfennig, he said in a weak, measly way, "Affection." And he tilted down to forcefully kiss the pink flannel over her pubic bone, his mustache prickling her.

She felt a thrill flow up her spine, but she held his head and gently lifted it. "We can't have you kneeling here like this. The ladies."

Worriedly, Hitler glanced down the hallway toward the quarters of Maria Reichert and her mother. There was a faint hint of a Christmas concert on Maria's wireless; otherwise all was dark. Squatting back on his heels, he groomed his forelock, then gripped the doorjamb and Geli's offered forearm to find his way up to his feet. And then he focused on her and she felt pinioned, his stunning irises as silver as mercury, his face wolfish and stern and full of control. Wordlessly overmastering her. Others in the party talked about his Svengali eyes, and now she knew what they meant. Within a few seconds she felt so enfeebled she feared she'd slide to the floor.

"We have both been depriving ourselves," he said. "We haven't given our love an outlet."

Was she in love? She knew she was confused and sad and yearning. Was that love? She wanted to be inward and alone with her emotions for a while, but he took her hand and tightly held it behind his back as he forthrightly walked them to his red-walled room.

She stood there in the coldness as he shut the door and tore loose his black bow tie. She felt adrift in the geography of dreams, somewhere between fright and fascination, where she seemed to have no volition, where she seemed to watch herself as she watched him.

He sat in his fire-red wingback chair to take off his shoes and stockings and stocking garters, and he focused on her with great seriousness as he twisted the studs and cuff links from his formal shirt. "Are you just going to stare?" he asked.

"I have no idea what else to do."

"Aren't you a child of nature?"

She'd never heard the words "child" and "nature" voiced with such snide criticism. She said, "I don't know what you have in mind."

With flat, tan teeth, he smiled. "Oh yes you do." He stood and strode to his closet and found a wooden hanger for his tuxedo jacket. Without turning, he said, "Lift off the nightgown, Geli."

"Uncle Alf, I'm not sure—"

In a tolerant, teacherly, quiet way, he told her, "Do as I say."

She did. She was in free fall and knew it. She felt hellbent and unruly, as if she were riding a flood that was seeking the sea, the wild tide of it erasing all fences, boundaries, government, calendars, plans, and intentions. She heard a male voice in her head say, *Aren't you the fat cow?*, and she flicked off the overhead light so that there was only the yellow glow from the wall sconces. And then she walked naked to the high, wide, feather bed and sat with primly crossed legs on the gold satin quilt.

"Don't look," he said, so she held her stare on the floor as she understood him to be shaking the trousers off his skinny legs and folding them onto a hanger. She'd forgotten that he wore long underwear in winter. She stole glimpses of the jiggle of his soft flesh as he shrugged and fought and jumped his way out of the underwear and jammed it into a laundry basket. Eyeing his niece to ensure her shyness, he posed as he did in his Brownshirt photographs, his features ferocious, his fists clenched, his flabby stomach sucked in and his chest inflated, his head haughtily high. And then he said, "Look now."

She found his pose ludicrous, but hid it, and she hid, too, the fact that his maleness was so odd and disconcerting, for he had skin so white it seemed powdered, no formation of muscles in his shoulders or arms, the hairless, female breasts of a girl in puberty, and a flaccid, purple, uncircumcized penis that was like a short thumb above a boy's compact scrotum. She shifted her gaze to Adolf Ziegler's healthy nude.

"I have had the benefit of seeing you," her uncle said. "And now we are on the same footing."

She asked in a flat voice, "Are we going to make love?"

She watched his shadow shift shapes on the floor as he crossed to her. She shivered with cold. She felt the feather bed sag with his weight as he sat just beside her. "Aren't you the randy harlot," he said with a smile. "To try to rush me like that."

She was exhausted and did not know why. "What then? Shall we kiss?"

Considering and striking various options, he finally said, "Walk to the closet."

She felt his leer like hands as she did.

"On the floor inside are my jackboots. Put them on."

She did.

"And hanging inside the door is my dog whip."

She got it but said, "I find this distinctly odd."

"Hush," he said. "Walk to me now."

The jackboots were so loose they fell from her feet as she walked, so she shuffled to within a foot of him and found herself giggling, and then she faced his hot glare and was silent again.

There was no letup to his glare as it journeyed down to the great curiosities of her breasts. Was he trying to make her feel ugly? Leaning forward, he laid out a gray-coated tongue and licked circles around her right nipple, then took it between his teeth and tugged until it hurt. Seeing her wince, he smiled and said, "Teach me."

"Tenderly," she said.

"With the whip, I mean. Teach me."

She heard the male voice in her head say, *Hit him.* "Hit you?"

"Yes!"

"I can't."

"Hit the side of your boot with the whip."

She stropped it.

"Oh, that's it. Again."

She did.

His jaws widened like a python's and he hideously took as much of her full left breast in his mouth as he could, hurtfully sucking and swallowing it until she whacked a jackboot with the whip and said, "No!"

Withdrawing his mouth from her breast, he smiled. "Aren't you quick."

"I don't like this game," she said.

"Well, it's not for you, it's for me."

"Don't you want affection?"

He smirked. His hand knifed between her thighs and found her vagina. She angrily squeezed her thighs tighter and fought off his hand with her own. Whining, he said, "Won't you make me obey?"

She stropped the whip. "Don't!"

He fell in a heap and held his head with his hands. "Oh, you're right! I'm a worm! I'm vermin!" Crouching at her feet, he started to masturbate, his head nodding up and down.

"I hate this," she said.

"Hit me then!"

"No!" She tried to squirm away from him, but his left hand forcefully held the jackboot at her ankle and she couldn't free it.

And then he was flat on his back, staring up at her vulva as he feverishly jerked at himself. "Oh yes, oh yes, that's it. Closer. Squat close."

She yelled at him, "I *hate* this!"

And he yelled, "Don't argue with me! I have the *right* to you after all these years!" There was an odd change in him that she couldn't identify; she only knew it was terrifying. She froze and his free hand lifted and fiddled with her labia as he warned, "If you say no one more time . . ." A finger found its way inside her, and she flinched. "We are lovers," he said. "And this is how we love."

She did as he ordered.

■ ■ ■

On the floor of her room the next morning Geli found his cartoon of himself naked and impotent, a long limp *wienerwurst* hanging low between his legs while a giant question mark and exclamation point seemed to spring from his head. Geli angrily left the cartoon on her desk so Anni Winter would see it as she cleaned.

She'd hardly slept, so she stayed in her bed, glumly paging through the score of Paul Lincke's operetta *Frau Luna* until she heard the hall telephone ring, and then she heard Anni just outside her door, calling, "Fräulein Raubal! It's your mother!"

She went into Hitler's office and held the black receiver in her hands until she was confident she wouldn't cry. She put it to her ear. "Hello, Mommy."

"Did Adolf tell you?" Angela asked.

She raked hair back from her face. "What?"

"He's going to buy me a car! A Wanderer! I just can't believe it! I'm so happy!"

She grimly faced his photograph. "Then I'm happy, too," Geli said.

Chapter Seventeen
Confessions, 1931

She flattered him with imitation: fuming, ranting, weeping, falling to the floor in tantrums, soaring giddily when things went well, sinking into full-day pouts over imagined snubs or neglect. She loathed him. She did not. She feared she was too prudish and timid. She felt sullied and odious. She screamed at waiters in restaurants. She would not pay a shopkeeper without complaining of piracy. She was becoming, she knew, a bitch, and she hated it, hated him saying, "We are so alike," hated his infatuation, his sticky enthrallment, his cruelty and unnaturalness, his unoriginality in choosing such a vulgar, bland face to offer the world.

In March, Hitler and Geli attended a Bavarian play by Ludwig Thoma at the Kammerspiele Theater, where he fancied his niece in a cloying way, finding reasons to confer with her, to fondle her, to angle his head childishly into hers, to just watch. Tiring of his scrutiny, she put a finger to her lips to shush him, and he folded his arms and sulked for a while before mooning over Geli again. And then he noticed Herr Doktor Hanfstaengl observing him from a side gallery, and his face took on the slaughter-of-the-innocents look of his publicity photographs.

Afterward they all dined together at the Schwarzwälder Café, where a continually yapping schnauzer so annoyed Hitler that he walked to the far table and truculently stared until the schnauzer cowered and was silent. And then he returned to the table, demeaned his niece by feeding pinches of cake to her, and flourished in front of Putzi his latest royalty statement from Eher Verlag. *Mein Kampf* was then nearly six years old and had averaged sales of just six thousand copies per year, but suddenly in 1930 fifty-four thousand books were sold, and with foreign rights, he boasted, he'd soon be a wealthy man.

"Well, that calls for some glasses of the finest fizz!" Putzi said.

Instead the führer fell into an hour-long monologue on the next elections in 1932, on the "clownish elements of salon bolshevism" who'd drifted into the party and would have to be weeded out, about his forbearance when being tested by the persistent conflicts between the hooligan SA and Heinrich Himmler's disciplined and increasingly formidable SS force, organizations faithful to him who were vying to be his favorites. "When a mother has many children, and one of them goes astray," Hitler told his foreign press secretary, "it is the wise mother who grips the child by the hand and won't let go."

Even then Putzi Hanfstaengl was aware that Geli was that child, for she was plainly bored by Hitler's monologue and was flagrant in yawning and tinking her forks and yearningly gazing over her fox stole at all the jolly couples around them.

At closing time at the Schwarzwälder Café, their still far-from-sleep führer persuaded Herr and Frau Hanfstaengl to join him and his niece in the Prinzregentenplatz flat for cordials. And when there he further persuaded Putzi to favor them with his famous piano playing, for he had the ability to flawlessly perform short pieces in any style or key, and he first entertained them that night by interpreting the trifle "Hänschen Klein" in five different ways, as if it had been scored by Bach, Mozart, Beethoven, Schumann, and Wagner.

Wildly applauding and gleeful, Hitler announced, "And now my niece will perform with you," and she dutifully got up from a floral sofa to join Putzi on the white piano bench.

"Sweet and short," she whispered, and Putzi told her to play the left-hand chords of the "Horst Wessel Lied" while he quickened the right-hand notes into a minuet. And then they both turned and bowed.

Eyes wet with pleasure, Hitler hurried to wake up Frau Reichert before they started another song.

Geli called, "It's two in the morning!," but Hitler ignored her.

Putzi said, "No one told me you were also a pianist."

She smiled. "Who can plumb the depths of my talents?"

"Do you and the leader often do duets?"

Geli's smile faded. She seemed to him to be communicating a secret in her stare. "We try," she said, "but it's hard. My uncle only plays the black keys."

■ ■ ■

She was invited to a grand costume ball at the Deutsches Theater, and she prevailed upon Baldur von Schirach, whose office was just above Hitler's in the Brown House, to wear down the führer until he finally agreed to let Geli go. If Heinrich Hoffmann took her, he said. And if she was home by eleven. And a day later he decided that Max Amann ought to go with them, too.

The theatrical designer Ingo Schröder costumed Henny as a white-buckskinned Indian princess as featured in the Westerns of Karl May, but four of his designs for Geli were rejected by Hitler for varying reasons, and Schröder would not try others.

Geli sketched a costume she'd sew for herself on her Köhler machine, and she took it to Hitler for his approval as he shared coffee and strudel with Ilse and Rudolf Hess in the parlor. On the wide, round mahogany table was a sheet of red poster board on which Hess had pasted famous faces and the lettering "*Wer ist der wichtigste Mann der Welt?*"—Who is the most important man in the world?

"We'll merely ask the question," Hess told her. "The conclusion will be inevitable. We wonder, though, if the faces aren't too hard for the man in the street."

"She's very smart," Hitler said. "She'll get them all."

She leaned over the poster. "Herr Gerhart Hauptmann, the playwright," she said. "Uncle Adolf. Leon Trotsky. Albert Einstein. And him I don't know."

"Our new friend Hjalmar Schacht," Hitler said. "The former president of the Reichsbank."

Geli shrugged a *you-could-have-fooled-me*. "Herr General Paul von Hindenburg," she said. "Max Schmeling."

Hitler asked, "What does *he* do?"

"Isn't he the heavyweight boxing champion of the world?"

"No," Hitler said. "He demonstrates the superiority of the Aryan race." And he laughed hard at his own joke as Ilse took Geli's sketch of her costume.

"Oh, I like it," Ilse said. "Who is it?"

"Diana."

"Diana who?" Hitler asked.

Ilse handed the sketch to her husband as Geli said, "The Roman goddess of the moon. The protectress of women."

Ilse asked, "What fabric?"

"A yellow chiffon."

"Won't that be lovely."

Rudolf silently handed the sketch to his führer.

Examining it, Hitler asked, "What's chiffon?"

"Oh, you see it in lots of dresses," Ilse said. "A sheer fabric."

"Meaning see-through," Hitler said. He tossed the sketch onto the poster and said, "If you want to wear something like that, you might as well go naked."

Geli stared at him in fury, flushing red. "I forgot," she hotly said. "We have the highest standards of decency to uphold." And then she took the sketch and ran to her room, volcanically slamming the door.

In silence Hitler dithered with his strudel, his gaze flying about in distraction until he formally excused himself and carried his whining contrition down the hallway.

■ ■ ■

She finally settled on a white ciré satin dinner dress by Mainbocher with a silver headband adorned with a white feather, though she thought it all wasted as she sat in a theater box with Hoffmann and Amann in their tuxedos, watching the fun others were having on the floor below them. Max Amann's hair seemed no more than a fallen leaf on his head, and he'd shaved off his Hitler mustache on Hitler's orders, so she was suddenly aware that his nude upper lip was as long as his foreshortened nose. She coldly asked, "How old are you, Max?"

"I'll be forty in November."

"Are you sure you're not older?"

"War changes you," Amann said.

"And you, Heinrich?"

Hoffmann finished popping a magnum of champagne, and reported that he was forty-five. "We're both short, too," he said. "We're both unattractive to you. And we already know we're spoiling your evening."

She said, "I'm hard to read, aren't I? I have subtle ways."

"I have a daughter," Hoffmann said.

She saw a pretty woman who was wearing only an eye mask and a man's striped tie around her waist. She saw a naked man painted in gold. A fan dancer was entertaining fraternity boys in their booth. She heard Hoffmann shout, "Ernst!"

Ambling to their theater box was Captain Ernst Röhm, who'd just returned from Bolivia where he'd been schooling mercenaries in the art of war. Röhm smiled at her like they were old friends, and she presumed he felt that way because he'd been a friend and mentor to Hitler since 1919, one of the few men with whom her uncle ever used the familiar "*Du*" for "you." She disliked him at once. Röhm was wearing the SA uniform at a fancy dress ball, for one thing, and he was a squat, fat, fanatical soldier with short brown hair, tiny eyes, and a flushed, round, piggish face made even uglier by the fact that the bridge of his nose had been shot off on the eastern front, and his left cheek had been cruelly torn by a Russian bullet. His shirt collar seemed to be choking him, and his handshake was moist as he told her, "So you are the famous niece. I have wondered if we would ever meet."

"Well, it's not like I've been hiding."

"Oh no?"

"Won't you join us for some champagne?" Amann asked.

Röhm did so, stiffly, as if he still carried a sword, and the former sergeant, Max Amann, who was all accounting and ambition, switched chairs to confer with him.

She couldn't fathom the men's fondness for Röhm, for she'd heard from Putzi Hanfstaengl, who hated him, that Röhm was an occultist who flaunted his predatory interest in boys, loved bloodshed and the heat of battle, and had many hatreds: Jews, Communism, Christianity, democracy, anyone in the officer corps above the rank of major, civilians in general, and females of any age. With the financial support of the Reichswehr and rich industrialists, she'd been told that Röhm had formed, just before the putsch, a civilian defense force of one hundred thousand former soldiers to crush any opposition and assassinate politicians, and a few years later he'd fled to Bolivia—she'd heard there was a threat of blackmail—and had only agreed to return to Germany when Hitler offered him the post of chief of staff of the Sturmabteilung.

Röhm finally turned to Geli. "And how is Leo?"

She was perplexed that they'd met, but then recalled her brother's visit for Reich Party Day in January 1923. She said, "Leo's fine. He's a schoolteacher in Linz now."

Röhm smiled with insinuation. "Of boys? What a pleasurable job *that* must be.

"Ernst!" Hoffmann said. "Manners."

"And Emil Maurice?" Röhm asked.

"I haven't seen him in months."

Röhm seemed to sink into his flesh with satisfaction. "*I* have. Driving for the leader."

"*Really?*"

"Really. A forgive-and-forget situation."

With sarcasm she said, "Uncle Adolf is famous for those."

Amann frowned at her until Röhm offered, "Emil told me you're a model now." And then Amann smiled.

Who else had seen her uncle's sketches? Was she lewdly talked about at his *Stammtisch*? Her face hot with embarrassment and betrayal, she found that Hoffmann was finishing his flute of champagne, and she fervently asked him, "Shall we dance?"

"Why not?" he said.

Walking her downstairs, his hand held her waist in a fatherly way, and he confided, "I have seen that expression of yours in Adolf. We call it 'seething rage.'"

With intensity she asked, "Will you please take me away from here?"

■ ■ ■

They were heading east, from Schwanthalerstrasse toward the flat, when Geli said, "Please, not home yet," and he obligingly turned north into the Englischer Garten. There they got out of his car and he escorted her to a food stall where he got them Paulaner beers and the food seller flattered Geli for her feathered headband and her fine dress. And then they strolled under the soft loom of night to sit beneath the timbers and yellow lanterns of the five-level Chinese Tower. Hoffmann swallowed half his first beer and pounded on a firm joist with his fist as he peered up inside. "They tell me this is modeled on the Pagoda in London's Kew Gardens."

She was quiet. She drank her Paulaner.

Sitting next to her, he said, "We try to get Adolf to England, but he won't travel outside Germany. Wants the world to visit him."

She sighed.

"An American laid out these gardens," Hoffmann said. "Benjamin something. Otherwise known as Count Rumford. My mother used to feed us Rumford soup when we were hard up. Mostly potatoes, just a hint of diced bacon, and barley, water, vinegar, salt."

She was silently crying, her tears shining under the lanterns.

"Oh now, what's this about? Röhm's just a fat pighound."

"I'm so confined," she said. "I have to make so many concessions. And they all hate me anyway."

"Who?"

"All his cold, pitiless, stupid friends in the Brown House. Am I not hated?"

"Cordially disliked," he admitted.

"*Why?*"

"There are those who think you confuse him," he said. "Who think he's distracted. Weak. And frankly there are hints of scandal. An uncle and his niece sharing a flat. We could be ruined."

"*Sharing a flat?*"

Hoffmann was flummoxed. "Aren't you?"

"My uncle's a monster!"

"Well, that's just the Communists—"

"Oh, you have *no* idea!"

She felt his discomfort and ambivalence, his wanting to flee with her accusations unheard, but the father in him said, "Tell me."

She stanched her tears. She jaggedly inhaled. "The things he makes me do are disgusting."

"Such as?"

"Whipping him and calling him names while he plays with himself. Wanting me to urinate on him. And worse. Unspeakable things."

"And he forces you?"

She nodded.

"Often this happens?"

"Four times now. Almost monthly." She saw that he wanted to question her further, but would not. Willfully, he stood and walked a few meters away, sifting what she'd confessed. After a while he seemed as stilled as a motor so long shut off that it would have felt cold to the touch.

Without facing her, Hoffmann said, "We all have secrets, Geli. I, for one, have not heard any of this. I shall never admit I have. And as a father I beg of you to say none of this to Henny."

She watched him seem to watch the moon, and she realized she was as alone as she'd ever been. She asked, "Are you crossing to the other side, Herr Hoffmann?"

"All my belongings are there," he said.

■ ■ ■

All through April and May she and Anni Winter screamed at each other; she scorned Maria Reichert as she cleaned; she claimed she'd seen Frau Dachs sleepwalking in the hallway with an ice pick in her hand; she sang so poorly that Adolf Vogl telephoned Hitler to report that he was wasting his money; she was felled by headaches or menstrual cramps whenever her uncle was free for the night. She was becoming so contrary that he began introducing her to cronies not as *meine Nichte* (my niece), but *mein nicht* (my not); she finally got what she wanted when Hitler shouted, "We have no peace in this apartment!" And it was he who suggested they go to Obersalzberg three weeks early.

With Angela, in Obersalzberg, she figured she'd be safe, and she was right. Angela shunted Hitler out of the kitchen, was there in the Winter Garden each night, was even pleased to be invited by her daughter on their picnics and hikes and afternoon outings in the Mercedes. Wholly absorbed in his niece, his hands flying onto her whenever he found an occasion, his hot eyes frequently communicating grievance and forsakenness and a hunger he thought was heartache, Adolf Hitler was nevertheless too pompous and self-conscious to be fully vulnerable to the foolishness of the lovelorn, and by the time Henny joined the family in Haus Wachenfeld for Geli's twenty-third birthday on June 4th, he'd sublimated his desire and seemed to Henny merely preoccupied, finicky, and avuncular, just a cross politician shouting into the telephone, shaking out a newspaper on the terrace, scouring medical journals to find out the names of his maladies and to discover which new chronic disease would next be poisoning him.

Angela was steeping orange pekoe tea for him when she heard her half-brother shyly hint at his interest in joining Geli and Henny for an afternoon at the movie palace in Berchtesgaden. And Geli oh so sweetly said, "Well, I really doubt you'd like it, Uncle Adolf. *Girls in Uniform*? An all-female cast? About a tyrannical headmistress in a Prussian boarding school?" And she added in the slang she'd gotten from Willie Hitler, "Not your cup of tea."

She saw his face reef with the hurts of isolation and dismissal that he must have felt as a child, and then he turned from her as quick as an affront, and loudly trudged up the stairs.

When they returned that night, Angela was standing in the kitchen with folded arms. "Your *fiancé* is on his way to Berlin," she said.

"We're not engaged. We're just related."

"Well, he's in a fury."

Rolling her eyes, Geli said, "What a rarity."

"I have no idea what you're doing, but I don't like it."

"We went to see a *movie*," Geli said.

Angela bent over and opened the oven where she was heating blinis for them, food as always her comfort and way out of a storm. She said, "The girls in your Gymnasium class are married now. Many already have more than one child. Are you trying to destroy your future?"

"I'm trying to determine it."

Angela shut the oven door and straightened up. "Don't toy with him, Geli," she said. "We'll find ourselves out on the street."

"We're already selling ourselves. Maybe we belong there."

Angela theatrically lifted a hand as if, were she any other mother, she'd have long since slapped her. And then she ordered, "Up to your room!"

"Oh please," Geli said, but she did as she was told, hearing her mother shout, as she found the upstairs landing, "He is the *patriarch*!"

She smirked at Henny. Who was solemn.

"Well, it's true, isn't it?" Henny said.

■ ■ ■

She still walked the Alsatians to the Hotel zum Türken each morn-ing to buy her uncle's newspapers, but now she'd linger there long enough to scan the front section of the leftist *Münchener Post*, or "The Poison Kitchen" as her uncle called it because of its frequent satiric attacks on National Socialism. She found in it weekly reports of cold-blooded political murders by factions within "the Hitler Party," whose crimes generally went unpunished or received insuffi-cient jail sentences because of a justice system that favored the Nationalist right. She also read in the *Münchener Post* her uncle's self-praise that, "Nothing happens in the movement without my knowledge, without my approval. Even more, nothing happens without my wish."

And she was cleaning his upstairs room in late July when she found hidden under his bed an illustrated book by Dr. Joachim Welzl called *Woman as Slave: The Sexual-Psychology of the Masochist.*

She couldn't say precisely what the connection was between the book and the newspaper articles she'd read, but she was confident there was one, and she was sick.

■ ■ ■

In June the failing economy had forced Chancellor Heinrich Brün-ing to issue an emergency finance decree that further slashed unem-ployment and welfare payments to millions who were already hard-pressed by the worldwide depression. Workers were soon call-ing him "Chancellor Hunger" and Hitler was finding many reasons to travel north and stir up further protests.

Probably at Hitler's behest, Doktor Goebbels mailed a friendly letter to Geli describing their frantic political tour of Germany. "*Endless traveling,*" he wrote her. "*Work is accomplished while stand-ing, driving, and flying. Important conversations are held in doorways or on the way to the railroad station. We turn up in a city a half hour before the speech is scheduled, he climbs to the platform and speaks. By the time he's done he's in a state, as if he'd just been pulled out of a hot bath fully dressed. Then we get into the car and drive another two hours. We need rest.*"

In August Hitler telephoned Edwin and Helene Bechstein to say he'd holiday at the Wagner Festival in Bayreuth, and he'd be staying at Wahnfried, the home of his old friend Winifred Wagner. And it was Edwin Bechstein who called Haus Wachenfeld and insisted that Geli join them for the festival, saying, "It really is *the* place to be seen." And then he insinuated that it was her uncle who was inviting her; he'd decided on a conciliation and accord.

On the way to Bayreuth, three hours north of München by car, Direktor Bechstein, as he liked to be called, stiffly sat across from Geli in his limousine, his spectacles on and his attention fixed on a sheaf of accounting papers in his lap. Next to her was Helene Bechstein's solidifying flesh, trussed in the strong barrel of a corset whose whalebones ribbed her navy blue dress, her softening face the color of lard and her voice just this side of a shriek as she chided Geli for the pain and anguish she'd caused her uncle. "Oh, how your heart would *break* if you'd heard him wailing as I did! Threatening to shoot himself! The indecency of putting our Wolf through all that! And you! Who are you? A girl who scoffs at her own good fortune, is who. A Slavic girl whose charm wears thin and whose beauty won't last. Who'll soon be back in Wien near the west railway station if she doesn't watch out."

Sighing, Geli asked, "Are you going to go on berating me like this?"

"We *can*," Direktor Bechstein said. "We're your hosts."

She laughed at the incongruousness of the statement, but Helene Bechstein forged ahead with, "Who is this Jewish boyfriend?"

"We've heard," her husband added.

Geli was shocked. "There's no one."

"Are you pregnant?" Helene Bechstein asked.

"Isn't it obligatory to have a male contribution?"

The old woman turned away. "Don't be vulgar."

"Wasn't he a pianist?" Direktor Bechstein asked his wife.

With certainty, she said, "An art teacher in Linz."

"I do hope he was good-looking," Geli said. "I hate being linked with toads."

Helene Bechstein stared. "Wolf urged us to bring you. To heal the wounds. Don't you see that he desperately wants a détente?"

But the Wagner Festival filled Bayreuth with Germany's rich and famous, and under those circumstances Hitler seemed to have qualms about associating himself with the scandal of his niece. She was avoided that afternoon as he waded through crowds, shaking hands and soliciting contributions. And so she visited Wahnfried just before the opera in a stunning red evening gown and red shoes and was told he was changing into his tails until finally she was told he was leaving. She was forced to share a box with the Bechsteins in the Festspielhaus for a flamboyant version of *Die Götterdämmerung* while she watched Winifred's faraway opera box as Hitler swooned with the music and flattered Richard Wagner's thirty-four-year-old daughter-in-law with affectionate hand pats, juvenile whispering, and the self-congratulatory talk that, for him, was flirtation. And then a message was sent to Geli's room in the Goldener Anker Hotel that she was to go back to Obersalzberg by railway car in the morning.

■ ■ ■

She was in the flat at Prinzregentenplatz in September when she finally saw her uncle again. Three weeks had passed. She was just leaving the breakfast room as he came down the hallway in his jackboots and Brownshirt uniform, and he bowed forward from the waist as he asked, "And how was your summer?"

"Quite calm," she said.

"Fully rested?"

"I slept well. And you?"

"Anni!" he called, and walked by her.

Anni Winter brought out his tea and biscuit tray from the kitchen.

There was a formality to their chance meetings in the flat, as if they were acquaintances who found they shared a floor in a grand luxe hotel. She still overheard him interrogating the Winters about what she'd done that day, and she noticed men she took to be SS who'd loiter for hours outside the *Drogerie* on Grillparzerstrasse, or walk a hundred meters behind her as she strolled along the River Isar to Müller's Public Baths.

A friend from the university named Elfi Samthaber telephoned her one noontime and Geli told Frau Reichert she'd take the call in Hitler's office. She sat in his chair as she chatted, and then she found in his wastebasket a handwritten note on orchid-scented Wedgwood blue paper that was just like the stationery she'd been given for her birthday. She read:

> Dear Herr Hitler,
>
> Thank you again for the wonderful invitation to the theater. It was a memorable evening. I am most grateful to you for your kindness. I am counting the hours until I may have the joy of another meeting.
>
> > Yours,
> > Eva

She tore the note into four pieces and in spite left it on the ink blotter. She continued her conversation.

■　■　■

She felt a flow of cold air river over her as she fitfully slept that night, and she reached for a fallen blanket until frustration woke her. And she saw that her uncle was kneeling on the floor beside her, fully dressed, and that it was he who'd folded the covers back, who'd softly worked the nightgown up to her waist. His hand found her mouth and held it shut as he bristled the skin of her buttock with smacking kisses.

"She means nothing to me," he whispered. "You do." His free hand forced itself between her clenched thighs and she felt chilled as he fluttered her sex. Worming his face into her flesh, he asked in the hushed voice of a lover, "Tell me what you want, Geli." And he lifted the hand that was quieting her.

She felt the hot slide of tears on her cheeks. She told him, "To get away from you."

Hitler halted for a second, and she was afraid he'd hit her, but then he continued as if she'd encouraged him. "Would you like to go to Wien?"

She felt like a child given a choice of presents. She said yes.

"Will you let me do what I want?"

She had no choice. She nodded.

■ ■ ■

On September 11th she went to the Brown House with Hitler for a short visit before the afternoon showing of a mountaineering film, *The White Hell of Mount Palü*, costarring Luis Trenker and Leni Riefenstahl. But the führer was in his office so infrequently that Rudolf Hess and Franz Xaver Schwarz hurried to take advantage of his being there to finally get his signature and have him review a calendar of forthcoming events.

Waiting in the hallway, she looked at an unskilled watercolor of Feldherrnhalle on November 9, 1923, featuring a fearless and far taller Hitler, his fist raised defiantly as he faced a fusillade from green-uniformed police and as his fellow putschists fell at his feet. Other faces were hard to make out, though the furtive, smallish man behind him seemed to be Erich Ludendorff. The quartermaster general and her uncle were not now on speaking terms, she knew, and she supposed the picture had been hung in the hallway to alter the memory of the putsch, when Ludendorff was the heroic one and some foreign correspondents had dismissed her uncle as "Ludendorff's noisy lieutenant." The facts, for her uncle, were instruments that merely needed management.

Carrying his leather portfolio, a jovial Heinrich Hoffmann walked down from the upstairs offices with the seemingly giant Putzi Hanfstaengl, whose hand was on the far shorter man's shoulder, but their faces fell when they saw Geli, they failed to offer greetings, and she thought she heard Putzi whisper, "Empty-headed slut," as they exited the building.

An officious Rudolf Hess found her in the hallway. "We have many transactions and deliberations that require the indispensable wisdom of the leader. With profound regrets he suggests you go on to the cinema without him."

Hiding her pleasure, she said, "Certainly."

The film had been his idea. She instead strolled south in fine weather to the fruit vendors' stands of the Viktualien Markt and to the hundreds of shops surrounding the gray bricks of city hall and Marienplatz. She was audience to fire-eaters, jugglers, accordion players, an old man who grinned as he chewed bottle glass, and a blond, burly woman who called herself "Madame Nobody" and would bend iron bars in her hands for ten pfennigs. At a bookstall she bought Erich Maria Remarque's best-selling antiwar novel *All Quiet on the Western Front,* and she was reading it with a tankard of Franziskaner at an outside table on Neuhauserstrasse, just across from St. Michael's Church, when she heard a man say, "We meet again!"

She shaded her eyes but at first couldn't find the man's face because of the fierce sun behind him. And then he limped to the shade and she saw that it was a tall, soldierly priest in his fifties wearing a black wool coat and fedora, the Jesuit she'd seen years before in the Hofbräuhaus, the one who'd regretted to say that her uncle was a dangerous man.

"Are you a Nazi now?" he asked.

She told him she wasn't. She then remembered his name: Rupert Mayer.

"The jewelry gives the wrong impression," he said.

She fingered the gold swastika at her throat. "A gift. Won't you sit?"

"I have confessions soon." With firmness the Jesuit said, "A Catholic cannot be an anti-Semite. Are you aware of that?"

She affirmed him with friendly uncertainty.

"Many aren't," Mayer said. He folded his hands. "And so, in spite of the political climate, are you liking Germany?"

"Yes. I find it beautiful."

"Good. You have been here for how long now?"

"Four years."

He frowned with further assessment. "Are you happy?"

She felt affronted in some way, and said, "Why do you ask, Pater Mayer?"

"The fräulein is not the woman I first met."

"I'm older," she said.

"No. I can tell. The yoke isn't easy."

Tears blurred her eyes, and she turned away to stall them. She seemed ready to cry at anything now. She heard the priest ask, "Are you all right, Fräulein Raubal?" and she nodded and fluttered her hand. Waving him off. She finished her Franziskaner and slid the tankard aside as he touched his fedora in good-bye and tilted on his cane in order to cross Neuhauserstrasse to St. Michael's. She watched him waiting for a fleet of trucks to pass, and she got up and hesitantly walked to him.

He smiled. "Traffic."

She told him, "It's true. I'm unhappy."

With sympathy, he said, "I'm not surprised."

"Would you please hear my confession?" she asked.

She'd decided. Although Hitler snidely objected, she was given his grudging permission to go to Mass at St. Michael's Church on Sunday, and afterward walked the few blocks to Adolf Vogl's house to cancel her September lessons and to inquire whether he knew of anyone she could study with in Wien. Because he was a party member, she told him she'd be there for just a few months. Vogl thought she should audition for his own former voice teacher, Professor Otto Ro, and he gave her a letter of introduction.

On Monday, September 15th, Willi Schmidt, an important music critic in München, welcomed Geli into his office and leaned to his side in his high-backed writing chair as he listened to her sing "Domine Jesu" from the *Requiem* of Mozart, and "Lacrymosa" from the *Requiem* of Verdi. And then he penned a three-paragraph recommendation that called the young lady delightful, graciously praised the beauty of her voice and the evenness of her breathing, and offered the opinion that she would be far better suited to lieder.

She agreed. She told Schmidt, who was *not* a party member, that she would be in Wien permanently.

"What a pity," he said. "Why are you leaving Germany?"

She frankly told him, "My uncle is molesting me," but she took no joy in Schmidt's surprise. She hurried out.

She strolled down Briennerstrasse to the Brown House, waving, as she went inside, to the SS man who'd been shadowing her. She found Hitler in the oak-and-gold elegance of the cellar restaurant just under an oversize portrait of Dietrich Eckart and holding forth to Otto Wagener, the party's economic adviser, whom he seemed to be striving to impress with his phenomenal memory of agricultural, financial, and industrial statistics. Without looking at his niece, Hitler condescendingly patted a spot beside him on the upholstered horseshoe bench. She seated herself and slid over.

Otto Wagener was a fat, friendly, chain-smoker with a face that would look fairly similar if it were upside down on his head. Changing the subject for fear of boring the fräulein, Wagener asked if she were a university student.

With false excitement, Geli said, "I was. But Uncle Alf always knows the right thing to do, and he decided I should be a singer."

"A singer!" Wagener said. "Really, Herr Hitler, it isn't fair. An abundance of talents have been apportioned to your family, leaving little for the rest of us."

In the famished, never-enough of his vanity, Hitler found a moment in which to smile. "We are good stock," he said. "It's true."

"And he is so generous," Geli said, "that Uncle Alf is sending me to Wien for lessons." She saw her uncle try not to look startled.

Wagener said, "There's no place like Wien for an opera singer. Are you leaving soon, Fräulein Raubal?"

"Wednesday," she said. She felt the scald of Hitler's eyes, but then a waiter was there, softly putting a saucer and teacup and spoon in front of her, and she paid attention to that.

Wearing a black SS uniform, a frail Heinrich Himmler hurried in and sidled up behind Hitler to whisper in his ear. His face seemed as wan and featureless as the sand dunes of the Chiemsee, and his pince-nez flashed with chandelier light so that they huddled against his nose like silver coins.

Staring at his niece, Hitler asked Himmler, "*Who?*"

Himmler said the name again in hushed tones.

And Geli turned to Wagener to say, "I have introductions to the finest teachers there, and the famous music critic Willie Schmidt has flattered me with a letter of recommendation."

With formality, Himmler offered a secret idea to his leader, and Hitler smiled. "She is going to Wien for a few weeks," he told Wagener, "for finishing touches only. And then, if she finds the courage, she'll be performing at the Prinzregenten Theater in December."

Wagener was not ignorant. Choosing to ignore the intriguing on both sides, he asked, "And what do you foresee in the crude-oil markets, Herr Hitler?"

Hitler expatiated. Calmly, Geli sipped tea.

■ ■ ■

Wednesday, September 16th, she left München with just one suitcase in order to make it seem she was indeed on a journey of only a few weeks. She had no savings; she'd given no thought to a job. She just wanted out.

She took the railway to Berchtesgaden, where Angela picked her up in the Wanderer automobile she'd gotten from her half-brother in January, and they talked about three women's boardinghouses where she could stay, if not with Aunt Paula. To hide her intentions from her mother, Geli packed only a few fall and winter clothes from the upstairs closet at Haus Wachenfeld, and she waited until after dinner to nonchalantly telephone the Salzburg railway station to find out about Thursday departure times for Wien. She whistled as she helped with the dishes.

Angela found a place for the leftover oxtail soup in the icebox and said, "I haven't seen you this happy in months."

Geli fanned the wetness from the dish towel, and folded and hung it as she fraudulently answered, "I was so homesick for Wien."

Angela smiled. "I ought to tag along with you and add some old-fashioned gloom just for balance."

"Oh, you needn't, really," Geli said. "I hear they have Nazis there, too."

Angela shifted a chair under the kitchen table. "We'll have none of that," she said. "I'm a Nazi."

"You're deluded, Mother."

"Oh, you. You think you know everything, you."

She smiled falsely and confessed, "Everything about Uncle Adolf, yes."

A flint of confusion nettled her mother's face, and then she got the meaning. She seemed staggered as she turned away from Geli and leaned over the kitchen table, flooding with grief, her red hands so flat on the oak she could have felt the whorls of the grain. "He's a *great* man," Angela said. "A *genius*."

"He isn't. He's evil. They all are. Don't you see how Uncle Adolf buys us off? If we like the good things, the money and fame, we have to forgive the bad. We say, 'Oh, that's just him,' as if it doesn't matter. But it *all* matters: the hating, the lying, the bullying—"

"Don't say anything more," Angela said, and tightly held her hands to her ears.

"The things he makes me do," she said, but softly, so it wouldn't be heard.

■ ■ ■

On Thursday morning they were just about to leave for the train when Angela got a telephone call from a frantic Adolf who said he'd changed his mind, he was too lonely already, Geli was not to go to Austria just yet. Julius Schaub, he said, was on his way to collect her.

Angela hung up the receiver and felt a pang when she saw Geli's face. In a weak effort to console her, she offered, "If he changed his mind once, he can change it again."

Crying with frustration, Geli tried, "We could go to Salzburg right now. Schaub won't be here for an hour, and by then I'd be on my way to Wien."

Angela hugged her and said, "I hear they have Nazis there, too."

■ ■ ■

She fumed in the front seat of the Mercedes as Schaub took his truant back to München. With fiercely crossed arms, she frowned out the side window at skies as gray as prison blankets and at fields of hay swaying beneath the *Föhn*, the hot, humid wind from the south. A farmer was waiting on a haymower and a hired man was holding the harnesses of the horse team as an old woman in a shroud of a dress hastily shuffled toward them carrying handled grocery bags that were so heavy with food her fingers seemed to drain from her hands. Geli told Schaub, "She looks just like me."

With his customary seriousness, Schaub considered the woman and decided Geli was joking. "Other women are begging to change places with you," Schaub said.

"Let them," she said. "I have had my turn."

"It isn't *all* bad," Schaub said.

"I am in chains."

With disdain, he said, "A Communist slogan." Intently watching the highway, he added, "The fact is, the folk don't know what to do with freedom. Choices confuse them. They wander aimlessly. They gain nothing but headaches and debts. They need a Hitler to think for them and tell them what to do. To force them to do it, if they object."

"And was it he who told you that?"

"Well, he's *right*," Schaub said. "The leader is always right."

She sighed. "You're hopeless. All of you."

Schaub seemed genuinely baffled. "We are *full* of hope!"

With effort, she fell asleep. She awoke in front of the flat at Prinzregentenplatz and found her uncle in his Brownshirt uniform, just outside her car window, worriedly staring in. Ever alert to her, her uncle seemed to notice she'd gotten rid of his gift of the gold swastika and was now wearing a crucifix at her neck. "Are you well?" he asked.

She didn't say. She opened the door and got out. She felt the
sting of his mustache as he formally kissed her cheek and in a
hushed voice asked, "Can I be the leader of a great nation if even
my niece will not obey me?"

"All I do is obey you!"

"Oh, but using your feminine wiles is the disobedience of women."
Avoiding touching her, Hitler sat where she'd been. "I have to pre-
pare a speech," he told her. "We're going up to Hamburg tomorrow to
launch my presidential campaign."

"We?"

"Well, not you."

Geli was outraged. "You brought me back so you could leave?"

Hitler failed to see the difficulty. "This way I'll know where you
are."

"Alone, in the flat."

Schaub was finishing setting Geli's suitcase down on the sidewalk.
Without turning to him, Hitler shouted, "Schaub! Are you available
tonight?"

"If you wish."

"Take your wife and my niece to a movie palace." And then he
grinned as if, in a flash, he'd solved everything; he'd even amazed
himself.

■ ■ ■

She'd heard that Hitler objected to it, so she insisted the Schaubs
take her to see M, a Fritz Lang film starring Peter Lorre as a child
murderer. Schaub later claimed his wife had noticed Geli was "inat-
tentive, sad, indeed almost tearful." She'd gotten chocolate with
Geli at the refreshment stall and had asked what the problem was,
but Geli failed to confide in her, merely replying, "I'm upset."
Schaub himself was forced to return to the Brown House for Hitler,
so when the film ended his wife and Geli shared a taxi to the flat at
Prinzregentenplatz 16 where Geli seemed not to want to go inside.
She took a long time saying good-bye to Frau Schaub and asked
"what she was going to do in the next few days because she was

alone, too." Schaub's wife told her to telephone their flat and, after a handshake, Geli headed into the building, whistling just as Peter Lorre did. She never called.

■ ■ ■

The *Föhn* winds continued, and just after breakfast on September 18th, Geli strolled along the Isar river to Karl Müller's Public Baths. She was wearing a pearl necklace and a taupe, short-sleeved afternoon dress with saddle shoes. She swam a kilometer and lolled in the pool with Elfi Samthaber, who was astonished to find her friend still in München. She told Elfi there'd been a hitch in her plans, but she expected to be in Austria soon.

The heat was wilting, the gray morning air felt as moist as steam, and the avenues were jammed with cars and tour buses filled with watchful people from elsewhere who were there for the first days of Oktoberfest. She walked to the Hoffmann house in Bogenhausen, but she was not invited inside even when the upstairs maid roused Henny from sleep and she appeared on the porch in a red kimono, with sleep-welted eyes and hair as wild as bramble. Camera cases were behind her in the foyer, and as Henny shut the front door and roosted with Geli on the porch steps, she yawned and said she'd decided not to go along and watch her father photograph the führer in Hamburg.

"Would you like to do something tonight?" Geli asked.

She was told that Henny was going to an Oktoberfest party with Baldur von Schirach.

"And Saturday?" She saw the traffic of fear and pity in her friend's stare, and she got up. "So, your father's given you instructions."

"Others, too," Henny said. "Weren't you going to Wien?"

"I still am."

"You should. I hear they're all uneasy about you now."

"Why?"

"I have learned not to ask questions."

"Maybe I'll stay in Germany just to be an annoyance."

"Don't defy them," Henny said, and then she noticed a Brownshirt slowly coast past on a bicycle, frankly watching them both, and she disappeared inside the house.

■ ■ ■

At one o'clock Geli ate a lunch of spaghetti and Chianti in the flat's dining room and was just finishing when she was joined there by Hitler, who'd returned from the Brown House in his Brownshirt uniform to have Anni Winter gather his things for the weekend. Schaub and Hoffmann, he said, would be coming for him at six.

She asked, "Will you go all the way to Hamburg tonight?"

"Well, at least as far as Leipzig. I hate being rushed before a speech. I make oratory look easy, but it's not."

She agreed that it must be difficult.

Scoffing at her sympathy, Hitler turned to the kitchen and shouted, "Frau Reichert! Shall I be here all afternoon?" Then he settled in his chair and sighed as he folded his hands atop his crossed thighs. "I have had such nasty feelings today."

She told him it was the *Föhn*. The hot winds unsettled people.

Snidely smiling, he asked, "Where would you be now? Well past Linz? A few hours from Wien?"

She didn't say.

Maria Reichert hurried in with a tray holding a silver tea service and a full plate of spaghetti and meatless tomato sauce. She reminded Herr Hitler that she was off duty from five that afternoon until Monday morning, but she'd hired a friend, Anna Kirmair, for the Saturday housecleaning. And the Winters would be in for half a day tomorrow to polish the silver and handle the laundry chores.

She was boring him, he told her, and she reddened with embarrassment and went out.

"And what about me?" Geli asked.

Quietly rolling strings of pasta with his fork and spoon, Hitler prematurely smiled at his wit and said, "Oh, you are anything but boring."

"Will you let me go to Wien?"

"I haven't decided."

She stupidly asked how he knew she wouldn't go while he was gone, and he laughed hugely for a while.

She felt tears of frustration filming her eyes, and hated the fact that it so manifestly gave him satisfaction. She stood in silence and walked to her bedroom. She didn't slam the door.

And then she found that he'd followed her. Worms of rage were there in his forehead and flames seemed to churn in his stare. "You have made me helpless and pitiful," he said. "You see that, don't you? I have fallen in love with you, and you have loathed and rejected me. And yet I am seized by you. I am lost and in ruins. Even now my throat tightens. My heart cracks in two. You cannot destroy Germany in this way."

"*You* hate! *You* destroy! You'll do to Germany just what you're doing to me! And I won't have it anymore!"

He screamed, "*My* will is your will! *Your* will is *not* mine!" And then he slammed her door and the foyer door and thundered down the stairs.

She was solemnly watching at the high window as Hitler's jackboots strode to his waiting car.

■ ■ ■

Maria Reichert later reported that she'd heard Geli weeping behind a locked door all afternoon, but Anni Winter said she went to the *Drogerie* for Zuchooh Creme and Carmol Katarrh-Pastillen. And when she gave it to Anni to add to Hitler's toiletries kit, she said, "I have no idea why he won't let me go; I really have nothing at all in common with him."

Anni later protected the führer by telling an interviewer she'd miserably said, "I have no idea why I can't let him go; I'm really getting nothing at all from my uncle." Anni further suggested that Geli was in a funk because of Hitler's heightened affection for Fräulein Braun, saying she'd found the note from Eva in his jacket as she'd helped Anni pack. She also said she'd gone past Geli's room just before leaving that evening and had found it locked from the inside. She had been listening to American jazz. Duke Ellington.

Widow Reichert got into a green Bavarian headdress and full-skirted dirndl that choked her waist but plumped up her breasts, and, after shouting the night's instructions to her deaf old mother, she went off at five to work in one of the giant beer tents of Oktoberfest.

At five-thirty the führer returned again to his flat to bathe and change into a fashionable navy blue suit and a homburg. And when Anni and Georg Winter left the building at six, Julius Schaub and Heinrich Hoffmann were loitering under the gray stone frieze of Wotan at 16 Prinzregentenplatz. The fine-boned *Haushofmeister* was tilting to the right with Hitler's suitcase, and Schaub took it from him to put it in the trunk of the Mercedes.

Upstairs in her room, Geli was paging through the fashion magazine *Die Dame* when she heard her uncle hesitate outside her bedroom door and softly knuckle it to offer his farewell. Without shifting on the sofa, she called out, "Will you let me go to Wien?" And she heard Hitler's heavy stride down the hallway.

She got up to raise the venetian blinds and watch Prinzregentenplatz, and she pushed up the sash on her window farther when she saw her uncle shake Heinrich Hoffmann's hand and mince his way toward the front-right passenger door that Schaub was holding open. She leaned out on the sill and shouted down, "*Will* you let me go to Wien?"

Childishly stamping his shoe, he shouted up, "For the last time, no!"

She withdrew from the window and heard him explain, "We have been quarreling."

She heard Heinrich Hoffmann coolly say, "She'll get over it."

Seeking to pacify his niece, Hitler said, "One minute," and headed inside the building again. And his official photographer followed just in case he needed to intercede.

She greeted the führer at the flat's door, and softly asked again, "Will you please let me go to Wien?" She chilled as she felt him fondly stroke her cheek, and then she heard him relent and say, "All right, Little Princess. You can go just as soon as I get back." She smiled. "Au revoir, Uncle Adolf. Au revoir, Herr Hoffmann."

And then the men left for Hamburg. She shut the foyer door and saw old Frau Dachs in the hallway, haltingly holding out a luncheon tray with a spoon and a bowl of potato soup on it. "Would you like?" she asked.

"I'll make my own dinner."

"What?"

With exaggeration, Geli shook her head.

"Well, I'm going to my quarters," the old woman said. "Don't stay up too late."

■ ■ ■

She strolled on Prinzregentenstrasse in the lukewarm zephyrs of the *Föhn*, buying a chilled brown bottle of Liebfraumilch, a hunk of Gouda cheese, and a waxed-paper funnel of fragrant yellow freesias that she carefully arranged in a Dresden vase and situated on her white dresser next to the framed photograph of her favorite Alsatian, Muck. She took a glass of wine to the foyer and sat on the herringboned oak as she telephoned Elfi Samthaber and genially chatted about the fall fashions she'd seen in *Die Dame*, promising to call Elfi again on Saturday. Maybe they'd go to the theater. She ate cheese and crackers and listened to Radio Berlin as she painted on nail polish. She leafed through magazines. She went to her desk and got out a sheet of Wedgwood-blue writing paper with "Angelika Raubal" printed on it in English script in the upper-left corner. She began a friendly letter to Ingrid von Launitz. And she was head-down and writing when she heard the shush of the front door opening, then heard it softly chunk closed. She looked at the Longines clock beside her bed. Half-past eleven. She called, "Maria?"

She heard no answer. She got scared.

Whoever it was seemed to be holding himself motionless, as if he were sensing if others were still up. And then he was walking down the hallway. She stared at her door but heard his shoes stride past it on the runner and go into the office. She heard the give of a drawer as he tugged on it, then the harsh grind and thump as his thigh bumped it shut.

"Uncle?" she called.

Stillness. Was he hesitating? Was he checking himself in the mirror? She was still holding her pen. She let it go. She fastened the free buttons of her dress and groomed a wing of hair from her face. And then she saw the brass door handle gently lower and the tall oak door fall open like a page of an old book.

Hitler was stolidly there, still in his fashionable blue suit, hunched forward a little and frowning, his hands behind his back. He looked like a banker who'd sought a theater exit and found himself onstage. His face was white. His forelock had fallen. He seemed full of sentences and huddled emotions. Embers of their argument still flared in the ash.

She asked, "Aren't you going to Hamburg?"

"We only got as far as Nürnberg," he said. "We registered in the Deutscher Hof Hotel, and Schaub took me to the railway station."

"Why?"

Wincing a false smile, he just stared at her for a moment. Knives in his eyes. And then he glanced away and asked, "What are you writing?"

"Just a letter." And though Geli knew she'd only attract further interest in it, she found herself folding her forearms over the page.

Hitler strolled forward like a skeptical teacher on the hunt for insurrection in his class. "To whom? You have a friend to write to far from here?"

"Ingrid. In Wien."

She shied from him as he sidled around the desk. His flank familiarly leaned against her, and she gave way. "'Dear Ingrid,'" Hitler read. He tilted away to try to make out her handwriting without his glasses. And he quoted, "'When I come to Wien—I hope very soon— we'll drive together to Semmering an—'"

"'And' is where you came in."

"And what?"

"Have fun," she said.

"Semmering. The health resort?"

"Yes."

"I was too poor to visit health resorts when I was twenty-three. Where will you get the money?"

She was not stunned that he'd no longer fund her. She was stunned that she'd failed to consider it.

Eyes shining with tears, he asked, "And what will you tell your friends in Austria about me? Will you also tell Professor Otto Ro that your uncle has been molesting you?"

Of course he'd find out, she thought. She was frightened he'd hit her, but his hands were still behind his back. She quickly said, "I'll say nothing about you. I promise."

Saying nothing more, he shifted his right hand from behind his back and laid a gun on the letter, his Walther 6.35, as ugly as sin, her mother would say. Collecting attention. Everything else in the room seemed diminished by it.

"Hold it in your hands," he said.

She fabricated an offhand tone, full of innocence and what he'd think of as feminine wile as she told him, "I'd rather not." And then she got up and fitted the chair within the kneehole of the desk. She withdrew from her uncle before sitting on the sofa as she'd seen his favorite movie stars do, her left arm angled high on the sofa back and a hand in her hair, as blithe as a girl on a picnic, her face serene in the sunshine. She nonchalantly asked, "Why the gun?"

Without smiling, he said, "It's a sex toy."

She giggled out of sheer nervousness. She felt a change in him, a cold, machinelike subtraction of emotion, as if he himself were the gun. "Will you kiss me good-bye?" he asked.

She was amazed. Had she finally won the argument? Was she going? She grinned. Anything now seemed easy. "Of course."

She walked toward him and tilted her face as his soft belly jellied against her, and he quickly stabbed his pursed lips against her full, pliant mouth before finding formality again. "And now for this one last time," he said, "I would like you to excite me."

She tried not to show her dismay. "How?"

Shifting the weight of the Walther in his right hand, he touched the gun's cold barrel to the neck of her dress. "Undo it," he said.

Tentatively she undid the collar and then the two buttons below that.

But he said in his soothing, dog-calming voice, "A little further, Princess. Show me your titties."

She felt insulted but did as he said, widening the front of her dress around her filled brassiere. His face was cold-blooded as he stared, and she flinched when she felt the chill steel of the Walther handgun drawl over the roundness of each breast as if he were sketching a cartoon, even touching the barrel to the fabric over her right nipple while saying "Bip," and then her left, saying "Bip" again. He seemed to want her to smile, so she did.

And then his free fist flashed out and hit her face hard. She reeled against the sofa and heard a jangle of bells in her brain, and then a fainter ringing. When she felt her nose, hot blood twined through her fingers, and she knew at once that her nose was broken. She was so shocked she did not scream.

"Look what you made me do," Hitler said. "Talking about me." He was shaking the sting from his hand.

She was on her knees and thinking irrationally that she could stanch the blood from soaking her dress if she just found a handkerchief. She wondered if it were possible that her beauty was gone forever. And then she realized that it would not end with this.

His free hand forced her chin up and he frowned with dissatisfaction. "You needn't worry," he said. "I won't remember you like this."

"Don't," she said.

"The Japanese who have betrayed their leaders commit a suicide of honor," he said. "And now I would like *you* to kill yourself."

Wide-eyed, she scrutinized his face in the hope of finding out that he was kidding. But she knew he was not. She cried, "No, Uncle Adolf! No, no! Please!"

Calmly he said, "Aren't you pathetic. Suicide is just a flash of pain, a fraction of a second, and then there's nothingness. All problems vanish into the void."

In fury, she yelled, "Then you do it! Shithead!" Holding her hurting nose she flailed a fist at him, but she felt him catch her hair in one hand and yank her still as he held the Walther pistol just above her heart, then fired down.

She jolted with the force of the bullet slamming through her and saw his hands fly up to his ears to quell the gunshot noise. She fleetingly thought, *The canaries*, and fell unconscious to the floor.

Worriedly, Hitler looked to the hallway, then reminded himself that only Frau Dachs was still there with them in the flat, and she was deaf. Locking the bedroom door from the inside, he squatted above his niece as if she were horticulture he couldn't quite name, his hands loose but for the gun, his forearms on his knees, his face fascinated. She was still breathing, but with great effort, a watery sigh as she exhaled, then a faint screaking noise in inhalation, as of an old, unoiled hinge. Leaning farther over, he saw that blood bubbled up from her lung wound as she breathed, staining maroon the front of her taupe afternoon dress. A frail tear formed in Geli's right eye and trickled down her cheek. Hitler wiped it away with his thumb, then stood, his back aching, and sat heavily on the sofa with the gun still hot between his thighs. She was strong. She was hanging on to life, like his mother. Watching her faint twitching movements, he was sure she was dying. And then he was sure Angelika Raubal was dead, and there was nothing further to do but cry with self-pity for his loss and love and misfortune.

CHAPTER NINETEEN
AFTERWARD

Waking at sunrise on September 19th, he realized it was time to act, so he put the gun on a sofa cushion, gingerly stepped around the wide pool of blood, walked out to the hallway telephone, and called Rudolf Hess at home. "I shot my Princess," Hitler told him.

Shocked out of sleep, Hess was silent for a few seconds, assessing what had been said, and then he asked, "Where are you?"

"In the flat."

"Is she dead?"

"Yes."

"Am I the first to know?"

"Yes."

"Wait for me," Hess said. And he added, "You have done the right thing, my leader."

Hess got to the flat within twenty minutes, and found that the führer had already awakened Maria Reichert in order to have her make tea. Questioning her in the kitchen, Hess heard that she'd returned from Oktoberfest around two. She'd been *beschwipst* with drink and had gone straight to bed.

Was she aware of what had happened to Fräulein Raubal?

She said she'd been told she'd committed suicide.

"It's sad, isn't it," Hess said. And then he saw old Frau Dachs standing at the kitchen door in a hairnet and quilted robe.

"I'm deaf but I felt it," she said. "Around midnight. Windows shivering, and the whole flat shaking when she hit the floor."

Hess turned to the old woman's daughter. "Will you please see that she gets dressed and goes to a friend's? We don't want to further upset her."

"*Mutti*," Maria said. "Out."

Hess hurried to Geli's bedroom. She was lying facedown, with her legs folded off to the right as if she'd fallen from a kneel. She seemed to be fingering the confusion of her brown hair with her right hand, while her left arm was flat on the floor, as if straining for the Walther on the sofa. She was stiff with rigor mortis and the front of her dress was flooded in the darkening blood that widened out from the sofa to the four-poster bed. There were no shoe prints. A skeleton key was still inside the door, which was good. Walking down to Hitler's bedroom, Hess got the skeleton key from his door, found out that it fitted Geli's, and locked her door from the hallway.

Watching the Saturday traffic on Prinzregentenstrasse and sipping orange peel tea, the führer seemed fairly placid, but there was a shocking, crazed look to his eyes when Hess handed him the skeleton key. "Where are Schaub and Hoffmann?" Hess asked.

"Nürnberg," the führer said. "The Deutscher Hof Hotel."

"We'll take you away," Hess told him, "just as soon as the others arrive."

One by one they were joined in the flat by Heinrich Himmler, Max Amann, Franz Xaver Schwarz, and Baldur von Schirach. The führer was still not himself, so Himmler took him to his office in the party headquarters as the other gentlemen from the Brown House got together in the library to figure out a story.

Anni and Georg Winter and Anna Kirmair, the day maid, walked into the flat about fifteen minutes later, at nine, and found the four high-ranking Nazis in a heated argument. Georg asked Max Amann, "What's happened?"

And he was told, "We haven't decided yet."

Within a few minutes they had decided, and Baldur von Schirach telephoned Adolf Dresler in the Brown House and extemporized a press release stating that Adolf Hitler had canceled his speech in Hamburg and was in deep mourning over the suicide of Angelika Raubal, his niece, who had been living in a furnished room in a building in Bogenhausen where Hitler owned a flat.

Meanwhile, Rudolf Hess was instructing the staff that a scandal would wreck the party, and if they had faith in Hitler, and hated Communists and Jews like he did, and hoped for a glorious Germany, free of want, they ought to put aside their niggling qualms and give the police analogous statements. Each agreed to do that, but they were schooled at some speed and their stories either did not match or matched so well they seemed memorized.

And then Amann handed Hess the telephone and he heard Himmler screaming that Göring, Goebbels, and he were in agreement that calling the unfortunate occurrence that befell Hitler's niece a suicide might wreak nearly as much havoc for the party as calling it a murder. Would she, who knew her uncle so well, prefer to end it all? Wouldn't the proximity of the führer make her happy and optimistic?

Schirach called Adolf Dresler again to change the press release to say that it was "a lamentable accident" and that she'd killed herself while handling the gun; but he was too late, the first press release had been issued. With regret Schirach told Hess that the story could not be changed and they discussed a suicide motive that would not involve the führer. She'd discovered, they decided, that she wasn't a good enough singer. She was humiliated and ashamed.

Max Amann called the Deutscher Hof Hotel and was informed that the Hitler group had just checked out. A pageboy was sent in a taxi to flag them down.

Rudolf Hess handed Anni Winter the führer's teacup and saucer for washing, then rushed down the hallway and rammed into Geli's locked bedroom door, but it held fast. According to Ilse Hess, Georg Winter got a screwdriver and wedged it between the doorjamb and the lock as Hess flung himself at the door again. And this time it gave way, though he injured his right shoulder.

Franz Xaver Schwarz was a city councilor as well as the party treasurer, so it was he who was chosen to telephone the police and be in the flat when they came. Maria Reichert walked her mother down to the flat of friends on the first floor, so she was never questioned about September 18th though she'd been there the whole night.

And finally Heinrich Hoffmann called Rudolf Hess from the hotel in Nürnberg, about two hours to the north by car. Told of the murder, he was ordered to say Hitler had stayed with them in the hotel that night, and he and Schaub were to race back to München as if the führer were with them.

"And how is he?" Hoffmann asked.

"Stricken with grief, of course."

"I mean really."

"We'll be fine," Hess said, and hung up. He handed the telephone to Schwarz as he, Amann, and Schirach went to the Brown House for a conference with the führer.

Schwarz called Franz Gürtner, the Bavarian minister of justice who'd called the Nazis "flesh of our flesh," and he also called Ernst Pöhner, a former police commissioner and a patriotic nationalist who'd persistently excused the violence of the SA so long as it was directed against Communists. Many things went unspoken.

Doktor Müller, the coroner, and two criminal police inspectors from the Polizeidirektion München arrived at the flat shortly after eleven that morning and were politely escorted to the crime scene by Schwarz, who claimed he'd been called to the flat by Maria Reichert just as soon as she'd seen the body.

There were no photographs taken. There was no autopsy. Kriminal Kommissar Forster wandered around the room, pursuing evidence, but only collected the Walther 6.35, the brass bullet casing, and Geli's unfinished letter. Doktor Müller unfolded an oilcloth over the blood and crouched on it to examine the body, indicating to the police inspectors that the fatal shot had entered the female victim's chest just above the heart, which it had missed, and had penetrated vertically through the left lung and kidney before halting, wide left of the spine, just above the pelvic girdle, where the bullet could be felt beneath the skin. There was some tattooing near the entrance wound, meaning the Walther had been fired from a few inches away. The signs of rigidity in her face, trunk, and extremities would seem to indicate that she'd died between four and forty hours earlier. Rigor mortis, he said, was too variable to provide greater accuracy about the time of death. While he found some purplish bruising on her neck and thighs, he felt that was just postmortem lividity. Doktor Müller thought the grayish discoloration of the skin was probably due to the fact that death was primarily consequent to suffocation following the shot in the lung. A few days later, when there was a further investigation, he seemed to recall an injury to the nose, but insisted it was flattened by lying face downward for many hours. On Saturday, Doktor Müller got up from beside Geli and snagged off his rubber gloves as he told the policemen, "Suicide or homicide. Who knows?"

Kriminal Kommissar Sauer asked his partner to hold the Walther in a way that would produce such a bullet trajectory, and he finally did by facing the ridge of the barrel and inserting his thumbs in the trigger guard while gripping the gun butt with his fingers. Sauer asked, "And how does that feel?"

"Clumsy," Forster said.

"But it's possible?"

"If she wanted to kill herself, why would she want to do it that way?"

Sauer and Forster went out to interview the household staff as Franz Xaver Schwarz silently watched. Georg Winter offered little, only saying that he'd forced open the door with a screwdriver "and found Raubal lying on the floor as a corpse. She'd shot herself. I can't give any reason why she should have shot herself."

Maria Reichert would later assert that she'd been in the flat when the shot was fired around eight in the evening, but she'd thought the noise had come from partygoers in the street. She'd also maintain that in the morning she'd called Schwarz and he in turn had called a locksmith named Hatzk to open the locked door. With Sauer, on Saturday, however, she got Hess's instructions right, saying that soon after the spaghetti lunch, when the führer was gone, she'd heard a noise like a gunshot from Geli's room, but thought the fräulein had taken a perfume bottle from the dresser and furiously smashed it to the floor. "She was a wild one," she said. She hadn't seen Geli after that. At nine on Saturday morning, she'd knocked on the door to wake Geli and, hearing no answer, had called for Anni Winter, who in turn had called her husband. Georg Winter had broken the door down, and she'd screamed when she'd seen the corpse. "I can't explain why Raubal killed herself," she said, adding, "She was very agitated recently."

According to the police summary, Anni Winter testified that, "Raubal did not want to spend the weekend in Obersalzberg, as had been arranged, because she had no suitable dress to wear. She told me that her Uncle Adolf had refused to buy her a new dress, which also meant paying her fare to Wien, for she only bought her fancy clothes in Wien or Salzburg. But she did not seem unduly disappointed. Her moods changed so quickly. About three in the afternoon yesterday, I saw Raubal, very flustered, go into Hitler's office and then hurry back into her own room. This seemed to me rather extraordinary. I now presume that she was fetching his pistol. At about nine this morning I was trying to take the newspaper into her room as I usually did, but I couldn't get in, and no one answered when I knocked. I started to suspect that Raubal had been out overnight, but then realized the door was locked from the inside with the key stuck in it. I was present when my husband forced the door open. I don't know why Raubal shot herself."

Anna Kirmair only confirmed that the skeleton key was still in the door, which had been locked from the inside. "Why Raubal took her life, I don't know."

There would also be many and varying accounts of a savage argument between Hitler and his niece on the afternoon of September
18th—because she was pregnant with Adolf's child, with the child of
a pianist, she was jealous of Eva Braun, she had a Jewish lover in Linz,
a Jewish lover in Wien, she wanted desperately to see her Aunt
Paula—but those were fictions and phantoms calculated to create
the impression of a dispirited and disintegrating young woman,
and the sheer variety of the stories illustrated how little anyone
believed them.

At two in the afternoon Maria Fischbauer, a paid preparer of
corpses, got to the flat with a tin pail, hard bar soap, and a hand
mitt. She washed Geli's body without stripping off her clothes, and
with the help of Anna Kirmair laid the body into a wooden coffin
that three men from the East Cemetery had hauled up the stairs.
And then they were permitted to quietly bear her away. Questioned
later, Frau Fischbauer said, "Apart from the entry wound on the
breast, I noticed no injuries and in particular I did not notice that
the bridge of the nose was broken or that the nose was injured in
any other way."

Rosina Zweckl worked in the East Cemetery where she shifted
Geli's body to a finer zinc coffin furnished by the party. She said
she'd carefully scrutinized the body because she'd heard the woman
was Hitler's niece. She'd been told she was a virgin—possibly to
quell the gossip of a pregnancy. "She was very blue in the face,"
Zweckl told investigators, but she could say little more. Then, as if
prompted, she oddly paraphrased Maria Fischbauer, saying, "Apart
from the entry wound in the breast, I noticed no injuries and in particular I saw nothing suspicious about the nose."

Sauer went back to the flat on Prinzregentenplatz at half-past
three, and found Adolf Hitler and Heinrich Hoffman there, as their
friends had promised.

The photographer lit a cigarette in what he called the "coffee and
cakes room," off the foyer, and fell right into his *Stammtisch* role of
garrulous storyteller, saying they'd left München around dinnertime
on Friday, but that they were all tired and uneasy because of the

Föhn, and so they'd journeyed only as far as Nürnberg before decid-
ing to stay the night at the Deutscher Hof, the party's hotel.

Sauer wrote that down. "All three of you registered there?"

"Well, just me. We shared the Hitler suite."

"And what time was this?"

"About eight."

Sauer asked him to please continue.

Well, they'd been heading north from Nürnberg this morning
when Hitler had noticed the pageboy from the hotel waving for
them to pull over. Hearing that Rudolf Hess urgently sought him,
Hitler rushed back to the hotel, threw his dog whip and homburg on
a lobby chair, and squeezed into a telephone booth. Hoffmann
heard him say, "Hitler here. Has something happened?" And then in
a hoarse voice he'd replied, "Oh God! How awful!" Hoffmann had
been trying to put it together in his head, but had heard only, "Hess!
Answer me—yes or no—is she alive or dead?"

The photographer lit another cigarette with the fire from the first
and continued, "Afraid of Hitler's legendary fury, Rudi naturally
hung up. Who wouldn't with such unhappy news? And Hitler
headed toward the Mercedes, his hair awry over his forehead and a
wild and glazed look in his face. 'Something has happened to Geli,'
he said. And then he told Schaub to go back to München, shouting,
'Get every ounce you can out of this car! I must see Geli alive again!'

"Hitler's frenzy was contagious," Hoffmann told Sauer. "With its
accelerator jammed to the floorboards, the great car screamed its
way back to München, but near Ebenhausen we were stopped for
speeding by Hauptwachtmeister Probst."

"We'll check on that, of course," Sauer said.

With self-satisfaction, Hoffmann said, "Schaub has the ticket to
prove it. We were going twice the limit."

"And you only heard the dread news when you got here?"

"Well, we went to the Brown House first. We heard then."

"She was alive and well when you left on Friday?"

"Oh yes. She'd fondly kissed the leader good-bye."

"Was she the suicidal type?"

The photographer slyly said, "The very reverse. Completely unhysterical. She had a carefree nature. She faced life with a fresh and healthy outlook. And that's what makes it so puzzling to her friends that she should have felt impelled to take her own life."

Sauer went to the office next to Geli's bedroom to question Hitler, who was now in a gray suit and yellow tie with a gold swastika on the lapel. Sauer underestimated him. "Where are your homburg and dog whip?" he asked, as if he'd caught him out.

Unflustered, Hitler tilted back in his office chair and said, "I have a change of clothes at party headquarters. The tragedy put me in a foul sweat, and I did not wish to offend."

"A tragedy? I just heard you thought your niece was still alive."

"Oh, deep down one knows these things, even while hoping otherwise. We were quite fond of each other."

"Were you told how she died?"

With stunning aplomb he said, "She wrapped my Walther in a facecloth to muffle the explosion. And then she fired into her mouth."

Sauer stared at him, but Hitler offered nothing more. "Tell me about her."

"She was born in Linz, Austria. She was the daughter of my half-sister. She was twenty-three years old." And there, too, he halted, as if that were enough—he who was known for hour-long monologues.

"And?" Sauer asked.

Worrying his forehead with his hand in his sadness, he sighed and said, "My niece had been a medical student at the university, but she hadn't taken to it. She therefore turned to singing lessons. She was soon to make her operatic debut, but she didn't feel quite ready and beseeched me for further lessons from a Professor Otto Ro in Wien. Quite naturally, as her male guardian, I was concerned that she would be defiled by wild and unsavory influences in that sink of iniquity, and I agreed to the journey only on the condition that her mother, now in Obersalzberg, went with her. Geli did not, for some reason, choose to oblige me, and I declared myself to be quite against the plan. She may well have been annoyed about that, but she did not seem particularly upset, and she'd taken leave of me quite calmly when I left for Hamburg on Friday afternoon."

"At what hour?"

"Around three."

"And you went less than one third of the way?"

"We had plenty of time. My speech was to have been at eight o'clock this evening."

"Are you aware of anything that may have driven your niece to suicide?"

"She may have felt she'd disappointed me. She'd begged for singing lessons, and out of generosity I'd paid for them, but she was discovering she was not talented enough. To be frank, I think she was frightened of going onstage. Or there may have been a conflict over love. One hears so many rumors. And yet as her uncle I felt constrained by propriety from a natural curiosity about my niece's private affairs. In fact, I was forced to be rather more aloof than I wished, and I was not always privy to intimate details of her life."

"Anything else?"

Scanning the gray skies through his office window, Hitler sucked thoughtfully on his right little finger and said, "It occurs to me now that she'd once taken part in a séance where tables moved and there she'd been told she certainly wouldn't die a natural death. And she was always afraid of guns, possibly out of foreboding."

Sauer asked, "She knew where your pistol was kept?"

"Oh yes." And then he held his famous mesmerizing stare on Sauer, a film of tears welling up on cue. "You must understand Geli's death has affected me very deeply. She was the only relation with whom I was ever close. We were inseparable. And now *this* has to happen to me."

■ ■ ■

Frau Angela Raubal was summoned from Obersalzberg on Saturday and her train was met by Rudolf Hess, Franz Xaver Schwarz, and Anni Winter. She fainted when she viewed Geli's body in the East Cemetery. When she awoke she was in a parlor and Rudolf Hess was watching her with overdone worry and sympathy. She was told that the police and the coroner had just completed their investigation. All agreed that it had been a suicide, so Angelika Raubal, medical student, was listed as number 193 in the München *Selbstmörder* register for 1931. Angela was not told that a public prosecutor named Gläser had been offended by the hastiness of the judgment and had urged a further inquest, but he had been overruled by Franz Gürtner, who would become Reich minister of justice when Adolf Hitler came to power.

The *Völkischer Beobachter* failed to mention Geli's death, but on Monday, September 21st, the *Münchener Post* carried news of what they called "A Mysterious Affair: Suicide of Hitler's Niece." Their journalist was factually wrong in thinking Geli lived in a flat on Prinzregentenplatz that was other than her uncle's, and he fell for the gossip that she wanted to go to Wien in order to become engaged, but he seemed to have been informed of the quarreling between Hitler and his niece, and he hinted at manslaughter rather than suicide in writing that "Fräulein Geli had been found shot in the flat with Hitler's gun in her hand. The bridge of the nose was shattered, and there were other serious injuries on the body." And he knew that on Saturday morning "gentlemen from the Brown House conferred on what should be announced as the motive for the suicide. It was agreed that Geli's death should be explained in terms of frustrated artistic ambitions."

The Monday story by the *Münchener Post* forced the police to order a further investigation, but nothing would change. The Walther pistol was returned to Hitler on September 21st, and by then the zinc coffin containing Geli's body was being shipped by railway from the East Cemetery in München to the Central Cemetery in Wien.

Leo Raubal got on the train in Linz and found that his mother had been joined in the funeral journey by Captain Ernst Röhm and Heinrich Himmler, who'd offensively presumed to act as old family friends. Owing to his revolutionary putsch in 1923, Hitler had lost his Austrian citizenship and was forbidden to enter the country, hence Leo thought it strange that his sister wasn't being buried in München or Berchtesgaden; but when he asked his mother why, she vaguely said, "Oh, I don't know," and whenever Angela talked about the suicide later, it seemed to him that she was concealing.

She'd chosen Pater Johann Pant as the officiating priest for the funeral in Wien, for he'd met Adolf thirty years before when he'd been a hostel chaplain and young Adolf was selling hand-painted postcards, and he'd hunted down funds for Geli's education when Angela couldn't afford tuition. The priest confided to Leo that there was an official difficulty, for the Church considered any suicide a grave offense against God; he would have to deny Geli a Catholic funeral service and burial in consecrated ground.

Heinrich Himmler had grown up as a pious Catholic, but he'd fallen as far away from the Church as Hitler had. And yet, hearing about the obstacle, and confident that the priest could reveal nothing that was said in the confessional, Himmler chose, in a spasm of decency, to help out the Raubal family by secretly visiting the rectory and asking Pater Johann Pant for the sacrament of penance. That night the priest told Leo that his sister would be buried with the full funeral rites of the Catholic Church, and "from this fact you may draw conclusions which I cannot communicate to you."

■ ■ ■

She was buried grandly in a shrine at Arkadengruft 9, facing the Lüger Church. Aunt Paula Hitler was there with the Raubals, Ernst Röhm, Heinrich Himmler, Adolf Müller, the *Völkischer Beobachter*'s printer, and the self-appointed National Socialist *Gauleiter* of Wien, Alfred Frauenfeld. A fine, inscribed marble slab would later be sited there:

HERE SLEEPS OUR BELOVED CHILD

GELI

IN ETERNAL SLUMBER

SHE WAS OUR RAY OF SUNSHINE

BORN 4 JUNE 1908   DIED 18 SEPTEMBER 1931

THE RAUBAL FAMILY

■ ■ ■

Angela Raubal would continue to be a faithful member of the National Socialist German Workers Party and would stay on as chatelaine of the chalet in Obersalzberg, which would be grandly remodeled as the Berghof, but she would quit the job in 1935 because she so disliked Eva Braun, whom she called "the stupid cow," and she would marry a Professor Martin Hammitzsch, who was the sixty-year-old director of a school of construction engineering in Dresden. Citing pressing affairs of state, Adolf failed to attend the wedding. When the führer committed suicide with Eva Braun in 1945, Angela found that the wealthiest man in Europe had left to the party the Berghof, his furniture, his pictures, and some personal items, but that she and Paula were to be given only twelve thousand reichsmarks per year for life. She received none of it. Interrogated by the American OSS in the aftermath of the war, Angela still exonerated Hitler for the death of her daughter and said she'd been murdered by Himmler. Frau Hammitzsch also felt Hitler had intended to marry his niece, but had delayed, she said, because Geli was in love with a violinist in Linz. Angela died in 1949 at the age of sixty-six.

Alois Hitler Jr. had little further contact with his half-brother after 1933, was never even mentioned by Adolf to his friends, and never once was seen in the chancellery in Berlin. Alois lost his son Heinz in the war, and lost his restaurant in the Wittenbergplatz afterward. In his half-brother's last will and testament, he was given sixty thousand marks but at the time of his death in 1956 had received none of it.

Paula Hitler stayed on in Wien, living shyly and worriedly in a shade-drawn flat under the name of Wolf. She died in 1960. She never married.

William Patrick Hitler emigrated to America, changed his last name, and served in the United States Navy, informing on his family for the OSS. After the war he settled just outside New York City. He named his son Adolf.

While teaching in a *Realschule* in Linz, Leo Raubal married his fiancée, Anne, fathered two children, and graduated from a reserve officer candidate school. Called into the Luftwaffe in 1939, less than a month after the onset of war, he served as a lieutenant and adjutant to the regimental commander. At the seige of Stalingrad in January 1943, he was wounded and taken prisoner by the Russians, and an offer was made to his uncle that Leo would be released in exchange for the son of Josef Stalin. Hitler refused, saying, "War is war," and then so did Stalin. Sentenced to twenty-five years in prison—for execution was officially forbidden in Soviet Russia—Leo was one of the few to survive the Russian gulag and was released in 1955, his faith in Adolf Hitler perversely unshaken and, in spite of all the damning evidence, firmly persuaded that his uncle was innocent of his sister's murder.

Putzi Hanfstaengl fell out of favor with the party for his insistence that the führer ought to soften his religious and racial views, and found the temerity to publicly call Doktor Goebbels a swine. Convinced that he was about to be "neutralized," he fled to England in 1937, and then, under the name of Dr. Sedgwick, he served in the American White House, furnishing President Franklin Delano Roosevelt, his old Harvard classmate, with information on the Nazi hierarchy as an adviser on psychological warfare. After the war, he was repatriated to Germany and died there in 1975.

Heinrich Hoffmann took more than two and a half million photographs of Adolf Hitler between their first meeting in 1919 and the führer's suicide in 1945. When the Reich chancellor's face was put on postage stamps, royalties were paid to them both, and Hoffmann became a far wealthier man, though he was already rich because of best-selling picture books such as *Germany, Awake!*; *Hitler Conquers the German Heart*; *Hitler As No One Knows Him*; *Youth Around Hitler*; *Hitler in His Mountains*; and *Hitler Liberates the Sudetenland*. Hitler named him a professor in 1938, and in 1940 he was elected as a Reichstag deputy. After the war he was judged a "beneficiary" of the Third Reich and was sentenced to hard labor and loss of property. He died in München in 1957 at the age of seventy-two.

With Hitler's blessing, Henrietta Hoffmann married Baldur von Schirach in March 1932, and the wedding reception was held in the

flat at Prinzregentenplatz 16. She changed clothes in Geli's perpetually locked bedroom and found it had been turned into a shrine or,
as she put it, "an Egyptian burial place," with Geli's pullovers and
pleated skirts still in the wardrobe, the sheet music and librettos of
operas just where they'd been when she died, and an affecting full-
length portrait of Geli by Adolf Ziegler hanging on the wall. The
bloodstains had been washed away, and the air was perfumed with
fresh freesias that Anni Winter put there when she cleaned. She
heard that there were paintings or sculptures of Geli in all Hitler's
offices.

She always maintained that her friend had committed suicide.
"Hitler fenced in her life so tightly," she said, "confined her in such
a narrow space, that she saw no other way out. Finally she hated her
uncle, she really wanted to kill him. She couldn't do that. So she
killed herself, to hurt him deeply enough, to disturb him. She knew
that nothing else would wound him so badly. And because he knew,
too, he had to blame himself."

She noted that "there were no more happy picnics" after Geli
died, and no one felt free to mention her name. Hitler never again
played the piano, he was more slovenly in his grooming, he gave up
all forms of alcohol, the anarchy of his allocation of time just got
worse, and on September 18th and Christmas Eve each year until
1939, he would keep a self-pitying all-night vigil in his niece's room.

In a face-to-face confrontation with Hitler at the Berghof in
1943, Henny von Schirach criticized the harsh treatment of the
Jews in Austria, and she fell foul of the führer. A few months before
the end of the war, she and her husband were divorced. She'd had
four children with Baldur von Schirach, and had named the first
one Angela.

In 1933 Chancellor Hitler made Baldur von Schirach, then
twenty-six, his Reich youth leader and offered him to the public as an
Adonis who embodied all that was fine and glorious in the young.
Soon his picture was nearly as widely displayed throughout Germany
as Adolf Hitler's. Jealousy led to vilification from other Nazis and
jokes about his effeminacy, and in 1941 he was ousted from the hier-

archy and sent to Wien as *Gauleiter* and Reich governor. Schirach defended the eastward deportation of nearly two hundred thousand Austrian Jews as "a contribution to European culture," but later, in the Nürnberg trials, he denied he knew of their extermination and called the annihilation of European Jewry "the greatest and most satanic murder in world history." Sentenced to twenty years in prison for crimes against humanity, he was released in 1966 and died twelve years later.

Julius Schaub became an SS *Obersturmführer*, or first lieutenant, and Hitler's aide-de-camp throughout the war, and as the führer's health faded, his crutch. While in prison he wrote his unpublishable memoirs, then fell into the obscurity that his character warranted.

In 1935 Emil Maurice was condemned by the Gestapo for having Jewish ancestry, but the führer intervened for the Old Combatant, and in 1937 even made Emil the head of the Landeshandwerksmeister, a society of professional handicrafts workers, a job for which he was particularly unsuited. In the war he became an SS *Oberführer*, or brigadier general, and he survived it. Eva Braun's biographer interviewed him in 1968, and found that thirty-seven years after her death, he was still in love with Geli Raubal.

■ ■ ■

As minister of public enlightenment and propaganda, Joseph Goebbels once cynically admitted that the way to attract new members to the party was to excite the most primitive instincts of "the stupid, the lazy, and the cowardly," that hatred was his primary trade; but by 1945 it was he who was hated and ridiculed throughout Germany as "the malicious dwarf" and "Wotan's Mickey Mouse." A friendless man all his life, he still venerated Adolf Hitler as a Teutonic god, and held him in such unfathomable awe that he felt priviliged to have his wife and six young children invited to suffer the grim final days in the bunker below the Reich's chancellery in Berlin.

Magda Goebbels had long been so strangely in love with Hitler that she'd agreed to marry the faithless Doktor Goebbels just to be closer to him, and frequently thought of herself as "First Lady of the Reich." She, like her husband, could not conceive of life without the führer. Within hours of Hitler's suicide, Magda had her one son and five daughters injected with morphine to calm them, then fed them poisoned chocolate and watched them die. Then Doktor and Frau Goebbels walked up the four flights of stairs to the night of the chancellery garden where Magda bit into an ampule of potassium cyanide as her husband stood behind her and fired a bullet into her brain. Doktor Goebbels then chewed an ampule as he fired his Walther P-38 pistol into his right temple. An SS guard fired twice into the fallen bodies to make sure they were dead. Imitating Hitler in all things, Doktor Goebbels had left instructions for SS orderlies to douse their bodies in four jerry cans of gasoline before setting them aflame, but the job was incomplete and their faces were skinless but still recognizable when the invading Russians found and photographed them.

On May 21, 1945, British soliders at a checkpoint between Hamburg and Bremerhaven halted a car in which was cowering a man who seemed familiar. Crazed with failure and in ill health, his gray mustache shaved off, his pince-nez forsaken for a fake eye patch, his clothing that of a janitor, he was still unmistakably Heinrich Himmler, minister of the interior; Reich commissar for the consolidation of German nationhood; *Reichsführer* of the SS, the security service, three million policemen, the prisoners of war camps and the extermination camps at Kulmhof, Belzec, Sobibór, Maidanek, Birkenau, Treblinka, and Auschwitz. In jail a doctor examined him and saw in his mouth what seemed to be a black and carious molar. It was, in fact, a vial of cyanide. Immediately Himmler bit down on it, swallowed the poison, and writhed on the floor in agony for twelve minutes—many would say not long enough—until he was finally dead.

Collecting offices and titles just as he collected looted masterpieces, Hermann Wilhelm Göring was, before he fell out of favor with Hitler, Prussian minister of the interior, president of the Reichstag, chief of the Luftwaffe, head of the Gestapo, and *Reichsmarschall* of greater Germany, the fat Falstaff in many malicious jokes. Com-

bining flamboyance, greed, hedonism, joviality, cruelty, and misan-
thropy with a love of deer hunting and the shrewd eye for art and
jewelry of a connoisseur, Göring was thought of, in Nazi circles, as a
Renaissance man; but with no education, no ethics, no second
thoughts, no skill in administration, no understanding of technology, no perseverance, and with frequent miscalculations of Allied
strength, his many organizations faltered and failed in the war, and
on May 9, 1945, he was taken prisoner by soldiers of the United
States Seventh Army. Convicted of war crimes and crimes against
humanity by the international military tribunal in Nürnberg, he was
sentenced to death by hanging in 1946, but instead, as the scaffold
was readied in the jail yard at Spandau, he managed to commit suicide with the help of a hidden poison. In his death photograph he is
winking.

Alfred Rosenberg, who was called "the intellectual high priest of
the master race," continued to publish widely in the thirties on
racist, anti-Semitic, and anti-Catholic themes, and was rewarded
with the title of "Deputy for the Entire Spiritual Development and
Ideology of the NSDAP," and then Reich minister for the occupied
eastern territories, jobs that allowed him to liquidate the Jewish
ghettos, to plunder fine art from Jewish collections, and to write
memoranda that no one read. At the Nürnberg trials he claimed his
writings had been shamefully misused, that he'd wanted a "chival-
rous solution" to the Jewish question, that concentration camps and
gas chambers were inconceivable to him and to Hitler, who'd only
intended to give the Jews "harsh warnings." Rosenberg was found
guilty of crimes against humanity and was executed by hanging in
1946.

Rudolf Hess was deputy führer and Reich minister without portfolio when, in 1941, he crazily flew a Messerschmitt over the North
Sea and parachuted into Scotland in order to independently negoti-
ate peace with Great Britain and demand that Winston Churchill
resign. Jailed in the Tower of London until 1945, he feigned insanity, amnesia, and sheer disinterest at the Nürnberg trials, whined
continually about his health, and was shunned by the other prison-

ers, who called him "Fräulein Anni." Claiming he'd worked "under the greatest son Germany had brought forth in its thousand-year history," he once wrote that, "Even if I could, I would not want to erase this Nazi period of time from my existence. I do not regret anything." When eleven of his codefendants were executed, Hess was amused. Even after the war he was still insisting that the Jews in Germany should be imprisoned "for their own protection." Only when he was seventy-five years old did he allow his wife Ilse to visit him. Rudolf Hess, Hitler's Hesserl, his Rudi, was the sole prisoner in Spandau jail when he died in 1987 at the age of ninety-three, and after that the jail was destroyed.

■ ■ ■

On April 20, 1945, Adolf Hitler celebrated his fifty-sixth birthday in a confining and unfinished concrete bunker of thirty rooms far below the garden of the Reichs chancellery in Berlin. Walls sweated, old food littered the hallways, floors were tangled with electric cables, the Red Army's shelling of the city was a worrying noise overhead, and with seventy people crowded underground and too few lavatories, the smell was so foul that a staff member later said "it was like working in a public urinal."

A flighty and lovesick Eva Braun joined Adolf down there and found a screeching, hysterical, stooped, and prematurely senile old man whose once stunning eyes were now teary and shot with red veins, whose skin was sallow, whose hair had turned suddenly gray, whose hands trembled, who stank, who shuddered, who could no longer even hold a rifle, who lost his balance when he walked, whose feet had to be lifted onto his bed by his valet. The front of his brown uniform jacket was stained with soup and mustard. Spittle was often on his lips and he drooled or whistled through his false teeth when he talked. Imaginary armies ignored his commands; treachery was everywhere; his dearest friends had failed and undermined him.

Eva Braun had been his secret mistress for thirteen years; she was his "girl at my disposal in München." Even as late as April 1st he'd confessed to his secretary, "Eva is very nice, but only Geli could have inspired in me genuine passion. Marrying Eva is out of the question. The only woman I would ever have tied myself to for life was my niece."

And yet he did marry Eva Braun in the map room of the bunker just before midnight on April 28th. She was wearing a black silk taffeta gown. A city official heard them swear they were of pure Aryan descent and free of any hereditary disease, and as quickly as that it was done. Afterward Hitler drank Tokay and joked with Joseph and Magda Goebbels about happier times while Eva sent for the phonograph and "Red Roses," the only record down there. Officers danced with the cooks and the secretaries. Eva and the others dared, for once, to smoke. At four in the morning Hitler signed his last will and political testament, in which he distributed his holdings and property, denounced Reichsführer Himmler and Reichsmarschall Göring because of their rumored overtures of surrender, claimed the Luftwaffe, the army, and the SS had all betrayed him, and congratulated himself for his part in the annihilation of international Jewry while counseling other nations to ruthlessly do likewise.

"And now," he said, after he'd signed, "there is nothing left to do but die."

Eva wrote a letter to her sister, announcing the wedding but admitting that all was lost, and saying, "I can't understand how all this can have happened; it's enough to make one lose one's faith in God!" She wrote other letters to friends that were so adolescent and cloyingly sentimental that the aviatrix who'd said she'd deliver them instead tore them up in disgust.

When he was made chancellor in 1933, Hitler acquired an Alsatian he'd named Blondi and it was she who was featured in the Heinrich Hoffmann photographs that sought to portray the führer informally as a friendly, affable human being. And now in order to test the effectiveness of the poison, Hitler studiously watched as a doctor crushed a glass ampule of potassium cyanide into Blondi's mouth and held her muzzle closed. She shocked Hitler with wild, whining convulsions before she fell over, dead. Immediately he offered the Hitler salute and SS soldiers hauled Blondi away.

On the afternoon of April 30th, Hitler and Eva shook hands with their friends in farewell, and Eva followed as her frail husband tottered into his private suite and sat on a wide settee upholstered in a fabric of leaping antelopes and medieval warriors in Russian boots. She was thirty-three, and still pretty, wearing a blue dress, a raspberry-colored silk scarf, and buckskin pumps; he wore a fresh brown uniform from Wilhelm Holters' tailor shop in Berlin, a red swastika armband, a fine gold wristwatch, a medallion given him by his mother when he was nine, his Iron Cross for bravery, and his Medal for the Wounded from 1916. A framed photograph of Klara Hitler was near him. Hitler handed his new wife the 6.35 Walther pistol that he'd killed Geli with, that he holstered under the waist of his trousers whenever out, and Eva laid it next to her on the settee. She listened to his instructions. They did not kiss. Eva was, others later said, in a controlled state of terror. She put a Zyankali ampule containing potassium cyanide into her mouth and hesitated a moment before breaking the glass with her molars. She cried out when the shards cut her cheek. She then was supposed to shoot herself with the pistol, but the poison acted too quickly and she collapsed to her right. The scent of bitter almonds floated on the air. Hitler put a Zyankali ampule in his mouth, fastened it between his upper bridgework and lower false teeth, and held just beneath his chin a Walther 7.25 pistol that he immediately fired upward into his head, the shot jolting his jaw shut so that the glass ampule shattered. When he fell to the side, he knocked over a flower vase that sloshed water onto the front of Eva's dress so that she seemed to be bleeding.

An adjutant hurried in after hearing the gunshot, then other SS soldiers, and the führer and his wife were laid in gray woolen blankets and with difficulty hauled up four flights of stairs and outside into the chancellery garden. There four jerry cans of gasoline were used to thoroughly soak them and they were ignited with a flung rag. A foul black cloud bloomed overhead as flames ate skin, hair, and clothing, and then the fire slowly subsided. Occasionally soldiers would hurry back out under the Russian shelling to douse the suicides with more gasoline, but the heat wasn't great enough to fully cremate the teeth and bones, and after six hours the charred and smoldering remains were hastily buried in a shell hole where the Russians later found them, just as Hitler had feared.

■ ■ ■

If only he'd done it fourteen years earlier. On September 20, 1931, Hitler passed a sleepless night at Prinzregentenplatz 16, nearly surrendering to notions of joining his niece in death. But he strangely flew into a rage when he found out that party members were talking of his Angelika Raubal as a suicide, and he fell into Hermann Göring's huge hug, weeping with gratitude and relief when Göring suggested that it was just as likely to have been an accident. Sniveling and sighing, Hitler said, "Now I know who is my real friend."

The gentlemen from the Brown House decided that their leader should be closely watched, and called for Julius Schaub and Heinrich Hoffmann to accompany him to Adolf Müller's villa at St. Quirin, near the heaths and blue waters of the Tegernsee. Worrying aloud about his health on the ride there—night sweats, nervous tension, queasiness, a peptic stomach, twitching muscles, difficulty in swallowing—Hitler concluded that they were the first signs of stomach cancer and that he had only a few years left in which to fulfill his agenda. "But the task is too gigantic," he said. "And the goal is too far off. Why don't I just die now?"

The photographer feared the führer was not far from a nervous breakdown, and when he found out he'd brought his Walther pistol with him, he was afraid Hitler would kill himself, and so Hoffmann hid the pistol in a Nettel camera case. Hitler would not talk, he would not eat. Alone, for hour after hour he paced in his upstairs room.

Writing of the night in his postwar memoirs, Hoffmann stated, "Geli's death had shaken my friend to the depths of his soul. Had he a feeling of guilt? Was he torturing himself with remorseful self-reproach? What would he do? All these questions went hammering through my head, but to none of them could I find an answer."

The following morning, he took milk, ham, and biscuits to the führer. "Won't you try to eat something?" he asked.

In silence, Hitler shook his head and continued to stride back and forth across the room.

"Something you must eat or you'll collapse," Hoffmann said, and held out the ham.

Hitler glanced at the pink meat and objected, "Eating that would be like eating a corpse!," and said that nothing on earth would ever entice him to eat meat again, a promise he henceforth kept but for the occasional liver dumplings.

At dinnertime, Hoffmann recalled how the führer loved spaghetti, and he telephoned Henny to obtusely ask how it was made. Trying his hand for the first time in his life at the art of cooking, he felt his effort praiseworthy, but still Hitler would not eat, and again he filled the night with his footfalls.

At last, on Tuesday afternoon, Adolf Müller, the printer of the *Völkischer Beobachter*, arrived at his St. Quirin villa and informed the führer that the funeral of his niece had been held that morning. Although he'd hardly slept for three days, Hitler determined that the Austrian authorities would no longer be waiting for him, and a party that included Emil Maurice, Julius Schaub, and Rudolf Hess immediately headed off for an all-night journey to Wien.

At sunrise on Wednesday the party was met at the Central Cemetery by the Nazi *Gauleiter* Alfred Frauenfeld but, humming the funeral march from *Die Götterdämmerung*, Hitler strolled through the tall iron gates alone, and laid on Geli's grave twenty-three red chrysanthemums, her age and her favorite flower. And then, since he would not pray, he was soon outside the cemetery again. "She's the only woman I'll ever love," Hitler said. "Germany shall now be my only bride."

The men just looked at each other for a while until Heinrich Hoffmann suggested they all go out for breakfast, and Frauenfeld invited them to his flat. The führer agreed as long as he could first be driven by the Belvedere Hotel, inside the Ring, where there was a frieze of a sphinx whose face reminded him of Geli, and then past the magnificent Opera, where he sighed theatrically and talked about hearing Wagner there with August Kubizek just before Geli was born.

Schaub, Hoffmann, Hitler, Hess, Maurice, and Frauenfeld gloomily trudged up the stairs to the flat and took seats at a wide, round table as the *Gauleiter* shook his wife awake in order to have her cook. There was no conversation for a while, only the sounds from the kitchen. She was cracking eggshells, she was grinding coffee beans. And then, to soften the führer's mood, Heinrich Hoffmann reminisced about the first time he'd met Geli. "She was singing in München with a high school group called Seraphim and she'd been invited to hear you speak."

Hitler smiled. "I remember."

"And then Emil brought her to my birthday party for you. She was so lovely. My flabbergasting daughter was blue with champagne and told Geli she had beautiful breasts. She just said, 'Thank you.' I wanted to take her picture right away."

Seeing the führer's appreciation of that, Julius Schaub said he'd given Geli a tour of München that day; he'd helped her buy fine clothes. "She wasn't inhibited with men like some girls are. She was open, and full of high spirits, and always ready for a joke."

Rudolf Hess said he'd first seen her in 1924. "We were in Landsberg Fortress, and she'd come to visit with Angela. She was fifteen. And so fetching. We talked about astrology. I'd just begun typing out *My Struggle* on that old Remington."

Emil said, "She had eyes like a poem."

The heavy wife of the *Gauleiter* poured tea and a shot of vodka into Hitler's cup, and coffee for the others. She went away.

And finally Hitler said, "I first saw Geli at her christening in Linz in 1908. She was just a baby, of course. She gripped my finger in her little hand and I introduced myself as Adolfus. That's my name in the baptismal registry. August Kubizek and I shared a flat here then. We lived in poverty and squalor. My life is a miracle."

Others concurred.

Then Hitler began talking not of his niece, but of the possiblity of campaigning against the old general Paul von Hindenburg for the presidency. And he hesitated, and held his stare on the wall beside Hess's head as if on a doorway with a loved one behind it and just about to enter, or as if he were imagining a history still to be written, imagining *six million Jews*. With a firm and confident voice he said, "And now let the struggle begin."

THE END

AUTHOR'S NOTE

This is a work of fiction based on fact. I have stayed faithful to the history of the period as often as possible and, especially in Hitler's case, freely incorporate actual quotations from him into the novel's dialogue. But of course many of the most consequential moments of any person's life go unglimpsed by either historians or journalists, and those intimate moments are where fiction finds its force and interest. I have felt free to invent in those instances, but always in the spirit of likelihood and fidelity to the record.

To spare the reader the confusion of tracking the crowds of people who habitually surround politicians, I have either failed to mention a personality—there is no mention of the Strasser brothers, for example—or in a few instances I have combined two characters into one—as in the case of Hitler's chauffeurs Julius Schreck and Julius Schaub, who are here, for convenience, only Schaub. Missing for similar reasons is Hitler's other niece, Elfriede Raubal, Geli's younger sister. Quite little is known about that sister, and she did not figure in the major events on which this story concentrates, so I thought it best to be silent about her. Ingrid von Launitz and Christof Fritsch are fictional stand-ins for those female friends in Vienna and male friends in Munich who are often associated with Geli but are never named. I have no idea whether Geli ever met Rupert Mayer but it did not seem far-fetched, and as he was known as an early opponent of the Nazis and the conscience of Catholic Munich, having them meet was hard to resist. The letters written to Adolf by admiring women are adaptations of actual letters sent to him, but later, during the war; and I have slightly altered the chronology in other ways that I hope historians and those acquainted with the facts will agree is minor.

I first became interested in the subject of Adolf Hitler's love affair with his niece when I read *Hitler and Stalin: Parallel Lives* by Alan Bullock and found in it the mention that Geli Raubal, who was a mystery to me at the time, was the only woman Hitler had ever really loved or wanted to marry—Eva Braun was no more than his secret mistress. Curiosity sent me to other biographies of Adolf Hitler, including a major one by John Toland in which he indicated that "there were innuendoes that the Führer himself had done away with his niece, and allegations that Minister of Justice Gürtner had destroyed the evidence." In a footnote, Mr. Toland stated "Hitler could not have killed Geli since he was in Nuremberg," and I wondered how Mr. Toland and his fellow biographers could be so sure. Whose testimony corroborated that alibi? Hitler's and his friends'? Why believe them?

Two primary sources that were important for me early on were *Adolf Hitler: The Missing Years* by Ernst Hanfstaengl and *Hitler Was My Friend* by Heinrich Hoffmann, both of which hint at an odd, if not perverse, relationship between Hitler and his niece, and heightened my suspicions about a possible murder and cover-up. In fact, the further I investigated the accounts of the purported suicide, the more I found contradictions, discrepancies, evasions, and lies, and homicide seemed increasingly likely.

I was perhaps eighty pages into the writing of this novel in the spring of 1997 when my editor sent me the at first unwelcome news that there was a nonfiction book being published in England on the same subject: *Hitler & Geli* by Ronald Hayman. Quickly getting hold of a copy, I was fascinated, and gratified, to find out that Mr. Hayman shared my suspicions of murder and, as he had done far more research into the matter than I'd been able to do up to that point, his fine book became a significant resource as I forged ahead with this novel. Mr. Hayman's bibliography also alerted me to "Hitler's Doomed Angel," a ground-breaking *Vanity Fair* magazine article on Geli by Ron Rosenbaum that I'd managed to miss until then. And as I was finishing the first draft of the novel, Mr. Rosenbaum's superb *Explaining Hitler* appeared. It, too, was tremendously helpful in shaping my opinions of the personae, the historical period, and the persistent gossip about what really happened in Hitler's apartment at Prinzregentenplatz 16. I also found great profit in the holdings of the stunning United States Holocaust Memorial Museum in Washington, D.C., as well as in the first biography of Hitler, *Der Fuehrer* by Konrad Heiden, *The Making of Adolf Hitler: The Birth and Rise of Nazism* by Eugene Davidson, *Hitler* by Joachim Fest, *Young Hitler: The Story of Our Friendship* by August Kubizek, *Where Ghosts Walked: Munich's Road to the Third Reich* by David Clay Large, *The Psychopathic God: Adolf Hitler* by Robert G. L. Waite, and *The Death of Hitler* by Ada Petrova and Peter Watson. While in some ways my conclusions may differ from theirs, I could not have arrived at those conclusions without them, and so to all of these authors, and many more, I am profoundly grateful.

My thanks to the Lila Wallace-Reader's Digest Foundation for financial assistance in the research and writing; to my editor, Terry Karten, for her tender discernment and advocacy; to my agents, Peter Matson and Jody Hotchkiss, for their unfailing enthusiasm and support; to Dr. Dan Caldwell of Pepperdine University for his generous help with research; to Reverend Paul Locatelli, S.J. and Santa Clara University for the gracious gift of time in which to write; to Dick and Elizabeth Moley for their friendship to my work; and to John Irving who, when I told him about my idea for a short story based on my initial findings, instead suggested, "You may have a novel there." My thanks especially to Jim Shepard. This book had its origins in many years of our late-night conversations about the films and history of Weimar Germany and the Third Reich, and is the better for the learning, insight, correction, and humor he benevolently brought to the criticism of each chapter as I finished it. And finally my gratitude to the first reader of these pages, my wife, Bo Caldwell, whose faith in the project and whose praise, questions, and optimism were just what I so often needed.

"Hansen's fictional tour-de-force." — *Time*

Listen to

HITLER'S NIECE

by

RON HANSEN

as read by Academy Award®–nominated actress
JANET MCTEER

"This haunting audiobook is well entrusted
to the voice of Janet McTeer."
— *AudioFile*

The story of the intense and disturbing relationship between
Adolf Hitler and the daughter of his half-sister Angela, this drama
evolves against the backdrop of Hitler's rise to prominence and
power from particularly inauspicious beginnings. In a carefully
researched historical novel that is funny, unflinching, shocking,
profound, and as compulsively readable as a psychological thriller,
Ron Hansen presents Adolf Hitler as he's never been seen before
in fiction, but as his intimates must have seen him.

ISBN 0-694-52198-1 • $25.00 ($37.50 Can.)
6 hours; 4 cassettes
ABRIDGED

Available at your local bookstore, or call 1-800-331-3761 to order.

HarperAudio
A Division of HarperCollinsPublishers
www.harperaudio.com